HE'S NOT MY TYPE

USA TODAY BESTSELLING AUTHOR

MEGHAN QUINN

Published by Hot-Lanta Publishing, LLC

Copyright 2023

Cover Design By: RBA Designs

Cover Illustrations By: Gerard Soratorio

Prologue

HALSEY

Over a year ago . . .

"Are those new loafers?" Posey asks as we make our way down the hallway of the Agitators arena toward our locker room.

I glance down at my probably year-old shoes, then back up at him. "No."

"Huh." He takes another sip of his Gatorade. "They look new."

Levi Posey, one of my best friends and teammates. The self-appointed bruiser on the team acts like a devil in skates, but off the ice, he's a cinnamon roll—all ooey and gooey on the inside. He has made it quite clear his first love is bologna, and his second love is hockey.

And he can be the most annoyingly invasive human being you'll ever meet.

"Are you sure?" Posey puts the cap on his Gatorade. "They're very shiny."

"Positive," I answer.

"Do you not wear them often?"

Jesus Christ, what is happening?

"Dude," I say, stopping in the hallway. "What's with the shoe talk?"

Posey stops as well and shrugs. "Just trying to make conversation with my buddy." He pokes me in the arm. "My good old pal. Don't you want to have a conversation with me?"

Yeah, not buying it one bit.

My eyes fall to where he poked me, then back to him. "What's going on?"

"What do you mean?" he asks, looking anything but innocent. "Nothing's going on. I'm just talking about shoes."

"Did the boys put you up to something?"

He rolls his eyes dramatically. "I don't know what you could possibly be talking about." He goes to uncap his drink again, but I swat it out of his hand, sending the bottle straight into the wall next to us. "Hey!" he protests. "That's for preventive cramping, treat it with respect."

He picks up his bottle as I say, "Don't bullshit me. Why are you being weird?"

"Can't a man ask another man about his shiny loafers without being questioned?"

"No," I answer.

He sighs and tosses his hands up in the air as if surrendering. "Fine, but if they ask, tell them I was smooth about this."

Levi Posey is anything but smooth.

Also . . . I knew something was up.

"Sure. Now, what's going on?"

Posey glances over his shoulder, looking around to see if we're alone, then he leans in with a conspiratorial tone. "Well, we had a meeting the other night——"

"Who is *we*?" I ask, a brow raised.

"Pacey, Hornsby, and Taters."

Typical.

Eli Hornsby—the pretty boy.

Pacey Lawes—the elder of the group.

And Silas Taters—the asshole.

My other three best friends like to stick their noses in my business whenever they get the chance.

I lean against the wall and cross my arms over my chest. "And what exactly was this meeting about? And if you say you're worried about me, I'm walking away."

He winces and looks toward the ceiling. "Uh, well . . . okay, we were, well . . . we were talking about how we're . . . uh"—he scratches his chin—"we were conversing about certain things that pertained to you, but we didn't particularly mention worried . . . more *concerned* about you."

I push off the wall and walk away when he stops me by gripping my arm. "I didn't say worried, I said *concerned*. Not the same thing."

"It *is* the same thing."

"Whatever, we're just worried." I raise my brow at him. "I mean concerned . . . we're concerned." He grips me tighter, preventing me from leaving.

"There's nothing to be concerned about. I'm fine."

"You're not fine," he groans in frustration. "You barely hang out with us outside of the arena. When we were in Banff, you just read the entire time. We feel like you're pushing the world away and—"

"Hey, sorry, am I interrupting?" a female voice says, cutting Posey off from talking about shit I don't want to talk about.

I glance to the right, down the hall to where a tall brunette stands, holding an iPad to her chest. It takes me a second for my eyes to focus, but once they do, every muscle in my body softens. *Because . . . holy . . . shit.*

I don't know who this is or what she's doing here, but she is easily the most beautiful woman I've ever laid my tired eyes on.

Long, dark eyelashes frame sage-green eyes so light that they almost look gray. Rosy cheeks and painted pink lips draw my attention from her soul-rendering eyes, where I feel this deep ache to get closer to see if her lips are naturally glossy. Her slender neck is just the right length for a man to explore . . . to hold . . . to mark.

Her gray dress leaves nothing to the imagination as it clings to her longer, curvy frame. The hem falls to her mid-thigh, showing off her tan legs propped up by a pair of gray heels with tiny bows on the back.

Jesus Christ.

She's so fucking pretty.

"Not interrupting at all," Posey says as he steps forward and lends out his hand. "Hi, I'm Levi Posey."

The brunette takes his hand, stepping forward as well, sending a wave of her perfume in our direction. Not overly sweet but just the right mix of earthy and feminine. The lethal combination has my heart racing.

"Oh, I know who you are." Her smile stretches across her face, twinkling under the fluorescent lights of the hallway. Christ, that smile. Like a goddamn warm hug on a cold day. "I'm Blakely White. I work in the VIP relations and marketing department."

Blakely.

Hell, I like that name.

She turns toward me, her eyes connecting with mine, and fucking hand to heart, I feel this jolt of possession rock through me so fucking hard that I have to catch my breath. I can't tell you the last time I felt something like this.

Ever since I lost Holden, I've felt . . . empty. Like the only reason my body has functioned is to play hockey and nothing else.

Not to feel.

Not to experience the journey of life.

And sure as fuck not to fall in love.

"And you are the hands and skates of the team," she cutely says. "Halsey Holmes, it's so nice to meet you."

She holds her hand out to me, and I attempt to calm my nerves as I take her hand. When our palms connect, and I look her in the eyes, I feel this powerful, electric force bounce between us, jump-starting my heart from its nearly catatonic state. What the actual fuck?

My mouth waters.

The back of my neck starts to sweat.

And a visceral feeling of life pulses through me, reawakening me in a way I never fucking saw coming.

"N-nice to meet you," I say, hating that I stumbled over my words.

She releases my hand and returns to holding her iPad to her chest. "I was hoping I could borrow Halsey for a second."

"Sure." Posey slaps me on the back. "I'll catch you in the locker room, man." He moves around Blakely and says, "It was nice meeting you."

"You too," she says sweetly before turning toward me. "Do you mind coming up to the VIP suite with me?"

I swallow hard, my tongue sticking to the roof of my mouth and my palms sweating. "No, that's fine."

"Great." That smile reappears, and my mind immediately commits it to memory. Blakely's smile would give Julia Roberts a run for her money. Beaming . . . radiant . . . yet delicate, like she reserves it for certain people. "Let me lead the way."

Her heels click against the concrete floor, and I attempt to keep my eyes level as I walk behind her, but they greedily betray me as they fall south, right to her heart-shaped ass.

Fuck . . .

With a harmonic sway, she steps one foot in front of the other, and with every shift, her dress curves around her tight, shapely ass. Gently sculpted lines, plump cheeks, the perfect ass to hold.

Or spank.

Yes, the perfect ass to spank.

Jesus, what am I even thinking?

She glances over her shoulder, giving me just enough time to avert my eyes as she says, "I just have a few things for you to sign if that's okay? I considered bringing them down here, but I figured this might be easier. At least for me." She winces. "Maybe not for you."

"It's good," I reply, reminding myself she didn't retrieve me to stare at her ass. *You're in a professional setting, you fucker, remember that.*

She falls in step with me so we're walking side by side. When we reach the elevator that leads to the VIP level, she asks, "I'm not messing up your pregame routine, am I?"

"No." I shake my head, place my hands in my pockets, and stare at the floor. If you look at the ground, you're not leering at her.

"Oh, good. I know how superstitious players can be." She leans in close and whispers, "Are you one of them?"

I lift my eyes to hers, and fuck me . . . she's so beautiful, it's impossible not to stare.

Those eyes, I've never seen anything like them before. So light with barely a blip of color but so lively at the same time. There's an energy in her irises that has tapped into a part of me I thought was nonexistent.

That died the night my twin brother died as well.

"Superstitious?" I ask just as the elevator opens. I hold the door for her, and she steps on first before I follow her. "Not really."

"That's good. Then I don't feel that bad pulling you away from the locker room." The elevator starts moving, and she asks, "Is it true that Levi Posey has to eat a bologna sandwich before every game?"

"Yeah," I say, leaning against the elevator wall. "There's always a stack of bologna in the players' cafeteria for him."

"I don't think I've ever heard of a grown man eating bologna. But he kills it on the ice, so he should keep doing what he's doing."

The elevator doors open, and I block them as she exits. I follow closely, and we make our way down the hallway, past a few suites, and straight to the VIP suite that overlooks center ice.

She props the door open for me, but I quickly grab it and

gesture for her to lead the way. She smiles sweetly and, as I follow her, I notice how long her legs are. Even with heels, I'm still taller than her. She's much taller than every other woman we've walked by, but that doesn't prevent her from wearing the shoes she wants, which makes her calves look insane.

"Right over here," Blakely says as I lift my eyes again, refraining from staring.

There's a table full of pucks, jerseys, hockey sticks, and pictures. When I glance at her in surprise, she says, "I know, it might be a little much, but this group is a huge donor and massive fans. Is it okay?"

"It's fine," I say. Just means I get to spend a little more time with her. If only I could pull my head out of my ass long enough to actually strike up a conversation, something with more substance than Posey's bologna sandwiches.

But hell, this girl has me all twisted up inside. One look and my palms started sweating, I felt tongue-tied, and my heart raced faster than when I was chasing down a puck against an opponent.

With one look, she brought me back to life.

"You can sit here," Blakely says, patting a stool in front of the memorabilia. She uncaps a Sharpie and hands it to me before placing a small stack of photos in front of me.

That dreaded fucking picture.

I hate this picture.

Not because I look bad in it or any narcissistic thoughts like that.

I hate it because I know the exact game when this photo was taken.

I know it so well because it was a game-winning shot on the night Holden died.

Unfortunately for me, the team uses this picture for every promotion under the sun. For them, it's a moment in Agitators' history that comes with great celebration. For me, it's a reminder of the dark, life-altering night that I lost my brother . . .

"Are you okay?" Blakely asks, startling me from my thoughts.

7

"Yeah." I take a deep breath. *Don't go there, Halsey. Don't fucking go there.*

"You sure?"

"Yup." I sit taller, pushing away the darkness clouding my mind, flooding my spirit. But unlike every other time, I push it away. I can't sit in it. I can't wallow in the pain and let it consume me. Not in front of her.

So I sign the first picture.

"Okay, because if this is too much, I can pare down—"

"No, you're good," I say, trying to use a lighter tone. When I see she's still concerned, I try to change the subject. "Have you worked here long?"

"Not too long, but long enough to become immensely involved in the outcomes of the games." She helps me with the photos, pulling them away after I sign them. "The other night, when you scored that goal with only forty-five seconds to spare, I nearly ripped my pencil skirt from cheering so much. Between you and me and the skirt, there was a slight tear near the zipper."

And just like that, I don't have to be the one to pull my mind from that dark cloud. I don't have to push it away all on my own.

She did it effortlessly with her real, unfiltered response.

"How did you manage that?" I ask.

She cutely shrugs. "Apparently, I like to do lunges while celebrating. Let's just say the skirt has been retired. I told myself I'd hold off on wearing form-fitting clothes on game days, but here I am, in a dress bound to rip if you score again." She points at me. "So if you see me waddling away with a towel wrapped around my waist after the game, you'll know the celebratory lunges struck again."

A light chuckle falls past my lips, the sound so fucking foreign to me.

"Gives me more reason to wait until the last second to score."

"Please don't." She clutches her heart. "I can't take that kind of anxiety and excitement all at the same time . . . neither can my clothes."

She's so easy to talk to.

"Might need to ask for hazard pay for more clothing."

"Now there's an idea." She takes the photos and stacks them together before handing me a jersey. "Here, let me stretch it out for you. I've learned these are a pain to sign."

"I always sign on the number for that very reason," I say while I scroll my name across the raised number on the back of the jersey.

"The veterans on the team know best." She winks at me, and my stomach bottoms out from the innocent gesture.

Jesus, is that all it takes, Holmes?

A pair of pretty eyes and you're a goner?

I glance up at her while she shuffles for the next jersey, her lips quirked to the side in concentration, her tongue peeking out in the corner.

Yup . . . that's all it takes.

One look into those eyes and I'm fucking lost.

So lost that I want to prolong this interaction. I want to get to know her more. I want to . . . hell, I think I want to ask her out.

But am I mentally ready to even handle something like that? Taking a girl out?

I've had one-night stands just to expel adrenaline after a game.

But am I going out on a date? Possibly starting a relationship? That's a level I'm not sure I'm ready for.

I glance at her again, taking in those tempting lips. Yeah, I don't think I could walk away and not ask for more.

"Okay, this is going to be very brazen, and I swear, I'm not trying to hit on you or anything." She hands me a hockey stick, and my brain inwardly begs her to hit on me. It would make this so much easier. "But your hands are huge. I mean, I don't think I've ever seen hands that big before. No wonder you can handle your stick so well . . ." Her eyes widen, and she quickly says, "Hockey stick. I mean hockey stick, not like . . . you know . . . penis stick."

A snort pops out of me, and a genuine smile crosses her lips.

"Did I just make you snort?"

"Unfortunately," I answer as I swipe at my nose.

"And they told me you were the toughest to crack." She flips her hair over her shoulder. "Looks like I have something to add to my résumé. Made Halsey Holmes snort. Who knew all it took was to say penis stick."

Penis stick and a fast-growing crush.

That's exactly what this feeling is: a crush.

But how could I not?

She's funny.

Cute.

Fucking adorable.

Gorgeous.

A breath of fresh air.

I need to see more of her.

It might be scary as shit, but I can't end the interaction here. I have to ask her out.

Adrenaline pumps through me as I realize that I'm taking that first step to living my life for the first time since I lost my brother.

"Can I tell you something that might scare you off, and you might never want to talk to me again, but I have no filter and can't seem to control myself?" she says, breaking into my thoughts.

"Sure," I say while in the back of my mind, I try to figure out how to ask this girl out. Maybe I should talk to Posey first, see what he thinks the best approach is . . . eh, maybe not Posey. Hornsby might be better; he always has the best of luck with women, and I don't think he'd make a big deal about it. Posey would probably clap like a moron and praise the bologna gods for answering his ridiculous prayers. I'm not sure Pacey would have much to say—he usually doesn't care about this kind of shit —and Silas, well, he's going through his own personal hell, so he's not the one to talk to.

Yeah, I'll ask Hornsby. It's not like Blakely is going anywhere.

"Okay, but you can't judge me," Blakely says, tearing me away from my thoughts again.

Pay attention, you fucker. If you want a chance with her, you need to make sure she knows you're interested.

"Would never consider judging you," I say.

"Thank you." She hands me the last item to sign. "So the other night, I was playing fuck, chuck, and marry, and I'm ashamed to come clean, but I chucked you." I lift my gaze to hers, my eyebrows shooting up. She holds up her hand. "Before you get mad at me, I need to explain that I was under pressure and I didn't know much about you, but then my boyfriend went on a tirade about how perfect you are—he has a huge man crush on you—and he convinced me to marry you."

Boyfriend?

She has a fucking boyfriend?

"I know, I know. Why am I telling you this? Like, why would you want to know that I chucked you when my boyfriend married you? An odd thing to say to someone, but I feel like it was sitting on my chest this entire time, and I had to come clean." She lets out a long breath. "Ooof, feels good to admit that."

A boyfriend.

Fuck.

Of course she has a boyfriend.

Why wouldn't she?

She's perfect. Girls like her are snatched up quickly.

"And I know what you're thinking: who did I fuck? Well, it was Rivers. And I know he's gay, but that's where the curiosity came about. I wanted to see what kind of moves he'd have. I married Posey, and my boyfriend quickly corrected me and said Posey would have way too much bologna in the house. He then told me that you would be a loyal husband and went into great detail about it, so . . . yeah, I was convinced otherwise." She winces at me. "Are you mad?"

Mad at her?

No.

Mad that she has a boyfriend?

Fuck yes.

I snap out of my disappointment and say, "No . . . seems like your boyfriend knows his stuff."

"He does. And trust me, I won't make that mistake again." She claps her hands together. "Well, it looks like we're done here. Do you want me to walk you back to the locker room?"

"Nah, that's okay," I say as I stand from the stool, disappointment heavy in my chest.

"Okay. Well, thank you so much for taking the time to do this for me. I really appreciate it, Halsey."

"Sure, any time." I offer her a generic smile.

"And I'm sorry if I made you uncomfortable with that whole fuck, chuck, or marry thing. I realize maybe that wasn't professional."

"It's fine." I take a step away. "Glad your boyfriend taught you a lesson."

"Lesson learned, won't make that mistake again." Her smile nearly cuts me in fucking two. "Well, good luck today, Halsey. Please no skirt-splitting end-of-game goals."

"I'll do my best." I wave and take off out of the room, my heart beating so fast that my breathing feels labored.

A boyfriend.

The perfect girl has a boyfriend.

Fuck . . .

Just my luck. The one girl who made me feel something for the first time in a while has a boyfriend. That seems to be my luck in this fucking life. The ounce of hope, of finding my way out of this fog, is so quickly squandered the minute I give in to it.

Let's just fucking pray I don't see her again because I don't think I could stomach being around her knowing I can't ask her out. That I have no chance of claiming her as mine.

Fuck . . . me.

All I can ask for is that this was a one-and-done interaction.

Narrator: Unfortunately for Halsey Holmes . . . it wasn't a one-and-done interaction. In fact, he's seen her almost every day in the hallway of the arena, which has only enabled his crush to the point that when he runs into her . . . he burns. Poor, poor Halsey.

Chapter One

HALSEY

"Want one?" Oden asks, holding out a piece of gum to me.

"I'm good," I answer as I focus on wrapping the blade of my stick with tape.

He leans back against the locker bench and sighs heavily. "Do you ever get nervous before a game?"

Oden O'Connor was our newest acquisition this January. The front office made some moves to stack our team leading into the second half of the season, and one of the biggest ones was OC. With Rivers's recent knee injury, OC was the perfect fill-in. Although on the younger side, he has impressive puck-handling skills and powerful legs underneath him.

"No," I answer, not really in the mood to talk but also not wanting to come off as an asshole. "Why, you nervous?"

"Yeah." He crosses his arms over his chest. "I only get nervous on special occasions, though. This is my first home game with the Agitators. There's that unsaid pressure in the air that I have to prove myself."

"Proved yourself last game with a goal and an assist," I say as I snap the tape off and check my blade, making sure to secure the tape.

"Nah, it takes time to earn the trust from the fans." He leans forward, resting his arms on his legs. "I know trust doesn't come easy, especially when you're filling in for a team favorite."

I glance at OC and notice his tight shoulders and the worry on his brow. He hasn't spoken to many of the guys on the team. I know Posey was trying to get to know him the other night but couldn't break through his shell. He's kept to himself a lot, but I've seen this tactic before—he's easing himself in. I can tell he has a fun personality just from how he skates around during warm-ups and from his previous interviews, but he's holding back as he immerses himself into the team. Probably smart.

"Don't put added pressure on yourself that's unnecessary," I say.

He glances over at me. "You're telling me if you were in my position, you wouldn't feel the pressure of proving yourself?"

Hmm, great question.

If I were in his skates and traded mid-season to a new team, I'd probably feel the pressure. But I don't think I'd let it get to my head, not how it seems like he is.

"I would," I answer honestly.

He nods and pauses for a moment before turning toward me. "Jesus, I half expected you to tell me you wouldn't feel the need to prove yourself and get my head out of my ass. What kind of pep-talker are you?"

"What?" I ask, surprised by the liveliness in his voice. See, I knew something was in there.

Eli Hornsby walks over and pats OC on the shoulder. "Leaning on the wrong guy if you want someone to tell you to take your head out of your ass. Holmes is on the gentler side. If you want someone to give it to you hard, ask Taters. He'll punch you right where it hurts."

"Not since he's fallen in love," Pacey, our goalie, says as he pulls up a chair and sits in front of me. "We've all softened since falling in love." He looks at Eli. "Especially you." He's not wrong. Hornsby is completely gone for his girl, Penny, and now his little boy, Holden.

"Oh fuck off, you're the softest of us all," Eli says to Pacey.

I might agree with that. It didn't take Pacey long to fall for Winnie. They're now engaged.

"Nah . . . the softest, that would be Taters."

Silas Taters, also called Potato by Winnie, a nickname that has now started to catch on in the group. He's one of our wingmen and fell fast and hard for Ollie. She now lives with him, and we barely see him.

"So all of you have girls?" OC asks.

"Not our friend Holmes." Eli pats me on the back with a knowing smile crossing his lips. "Although, there's a girl he wished—"

"Can you shut the fuck up?" I ask, knowing exactly where that was headed.

Jesus Christ. I never should have told these idiots about my crush on Blakely because they haven't been able to shut up about it. They think in some miraculous fashion, if they talk about it enough, she'll become single, and I'll get my chance. Manifestation, they tell me. They're all fucking morons. Blakely is not breaking up with her boyfriend.

She's madly in love—something I've not only heard from the source itself but also from Penny and Winnie.

And because of that, I've moved on. A crush is just that, a crush. I can walk away from it . . .

At least that's what I'm trying to convince myself.

"You have a crush?" OC asks. "On whom?"

Great, now the new guy's involved.

Feeling the tension grow in my shoulders, I say, "Doesn't matter. She's—"

"Halsey!"

My name is projected from the hallway, drawing all of our attention toward the locker room entrance.

"Halsey!" The scream is shrill, practically at a pitch only dogs can hear. "Hallllllllsey!"

"What the fuck is that?" Hornsby asks.

"Is that . . . Posey?" Pacey asks just as Posey comes barreling into the locker room, looking slightly disheveled and breathing heavily.

"Halsey," he repeats, this time out of breath.

"What the hell is going on?" Hornsby asks before I can.

Posey hangs on to the open doorway while his lungs work overtime. "It's happened."

"What's happened?" Pacey asks.

Posey presses his hands to his knees while bending over. The fucker skates for a living, and he's out of breath? That doesn't bode well for our defense.

"Fuck, the adrenaline," he mutters, then stands tall again. Hands on his hips, he says, "The news we've been waiting for." He takes a few steps into the round locker, and with a bizarre expression of glee, he announces, "The time has come."

We all look around at each other, trying to see if anyone understands him.

That would be a no.

"The time has come for what?" Hornsby asks, his patience wearing thin just like the rest of us.

"Stop being a nitwit and fucking tell us," Silas says, walking up to the group. When did he get here?

Posey looks me dead in the eyes with a huge smile and says, "She's a free woman, man."

Silence falls over the locker room once again as we all attempt to decipher what the fuck he's talking about. Did he eat some bad bologna?

Finally, Pacey—while pinching the bridge of his nose—says, "For the love of God, make sense."

"I am," Posey says in defense. "Blakely . . . she's a free woman."

Wait . . . what? Blakely?

Free?

As in . . .

"Holy shit," Hornsby says while gripping my leg. "Dude . . ."

"Who's Blakely?" OC asks, looking confused.

"You have to ask her out," Posey says, approaching us now. "Want me to formulate a plan?"

"Yes, a plan. That's what we need," Hornsby says.

"We could do a flash mob," Posey suggests.

"Over my dead body," Silas replies. "Don't be a douche about it. Just ask her out."

"Don't be a douche?" Pacey asks with a shake of his head. "Coming from the guy who had to fake-date someone to fall in love."

"You fake-dated someone?" OC asks. "What the hell is going on here?"

"It's simple," Posey says, leaning against Pacey's chair. "Pacey, here, was the start of the love train. He fell in love with a hopeless wanderer up in Banff. Her name is Winnie, and she got lost in the woods, stayed the night in Silas's cabin with the rest of us like the true champ that she is, and Pacey peed on her, said she was his, and now they're engaged."

"I didn't pee on her," Pacey interjects.

"That brings us to Eli Hornsby. Our former ladies' man—"

"Coming from the biggest ladies' man on the team," Hornsby says, gesturing to Posey—which, that's a fact. He is. He just doesn't get called out for it.

Posey continues. "On his birthday, he was looking for someone to bang, and he found her, Pacey's sister."

"Can you not say it that way?" Hornsby asks.

"And he got her pregnant," Posey says with gusto. The fucking storyteller of the group. "It was a long road for them. Jesus, the amount of time it took for Eli to finally realize he could give in to loving her. Some might say the author of his story could have cut out the last fifteen percent, and everyone would have still been pleased with the outcome."

"Not everyone can magically fall in love like Pacey," Hornsby complains. "Love isn't always perfect all at once. You have to earn it."

Ignoring him, Posey moves on. "But with Penny in our life, we met Blakely, who works for the team in VIP sales and marketing. We got to know Blakely even better when she filled in for Penny during her maternity leave. I thought our friend Halsey was next when it came to hopping on the love train, but nope, Silas pops in with a fake-dating relationship with . . ." Posey leans in and whispers, "A girl ten years his junior."

"You're an idiot," Silas says.

"And he almost didn't win her over, but thanks to my clever text messaging, he now has a live-in girlfriend, apparently the best sex he's ever had."

"Dude . . . be respectful," Silas growls.

Posey holds his hands up. "Your words, not mine." He smirks like the dick he is and continues. "But this entire time, we've watched Halsey slowly grow more and more infatuated with Blakely, trying to pretend he doesn't care about her by masking his love with late nights with random women, but we all know he wishes those women were Blakely. And that he could hold her hand and go home to her warm, tender arms and bury his head right into her ample—"

"Enough!" I yell.

Posey continues to smirk. "And today, fellas . . . well, today is the day. Halsey Malachi Holmes is finally going to ask her out."

All the boys turn toward me. Their waiting faces ready as if I'm about to raise my pointer finger and proclaim that today is the day.

Not going to fucking happen.

I shake my head. "No, I'm not. And my middle name isn't Malachi."

Posey's gleeful expression falls flat. "What do you mean you're not? Dude, she's a free woman, ask her out."

"Ooo . . . who are we asking out?" that very familiar female voice, who haunts me late at night, says as she enters the room.

Motherfucker, did she hear us?

My face turns beet red as Blakely steps up to our circle, looking so fucking beautiful in a pair of dress shorts with a white blouse tucked into her waistline. Her three-inch heels make her legs look so damn long it's almost as if they have no end.

Will I ever stop getting butterflies whenever I see her?

Probably not. I'm doomed.

Silence falls over the locker room as all six of us idiots stare her down, the realization that she could have heard the whole conversation hitting us simultaneously and causing us to scramble to find our words.

Pacey's lips seal shut, and his eyes widen as he looks at me for answers. He's no help.

Silas crosses his arms and grins, probably enjoying this far too much.

Eli shifts next to me, bowing his head and almost trying to sink back into nothing as if he was never here. Count him out as well.

And then there's Posey, mouthing . . . "She's here. She's here," while subtly pointing to the side, right at her.

I know, you fucking moron, I have eyes!

"Did I . . . interrupt?" she asks, looking insecure now.

Christ.

Someone needs to say something.

Anything to make it seem like we weren't talking about her.

Because the longer this silence goes on, the easier it will be for her to believe we were talking about her, which we were.

I take one more look at my boys and realize they have all abandoned me. What fucking friends they are. I rack my brain for something to say . . . anything that makes sense. But I come up short, and that's when a bead of sweat trickles down my back, making me painfully aware of just how awkward and uncomfortable I am.

"Uhh . . . you know," OC chimes in, immediately making him my favorite. "We were talking about a girl I know." What a fucking champion. "I'm Oden O'Connor, by the way."

"Blakely White," she says, leaning in to shake his hand. Her

long brown hair brushes near me, sending me into a near catatonic state from the lavender scent. "It's so nice to meet you."

"You too," he says while dropping her hand quickly.

Blakely then looks at Posey and says, "What happened to
you? We were talking with Camper over in marketing, and you
just took off in the middle of a sentence."

Jesus Christ, Posey.

He nervously smiles and says, "Bathroom emergency." When
her cute nose scrunches, he adds, "False alarm, but glad I
hustled, you know just in case. Sorry about that. I think you were
saying something about moving out of your apartment because
you broke up with your boyfriend?"

That's when he cut out and left? Right when she was talking
about her breakup? Could he be any more fucking obvious?

Blakely sighs heavily. "Yeah, I had to find a cheaper place."

"You, uh . . . broke up?" Eli asks. "Penny never said anything
to me." And this is why I like Hornsby. He'll wiggle out the truth
in a conventional, non-evasive way—unlike Posey.

"I haven't really said anything to anyone," Blakely says,
"which seems weird that I'm talking to you guys about it, but
yeah, we broke up a few weeks ago. I know Penny's been busy
with the baby, so I didn't want to bother her. Anyway, I found a
new place, but this morning, the pipe above my apartment burst
and flooded my place. It's been a nightmare, but you don't need
to worry about that. I came here—"

"Where are you going to stay?" Posey asks. "Clearly not there."

"Oh, uh, trying to figure that out."

"Does Penny know?" Eli asks. "I'm sure she would offer up
our place."

"Or ours," Pacey adds, knowing Blakely is also good friends
with Winnie.

Silas scratches the back of his neck and says, "Ollie would
probably do the same."

Blakely shakes her head. "No offense, Eli, but I'm not going
to room with an infant. I love him, but not that much. And

Winnie and Ollie would offer, but I'm also not going to stay with two happy couples having sex every chance they get."

Understandable—

"Holmes isn't happy, and he doesn't have a lot of sex," Posey says out of fucking nowhere.

Uh . . . what?

Blakely brings her attention to me with a tilt of her head. "Not having a lot of sex, Holmes?"

Kill me.

Kill me right fucking now.

"I mean, he has sex," Posey interjects. "But not like the other guys, you know? He's not a virgin if that's what you're thinking. Far from a virgin. Although there was a point in time when I wondered if he even had genitals—"

"Shut . . . up," Silas mutters, thankfully.

"Right." Posey clears his throat. "Anyway, he has a spare bedroom, and he's not part of a happy couple, and for all we know, he doesn't have an infant, so you know, you could stay with him."

What the actual fuck is he doing?

Blakely, stay with me?

I can barely look at her or talk to her. Sharing a living space would probably send me into a nervous breakdown.

"Are you his landlord?" Blakely teases.

"More like his hairy godmother." Posey makes himself laugh . . . and only himself.

Either Blakely is being polite or she's unaware of the tension building in our circle. As much as I love Posey for everything he is, he's putting me on the goddamn spot right now. I'm pretty sure it's not something I can handle.

Hell, I know it's not something I can handle.

What if she accepts? What the hell am I supposed to do? Live with my crush?

How would that fucking work? Me walking around the apartment, stumbling over my words and trying not to stare at her too much while she lives her life, probably taking on the opinion that I'm some sort of a goddamn nutjob?

No . . . this can't happen.

Not to mention, there's no way she would ever live with someone she barely knows. She has a good head on her shoulders, so she'll probably find a hotel or—

"Is it a real offer?" she asks.

My gaze snaps up to hers, and from the corner of my eye, I can see Posey's obnoxious smile. The satisfaction that must be running through him right now.

"Huh?" I ask, blanking completely.

"The offer to stay at your place, is it real?"

She can't be serious.

No way does she want to stay with me. She barely knows me. Sure, we've talked here and there, and I've told her she looked beautiful in her dress a couple of times. But stay with me? She might be desperate, but not that desperate.

"It is," Posey says. "He was telling me the other day that he wishes someone could water his bonsai tree when he's on away trips. He's always worried it will die when he's gone."

What the fuck is a bonsai tree?

"Don't you have to spritz them with water gently?" she asks.

"You would think," Posey says, "but I believe Holmes lets his soak up its own water, don't you?"

Where the fuck does he come up with this shit?

"Uh . . . yeah," I answer like an idiot.

"And he has the cutest name for his tree too, don't you?" Posey asks me.

Why is he doing this to me? Have I done something to hurt him? Have I somehow embarrassed him in a way that I'm unsure about? Is this revenge?

"Sherman, right?" Silas asks, getting in on it. Oh, look who's dead to me as well. Posey and Silas, both dead to me.

"Aw, Sherman is such a cute name for a plant." She smiles that smile that haunts me in my dreams, the one that grips my balls so fucking tight that I almost can't breathe around her.

"His pride and joy," Posey says. "And given the drought scare he had with Sherman a few weeks ago, I'm sure he would love someone to look after him."

Blakely locks eyes with me and says, "Well, if you truly want someone to watch over him, I'm your girl. I could use the room because the hotel I'm staying in tonight is way more than I can afford for weeks on end. And I'd pay you for rent."

"He doesn't need your money," Eli chimes in. "He's loaded. The man has one of the best contracts in the league."

Not necessary to put out there, but yeah, it's true.

"Okay, well, I can take care of Sherman for free. That's if . . . you'll let me."

Everyone in the circle turns their attention to me. I swear this feels like I've been sucked into an alternate universe where professional hockey players have pet bonsai trees with old man names and toss around spare bedrooms like candy. I woke up this morning thinking I have a game to prepare for, and that's it. Now I might have a temporary roommate, but not only that. A roommate whose beauty and sweetness make me fucking lose all sense of myself.

Eli nudges me with his elbow, and I clear my throat. "Uh, yeah. That would be cool," I say even though I can feel my entire body break into a full sweat.

"Amazing." Blakely brings her hands together, grateful to me for saving her day. "Let me have your phone so I can plug in my number."

I'm shell-shocked, still unsure how this happened, so Eli grabs my phone from next to me, flashes the face ID at me, and hands it over to her. She types her number in, and when I look up at Posey, he's giving me a thumbs-up while wiggling his eyebrows.

I hate him so much.

"Here you go." She hands me my phone back. "I sent myself a text, so I have your number too. Oh wait." She reaches for my phone and taps away on it before holding it up and taking a picture of herself.

"There, now you also have my picture as the contact." Yeah, I won't stare at that all night. "I hate when it shows up as just the initials in the contact." She hands me back my phone. "I have the hotel for tonight, but I'll move in tomorrow. Thank you so much, this is a huge lifesaver, not to mention . . . wallet saver."

"Yeah, sure. Of course," I say while shifting uncomfortably.

"Okay, well, I came in here for Pacey. Would you be able to meet us in the media room? There's a family who made a wish to meet you, and I want to brief you."

Pacey stands. "Sure, no problem."

I watch them leave together, and when they're out of sight, I look straight at Posey. "What the fuck was that?"

"Uh, me doing you a favor. A thank-you would be appreciated."

"That is not doing me a favor." I lean back on the locker bench. "That is setting me up for failure."

"How is that setting you up for failure?"

"I don't know," I say sarcastically. "How about the fact that I can barely talk to her, let alone look her in the eyes? Or that I don't want to have her as a roommate because I have no fucking clue how to handle that. Or that I don't have a fucking bonsai tree or know where to even get one."

"Yeah, I went a little loose on the bonsai tree," he says while rubbing his palm against his jaw. "But come on, this is your moment. She's a free lady and now indebted to you. What more can you ask for?"

"I don't want her indebted to me," I say. "Jesus, that's not how . . . that's not how I want to handle this."

"And how do you want to handle this?" Eli asks. "Because as far as I know, you'd never make a move."

"You don't know that," I say defensively even though I think it's true, given my current state of life as a hermit. Call it gut instincts, but I was ready to ask her out when I first met her. Then the more I got to know her, the more I realized she's way out of my league. She's bright, and fun, and free. I'm the complete opposite. I can't even remember what fun is. I live to

24

play hockey, and when I'm not playing hockey, I escape into books. I keep a solid regimen so I don't have to think or battle the thoughts in my head. I don't know how to be any other way.

I don't know how to survive any other way.

And throwing Blakely into the mix as my roommate? That will mess everything up.

I can feel it already.

"You wouldn't have ever asked her out," Silas says, arms folded. "Sorry, but it's true. I usually don't agree with Posey and his shenanigans, but I kind of agree with this move."

"Thank you." Posey bows like a moron. "Just doing the heavy lifting over here. I'll take thank-yous whenever you want to toss them my way in forms of cash or bologna."

"The only thing you're getting from me is a trip to the plant store. You got me into this mess, and you're going to help me get out of it," I say.

"Get out of it?" Posey shakes his head. "Oh no, we're going to find a way to make this permanent. Mark my words, you and Blakely are going to be boyfriend and girlfriend by the end of the season. There will be so much kissing in your future that you'll beg me to clue you in on what kind of lip balm I use to keep things so fresh."

"You're an idiot," I say, blowing by him and heading straight to the restroom where I might dry-heave because, holy shit . . . Blakely will be living with me.

Chapter Two

BLAKELY

"Surprise," I say, holding up two pints of ice cream and plastering a smile on my face.

Penny stares me down and deadpans, "I'm not happy with you." Then she turns around and heads into her apartment with me following her.

She's angry with me because she had to hear from Eli that Perry and I broke up a few weeks ago. I should have told him not to say anything, but I was so thrown off and relieved by Halsey's offer that I blacked out for a moment. The next thing I know, I'm getting a text from Penny about my breakup.

Since she was still on maternity leave, the Agitators gave her an extended leave, which is so freaking amazing, so I told her I'd explain everything after the game. The ice cream is to soften her up, although I'm not sure the tactic will work.

She takes a seat on the couch and folds her arms while staring me down.

I laugh nervously. "Is Holden asleep?"

"What do you think?"

"I'm going to assume yes. Such a shame he doesn't get to see the she-beast his mother turned into tonight."

"She-beast?" she asks as I offer her the pint of ice cream I got her—mint chocolate chip. She swats it away and takes my pretzel caramel that I've been looking forward to on the way over here. "You're lucky I didn't kick you right in the crotch when I opened the door."

I grab spoons for us from the kitchen, hand her one, then take a seat on the couch as well. "A kick to the crotch seems a bit extreme for the circumstances, don't you think?"

"No," she says. "I had to hear from my boyfriend—"

"Fiancé, technically," I say for God knows what reason, and that only pisses her off more.

"I had to hear from him that my best friend broke up with her boyfriend that she's known since college. How do you think that makes me feel?"

"Sad?" I ask with a wince.

"Pissed," she replies.

"Ah yes, I can sense the anger."

"Blakely, stop joking around. This is serious." She leaves her ice cream unopened, and I swear to God, if she just lets that melt and doesn't eat it out of spite, I'm going to be the one who's pissed. "Are we not close anymore? I know I had a baby, but I feel like I've still been a good friend. Am I not there for you like you need me to be?"

"What?" I ask. "No, that's not it." I sigh and leave my ice cream unopened as well. "I didn't tell anyone. I think I'm still trying to make sense of it all. I loved him, and I thought we were going to get married, but then it just . . . ended."

Her expression softens, and she says, "What happened?"

Needing ice cream now, I pop off the lid, and she does as well. Together, we each take a large scoop and stick them in our mouths. Mint is okay. It's not my favorite, but it will do for now.

"Perry came home one day from work and told me he had exciting news."

"What was it?" she asks.

"He got a new job . . . in Australia."

"In Australia?" she asks, eyes wide.

"Yeah, and he thought that was exciting. Sorry, but I beg to differ. I mean, sure Australia is amazing and beautiful, and I'd love to go there one day really for the kangaroos and backward flushing toilets—"

"You realize that's such a generalization. I mean, Australians probably think we're all really loud, turkey chasers, and only drive pickups."

"Either way . . ." I say, continuing, "I don't want to live there. My life is here. My job that I've worked so hard to land is here, and I love it. I love my job so freaking much. He just assumed that I wanted to go wherever he wanted to go."

"He never talked to you about it?"

I shake my head. This is what surprised me most of all. He didn't ask. He hadn't even talked about the new job. At. All. "And that's where the miscommunication is. He didn't think I cared, and he wanted something new and different. I'm all for spontaneity, but I also like to be grounded with familiarity. I don't want to leave you and the baby and my other friends and the job. I like it here. Anyway." I pick at my ice cream with my spoon. "We got into a big fight. He said if I truly loved him, I'd go anywhere to be with him, and I told him if he truly loved me, he wouldn't make assumptions about our life. That he would have talked about the possibility and asked me what I thought rather than searching for something else. It was a big blowup, and he left that night."

"To Australia?"

I shake my head. "To a hotel. When he came back the next morning, he apologized for what he said. He'd thought about it and couldn't let this opportunity pass him by. I told him I couldn't let my career take a back seat to what he wanted, so . . . we decided to break up." I shove a spoonful of ice cream in my mouth, very unsatisfied with the mint chocolate chip. What's baffled me has been the fact that I haven't felt absolutely ruined and devastated by this. We've been together for so many years. *Why am I not a mess? Was I not passionately in love with Perry?*

"I'm so sorry."

I shrug. "It is what it is. He left to go to Australia. I said bye and gave him a hug. He asked me if I was sure, and I nodded. I had to move out of our apartment because even though I loved it, I couldn't afford it on my own and the lease was up."

"Wait, so you moved too?"

I nod. "Yeah, to a new place, not far from here, but yesterday, I noticed water leaking down the wall. Apparently, it was from a clog in the dishwasher upstairs. Flooded my apartment, so now, I have to wait for them to fix it, which will take a couple of weeks."

"So where are you staying? Here?" she asks with excitement.

I shake my head. "There is no way I'd stay here, not with Holden. It might be fun for a second, but after a few nights of hearing him cry, you might have to start nursing me too."

She cringes. "Ew, don't say that."

I chuckle. "It's true. And before you say it, I also won't be staying with Ollie or Winnie. I know the kind of sex lives they have. I refuse to be a witness to that, especially when I'm nursing my wounds over here."

"So what are you going to do?"

"Well, I'm staying in a hotel tonight, but tomorrow . . ." I pause because I'm still kind of stunned I took him up on his offer. "I, uh . . . I'll be moving into Halsey's place."

Penny pauses, her spoon halfway to her mouth, and stares at me, confusion in her expression. "Halsey? As in . . . Halsey Holmes?"

"Yeah," I say, eating a scoop of ice cream while I watch her process what I'm saying.

"What? How? Why?"

"It all happened kind of fast, but I was attempting to grab Pacey for a VIP family, and it came up that I broke up with Perry and needed a place to stay. Posey said Halsey had an extra room, and I don't know, desperation hit me hard, so I asked him if he was okay with that."

"Was he?" Penny asks, leaning forward in disbelief.

"Apparently, because he said I could stay there as long as I watered his bonsai tree."

"What's a bonsai tree?"

"Uh, some fancy little tree that lives in a pot. I looked it up during the game. They're kind of cute. Halsey named his Sherman. From what I could tell, he seems quite attached to it."

"Wait, I'm so confused. We're talking about the same guy, right? Halsey Holmes, center for the Agitators?"

"Yup, that's the guy."

"But . . . he barely talks. You've barely spoken to him. He's the least outgoing guy on the team, and he just so happened to offer you a place to stay?"

I shrug. "Probably felt bad for me. Whatever. I'll take his pity. I bet he has a nice place. Plus, since they're in and out of town, I'll have his place to myself a few times, which will be nice."

"And what about the times when he's there?"

"I guess I'll get to know him. And hey, it's only for a few weeks. I can nurse my wounds, wait for my apartment to be fixed, and enjoy whatever high-rise fancy apartment he's living in. It'll be nice."

"Will it? Or will it be awkward?"

"Maybe a little awkward, but I can deal with that. Plus, who knows? Maybe I can help him come out of his shell. He's so guarded and quiet, so maybe he just needs a little bit of Blakely to liven him up."

"You realize that it's not just bringing someone out of his shell. He lost his twin brother in a car accident. Eli told me Halsey used to be really outgoing and fun, just like Holden. It's not his personality that's shy." Her voice turns softer as she says, "He's grieving, Blakely, and slightly broken. I don't think you should mess with that."

My brow creases. "I would never mess with that and the obvious pain he sits with every day, but I don't know, maybe it might be nice for him to have someone to talk to if he wants to talk. And if not, maybe the company will be nice for him. Either way, he said it was okay."

"Maybe he was just being nice."

I quirk my mouth to the side in confusion. "Do you not want me to live with him?"

"I just want you to be careful. You're hurting; he's hurting. I think it could be a recipe for disaster."

"I'm fine," I say. *Kind of.* Maybe I'm still in shock. It's been so weird not seeing Perry each day . . . Perhaps I'm also still angry. Blindsided. "If anything, I'm just slightly bitter, but the way I see it is if we were meant to be together, Perry would have never taken that job in Australia, or I would have felt like I didn't have any other choice but to leave with him . . . and I didn't feel that. I felt like leaving here would have hurt more. So . . . yeah, it just wasn't meant to be."

"Well, I'm glad you have that mindset. I just want you to make sure you come to me if you feel differently. I think Halsey has a lot going on mentally, and I'm not sure he could handle your breakup."

"Oh, I wouldn't impose that on him," I say. "We might be roommates soon, but I also don't think we're going to end up being that close."

"Okay." She places some ice cream in her mouth before shaking her head. "I can't believe you said yes to his offer."

I chuckle. "You know me, I'm up for anything . . . other than moving to Australia on a whim."

"Apparently, you have your limits."

Chapter Three

HALSEY

"You know, I thought it was homier in here." Posey looks around my apartment. "It feels . . . cold. Is it the concrete walls and floors or the lack of area rug? Maybe both."

"Can you shut the fuck up and just help me?" I ask as I place a bonsai tree on the kitchen counter along with some of the supplies needed to take care of the stupid thing. I opted for the juniper bonsai tree because Posey insisted it looked more like a Sherman than the other varieties. The fucking thing was fifty dollars.

Fifty dollars for a miniature tree. Sure, I can afford it, but I was annoyed I had to purchase it in the first place.

I told Posey after our game last night that he was meeting me first thing in the morning to help me get groceries and some necessities for Blakely's arrival, as well as a bonsai tree.

We're running late because he made us examine the feminine products for ten minutes and what I should stock in my bathroom until I finally told him she was probably coming with her own. He agreed, that made the most sense.

We then smelled every candle in the candle aisle despite me telling him I had candles, and he ended up picking the scent that I already have in my home. This was followed up by him thinking I needed lots of snacks to make it seem like I was human. Pretty sure my walking body portrays that, but at that point, I was exhausted, so I let him fill up the cart.

Looking at the full reusable bags in my apartment, I'm guessing that was a big mistake.

"You know, I'm getting tired of the attitude," Posey says as he comes up to me with a bag full of miscellaneous things like notepads, pens, lotion, and a whisk. He asked if I had one, and when I said no, he put it in the cart. You have to make it homey for her, he said. You have to make sure she doesn't need a whisk and comes up short, he said.

Guarantee, she won't even touch the fucking whisk.

"Then you never should have offered up my place to stay." I fill up the sink with two inches of water and put Sherman—yup, that's happening—in the water so it can soak up whatever it needs.

"You can act all grumpy about it, but you know deep down, this was a great idea."

"How?" I ask. "How was this a great idea?" I motion to my apartment. "If you haven't noticed, I keep it pretty plain here. I don't need much, just a place to read and sleep. She's going to come here and think it's some sort of jail cell."

"Not with the new Egyptian cotton sheets we got for her bed." He pats me on the shoulder and says, "And can I just say, it's really white knight-ish of you to give her your bed since you don't have one in her room. Sleeping on an air mattress is a real commitment and making sure she doesn't have to suffer through that truly shows how much you like this girl."

"I wasn't going to make her sleep on an air mattress," I mutter. Nope, that will be me, which should be fun given I have lower back issues from playing hockey my whole damn life.

"That being said, we should probably move the bed, right?" he asks.

"Yes," I answer. "We have about an hour to get this shit done, so put away the cold food and I'll work on everything else, then we'll do the beds."

"Right, okay." Posey peeks into the sink. "Is that too much water for Sherman?"

"No, that's what the girl at the nursery said to do."

"Are you sure?"

"For the love of God, Levi," I shout. "Please just put away the fucking cold food."

"Sheesh, okay." He moves toward the bags and starts unloading them as I try to calm myself.

Am I stressed?

Yes.

I'm beyond stressed. Blakely will be here in an hour. I have to move my bed to her room, try to make this concrete sanctuary not look so . . . sterile, and mentally prepare myself that Blakely White will *temporarily* share my space. My private, bland, and quiet space. *And if there are two things Blakely is not, it's bland and quiet.*

"You know, you should probably iron the curtains you got for her room."

I move past him and start placing crackers, chips, and whatever food Posey thought she might like in the pantry. "We don't have time to iron, they'll shake out once they're hung."

He's stacking the cans of lime La Croix very carefully, making me want to scream at him. "I don't know, it's risky."

"We can steam them then, but you need to fucking hurry up."

"Dude, we need to make it look presentable. The last thing you want is for her to think you're some careless bachelor. Trust me, I know what I'm doing."

"Do you?" I ask. "Because I don't see you with a girlfriend?"

"Because I haven't pulled the trigger yet. Once I do, I'll have my girl in the palm of my hand."

I highly doubt it. If anyone is a hot mess on this team, it's Levi Posey.

Together, we unpack the food and—carefully—stock the kitchen, including the whisk he made me buy, as well as the colorful cutting knives that are pink, purple, and blue. He claimed it was a nice, feminine touch that I could afford since I was brimming with masculinity. Once again, his words, not mine.

"Now, we don't want to light the candle, but we need to place it somewhere," Posey says, holding up the rich mahogany-scented jar. "Silas told me that sometimes it can look too desperate if you actually light the candle." He glances around the barren living room. "Where are your coffee table books?"

"I don't have any."

"Then where are your actual books? I know you have them, as you read all the time."

"They're in my room. Why?"

"Because, Joanna Gaines likes to stack books and put a candle on top. It looks nice."

"Who is Joanna Gaines?"

"Jesus." Posey moves past me, bumping my shoulder, and heads toward my bedroom. He stops immediately and takes it in. "What the hell is this?"

"My room."

He glances over his shoulder at me. "It's a bed with stacks of books piled on the floor. Where is your dresser? Your curtains? Perhaps a rug to keep your feet warm when you first pop out of bed?"

"Don't need them."

"What the hell do you do with your money?" he asks with a shake of his head.

"Invest. Save. I don't know. Buy books."

"How about some shelves, huh? That might be nice. Look at these stacks and stacks of books. Don't you think they would want a place to live? What kind of bookworm are you?"

"It doesn't matter to me. They're fine as is. Stop stalling." I walk over to my bed and strip the sheets off as well as the blan-

35

kets and pillows while Posey studies my stacks and stacks of books.

"This might work." He picks up a thick black book with no dust jacket. I hate them and always Terracycle them when I get the book. "What is this? A thriller? Doesn't matter, it will go with the living room aesthetic." He takes off, and I clench my jaw, keeping my mouth shut so I don't fly off on him.

I've been close with Posey for a while now, and you wouldn't think that our personalities would mix well. He's kind of out there, odd at times, and a fucking monster while playing hockey. He's also an instigator but with a heart. Hard to explain him. He's all over the place, like right now, thinking he's some sort of God's gift to interior design. Funnily enough, he reminds me a lot of my brother Holden. He was the same way. Outgoing, always instigating shenanigans—something that used to get on our older brother's nerves—but had a fucking heart of gold.

Levi Posey might drive me nuts, and I might want to murder him at times, but it's almost as if Holden has pushed us closer.

Fuck, if Holden were still here, he'd be laughing his ass off in the corner, enjoying every second of my scrambling. He would egg Posey on. And he'd definitely be waiting off to the side, watching this entire circus unfold.

"The candle is set." Posey walks back into the room, dusting off his hands.

"Well, thank God for that."

"I also took Sherman out of his water because the dirt was saturated. His new home is on the console table behind your couch for better light. Which by the way, you have a console table, but you don't have bookshelves? Make that make sense."

"Just help me with this mattress."

Posey grabs one end and tugs it toward him, grunting in the process. "Why the hell is this so heavy? Do you sleep on concrete as well?"

"It's a custom mattress for my lower back. Use your fucking muscles."

"I am," he grunts as he tugs it across the floor while I push. "I was expecting something lightweight."

"Well, it's not, so keep tugging."

"Are we going straight to the other room, or do you want to make a pit stop and move half of the bed so we can move the bottom and place it in the room first?" Why does he have to make things so complicated? I swear to God, when you work with Posey, you need to be prepared for an extra step in everything you do, including talking about it.

"Just move it to the other bedroom."

Together, we drag the mattress into the living room.

"Are you sure? Because if we do this properly, we could unravel the bed and put it back without being clumsy about it. We could be efficient." He tugs; I push. "And are we really clumsy people? Or are we efficient motherfuckers?"

"Does it fucking matter?" I push hard on the mattress with my shoulder, scooting it a good two feet.

"Whoa, man," Posey says. "You almost knocked me over."

I shove again, sending him to stumble backward and hit the console table behind the couch.

"Ah," he yells. "You almost made me knock over Sherman."

"Grip the mattress and keep moving." I push again.

"I am, but you're being aggressive."

"Because we have like forty minutes until she's here, and you want to steam the goddamn curtains and talk about efficiency. Just get it the fuck done."

"Don't fucking get mad at me for setting standards."

"Just . . . pull . . ." I give the mattress a shove, and once again, I knock Posey away, but in the process, I lose grip of the mattress, leaving it tilting on its own. "Shit," I say just as it starts to tip over. "Grab it," I yell as I stumble forward but trip over some of the reusable bags we didn't put away.

"I can't," he yells back.

We watch in horror as it tips all the way over, right onto the console table and flat onto Sherman.

"Nooooooo," Posey yells as the plant topples to the floor, and with a loud crack, the pot breaks. Wet soil scatters all over the floor along with a smushed plant. Posey falls to his knees and holds up the dilapidated bonsai tree. He glares up at me, clutching the plant to his chest. "You monster."

I grip my forehead, staring at the mess. Fuck, I don't have time for this.

"Don't you have any remorse?"

Feeling panic start to take over, I step back and press both hands to the top of my head. "Fuck, we won't get this done in time."

"He was so innocent." Posey strokes the plant.

"Can you stop that," I yell, my chest filling with anxiety. "Fuck, what are we going to do? We don't have time for this." I shake my head. "This . . . this was a bad idea. I . . . I have to call her, tell her she can't come. I can't do this. I can't—"

"Whoa, whoa, whoa." Posey stands from the floor, holding the bonsai tree by the broken trunk. "You're freaking out."

"Of course I'm freaking out!" I yell. "I just broke the bonsai tree that I never wanted in the first place, soil is everywhere, and I don't have a goddamn vacuum to clean it up. Blakely will be over here in forty minutes, she doesn't have a bed to sleep on, and the curtains will be fucking wrinkled! Not to mention, what the hell am I going to do with a girl in my apartment? I don't know how to act around her, talk to her . . . not fucking stare into her gorgeous eyes every chance I get. She's going to think I'm some sort of stalker. And I'm not a stalker. This is your fault. You're the one who made me do this. You're the one who—"

"Okay, okay. You're on the verge of what some might call a mental breakdown. And I'll tell you this, pointing the finger won't solve the problem." He pulls his phone out of his pocket and says, "This is why we're a band of brothers. I'm just going to shoot over a quick text and all will be right with the world."

He types away on his phone. I watch his face scrunch in concern as he types, and I take in the mess. There is no way we're going to get this done. No fucking way.

38

My phone chimes with a text, and when I lift a brow at him, he winces. "Shit, was that to the group chat with you in it?"

I pull my phone out of my pocket and read his text.

Posey: *You guys, we're at DEFCON 1 over here. Holmes is about to wee himself from nerves. We need help. Taters, please grab a juniper bonsai tree and have it here in twenty minutes. Pacey, we need a vacuum cleaner like ten minutes ago. Get it here. Hornsby, we need two nightstands, preferably a white oak or black iron. You also have twenty minutes.*

I glance up at him. "I'm not going to wee myself."

"Say that to your quivering legs."

———

"THE CURTAINS LOOK LIKE SHIT," Silas says as all five of us stare at the room we haphazardly put together.

"You think I don't know that?" I ask. "Fuck, should I take them down?"

"No," Pacey says. "You don't have blinds, so she'll want curtains for privacy."

"Told you they needed to be ironed." Posey leans against the wall, arms folded.

"You are literally not allowed to say anything to me anymore." I point at him and move out of her bedroom and into the living room, where the soil has been vacuumed by a brand-new vacuum courtesy of Pacey. Sherman has been replaced. Posey stupidly said he feels more attached and bonded to the new one. I punched him after that comment.

My air mattress is blown up, but not made with my sheets. I didn't want her hearing the air mattress being blown up, but I didn't have time to put the sheets on. I'll have to do that later.

The stupid candle is on the book on the coffee table as well as a figurine of a hockey player that Eli insisted I have after Posey bitched about my apartment being too bland.

So . . . that's what I have in my living room. A fucking sofa, TV, coffee table, candle with a book, and a hockey player figurine. It looked better without the extra shit. Now it looks like I'm trying too hard and the other things are out of place.

Not to mention, New Sherman, or Sherman as we're going to refer to him from here on out, looks stupid as the only thing on the console table.

It all looks stupid. Everything.

The curtains.

The nightstands that don't match because Hornsby doesn't know what white oak is.

The disheveled and wrinkled bedding on her bed because we all tried to make the bed together, but none of us were taking directions from each other.

It's a fucking disaster.

I move my hand over my forehead, my nerves completely shot, as the boys join me in the living room.

"I never noticed how uninspiring your apartment was until you added that candle," Pacey says. "Now I'm questioning if you should have it at all."

"See, I fucking told him that." I gesture to Posey.

"Nah, I think the candle is a nice touch," Silas says.

"Thank you." Posey throws his arms up in exasperation.

We all turn to Hornsby, who looks between us. "Uh . . . I don't know much about candles. Penny is really in charge now."

I'm just about to pick up the candle and hand it off to Posey when there's a knock on the door.

"Fuck," I whisper.

"She's here," Posey says.

"Shit, am I sweaty?" I lift my arms and turn toward the boys.

"Oooo, giant pit stains," Pacey says. "Go change your shirt."

Hornsby leans in and sniffs me. "And throw on more deodorant."

Taters slaps me in the ass. "Hurry. We'll distract her."

Too fucking flustered to even ask if all four of them greeting her would be weird, I run down the hall to my disheveled room and tear my shirt over my head. I toss it in my hamper in my walk-in closet and quickly grab a black Agitators shirt and toss it on. I hear them open the door and greet her, so I quickly grab my deodorant, swipe it on, then, for the hell of it, swish some mouthwash around, too.

When I spit out the mouthwash, I look up into the mirror and adjust my hair with my shaky hand.

Jesus, man. Calm the fuck down.

The last thing you need to do is stumble over your words and look like a bumbling mess.

I take a few deep breaths and then head out to the living room, making sure to shut my bedroom door behind me. The boys part, and Blakely is there, two large suitcases by her side, looking so fucking good in a black hat with her hair curled over her shoulders. She wears a pair of leggings and a long-sleeved sweater that hangs slightly off her shoulder, revealing some lacy strap hugging her shoulder.

Fuck.

Me.

"Hey, there you are. Posey told me you spilled a smoothie all over your shirt so you had to change."

Jesus fucking Christ.

Unsure of what to do, I stick my hands in my pockets. "Yeah . . . I changed." I swallow the saliva building up in my mouth from the anxiety ripping through me.

She smiles. "Well, I didn't think half the team would be here to greet me, so what a surprise."

"We were having a team meeting," Taters says. "We like coming to Holmes's place because it just has that cozy feel to it, don't you think?"

Blakely looks around and I can see the confusion in her eyes as she takes in the cold concrete walls and floors. But because she's nice, she says, "Oh yes, very cozy."

"Well." Posey claps his hands together. "We should get going. The ice isn't going to skate on itself. Got to keep our legs warm."

"Oh right, you have practice."

"More like treatment today and keeping our legs moving," Pacey says. He glances at me. "See you at the arena."

"Yup." I nod, and one by one, the guys filter out of the apartment. Posey gives me a subtle thumbs-up right before he closes the door, leaving me alone with Blakely.

When silence falls over us, she says, "Well, thanks again for letting me stay here."

"Yeah, sure. Of course."

I awkwardly shift, she awkwardly grips her purse and we just . . . stand there, unsure of where to go from here.

Finally, she says, "How about a tour?"

Fuck, that's right. That would be the next step.

Pull your head out of your ass, Holmes.

"Right, yeah, good idea. So, uh, this is my place." I gesture to the open space.

There's a smile in her voice as she replies, "I can see that."

Yup, she knows this is your place, dumbass.

Be better.

"And, uh, this is the living room. I don't have cable or anything like that, but I have all the streamers. If you want to watch the hockey games, if you're into that, I have ESPN+."

"So I can watch your away games and see if you have any last-minute goals."

"Yeah," I say, gesturing to the console table. "That's the plant."

She turns and gasps. "This is Sherman? Well, I can see why you're so attached. He's very cute." She squats down to get a better look. "He looks like a real tree, just shrunk down to be a foot tall. I love it."

I've never been into plants, but sure, Sherman is kind of cool.

Am I attached like Posey? No, but I can see the interest there. The thing is interesting to look at.

"Have you always been into bonsai trees?" She stands up and turns toward me.

"Uhh, not really."

"Oh, then what got you into them?"

Yeah, Holmes, what got you into bonsai trees?

I scuff my foot against the floor and say, "Read about one in a book. Sounded interesting, so I grabbed one."

"And you've been friends with Sherman ever since. That's so sweet."

Yup, not looking like a fucking loser at all.

Friends with a goddamn tree. Thank you, Posey.

I lead her to the kitchen and say, "This is the kitchen. Help yourself to whatever you want. I stocked the pantry and fridge with food. I just guessed what you might like. Please don't feel shy to eat and drink things. I won't be around to do it myself."

"Well, that was sweet." She opens the fridge. "Ooo, lime La Croix. My favorite." That puts a little pride in my chest. The lime was my idea. She opens the pantry and smirks. "I can see what you bought and what you already had. The top shelf full of protein bars and powder is obviously what you live off, and the fresh bags of pretzels, crackers, and cookies . . . those are for me."

I pull on the back of my neck. "I wanted to make sure you had something."

"Thank you. Trust me, I'll eat it."

"Cool." I move over to the kitchen drawers and pull them open. "Oh, your keys." *Why the fuck are they in the drawer?* "Here you go."

"Thanks." *Right. Move on.*

"Silverware is here. Utensils in this one." I lift the whisk. "You can use this, feel free to whisk anything you need." I notice the tag dangling off the end, and I curse myself for leaving it on there.

Her smile grows even wider. "Oh, I love a brand-new whisk. I'll get good use out of that. Thanks."

She's being sarcastic. I can tell by her expression and tone.

It makes me sweat.

I point rigidly behind her. "And that's the balcony. I don't have any furniture out there because I don't use it much, but I can buy some furniture if you want to go out there."

"Oh, don't worry about it. I can just lie on a blanket and enjoy the balcony like that. No need to buy furniture."

Fuck that. I'm buying furniture the minute I'm done with the tour.

I should have had it to begin with.

Blakely deserves furniture.

"And down the hallway is your bedroom." I head that way. "You have your own bathroom, so no need to worry about sharing one with me."

"Oh great." I open the door to her bedroom and cringe at the sight of the cumbersome bedding and wrinkled curtains. It's painfully obvious that I just set this up and did a terrible job at that. "Aw, it's so nice in here." She takes a look around.

I run my hand over my jaw nervously. "Sorry about the wrinkles. I didn't have time to iron everything."

She turns toward me and, to my surprise, places her hand on my arm. "Don't even worry about it. It looks great. Thank you."

"And the nightstands don't match," I blurt out. "Sorry."

She chuckles. "Seriously, Halsey. It's fine. This is perfect. I really appreciate you offering up your place. I know it must feel like an invasion of your privacy and all that, but I promise you'll barely notice I'm here. I'll be sure to watch over Sherman while you're gone on your away trips."

"Thanks," I say, feeling defeated and exhausted. No need to head to the freaking arena today. I got my workout through worrying. "Well, I guess I'll leave you to it."

"Thanks. I'm just going to grab my bags."

"Oh, I can help you with that."

"That's okay, I can do it."

We both head out of her room toward her bags. "Seriously, I got it." I grab both of the handles.

"Halsey." She smiles softly. "You've done enough."

"This is no big deal." Why am I fighting with her over her bags?

Because I'm sad and pathetic and want her to know that I'm a good guy who would help a girl with her bags.

Despite her protest, I move the bags down the hallway, pushing one and pulling the other, and I set them to the side in her room.

"Thank you," she says softly.

"You're welcome. Uh, and you have my number so if you need anything, just let me know."

"Great. Thanks. I'll probably be unpacking and settling in tonight but let me know if you want me to grab dinner or something."

"Nah, I'm good. Probably will go out with the guys."

"Oh, have fun." I nod, and just as I walk away, she says, "Quick question, what's your policy on me having people over?"

Uhhhh . . .

Like men? Because I know the answer to that, and it's not positive for her. There is no way in hell I'd be able to sit in my apartment knowing she has a man in her room with her.

"I mean like friends . . . just to clarify," she says. "I have no intent of having men here, but if I were to have Penny over, would that be okay?"

Thank fuck.

Blakely and a man here? Yeah, I wouldn't have been able to suffer through that. I'd move out first.

"Oh yeah, that would be fine," I reply. "Treat my apartment like yours."

Just don't bring men home.

"Well, thank you. I appreciate it."

"Of course." I glance over my shoulder and thumb toward the door. "Well, I should get to the arena."

"Okay, have a good treatment." She cutely waves, then lays down one of her pieces of luggage and unzips it.

That's my cue to leave . . . and to fucking breathe for a second.

Chapter Four

BLAKELY

"I half expected Holmes to be a little more . . . homey with his place," Penny says, glancing around his apartment. "I mean, not even a picture on the walls."

"Can you hang pictures on concrete walls?"

"I have no idea." She runs her hands over them. "I've never seen them before unless I was in a basement, but we're not in the basement. We're in a high-rise. Frankly, the whole thing is confusing."

"I know, but I also kind of like it," I say, examining his space. "It's simple. I would have pictured a rug for him at least, but the clean lines and simplicity of it all make sense for the kind of man Halsey is."

Holden stirs in his car seat but remains asleep as Penny walks over to the large sliding glass door that opens to the balcony.

"No furniture? This is an amazing balcony, and he doesn't have any furniture?"

"He said he would get some, but I don't think it's necessary, especially since I won't be here that long. He doesn't need to get it for me."

"He needs something out here. What a wasted space." She walks around, taking in the view. "You could fit an outdoor dining table out here, a few planters, an L couch. It's the perfect place for him to read his books. I don't understand why he wouldn't take advantage of it."

"I don't know. It doesn't seem like he . . . does much outside of hockey. You know?"

Penny pauses, then nods. "Yeah, I should have thought of that. Eli always talks about how different Halsey is from how he used to be. Makes me sad." She turns toward me. "I still can't believe you said yes to living here."

"Now that I'm here, I can't believe it either." I sit on the edge of his couch and look around at the plain gray walls, the matching floors, and the empty space. It could be warmer if Halsey allowed warmth in his life.

I don't know much about him, but I do know he's been through a lot. He's shut down, and not even his friends can bring him back to the guy he used to be.

Penny takes a seat next to me. "Want to talk about Perry?"

"Not really," I answer.

"Too bad, because I do. Do you miss him?"

Should have seen that coming.

I sigh and lean back on the couch. "Not really. I don't know . . . the whole thing feels so weird. I still can't believe he just left and didn't even look back. Here I thought there was actually something special between us, but boy, was I wrong."

"If he decided he made a mistake and returned, would you take him back?"

I shake my head. "No, I don't think so." And that is what's so strange. But every time I've stopped and thought about Perry, it hasn't been feelings of sadness that I've felt. In some senses, I dodged a bullet. Perhaps this sounds wrong, but I want to be someone's world. *Not someone who's easy to leave.* "I think he showed his true colors by leaving, Pen. If I'm honest, I don't want to be with a man who can walk away from me so easily. So I can't see why I'd take him back."

"That makes sense. In my humble opinion, he's a fool to let you go." I smile. Penny would say that. She's such a loving person.

"So does that mean you're going to move on?" *There's no other choice.*

"Move on with my life, yes. If you're implying moving on with dating, I'm pretty sure I'm done for now."

"Such a shame." She smirks at me. "I bet Halsey would be a lot of fun to mess around with."

"Don't even start with that," I say, pointing at her in warning.

She innocently shrugs. "What? I'm just saying . . . might be a good time to get to know him. And you have to admit, he's really hot."

My mind brings me back to Halsey in his black Agitators shirt, standing in my new room, apologizing for the non-matching nightstands and wrinkled curtains. Despite looking morose, the pull in his brow and the clench in his jaw gave him a broody, almost bad boy look, but the apology coming out of his mouth completely contradicted that notion. And then there was the way his shirt clung to his body. Tight around his arms, his chest . . . but it flowed around his tapered waist. And every time he stuck his hands in his pockets, his triceps flexed, tugging even more tightly on the sleeves. He had a boyish charm with a devil's body.

Really hot . . . not sure I'd describe him like that. It's too simple of a word. He's more than hot. He's handsome with an edge. Attractive with a heart. A combination of both, which I know would be devastating to anyone willing to place their heart in his standoffish hands.

"You've been thinking for a while there," Penny says with a nudge.

"Oh sorry." I chuckle. "Just thinking about Halsey."

"Oh, are you . . ." She wiggles her eyebrows.

"Not like that." I mean, sort of like that, but she doesn't need to know exactly what I was thinking. "He's hot, but there's nothing between us, so don't even start. This is a simple arrangement that will help me with my housing needs. That's it."

"Okay, but don't you think it would be so cool if you two, I don't know, fell for each other and got married and had a baby, and your baby could marry my baby, and we would be in-laws? Wouldn't that be great?"

"You need to come back to the office. That imagination is working hard."

She laughs. "Just one more week, and I'm back."

"Are you going to miss staying home with Holden?"

"Yes and no. Eli and I sort of got into a bit of a fight the other night because I told him I felt sad about leaving Holden, so he suggested I not go back to work since I didn't need to work."

I wince. "What a moron."

"Exactly. He went off about how he makes more money than we will ever need, and my working doesn't matter."

"Please tell me you set him in his place," I say.

"Oh, I did. I told him working isn't just about money. I like what I do. I enjoy working with the players and the team. That I love being a mom more than anything, but I also want to have something that's for me, and that's my job."

"Please tell me he understood."

"Not at first, but once I told him he was sleeping on the couch, he sat and listened some more. You know Eli; he's really protective and wants to provide for me, for the family. He wants to be the stupid alpha who does everything for his woman."

"Too bad for him, he fell for the wrong girl."

"Yup." Penny smirks. "Speaking of work, how is everything going?"

"Good." I shift so I'm facing her and lean my side against the back of the couch. "I have a meeting tomorrow with a high-profile donor."

"Why are you working with donors?" Penny asks.

"He came through the VIP relations to grab seats in our center ice suite and loved working with me, apparently. I'll loop in Wills once I find out what's going on, but I've researched him, and he's pretty impressive."

"What's his name?" Penny asks.

"Huxley Cane. Have you heard of him?"

Penny shakes her head. "No."

"Well, he has a business with his two brothers, and they've made some impressive moves. They're investors in The Jock Report."

"Oh wait, I do know about them. Didn't Ollie go to one of them for a job?"

"Yes, she went to JP Cane, who connected her with Ryot Bisley. Anyway, they run a few charities, and being that they're now friends with Silas, I'm trying to pull all the connections together. And to be honest, I'm slightly intimidated."

"Why?" Penny asks.

"During my research, I learned very quickly that Huxley Cane is the type of man who doesn't take shit from anyone. He's very cutthroat in the boardroom. He's made moves to benefit his company and his brothers, and he did it at such a young age. Not to mention . . . he's very good-looking."

"Is he married?"

I nod. "Yes, recently, and I believe his wife just had a baby. I swear I've seen his wife before."

"What do you mean?"

"I saw a picture of her, and she looked so familiar. I couldn't place her, and it's still driving me nuts." I shake my head. "Anyway, it should be interesting. I want to get settled in here and prepare for tomorrow's meeting."

Penny glances around. "Well, then let's get you set up and unpacked. Maybe run to the store and grab a few things to liven this space up a bit."

"No, I don't want to disturb his peace. He probably has it empty for a reason."

"Does he?" Penny stands and moves around the living room. "Or maybe he needs someone to come into his life to brighten things up because he'd never do it himself."

"Either way, I'm not going to be that girl. This arrangement is purely so I have a place to stay. I have no intention of trying to help Halsey with whatever is going on in his head. I doubt I'll even see him that much."

"You say that now . . . until he starts walking around the apartment without a shirt on."

"Doubtful," I say, standing as well. "Halsey doesn't seem like that kind of guy. Anytime I've spoken to him, he's either really quiet, stumbles over his words, or is soft spoken. He's not like Eli who would walk around without his shirt on because he's a conceited idiot who thinks everyone will fall to their feet over the placement of his nipples."

Penny chuckles, and in a swoony voice, she says, "Eli does have great nipples."

I roll my eyes and move toward my bedroom. "Please don't start on those again."

She follows me. "You're the one who mentioned them!"

⊏⊐

I STARE into the full-length mirror on the back of the door of my new bedroom, grateful there was one here. I feel like that's not something you think about until you don't have one.

I smooth my hands over my long navy skirt that flows down to my ankles. I paired the skirt with a white sleeveless bodysuit that I've left unattached at the crotch because my torso is too long to snap comfortably. No one likes a frontal wedgie, not even the kinkiest of ladies. Self-induced camel toe is never comfortable.

I spent a good portion of my night working on my fake tan. After washing it off last night, this morning has left me with the perfect golden bronze glow. It's taken me a few years and a lot of tutorials online to master my fake tanning routine, but now I have it down to a science, and it's looking good, giving me the confidence I need for this meeting today.

And to top everything off, I slicked my hair back into a low ponytail, leaving it parted in the middle, and added some dangling blue earrings that pull the whole outfit together. I think I'm as ready as ready can be.

Nerves bloom in my stomach, but I push them down as I grab my neon-green bag with a thin gold chain strap and cross it over my body.

I didn't see Halsey last night because he got home late, and I decided to hide away in my room, working on my tan. But as I open my bedroom door, I smell coffee, indicating he's awake and, for some reason, seeing him this morning makes me nervous. Maybe because I haven't really hung out with this man, and I'm about to see him in a vulnerable state, fresh and early in the morning.

But as I move into the main living space and spot him in the kitchen, leaning against the counter, staring ahead with a cup of coffee in hand, I realize that maybe this won't be as awkward as I'm anticipating.

He seems . . . relaxed, lost in his own thoughts.

And just like I thought, he's wearing a shirt. I'd have been shocked if he had been standing there without a shirt. It's such a shame. I'm curious about what he's hiding under that gray T-shirt. I mean, professional athlete, so his body is probably insane. And not that I'm staring, but not only is the man wearing a pair of black athletic shorts that hit him just above the knees, but his feet are also bare.

Yup. Bare.

In my opinion, revealing a man's bare feet is as scandalous as a brief glimpse of a woman's ankle back in the 1800s.

Since we're, you know, here and examining, I'd hate to leave out his sandy-brown hair that's sticking up in the front but flat in the back. Clearly, he sleeps on his back. And the grand finale, the thing that will make all ovaries join fallopian tubes in a collective weep, the thick layer of morning scruff that lines his square jaw.

Ooof, yup, that is . . . nice.

Okay, sure, the man is incredibly handsome. I'll give him that. But he's also extremely closed off and quiet, so I doubt I'd ever consider dating him. I need someone who can match my energy. Not that I'm looking for someone to date.

I move toward the kitchen and say in a cheery voice, "Good morning."

Startled, he glances to the side and straightens up. "Good, uh . . . good morning." He pats his hair, trying to straighten it out, but has zero control over it with his dry palm. It's cute.

Who would have thought such a giant man—six foot four, to be exact—would be such a cinnamon roll.

"Sorry, did I startle you?" I ask.

"No, you're fine." His eyes briefly scan me before moving back up to my face. The brief glance gives me a touch of satisfaction that I shouldn't be happy about because, like I said, I'm not interested. "Are you heading out?"

"Yeah, early morning," I say as I reach into my purse and grab my phone. "Have a big meeting that I want to prepare for in the office."

"Cool. Yeah, well, good luck with your meeting."

"Thank you. It should be—" My phone slips out of my hand and, in grand fashion, falls straight to the hard concrete floor with an agonizing smash. "Nooo," I say as I bend down.

At the same time, Halsey rushes over to help. I reach for it while he does as well, but I beat him to it.

The screen is completely cracked and black.

"Is it broken?" he asks, very concerned.

I try to turn it on, but the screen remains black, and I know there is no way it survived the fall.

Damn these concrete floors.

"Shit," I mutter. "Yeah, I think it is." I sigh and stare down at my lifeline. "I'm going to have to get a new one after work. I don't have time to do it this morning."

"I can run and get one for you."

I look up at him, surprised by his offer. "Oh, thanks, but it's okay. I appreciate it, though." I'm not sure if it's the mixture of hazel in his eyes, the balance of gold and green, or the concern in his expression, but for a moment, it makes me lose my balance, and while bending, I step forward, nearly falling into him.

He quickly reaches out to steady me with his hand on my arm.

"Whoa, you okay?" he asks.

"Yes," I answer. "Sorry about that." I push up to stand. "These shoes are hard to bend over in." I lift completely, unaware that my foot is stepping on the front of my skirt, so as I straighten myself out, my elastic-waisted skirt doesn't straighten out with me.

Instead . . .

It's pulled all the way down my body to the floor, where Halsey is still bent over, leaving me exposed in my unsnapped bodysuit and thong.

Dear Jesus, what have I done?

Horrified, I take inventory of what I'm dealing with as Halsey looks up, his eyes connecting with my unsnapped bodysuit that's acting more like a flowy loincloth than a fashionable garment.

"Oh God," I shout as I bend back down just as Halsey stands upright, like we're on a damn invisible seesaw. "Oh my God, I'm sorry. I flashed you."

He spins around, turning away, his hand in his hair.

"I didn't . . . I didn't do that on purpose," I say as I tug on my skirt, but since it's stuck under my foot, it only throws off my balance, causing me to topple backward on the floor and right out of my platform sandals that clunk to the floor.

Halsey turns around from the ruckus and finds me lying back on the floor, hands propping me up, my now loincloth barely covering my thong-covered crotch. Thank God for laser hair removal or else Halsey would be enjoying quite the scene.

His eyes fall to me, and when his head processes the hot mess in front of him—me completely out of my skirt, sandals splayed across the floor, and major crotch exposure on full display—he closes his eyes.

Mother of God, this is not what he signed up for.

"I . . . I didn't see anything," he says quickly, which of course sends me into a tailspin of embarrassment because whenever someone says they didn't see anything . . . we all know . . . they saw something.

No . . . they saw everything!

And I'm not one to get embarrassed, but this is a moment in my life that I know will sit heavily as my top core memory, never to be replaced until my very last breath.

Yup, branded in my brain forever.

"I want to, uh, help you, but I want to give you privacy."

How about one of those *Men in Black* memory erasers? Does he have any of those? That would be better than privacy right now.

I take a deep breath because it can't get worse than this and say, "Pretty sure privacy is a moot point by now." I struggle to stand as his eyes remain closed. I shake my skirt out and step into it, being very careful not to stand on it. Once it's slipped on, I say, "Okay, I'm no longer flashing you."

His eyes peer open as I catch a twinge of red staining the apples of his cheeks. "I'm sorry."

"What are you sorry about?" I ask. "I should be the one apologizing." I slip my shoes on. "Not every day the random person you have staying in your spare bedroom tries to flash you with their unsnapped bodysuit. I just want to state for the record, if I had it snapped, you would have been exposed to the inner depths of my nether regions. Think wedgie but in the front. No one wants to see that kind of crevice. And I know for damn sure you didn't think to yourself, oh, let me invite this girl to live with me, only to be flashed an unwarranted camel toe. Trust me, the loincloth was way better, and I don't know why I just said crevice because crevice is not a great choice of wording when talking about you know . . . the crotch area—ew, I hate the word crotch. I don't know what's worse, crotch or cervix. Both are just awful. But, God, I just flashed you, which probably woke you up faster than the caffeine in your coffee, and I swear I didn't do that on purpose. I didn't think this morning, you know what? Let's see how we can make the hairs on the back of Halsey's neck stand straight with horror—ah yes, step on your skirt and flash him your loincloth. Not on the plan this morning. And I'm rambling, I understand that, but I'm slightly horrified that I nearly slapped you in the face with my crotch . . . Ugh, that word . . . so . . . yeah."

If he wasn't rethinking his decision of having me as a room-mate when I whipped my loincloth at him, he's definitely rethinking it now after that unnecessary speech that offered no value to the world in the slightest.

"It's fine," he says, looking so uncomfortable. I'm sure he wants to slink away and retreat into one of his books so he can forget this ever happened. "Are you okay?"

"Only mortified, but it's nothing a heavily frosted donut and cup of coffee can't fix," I say as I take a deep breath. "Wow, okay, what a way to start the morning, huh?"

"Yeah." He leaves it at that but keeps eye contact, a strong eye contact that makes my stomach jolt with nerves.

"Anyway." I thumb toward the front door. "I should be going so I can call Penny and tell her my life is over now."

He nods toward my phone. "It's broken, remember?"

I glance down at it, then back at him. "Dammit. Well, I'll call her from the office. I guess better to get my clumsiness out now rather than in my meeting. Anyway, enjoy your coffee, good luck tonight, and yeah . . . sorry."

I head toward the front door as he says, "It's fine."

But I don't stay to hear him say bye because I just flashed Halsey Holmes—and I'm sure his little, innocent heart has been traumatized forever.

⎯⎯

"THANK YOU FOR MEETING WITH ME," Huxley Cane says as he unbuttons his suit jacket and takes a seat across from me.

When I say this man is on another level, I'm dead serious.

There is an air about him. His commanding presence

consumes your attention the minute he enters the room with his powerful stride, the deep, fixed expression in his eyes, and the way he subtly moves through the space with the knowledge that everything he glances at he owns.

Literally owns.

The walls.

The air.

He owns it all with one simple look.

And his suit, the fabric screams thousands of dollars. Stitching pristine, buttons sharply polished. His hair so perfectly styled, while his controlling eyes offer both a sense of welcome and the threat not to fuck with him.

He's intimidating, poised, and so handsome that I can't imagine what it would be like to be in a bedroom with him.

"Not a problem," I say as I fold my hands in front of me and try not to shiver from the way he so casually props his arm up on the armrest of his chair.

When I got to the office, I was so shaken from flashing Halsey that it took me a solid half hour to calm my racing heart. By the time I had my breathing under control, I only had twenty minutes before Huxley arrived, so I powered through my preparations, leaving me more frazzled than I care for.

"How was your trip up here?"

"Good," he says, his voice softening. "Lottie, my wife, and our baby joined me as well as my brothers and their wives. Lottie's cousin too. I appreciate tonight's tickets, by the way."

"Oh, not a problem at all. We put you in one of our best suites, right on center ice. It has a quiet area for the baby and a private bathroom, everything you need."

"Thank you." His eyes remain on mine as he speaks. *Man, he's intimidating.* "My wife's cousin is actually on the team."

"Really?" I ask. "I didn't know that. May I ask who it is?"

He nods. "Oden O'Connor."

"OC?" I ask. "That's so great. He's been an amazing addition to the team, especially with Rivers being out injured right now."

"We were excited to see him on the West Coast. He's close with his sister, so she's happy to have him an easy flight away."

"I get that. I have a sister who has kids, and they live farther away. It's sad not to be able to spend as much time with her as I'd like. You're lucky to have your family so close."

"I am." He clears his throat. "Well, do you mind if I switch this to business? I have some meetings after this, but I don't want to be rude."

"Not at all," I say. "I don't want to keep you longer than you can afford. I know your time is very valuable."

"I appreciate it." His expression gentles, only a touch. "Are you aware that we invested in The Jock Report?"

"Yes," I answer, marveling at the way he can go from a light conversation to business in seconds. His entire body changes from relaxed and easygoing to commanding and in charge. Yeah . . . he's really hot—not something I should be thinking about. Not even close.

"We're attempting to start a division from The Jock Report that helps the athletes with their individual charities and offering them a chance to have an option on their profile to donate. We're trying to figure out a lot behind it, like logistics and rewards for those who contribute, but we're looking to launch with a large kickoff party."

"Oh, that sounds really cool." I wince, not wanting to sound rude. "But where do I fit into all of this?"

"I want you to help head up the VIP relations for the Pacific division."

Uhhh . . . what?

Is he offering me a job?

I shift on my chair and try to find my words.

"You . . . you want me to work for you?"

"I do," he says. "Not only have I been convinced by the relationship we've developed over the past month, but I've also been thoroughly impressed with your attention to detail, accommodating personality, and people skills. You're exactly what we're looking for with this position." He reaches into his suit jacket and pulls out a business card. Sliding it across the desk, he says, "This is my email. I know this is a lot to consider, but I'll send you more information about the position when I return to the office." He stands from his chair, and I do as well. While he buttons his suit jacket, he says, "I pay extremely well and offer unmatched benefits. Think about it."

"O-okay," I say as I round my desk.

He holds his hand out to me, and I take it. He grips it softly and says, "I look forward to working with you, Blakely."

With that, he leaves my office and heads down the hallway, leaving me in a state of confusion.

Huxley Cane wants me to work for him?

How the hell did I manage that?

And how did I go from loincloth exposure to a job interview in a matter of hours?

Chapter Five

HALSEY

"Fuck yes, donuts," Silas says, approaching me and reaching for the box in my hands.

I swat his hand away. "They're not for you."

"Who the fuck are they for?" he asks, insulted.

"Not for you, that's all that matters." I head toward the elevators, nerves ripping through my stomach. I sat in my car in front of the donut shop for ten minutes to convince myself this was a good idea, not a creepy one.

And the phone I bought right before that wasn't a creepy, stalkerish move either.

"Why are you going up the elevators?" Silas follows closely. "Wait, are you going to go see Blakely?"

"Don't you have some warming up with an exercise band to do?"

"The elastic band can wait." He stands in front of me just before I'm about to press the up button to the elevator. "Are you taking donuts to Blakely?" A smile passes over his lips, and it takes everything in me not to knock it off his face.

"Can you just mind your own business?" I try to hit the up button again, but he blocks it.

"Why won't you admit it?"

"Because what does it matter?"

"You're making a move without telling your boys. That's why it matters. Don't you think you should consult with us? Hell, she's been there for one night, and you're already hitting on her?"

"I'm not fuckin' hitting on her," I say, feeling irritated. "And I sure as hell am not making a move. Also, you were the ones who told me to ask her out the day we discovered she was single."

"That's different."

"How?" I ask.

"It was our idea. We're always right."

"You're a goddamn idiot," I reply, my blood pressure spiking from this stupid conversation. "And if you must know, she had a rough morning that I won't get into because, frankly, you don't need to know, but she also broke her phone. She was stressed and mentioned needing a donut. She also needed a new phone, so I picked it up for her. The donuts were on the way."

"Luxe Donuts is not on the way to the arena, but nice try." He folds his arms at his chest. "So this isn't about making a move on her?"

"No."

He eyes me suspiciously, but that smile stays fixed on his lips. "I don't believe you, but tread carefully. You don't want to shoot your shot too soon."

"Trust me, I won't be doing that . . . ever."

"Okay." He chuckles and moves out of the way. "Keep telling yourself that."

I press the button, and when I expect him to walk toward the locker room, he doesn't.

"What?" I ask, feeling the pressure of his gaze.

"I think you could use someone like Blakely in your life. It would be good for you."

"Can you keep your fucking voice down?" I say, glancing over his shoulder to make sure no one heard him. "Jesus. Just . . . just drop it, okay?"

"Okay," he says with a shrug, and this time, he walks away.

Fuck, I shouldn't have done this. My friends are too involved in my life. They think they know what's best for me but don't know anything.

They don't know I'm absolutely terrified to give Blakely these things.

That this morning, when I saw her appear from her bedroom, I felt my heart stop beating from how goddamn beautiful she is.

That even though I felt bad that she was embarrassed this morning, I found it so goddamn endearing that she was flustered.

And they sure as hell don't know that I stood in the middle of my living room last night, staring at her bedroom door, wondering if I should knock on it and ask her if she needed anything.

I didn't knock.

I was too much of a chickenshit to take a step past my living room.

The elevator dings, and the doors open in front of me. I hesitate for a moment. *Maybe this was a bad idea.*

Maybe I should just head back to the locker room and pretend this never happened.

The thought of ignoring my brazen idea is really appealing until I realize I can't walk back to that locker room now with donuts and a phone after Silas saw me.

He would never let me live it down.

And not only that, but he'd also tell the other guys.

I have to go through with the idea, so I step onto the elevator and press the third floor where her office is.

As I ride up, I take deep, calming breaths, telling myself not to get too nervous and that everything will be okay.

When the elevator stops and the doors open, I run right into a familiar face. Familiar to what I've seen in the media at least.

"Halsey Holmes," he says while holding out his hand. "I'm Huxley Cane."

I take his hand and give it a firm handshake. "Yes, Huxley, how are you?"

"Great," he says. "It's an honor to meet you. You had me on the edge of my seat the other night with your late-game goal."

"That's what everyone's been telling me."

"Hell of a game. Plan on going tonight with some friends and family. Good luck."

"Thank you, I appreciate that," I say as he moves around me and walks into the elevator.

With a nod, I move down the hallway toward Blakely's office. When I see the office door is open, I steel my nerves and knock on the wood while poking my head in.

She's sitting at her desk, staring into space so my knock startles her. "Oh, Halsey," she says, making eye contact. "What are you doing here?"

I step into her office. "Uh, I thought you might need a new phone." I walk up to her desk and place it on the glass surface.

"Seriously?" she asks, looking stunned. "You got me a phone?"

I pull on the back of my neck while holding the donuts, starting to feel even more foolish from her reaction. "Well, I assumed you might need one for the game tonight and everything. You just need to insert your SIM card. I didn't know what case you'd like so I just grabbed this," I say while pulling a purple case from my back pocket. "Apparently it doesn't slip from hands easily. And there's a screen protector already installed on it as well. The purple is for the Agitators, but feel free to change it."

She stares at the phone and the case for a few seconds before looking up at me.

"If you don't like it or if it's wrong, I can take it back. I have time, so I can make the trip."

She shakes her head. "No, sorry, I love it, I'm just . . . stunned, is all. This was so nice of you. Thank you, Halsey."

"Oh sure." I set the donuts down as well. "And these are

because you said you needed a donut. Not sure if you were able to pick one up or not."

She offers me that beautiful smile, which makes me so goddamn weak that I grip the chair in front of me so I don't make a fool of myself.

"I wasn't able to grab a donut, so you just made my day."

"Well, I felt bad, so . . . hope your day goes better."

She stands from her desk and rounds it, coming right up to me. Unsure what she's about to do, I just stare at her as she loops her arms around me and pulls me into a hug.

A warm, genuine hug.

I'm quite stiff at first, but after one second of feeling her around me, my arms immediately circle her, and my head leans in, taking in the sweet scent of her shampoo—it's like a field of flowers.

"Thank you so much, Halsey. I appreciate it."

"Oh, you're welcome," I say as she pulls away. My fingers drag along her slender back before I let go.

Those beautiful eyes stare up at me as she says, "It's been an insane day, and I'm not sure I even apologized for flashing you. Did I? I blacked out. I know I spoke of a loincloth. Honestly, it wasn't my best moment." She flips open the donut box and pulls one out. She then takes a giant bite before letting her head fall back while she moans in delight.

Jesus . . .

"These are so good. Here, have one." She gestures toward the box.

"No, those are for you."

"Don't make me eat a donut alone, Halsey. Unless . . . will it mess up your pregame routine? If so, then don't take one. But if it will ensure you don't make me split my skirt, then do take one." She glances down at her skirt. "This is a frilly skirt, though . . . so I don't think I can split it, but I can flash people my loincloth, so . . . ugh, I don't know. Just eat a stupid donut."

I smirk and reach around her for a blueberry yeast donut.

She studies my choice. "Never would have guessed you'd choose that."

"I love everything blueberry."

"Really?" she asks, looking perplexed. "You don't look like a blueberry kind of guy."

I take a bite, then ask, "What does a blueberry kind of guy look like?"

She looks away for a moment, then, in question form, asks, "Blue?"

That makes me smirk. If only she knew the blue balls I have at the moment.

"I guess we can be deceiving."

"Apparently." She leans against her desk and blows out a long breath.

She studies the ground like something is on her mind.

"Is everything okay?"

"Huh? Oh yeah, just . . . kind of a crazy day." She glances at her open door. "Can I tell you something that you must keep within the roommate confidentiality agreement?"

"There's a roommate confidentiality agreement?" I ask, loving that she already feels so comfortable with me. Hell, if I flashed her my loincloth, I'm not sure I'd be able to act so casual an hour or so later.

"It's well known that the minute you share a space with a human, a confidentiality agreement is built in. Like if you happened to trip out of your shorts and show off your ding-dong this morning, I would have laughed hysterically and pointed, but then kept that close to my chest . . . possibly telling Penny, because she is technically attached to me."

"You realize anything you tell Penny is going to get to Hornsby, and there is no way Hornsby will keep that to himself. He'll announce it in the locker room."

Blakely shakes her head. "Trust me, the number of secrets we're able to keep to ourselves is unmatched. Your jiggling ding-dong would have gone into the vault."

"Good to know." *Although if she ever sees my cock, she better not refer to it as a jiggling ding-dong, that's for sure.* If my cock was in her sight, there'd be no jiggling. Period.

"So . . . are we in the vault?"

"You never have to worry about me talking about your secrets, Blakely," I say seriously.

She smiles softly. "Should have known. You're the guy people can trust."

I'm not sure how to respond, so I finish my donut.

"Anyway. Not sure if you ran into him in the hallway, but Huxley Cane was just here."

"Yes, I saw him."

"Well, he offered me a job."

My brow pulls together in a frown. "He did?"

She nods. "He did. I'm still unsure what he really wants me to do. Something with launching a new donation section of The Jock Report, and he wants me to be the VIP relations for the Pacific division."

My skin feels itchy from the thought of Blakely taking a new job. What would that entail? Would she have to move?

"He said he pays well, and the benefits are unmatched. He said he'll send over more information later."

"Um, let me get this right. He met you here, at the Agitators head office, and offered you a job? That's . . . well, that's ballsy."

"My thoughts exactly. But it's Huxley Cane. I guess that's what that sort of man does."

"Wow." I shift from one side to the other. "How do you feel about the job? Would you have to move?"

"I don't know," she says. "Does the idea of working for someone who has potential to truly grow my career sound appealing? Of course. But I love this job. I love working with you guys and with Penny. And I have no idea about moving. I guess if they asked me to move, I'd have to think about it. Which is crazy to say out loud since I didn't want to move with my boyfriend, but that was to Australia, and that was for his job. Maybe I'd move for my job." She shrugs casually. "I don't know."

Maybe she'd move for her job?

Panic immediately rushes through me, causing a light sheen of sweat to form on my lower back.

Not that I'm ready to make a move on her, or even really consider it, but if she moved . . . fuck, I don't know how I'd react to that.

You're fucking fooling yourself . . . you know how you'd react.

I'd regret never asking her out.

I know that for damn sure.

"Anyway, sorry to bother you with all of this. I'm sure you have things you have to do for your game. And listening to me talk about a new job is not one of them. And thank you for the phone. I'll pay you back."

"No need."

She gives me a cute side-eye expression. "Halsey, I'm paying you back. Also, thank you for the donuts. I plan on eating at least three more of these in the sanctuary of my office. Don't tell anyone." She squeezes my forearm, and I hate that my stomach nearly floats out of my body from the touch. "Good luck today."

"Thank you," I say, wanting to stay longer and talk through this new job thing. Convince her that moving probably isn't the best idea, that she has a life here and friends and people who like her . . . actually like her.

But I've been excused, and it's probably for the best because I need a game plan. She can't take that job. She can't move. And I need to give her a reason she can't.

⸻

"THIS MUSTARD IS AMAZING," Posey says with his mouth full of a bologna sandwich, some of the manufactured meat hanging out of the bread, flapping as he talks about it. Fucking vile. "It's new, and it's really adding a special . . . je ne sais quoi . . ."

"Don't be a douche," Silas says as he leans back against his locker.

"Do you really eat one of those before every game?" OC

asks, looking at Posey with a certain disgust in his upper lip. We all share the same sentiment.

"How do you think I'm able to hold my own on the ice?" He lifts his shirt, showing off his six-pack. "This is built on bologna."

"It's disgusting," Silas says, looking grumpier than usual.

"What's your problem?" Posey calls him out.

"Ollie and I got into a fight this morning, and I'm irritated," he answers.

"What was the fight about?" OC asks.

Silas stares up at the ceiling for a second. "She wanted to be on top this morning, and I wanted her from behind, so she ended up cutting me off and well . . . yeah."

The room turns silent, and after a moment, Posey says, "Do you really think we're going to feel bad for you that you're a dumbass and wouldn't let your girl ride you?"

"I wasn't looking for sympathy." He gestures toward me. "Focus on Holmes and the sour look on his face."

The boys turn toward me, and OC asks, "What's going on? You do look kind of . . . different."

"Ate something weird," I answer as I put on my shin guard.

"Liar," Silas says. And I know that tone. He's irritated, so he's going to make sure everyone around him is irritated. "He took donuts to Blakely, and it's obvious it didn't go well."

Yup . . . the motherfucker.

"Whatever happened to fucking privacy?" I ask him.

He circles his finger in the air. "Around here, there is no such thing."

Clearly.

"Dude, you took her donuts?" Posey leans in. "That's really nice. Did she not like them? Were they the wrong kind? Fuck, were they cake donuts, not yeast? Always go with the yeast, man. I don't know one person who will rave about a cake donut over a yeast."

"He's right about the yeast," OC chimes in.

"What about a sourdough?" Silas asks. "An old fashion? Those are good."

"You would eat that over a classic glazed?" Posey asks before shoving the rest of his sandwich in his mouth. "No fucking way."

"I mean, they're good," OC adds, "but I have to agree with Posey. They don't top a classic glazed."

"No one ever agrees with Posey," Silas says.

"Not true." Posey scrapes a drop of mustard from the corner of his lip. "A lot of people agree with me. I'm the smartest motherfucker on this team. It's why all of you are with women."

"If that's the case, then the donut situation wouldn't have gone bad. Ever think about that?" Silas asks. "This sorry asshole over here has his tail tucked between his legs because he tried giving a girl donuts, and it didn't work out. Where were you with that?"

"First of all . . ." Posey holds up one finger. "I can't be held accountable for when people go rogue. I had no idea he was taking her donuts, and if I did know, I'd have heavily suggested yeast donuts, not cake."

"They were not cake donuts!" I shout, feeling frustrated with this stupid back and forth.

The guys study me, then OC asks, "Were they yeast?"

"Yes, they were fucking yeast. This has nothing to do with the donuts. She actually liked the donuts."

"Huh." Posey scratches his jaw. "I could have sworn it would have been a cake versus yeast issue. Did you say something unsavory to her?"

"What would unsavory be?" OC asks.

"Like . . . let me fuck you from behind despite you wanting to ride me," Posey replies, glancing over at Silas.

"Jesus," he grumbles. "I wanted to spank her, okay? There are reasons for it."

"Ever think she didn't want to be spanked?" Posey asks.

"Trust me . . . she wants to be spanked."

"Who wants to be spanked?" Pacey asks, walking in from the training room.

"Ollie," Posey answers. "But not today. Silas is mad about it.

Also, something is going on with donuts and Holmes and Blakely, but we haven't gotten to the bottom of it."

"Were they yeast donuts?"

"For the love of fuck!" I shout, startling the guys. "They were yeast, okay? I'm not an asshole who thinks I can surprise a girl with cake donuts and make an impact. It wasn't the goddamn donuts."

"I think he's upset," Posey says, stating the obvious.

"If it wasn't the donuts, then what's going on?" OC asks, coming in with concern. He very well might be a welcome addition to this group. He seems more levelheaded than these other idiots I deal with.

I glance around the room, looking at my impatient friends. I shouldn't tell them, but I don't have the bandwidth to think up anything else. *And it was in the roommate confidentiality agreement vault.* But, fuck, I need the help. I hope she doesn't hate me if she ever finds out . . .

"She was offered a new job."

"Shit, that sucks," Pacey says. "Not being able to see her at work."

"Will just make it harder to make a move, but we can work around that," Posey says.

"She might be moving . . . back to the States," I add.

"Well, fuck," Silas says, his compassion starting to show.

"Man, I'm sorry," OC says.

"Leaving Vancouver? Really?" Posey asks.

"I think—"

"No!" Posey shouts, shaking his head. "Nope, it's not happening. I refuse to let it happen."

"As if you have control." Silas rolls his eyes.

"She seems dead set on being her own woman," Pacey adds. "Hence why she didn't move with her boyfriend. Do you think you can go up to her and tell her no? Not going to work."

Still shaking his head, Posey continues. "This is not how it was supposed to happen. She's not supposed to get a new job. Who's even offering the job?"

"Huxley Cane," I answer.

"Who the hell——"

"Hey, my cousin is married to him," OC says, cutting Silas off. Then he pauses for a second. "Hold on . . . Blakely. Jesus, that's how I know her."

Confused, I ask, "How do you know her?"

"My sister, Kenzie, was roommates with her in college. Fuck, that was driving me crazy."

"Your sister was roommates with Blakely?" Pacey asks. "Fucking small world."

"Yeah, kind of crazy. I'm not sure Kenzie even knows that. She's actually dating one of the guys who programmed The Jock Report. His name is Banner. They're making a lot of changes, so I could see why they want to hire Blakely."

Shit . . .

"Probably not what lover boy wanted to hear." Silas thumbs toward me. "Do you know anything about the positions?"

OC shakes his head. "Just that they have a big office in Los Angeles."

"Ooof, that doesn't bode well for the situation." Posey takes a deep breath. "Okay, the last thing we need to do is freak out and lose our minds over our perfectly executed plan not going our way."

"Are you talking about Holmes or yourself?" Silas asks.

Posey glares at him. "Both. We just need to find a way to make sure she doesn't move."

"Should we really attempt to repress her chances at growing her career?" Pacey asks, making me think the same thing. I mean, if she wants to grow, if she wants to move, who am I to stop her?

Then again . . . it makes me physically ache with the thought of her moving without at least telling her how I feel.

But telling her how I feel? Christ, that makes me even more physically ill.

"We aren't repressing her," Posey says. "We're just giving her options, is all."

"What do you mean?" I ask.

Posey looks me in the eyes and says, "We need to show her that you're boyfriend material."

"You know," OC says. "I'm not sure that's going to do anything. I don't remember much about Blakely except when I heard Kenzie tell Mom that she admired Blakely's determination to be a free spirit. To be her own person. I didn't really get what she meant at the time, but now that I know her a little, I do. I doubt anything you plan could 'change her mind.' She's going to do what she wants."

"Valuable information." Silas slips on his socks now, the game looming closer.

"We aren't going to try to tell her what to do," Posey clarifies. "We're just going to dangle a carrot in front of her and see if she bites. And when I say carrot, I mean Holmes's penis."

"We are not dangling my penis," I say.

Posey rolls his eyes. "Metaphorically. If she got a look at your penis, I'm pretty sure it would scare her away. That shit has girth."

"Can you not?" I ask.

"Please, everyone sees it in the shower, along with Silas's piercings and my perfectly shaped balls."

"When I say no one is getting a solid look at your balls, I fucking mean it," Pacey says. "But he's right, Holmes, you do have a lot of girth."

OC runs his hand through his hair. "Christ, didn't know we were sneaking peeks at everyone."

"You don't look?" Silas asks. "That's a fucking lie."

"I just went with the eyes-up policy."

"Apparently, we don't here," I say while pulling on my socks as well.

"Either way, we can't show her the penis yet, but we can devise a plan to show her how great you are and tempt her to be with you."

"I don't want to make a big deal of this," I say, regretting even bringing it up.

"But do you like her?" Pacey asks.

"We all know he likes her," Silas answers. "Every thread in the carpet knows that Holmes likes Blakely."

"Then why not even try?" Pacey asks.

"Because I don't want to bother her."

"How is it bothering her?" Posey asks.

"Oh, I don't know. Maybe because she lives with me now, and she doesn't want some hockey player fumbling around trying to make a good impression." I tug on my hair. "Not to mention, I just don't think I'm ready for that shit. I'm not . . . I'm not the same person," I say softly. *And that shuts every mouth.* No more sarcasm. No more ridiculous talk. Thank fuck.

"You're not," Pacey says. "And that's okay. We all change during our journey through this crazy world, but you can also veer from today's version of you. And I think I can speak for all of us when I say we don't want to see you alone. We want you to have someone you can talk to at night and share this life with. If any one of us deserves it, it's you."

"He's right," Silas says. "It's okay to recognize you're not the man you were a few years ago. Losing your brother . . . of course that will change you. But it's not good for you to just hole up in your room and not experience life outside of hockey. This is the first girl you've shown any remote interest in, in God knows how long. Don't let it slip by because you feel who you are now won't appeal to her."

"I know I'm new to this," OC says. "But I agree with them. My sister was very guarded, especially when she first met Banner, but he slowly eased his way into her life, and now she's the happiest I've ever seen. I think if you just . . . ease your way in, you'd at least see if there's something between you two."

"I agree," Posey says. "At least give it a shot. You'll regret it if you don't."

I sigh heavily, knowing they're right.

I'm not the same person since I lost Holden. He was . . . he was my other half. I won't *ever* be the same person, but I'm wasting away a life he could have had. I miss him. I can't fathom being happy with him gone. But if he saw me now, he'd be pissed. I know he would. He'd tell me to get my head out of my ass and stop letting the past haunt me—easier said than done.

I might be uncomfortable with the thought of easing myself in, but I know for a fact I'll regret not doing anything.

"Okay, what should I do?"

A large smile stretches across Posey's face. "First things first, you no longer wear a shirt around the apartment."

Oh hell . . .

Chapter Six

BLAKELY

"Yes, put the drinks right there, perfect," I say to one of the waitstaff manning the Cane suite tonight. "Can we please check with the chef on the food? I want to ensure everything is hot and the timing aligns with the game."

"Yes, of course," she says before taking off through the staff door.

I glance around the room, satisfied with how it's been put together. I've spent extra time on the suite, more time than the others I'm manning today, but you know, the man offered me a job today, so I feel like I have to live up to expectations.

I glance down at my new phone—actually loving the case Halsey picked out—and see that Huxley is supposed to arrive any moment. The boys are already out on the ice, warming up.

When I turn around to check the hallway for them, I see Huxley open the door for who I'm going to assume is his wife. Beautiful long brown hair, curvaceous body, and a baby strapped to her chest, she's positively gorgeous and exactly who I'd have pictured for Huxley's wife.

And Huxley, casually wearing a pair of black jeans and a black polo, is throwing me off from his regular business suit apparel—*but look at those arms . . . my God.*

"Miss White," he says with a smile. "So glad to see you."

"You too," I say, walking up to him. "You were able to find the suite okay?"

"Just fine," he says. "I want to introduce my wife. This is Lottie Cane."

"Lottie, it's so nice to meet you."

She offers me a warm smile. "You as well. I've heard a lot about you, Blakely. Seems like you've made a good impression on my husband." There's nothing malicious about her comment. It's very complimentary.

"Just doing my job," I answer.

"And doing it well," another man says, walking into the suite.

From the floppy yet sexy haircut to the same jawline and body, I can only assume this is one of Huxley's brothers.

His eyes land on mine, and that stir of intimidation from his gorgeous looks makes me feel slightly out of place. "JP Cane, it's so nice to meet you, Blakely. This is my wife, Kelsey."

Kelsey is also wrapped up with a baby, and I wonder just how far apart they were in their pregnancies.

"It's so nice to meet you. You have the best suite available. For the little ones, if you stay in this portion of the suite, with the doors to the arena closed, the crowd won't be loud at all, so the babies won't be disturbed."

"That's great," JP says while looking around. "Weird to think Kenzie's brother plays here."

"Oh, who is her brother . . ." The question falls off my lips just as a very familiar face walks through the doors. Holy shit.

"Blakely?" she says as my roommate from college comes into view.

"Kenzie?" I ask. "Oh my God." And then it hits me. Oden O'Connor. Duh. Jesus, why didn't I put two and two together?

I walk up to her and open my arms. Like in old times, she falls into my embrace and hugs me.

"Oh my goodness, it's been so long," she says, squeezing me tight. "Why has it been so long?"

"Because I'm a terrible friend," I answer before pulling away and looking at her. Still so freaking cute with her quirky glasses and Mrs. Frizzle-type attire. "Look at you, you look amazing."

"So do you." She takes my hands in hers. "Why didn't Oden tell me you were working here?"

"I don't think he realized because neither did I."

"How do you know each other?" Huxley asks.

I pull Kenzie in close and say, "Kenzie was my roommate in college. We were inseparable for four years. Even during school breaks, she'd come home with me or I'd go home with her. We spent an entire summer in her hometown, Almond Bay, hanging out on the beach, going to their cute town events, and buying a cookie a day from The Almond Store." I turn toward her. "I dream about those cookies."

She chuckles. "They now make cookie mix and sell it online so you can make your own at home."

"Well, sign me up." I bring her in for another squeeze and realize I need to pull it together and be professional. "Sorry about the gushing. I haven't seen this girl in a while, and it took me by surprise."

"Not a problem at all," Huxley says. "Feel free to reconnect and, Kenzie, don't be afraid to tell Blakely how wonderful we would be to work with."

She laughs. "They're demons. Don't even consider it." When Huxley raises his brow, she laughs again. "Just kidding. You would be very lucky."

"That's better," Huxley says before placing his hand on Lottie's back and leading her to a high-top table along with Kelsey and JP.

Quietly, I say, "I can't believe you're here. How long are you in town for?"

"For a few days."

"Really? We need to catch up. What are you doing tomorrow?"

"Planned on sightseeing, but you let me know when you're available, and I'll make time to see you."

"Perfect. I have some temporary housing at the moment, but you can meet me there, and either we can grab something to eat or stay in."

"Stay in for sure."

"I knew you were going to say that." I nudge her. "You haven't changed."

"Neither have you."

I pull my phone out and search for her name. When I find it, I flash her the screen and say, "Is this still your number?"

"Yup."

"Perfect. I'll text you."

"Sounds great."

"Well, enjoy the game, and if you guys need anything, I'll be in and out."

"Thank you," Huxley calls out.

I give Kenzie's hand one more squeeze before leaving, a smile on my face.

———

KENZIE: *Do you have time for lunch today? Not sure about your schedule.*

Blakely: *I don't have to go into the office today because the guys have an off/travel day. Lunch is perfect. I'll send my address. Want me to order some pizza with sausage?*

Kenzie: *Just like old times. I'll bring some cookies for dessert.*

Blakely: *Sounds great.*

I set my phone down and slip my robe over my thin pajama set. Normally, I wouldn't even consider putting a robe on, but given my new roommate, I figure I should respect his space and not walk around barely dressed.

Once the robe is tied, I head out into the kitchen where I can smell coffee, but instead of seeing a fully clothed Halsey in the kitchen, I'm stunned . . . *and breathless*. Halsey's standing there in low-hanging shorts that barely hang on to his narrow hips. And that's it. No shirt, no socks, no slippers, just his shorts.

Excuse my eyes, but they wander. They wander over the dimples right above his ass, the sinew that threads just under the surface of his skin, and the bulging muscles that climb up his back and over his shoulders, shifting and contracting with even the slightest of movements.

He's not wearing a shirt.

That's . . . that doesn't seem like him.

He's the shirt-wearing kind of guy.

I almost think he'd wear a shirt in the pool. That's how prudish he seems.

So to see him sans shirt throws me off. Until he slowly starts to turn around, coffee mug in hand, his head bent, blowing on the hot liquid.

Holy.

Fucking.

Shit.

The man is carved from stone with divots and curves I don't think I've ever seen in real life. Thick pecs, toned but boulder-like arms, and a six-pack that could do serious damage to any stain on a piece of fabric. And the V in his hips, it's cut so deep that I truly fear his shorts may fall off if he moves too quickly. Not to mention the short stack of hair that starts under his belly button and trails down to his waistline, disappearing where my eyes travel to an obvious bulge in his pants. Not the kind of bulge that screams morning wood but the type of bulge that says he's packing and can't do anything about it.

"Oh shit, you scared me," he says, startling me as well as my eyes shoot up to his.

"Sorry." I swallow hard, trying to rid my mind of thoughts of his bulge. *This is Halsey Holmes. You don't think about him like that, and you definitely don't think about him when you're sharing his apartment.* "I didn't mean to startle you."

"You're good," he says as he lifts himself onto the corner of the counter, his long legs hanging off the edge, his thick thighs pulling at the fabric of his shorts while his calves nearly share the same diameter as my quad.

Eyes up, Blakely.

Eyes up.

"Good game last night," I say as I move into the kitchen for some coffee. Hopefully, that will wake me up and keep me busy so I don't keep staring at the man in front of me.

Wait until I text Penny about this.

"Yeah, the boys played hard."

I reach for a mug from the cabinet and say, "Your two goals didn't hurt either."

"That's what happens when you have a flawless connection with your teammates on the ice."

I glance over my shoulder at him, and the cute way his bedhead makes him look sleepy and adorable at the same time. "Can't take a compliment, can you?"

"I can. Just put credit where credit is due."

"Just makes you a good teammate." I fill my coffee mug, then go to the fridge for some of the creamer I bought. I like the almond-flavored kind as it adds a nutty flavor to my morning nectar.

"Did you have a good day yesterday?" he asks. When I glance over my shoulder, I catch him carefully studying me while sipping his coffee. And I swear, something is different about him at this moment, other than the missing shirt. It's almost like he's . . . slowly trying to come out of his shell but is still nervous to do so.

I say that as if I actually know this man. I don't.

"I did. I surprisingly ran into my college roommate. She's OC's sister. I just made the connection. It's been a while since I've seen her or her family, so I didn't see it at first, but she was with Huxley Cane."

"Oh . . . really?" he asks, his brows pinching together. "How does she know Cane?"

"From what little I gathered last night, her boyfriend started

The Jock Report with his brother, which the Canes are investors in. And her cousins married Huxley and JP Cane. They're visiting for a few days. I invited her over here to catch up. I hope that's okay."

"Oh sure, of course," he answers. "You don't need to ask me."

"I know you said that earlier, but I want to be respectful."

"Seriously, have over whoever you want. I don't care. This is your place too."

"Thank you." I lean against the counter, enjoying this early morning chat with him. Perry used to wake up and start working so early that I'd always drink my coffee while scrolling through social media. It's nice to have someone to talk to while my body wakes up. "I'm excited to catch up with her. It was funny, Huxley was trying to get Kenzie to convince me to take his job last night."

Halsey pauses from lowering his mug and asks, "Did she convince you?"

"She barely said anything about it other than we would live near each other again. So I guess that answers the question of if I'd have to move. Either way, it would be fun to be near her again. We were each other's lifelines in college. Not sure either of us would have made it out of there without each other. I was wild and she wasn't. She helped ground me, and I helped her, for lack of a better term, blossom."

"Sounds like a good friend," he says while setting his mug down.

"She is. With our busy lives, we sort of lost touch, but she came back at the right time. I can't wait to catch up."

"Well, I hope you have a good time."

"Thank you." I nod toward his room. "Are you all packed for your away trip?"

"Just need to add a few things, but yeah, pretty much packed."

"Do you take anything on the plane to do?"

"Books," he answers.

"Oh duh, that was a dumb question. What are you taking with you this time?"

"Finishing up a thriller and bringing along the two others in the series."

"Carrying around three books? You know, that's what they make e-readers for."

"I have one, but I tend to feel less anxious about flying when I'm holding a physical book."

"You get anxious when flying?"

I see the regret in his eyes from divulging what seems to be a secret.

"Oh, yeah . . . just don't like not being in control."

Makes sense, given that his brother was out of control when he died in a car accident. God, this man, the demons that must rest inside him. And how sweet is it that a book is what calms him.

"Have you always been a reader?"

His hands rub over his legs, a telltale sign that maybe he's getting uncomfortable, but instead of shutting down, he stays with me emotionally and physically. Makes me feel like he sees me as a possible safe space. I don't know why that sends a surge of pride through me, but it does.

"I've picked up reading ever since I lost Holden," he answers. "Books have been my escape when I feel the world closing in on me." He tugs at his hair. "Sorry, didn't mean to make the moment sad."

"Oh my God, don't apologize. I'm the one who asked. I can't imagine going through what you went through, so I'm glad you found books."

"Me too." He hops off the counter but doesn't leave. He just leans against it while resting his hands on the edge behind him. The position makes the muscles in his chest flex differently, offering me an even better view of the work he does in the weight room.

Dragging my eyes away, I ask, "Have you had breakfast yet?"

"No, I actually ordered some egg sandwiches. Wasn't sure if you'd want one or not, but I got one for you."

"Really? That was nice. I'd love an egg sandwich."

Just then, the doorbell rings.

Great timing.

Pushing off the counter, he walks over to the front door and opens it, where he picks up a bag from the ground.

"Do people know they're delivering to you?" I ask as I pull out a plate for each of us and take them to the table along with my cup of coffee.

"No. I use a fake name."

"Really?" I smile. "What is it? Wait . . . let me guess. What does it start with?"

He sets the bag on the table and grabs his coffee from the counter. "F," he answers.

"Hmmm." I tap my chin while he sets a sandwich on the plate in front of me and takes a seat. The sweet smell of a fresh bagel combined with egg and cheese wafts into the air. Yup, this is exactly what I needed. "Frederick?"

His brows rise. "Did you read that on the bag?"

"Wait." My palm falls to the table. "Did I really just guess that correctly?"

"You did. Frederick Garrlo."

"Garrlo?" I chuckle. "Where the hell did you come up with that?" He takes a seat, and we both unwrap our egg sandwiches. It was so nice that he thought of me.

"I wish I could tell you it's a famous writer or character I loved, but it was a drunken decision."

"Ooo, tell me more," I say as I unwrap my bagel.

He does the same and lets the steam escape. "You know when we check into a hotel, we use aliases, right?" I nod as I take a sip of my coffee. He clears his throat and says, "Well, when, uh, when Holden was still around, we came up with our names together." His eyes drift to the side, remembering. "He was Frankie Garrlo, and I went with Frederick. I've never changed it."

And just like that, he mentions his brother again. Sure, he had to clear his throat and his voice softened when speaking about him, but I'm truly surprised. I wouldn't have expected Halsey to open up to me like this, to even bring his brother into the conversation because he's always so quiet. Maybe I've been looking at him completely wrong.

Maybe he doesn't mind talking about his brother but waits for the right moment.

"Where did Garrlo come from?"

Halsey shakes his head. "You don't want to know."

"I do . . . unless you don't want to tell me."

"It's really fucking stupid and immature." His eyes lift to mine, his unkempt hair flopping over his forehead. "You'll judge me."

"Um, are you forgetting how I flashed you my loincloth just yesterday? Pretty sure we established a judgment-free zone in this apartment. So please, regale me with the origin of Garrlo."

He wipes his mouth with a napkin and rests both arms on the table. "It was when Holden and I were in college. We talked about how when we made it professionally, we would need aliases. We started spitballing names back and forth, names that worked with each other because well, we were those set of twins that enjoyed dressing like each other, having similar names, you know, that shit."

"I think it's cute." And I can picture it. Holden and Halsey walking around in matching striped shirts while eating the same ice cream and trying to deceive people into who is who. I could imagine that side of Halsey.

He endearingly smiles at me. "He chose Frankie because there was this one place we went in Chicago called Frankie Donuts, and he was obsessed with it. I mean, like half a dozen donuts a day. The kid pounded them down. He would follow them on Instagram and drool all over the pictures, itching to see what special flavor they came up with for the week. So it was an ode to his favorite donut, and I needed a similar name, so Frederick it was."

I bet Holden was a good time. The picture Halsey has painted in my head has led me to believe exactly that.

"And what about Garrlo?"

He visibly looks uncomfortable. "This is where it gets really immature."

"Ooo, I can't wait." I gesture for him to go on. "Please, do tell."

He looks so uncomfortable as he says, "Garrlo is the last name of a girl who flashed both of us back in high school at the same time. It was our first time seeing boobs in real life." Halsey's face flushes to a beet-red color as he looks away.

A loud, obnoxious, and wet snort pops out of me right before I cover my mouth.

"I told you, it was stupid."

I shake my head, giggles falling past my lips as I think about two guys in college, looking back on their days growing up and coming up with a name that meant something to them.

Garrlo and an ode to her naked breasts. If only she knew.

"That's one of the best things I've ever heard," I say. "Donuts and boobs. I don't think I could have asked for a better connection. These egg sandwiches were delivered to a teenage boy's memory of donuts and boobs. I don't think I'll ever stop smiling about that."

"Glad I could make you smile," he says before taking a bite of his sandwich.

"You did, Halsey, and I appreciate it."

"THIS IS . . . not what I expected your place to look like," Kenzie says as she looks around the apartment.

"Oh yeah, I'd probably never choose an apartment like this. Too much concrete for me. This is actually Halsey Holmes's apartment."

"Halsey, as in the guy who scored two goals last night?" Kenzie pushes up her glasses on her nose, looking cuter than ever in a pair of leggings with books on them and a white crop top shirt. I've always thought of her as eccentric. It's one of the reasons we got along so well. I was obsessed with her polymer clay earring collection. We'd spend weekends not studying, coming up with new designs. I still have some. We went through a real pizza earring phase there for a second.

"Yes, that Halsey."

"Oh, I didn't know you were friends."

"Well . . . sort of." We take a seat on the couch after I got us both drinks. Orange soda, thought I'd throw it back to our college days. "I didn't know much about him other than he's quiet, plays hockey, and likes to read, but my apartment flooded, and I was desperate for a place to stay. I think I had a momentary lapse of judgment when his place was offered to me, but you know me, I just go with the flow."

"You do. I never would have been able to say yes to living with a stranger, let alone a man who was a stranger or one that attractive."

I chuckle. "But look at you now, dating someone. Let me see a picture."

Kenzie pulls up her phone and flashes me her screensaver. It's a picture of her being kissed on the cheek by a very attractive man with dark hair and a solid jaw full of scruff.

"Oh my God, Kenzie. He's hot."

"He is, so not someone I thought I'd end up with, but here I am."

"What do you mean by that?" I ask.

"I'm not blind. The man is way out of my league. Way too outgoing and loves every second of pushing me out of my comfort zone. Plus, he was a ladies' man beforehand."

"Stop. No one is out of your league. But the ladies' man thing, that's so not who I'd expect you to fall for."

"Me neither, but I met him at my cousin's wedding. It was kind of embarrassing at first because I was there alone, he was there alone, and my cousins asked if he would keep me company. I think we were both annoyed by the suggestion at first, but then we started talking, and I realized that he was not just very attractive but also very nice. So . . . I ghosted him."

My head falls back as I laugh. "Stop, did you really?"

"Oh yeah, I wasn't touching him with a ten-foot pole. I was not in a position to even consider going out with someone like him, but he wore me down, and we've been dating for a few months now."

"Do you think he's the one?"

She nods with a smile that reaches ear to ear. "Yeah. I know he wants to propose. His brother let it slip. I'm just wondering when it's going to happen."

"Is he not on this trip with you?"

She shakes her head. "He had to fly to New York for some meetings."

"Meetings . . . or to get a ring?"

Her eyes light up. "I don't know, I never thought about it . . . maybe a ring."

"That would be so exciting." I reach out and squeeze her hand. "I'm so happy for you. I know you struggled with guys in college, so I'm happy to see you with someone who loves you unconditionally."

"He does. I'm very lucky." She takes a sip of her soda and says, "I hope this isn't a touchy subject, but since you're living with Halsey right now, I'm going to assume you aren't with Perry anymore?"

"No, that ended a few weeks ago."

"Oh wow, really?"

"Yeah." I bring one leg up on the couch and turn completely toward her, draping my arm over the back of the couch. "He got a job in Australia, and he asked me to go with him. I didn't want to move, and I didn't think I had to give up everything I worked so hard for to follow him, you know?"

"I get that for sure."

"And he didn't have to take that job. It's almost as if he was looking for a reason to leave. We were happy, but I'm not sure we were fully invested in each other, if that makes sense."

"Like your careers mattered more than the relationship."

"Huh." I look away, thinking about that statement. "You know, I never thought about it that way."

"You and Perry were always very ambitious and goal oriented. There is nothing wrong with that, but if those ambitions outweigh the relationship, it seems like there was no relationship there. You have to see what's more important, and I think you both figured that out."

"You're right," I say. "Our work was more important than our relationship, more important than us." I wince. "What does that say about me?"

"It says that you know what you want, and nothing is wrong with that. I think when you're with the right person, you realize that you could live without the job, but you can't live without the person. I know that's the case with Banner and me. If he said he's moving to New York tomorrow, I'd jump on a flight with him."

I slowly nod. "God, Kenzie, when did you become so poetic?"

She chuckles. "I watch a lot of *Full House* reruns."

Orange soda nearly flies out of my nose from her response.

I cover my nose and take a deep breath. "You need to warn me before you say something like that next time." I wipe my nose. "It's when the music turns serious . . . right?"

"That's when I know I'm about to learn a lesson for the day. Danny Tanner with the wise advice."

"Always."

She crosses her legs and turns toward me. "So are you going to take Huxley's job?"

I roll my eyes. "Oh my God, please don't tell me he sent you here to ask me."

"No, not at all. But it would be cool if you were back in Los Angeles. I'd love to see you more. I can't believe it's taken us this long to see each other again."

"I know, I'm disappointed in us. But I don't know much about the job to make a solid decision. Still waiting on more details from Huxley. I'm flattered, that's for sure, but I do like my current job. I love spending time with the athletes and joking around with the boys. I like working with Penny, and I love it here in Vancouver. So it's tough."

She nods. "The love for where you're at right now outweighs the possibility to do something new."

"Perhaps," I answer.

"And does this decision have anything to do with the guy you're currently living with?"

"Halsey?" I ask, surprised by her question. "Oh, no. I barely know him. He's sweet and considerate, and I appreciate him letting me stay here for a few weeks. I'm between places at the moment until my new apartment doesn't have water running down its walls."

"Oh, no!"

"Yes, not ideal. But Halsey? Well, even though he's incredibly good-looking, I don't think there's anything there to explore. Where he's a tad . . . broody, I'm more sunshine and joy, you know?"

"Totally. You are that and more. Why is he so broody? Just an arrogant asshole or something?"

"No. Not at all. Sadly, he lost his twin brother in a car accident a while back. According to his friends, Halsey used to be fun-loving and outgoing, but ever since he lost his brother, he's shut down. But you know what has been sort of surprising?"

"What?" she asks.

"Since I've been here, Halsey has mentioned his brother a few times while we've spoken. Like I said, I don't know Halsey that well yet, but I've never heard him speak of his brother. So that makes me think he's comfortable around me. Even with that, though, with him opening up, there's still this darkness that rests behind his eyes. This mystery."

"Which means you're perfect for him."

"What?" I ask on a laugh. "How do you figure?"

"You're his opposite. Whereas he's dark and mysterious,

you're sunshine and fun. Maybe you can help him climb out of the darkness and see that there is life beyond the tragedy."

"I don't need any projects," I say. "I have enough to worry about. He's great, Kenzie, but yeah, not for me."

"Shame . . . everyone loves a roommates-to-lovers type romance."

"Ahh, I see you're still reading your romances."

She smirks. "They've come in handy."

Chapter Seven

HALSEY

"This is not going to work," I say to Posey, who just sat beside me on the airplane.

"What's not going to work?" He stretches his legs out and rests his folded hands on his stomach.

"This stupid plan you devised to convince Blakely I'm the guy for her."

"You mean the Break Blakely Action Plan?"

"I told you, I didn't like that name. And we shouldn't be naming it anyway. I can't go through with this."

Posey lets out a huge sigh, then at the top of his lungs, he shouts, "Frozen Fellas assemble."

I flinch from the projection of his voice before asking, "What the hell is Frozen Fellas?"

"You know in *Ted Lasso*. They have the Diamond Dogs and go over the problems they're facing. Well, I thought we needed a name, so I came up with Frozen Fellas. You know, because we're men and we play hockey. Catchy, isn't it?"

"No," I reply just as Pacey, Silas, and OC approach. OC sits across from us, and Pacey and Taters kneel in the seats in front of us but turn around so we can see them. Jesus Christ, they reported quickly. "Where's Hornsby?" I ask.

"He isn't officially a Frozen Fella yet. He hasn't signed the NDA. Something about him wanting his lawyer to look through it."

"You're an idiot," I say.

"Dude, I'm just protecting you and your interests. He's with Penny. If she found out about Break Blakely, you know she'd tell her. Is that what you want? You want Blakely to know that you purposely walked around this morning without a shirt on to entice her with your rippling chest?" He elbows me in the side. "You did that, right? You went shirtless?"

"I did, and I felt like the biggest douchebag."

"Did she check you out?" Pacey asks.

"I don't know. I was too fucking worried that I was making her uncomfortable to even notice."

"Did she look uncomfortable?" Pacey asks.

"No. I don't know. It was fucking weird, okay?"

"Did you get her breakfast?" OC asks.

"Yes, I did, and we sat and ate together and talked."

"Then what's the problem?" Posey asks. "It seems like you did all the right things. No shirt. Check. Breakfast. Check. Conversation. Check. How could this have gone any better?"

I rub my hand over my forehead and say, "I . . . I can't seem to control what I say around her."

"Uh-oh," Silas says while pointing. "I told you guys that was going to hurt him. We could plan all the ways he can get her to like him, but it comes down to his execution."

"What stupid thing did you say?" Posey asks. "Did you confess your love?"

"Or stumble over telling her how beautiful you think she is?" Pacey asks.

"Did you talk about your wiener?" OC asks, drawing all of

our attention. He shrugs. "I don't know, we talked about it yesterday, and I thought maybe it stuck in his head."

"None of that," I say before looking out the window, thinking about this morning and how easy it felt to talk to her. How I didn't even consider *what* I was saying and could just be me. "I talked about Holden."

The boys fall silent for a moment before Posey quietly asks, "Did you talk about the accident?"

"No, nothing like that, although I've mentioned it. I keep mentioning him, and the moments we shared."

"Is that a bad thing?" Silas asks, his voice gentler as well.

"That's what I'm struggling with. At the moment, it feels right. It feels like I'm supposed to be opening up to her because she makes me comfortable, more comfortable than I've ever felt. But afterward, I feel this anxious panic. It's a combination of regret and memories I don't want to relive, things I've stuffed away for so long, and every time they resurface, it's like I live through losing him all over again. And I can't seem to stop myself. Talking about him to her comes out so easily. Then there's the whole aspect of not wanting her to feel bad for me. I don't want to play the pity card. I don't want her looking at me as the guy who lost his brother, but then I can't stop mentioning him. I don't know what the hell is going on, and that's why we need to stop this. We need to cancel everything. I can't live with this pain at the forefront of my mind. I can't possibly deal with it and play fucking hockey at the same time."

The boys fall silent again, and I don't blame them. I don't know how to handle this situation either. I've been thinking about it all fucking morning, regretting talking about Holden, wondering if she thinks I'm seeking pity whenever I mention him. I'm not. I don't want anyone's pity.

I just . . . fuck, I just want her to like me.

I want her to see me as someone she can rely on and see herself with.

But fuck, I don't even know who I am anymore without Holden—*I don't like who I am anymore*—so how could I possibly get her to fall for me? Why would someone so vibrant and full of life consider me as boyfriend material? *Husband material?* She wouldn't.

"Maybe," Posey says, taking his time. "Maybe she's exactly what you need, and there's going to be some growing pains that go with it."

"What do you mean?" I ask.

"I think he's trying to say that Blakely might be the key to helping you through the trauma of losing your brother," Pacey says. "And I say this delicately, man, but none of us have been able to talk to you about Holden. It's rare if you ever speak about him, let alone hang out with us outside of hockey. Even when we're in Banff, you spend most of the time reading. It's not a bad thing, but we're also worried."

"He's right," Silas chimes in. "You've shut down, yet it seems Blakely pulls another side out of you. It's not bad, it's just different, but a good different."

I shake my head. "I don't want to go there."

"You need to," OC says, stepping in. "I lost a childhood friend back in college and I know it's not the same as losing your twin, but it was too easy to push the world away rather than fight against that feeling and live your life, a life my friend would have wanted me to live. This might be the first step of you coming out of that place of denial. And yeah, it's going to be really fucking uncomfortable and there will be days where you are sick to your stomach with reliving the pain you stuffed away, but dude, coming from experience, it's so much fucking better living on the other side."

Posey pats my leg. "He would have wanted you to live your life, man. We all know that about him."

"He's right," Silas agrees. "And you can't view talking about Holden with Blakely as a bad thing. Dude, don't you see how special that is? The kind of effect this girl has on you? This is just the beginning of talking to her, getting to know her, so imagine what will happen when you spend a few weeks talking to her on a deeper level?"

"Could be magic," Pacey adds.

And dammit, he could be right because that word . . . magic . . . I can't deny that's how it feels when I'm around her.

I feel light.

I feel safe.

I feel like she was brought into my life for a reason.

But the fear of giving myself over, that is buried so fucking deep.

I drag my hand through my hair. "So what, I'm going to grow an attachment to this girl, she's going to pull me out of this funk I'm living in, then she'll take a new job somewhere else, and I have to sit back and think, wow, that was fun, now what?"

"No." Posey shakes his head. "That's why we have the Break Blakely plan, because after we're done with her, not only is she going to want to stay in your apartment and in Vancouver but she's going to be head over heels in love with you."

"She is," Silas agrees, usually the most "realistic" one in the group. "Mark our words, you'll be proposing by the end of the season."

"And then the Frozen Fellas will be the groomsmen at your wedding. Eli pending with the whole NDA thing," OC says. He's starting to slip into the delirium that my guys live in, so I'm going to have to watch him. He's levelheaded, I don't need him being influenced by the others.

"So you good?" Posey asks.

"I don't know," I say on a huff. "I mean, fuck, do I really have a choice?"

"No, and I'm glad you see it that way. Now, where are we on the furniture? Did you order it?"

"Not yet," I answer.

"Why the fuck not? That was your homework. Pull out your phone, and we'll do it now so you won't have an excuse not to."

And this is why you don't let your friends get involved in your personal life.

MY PHONE CHIMES with a text as I shift out of the bathroom where I just took a shower. Towel wrapped around my waist, I pick up the phone and see that it's a text from Posey.

Jesus fucking Christ, this guy won't leave me alone.

Posey: *Text her tonight. Remember, tell her about the furniture and ask her how her day was.*

With one hand, I text him back.

Halsey: *You don't think that'll be weird? That's what a boyfriend would do.*

Posey: *A boyfriend would FaceTime, you are texting. And it's just being a friend. Now do it or I will run up and down these hallways screaming all night. Is that what you want to happen?*

Halsey: *Jesus, you're annoying.*

Posey: *I'm going to bed, don't fucking disturb me. You know how I need my sleep. If you require help with your texts, ask OC, he's the newbie, and he should be in charge of texts.*

Halsey: *I'll be fine.*

I sit on the edge of my bed and pull up her name in my phone.

Her beautiful face displayed in the thumbnail of the contact actually gives me butterflies.

Jesus, I'm so pathetic.

Taking a deep breath, I type out a text message and press send.

No going back now.

Halsey: *Hey Blakely. Heads-up, I have people stopping by tomorrow between three and five to deliver some furniture for the patio. Do you think you'll be home?*

I'm about to toss my phone to the side, not willing to wait around to see if she texts back, but then the dots indicate her texting, so I wait, my stomach twisting in a knot.

When my phone dings, my eyes immediately start reading.

Blakely: *Hey! How was the flight? I'll be home for sure. When you're out of town, we get to work from home, which is always nice. And you got furniture? Oh my God, I told you, you didn't have to . . . but also . . . please tell me a table was included in that purchase. LOL*

A genuine smile passes over my lips as I text her back.

Halsey: *Flight was good. Eli was nauseous on the flight for some reason, but other than that, it was smooth. And as for the furniture, I got a dining table that seats six, two lounge chairs, and a loveseat that rocks . . . oh, and a firepit for in front of it.*

Blakely: *Holy crap. That's a lot and, even though you didn't have to do that, I'm positively thrilled. A firepit? I'll grab the marshmallows and sticks. Was the lounge for you and your reading? If you tell me no, I might cry.*

Halsey: *I'll be using them for sure.*

Blakely: *Thank goodness. You could always use them for some naked sunbathing as well.*

Halsey: *Not really into that.*

Blakely: *Yeah, me neither. **sense the sarcasm***

Hell, she can't tell me that shit, because that's all I'll think about when on that lounger now.

Halsey: *Look out for peeping Toms.*

Blakely: *They wouldn't be looking for me. They'd be looking for Frederick Garrlo.*

Halsey: *Pretty sure they'd be looking for you.*

Blakely: *You flatter me. Well, I'll let the movers in with pleasure. Also, I watered Sherman today in the sink, as his soil was looking a touch dry. Once he soaked everything up that he wanted, I gave him some sun time. I'll be honest, he's the easiest, most calm plant I've ever had to take care of.*

Halsey: *Have you taken care of a plant that wasn't calm?*

Blakely: *A few. One of those Venus Fly Trap plants. They're unruly and rude. And then there was this donkey tail succulent that would shed a tail anytime you looked at it. I swear to God, they just fell off. My mom was livid when she came home. I told her I didn't touch the plant, that it was just revolting since she left. She didn't buy it. Fun fact . . . I stroked one of its strands unknowing that the tails easily fall off and they nearly shattered to the ground. I was so horrified I tried to glue them back, but the plant wouldn't let me.*

Fuck . . . she's cute. I move toward my suitcase for a pair of shorts as I type her back.

Halsey: Sherman is heartier than that. I don't think you'll have any problems with him.

Blakely: I sure hope not. I'd hate to mess up the only job I have when it comes to staying in this apartment. Which by the way, I had my friend Kenzie over and she was confused at first. She was like . . . this is not a place she would ever picture me in. She liked it, but I'm more of a white walls, fluffy blankets kind of girl.

Yeah, I could have told you that. My apartment is not particularly welcoming or a place that I could see Blakely wanting to rent, which makes me think, should I add more than just curtains? Was Posey right about a rug? If I got a rug now, would it be obvious that I was trying too hard?

Probably.

I slip my shorts on and type her back.

Halsey: Feel free to change anything you want. I'm not much of a designer. I'm pretty sure I haven't taken the tags off everything I've purchased.

Blakely: Like the whisk? I noticed. It's okay, I don't want to disturb your peace. I'm sure you enjoy the minimalistic look.

Halsey: I really don't care. The only reason it's so minimalistic is because I haven't cared enough to do anything to the place. I don't even have bookshelves for my books. Posey was disgusted when he saw my books stacked up.

I lean back on the mattress of my hotel bed, grateful for the departure from the air mattress back home. Those are made for maybe one or two nights, not as a regular bed, and I'm already feeling it.

Blakely: You don't have shelves? Halsey Holmes, that's sacrilege to a book lover. Don't you know the essentials to anyone who loves to read is a bookmark, a favorite snack, bookshelves, and a guilty pleasure genre that you read and don't tell anyone about?

Halsey: Guilty pleasure genre? I don't think I have one of those.

Blakely: Liar. There has to be a type of book you like reading but are slightly embarrassed that you read it. For example, I don't read much, but I am in the line of reading any autobiography from a reality show personality.

Halsey: Oh . . . well I guess there are a few things that I wouldn't read in front of the guys. I like this one author, Lynsay Sands. She writes

Scottish romances, and I can't believe I actually typed that out to you, but yeah. There's a series I like, one in particular where the heroine is shot in the boob with an arrow.

Blakely: *Uh . . . pardon me?*

Oh shit, you idiot.

See, this is what I'm talking about.

She just pulls it out of me. I say stupid things that I probably shouldn't say.

Halsey: *Maybe forget I said that.*

Blakely: *Ohhhhh no, that won't be forgotten. You like an arrow to a boob?*

Halsey: *No! I mean . . . it was funny. Unexpected. Never read anything that had no problem shooting an arrow to a boob is all. I was caught off guard and it stuck with me. I don't get pleasure over boob mutilation if that's what you're thinking.*

Blakely: *LOL. I was not thinking that, but now that you mention it . . .*

Blakely: *Just kidding. I don't think you could hurt a fly, unless you're on the ice. I've seen you check a few guys. That's if they can keep up with you.*

The flattery does obnoxious things for my ego.

Halsey: *I've been in my fair share of fights. Trust me, I can hurt someone.*

Blakely: *I don't believe it.*

Halsey: *Are you trying to get me to prove it to you?*

Blakely: *Maybe . . . how good are you at leg wrestling?*

Halsey: *Don't even try.*

Blakely: *I have some powerful legs and hips. I'd give you a run for your money.*

Halsey: *Like I said, don't even try.*

Blakely: *Well, now I feel like this needs to happen when you return. I'd say best of three but I'm not sure my stamina is as good as yours, so I think it'll have to be all or nothing.*

Halsey: *Not going to happen. We're not battling it out in a leg wrestle.*

Blakely: *Oh that's cute, you're scared. Anyway, I know you have to* *get to bed, get that beauty sleep and rest up those muscles. We need goals tomorrow. I'll be sure to look out for the delivery. Can't wait.*

Halsey: *Thanks. I appreciate it. Have a good night, Blakely.*

Blakely: *You too!*

———

"WHAT THE FUCK did you eat today?" OC asks as he sits next to me on the bench, the last minute of the game playing out in front of us. We're up four to one, two of the goals being mine, the other two belonging to Silas and OC, both with my assists. "I can barely keep up with your skating and I'm younger than you."

"No need to mention age," I say as Posey checks someone into the boards, causing the fans to boo. OC, Silas, and I are out of the game, giving our legs a rest, but hell, I think I could go another hour. My adrenaline is pumping, and my body is itching for more action.

"Seriously though, what's going on with you? Take an upper I don't know about?"

I shake my head and squirt some water into my mouth as sweat drips down my face, droplets falling off the ends of my hair. "I don't know, just have a lot of energy."

"That's apparent." He takes a deep breath. "Keeping up with you wore me the fuck out."

"Maybe you're out of shape?"

He glares at me. Seeing more of his personality makes me feel like we've been friends for longer than a couple of weeks. He feels so familiar, like I've known him for years. "I'm not out of shape. I can out lift you any day, outrun you."

"Clearly you can't outskate me," I say, even surprising myself.

"Oh, fucking cocky now?"

The timer counts down from ten seconds, and the guys casually skate around the rink, knowing we've secured the W. When the buzzer goes off, we lift from the bench and hop onto the ice to line up and offer each other fist bumps. That was an easier win than expected. Usually the Polar Freeze give us more of a headache on the ice.

We head into the locker room but not before offering some fist bumps to fans on our way in.

The clatter of pads and skates sound off in the locker room as we all take seats and start stripping down.

"Fuck, I'm exhausted," Silas says while glancing over at me. "I swear to God that felt like the most intense scrimmage of my life. What the hell got into you tonight?" He looks my way, and I shrug.

"Just doing my job."

Silas shakes his head. "No, man, that was another level. Even your passes were faster. They were zipping so fast across the ice that I barely had enough time to react. I probably would have scored two more goals had I been."

"Same," OC says. "Keeping up with you was hard tonight."

"Maybe you two should get your shit together then."

"Ooo, you hear that?" Pacey says. "Holmes is talking a little smack over there. Not sure we've seen that side of him in a while. He's always like . . . it's all about the team, I love the team, teammates are great. Yay team."

I give him an unamused look that makes him laugh.

"You know, he's right," Eli says, while tearing his jersey over his head with some help from Posey when it gets stuck on his pads. "You are all about the team, so what's the difference?"

"Nothing," I say, but when I glance over at Posey, I know he's concocting something in his head. He has that puzzling look in his eyes, like he's trying to solve the world's greatest math equation.

"Wait . . ." he says, silencing the room. "Is this because of Blakely?"

And there it is.

"No," I say. Even though, if I were honest with myself, talking to her last night felt really good. I went to bed with a smile on my face and a sense of fulfillment I haven't felt in a long time. Also, I got a texted photo of her on one of the loungers earlier today, smiling brightly with a huge thank-you attached to the image. I thought about saving the picture to my phone but decided that might be a little creepy.

"He's lying." Silas points at my face. "Look, he's holding back a smirk."

OC leans forward, getting a better look at my angled head. He raises his hand and points above my head. "I can confirm, he's hiding a smirk."

"Smirk is confirmed," Silas says while slapping the bench with his hand.

"Then it is Blakely," Pacey says.

"Wait, what about Blakely?" Eli asks, looking confused.

"Can we all shut up? It has nothing to do with Blakely," I say, not wanting the entire team to figure this shit out.

But of course my friends are idiots, and they come flocking in front of me with chairs where they form a circle.

"Does this have to do with the NDA?" Eli asks. "I electronically signed it before the game. Fill me in."

"Ah, our newest member of the Frozen Fellas," Posey says. "Welcome."

They all offer Eli a fist bump.

This has gotten out of control. Next thing you know, we're going to have branded shirts, notepads, and pens for our next meeting.

Jesus, I could actually see that happening. I wouldn't put it past Posey.

"Here is the gist of it," Silas says, getting more involved than I expected him to. Posey must have gotten to him. "Blakely is staying with Holmes. Holmes loves her. Blakely was offered a potential new job that could make her move, and Holmes is unsure if she's going to take it or not. He clearly doesn't want to lose her because he's madly in love. Therefore, Posey came up with an action plan called Break Blakely where Holmes walks around with his shirt off in the apartment and does nice things for her to show her that he's boyfriend material. We're in the early phases, but from the rocket in his pants today, and I'm not talking about the girth-o-nater, name courtesy of OC—"

"Thank you." OC bows.

"I'm going to guess that the earlier phases have started to make an impact, and our friend here is feeling the effects of some female attention from his unrequited love. And obviously, if you tell Penny any of this, we're allowed to cut off one of your fingers, courtesy of the NDA agreement you just electronically signed."

"The finger thing was a holdup for me. I thought it was kind of weird," Eli says.

"We decided losing a finger was a good threat. We kept toes for skating balance, dicks for pleasure, and hair wasn't threatening enough. A finger was a good option. It lets you know we're not fucking around. But there was the amendment to the finger. Did you see it?" Pacey asks.

Eli nods. "A trial of holding a stick without one finger. If it doesn't go well, the group collectively gets to pierce the offenders belly button and add a permanent charm that shall never ever be removed."

"Correct." Pacey nods. "Belly button piercing with dangly, glitzy charm seemed just as offensive, so either way, don't fuck up and tell Penny. Got it?"

With obvious strain, Eli pulls on the back of his neck and says, "I wish I'd known what the secret was about before I signed the NDA. This is dangerous territory for me. Is there an out where I can mentally erase what you just told me and not go any deeper? I mean, the Frozen Fellas feels like a band I want to be a part of, but given the circumstances, I don't think I can be involved and keep Penny out of it."

"I think that's fair," Silas says. "All in favor of excusing Eli from this discussion and all discussions involving Blakely and Holmes, say aye."

As a collective whole, the guys all say, "Aye," then wait for me.

Rolling my eyes, I say, "Aye."

"You are excused, but you will not utter anything you've heard to Penny regarding the Frozen Fellas and Break Blakely."

Eli holds up his hand as if he's on the stand and swearing in to trial. "I shall keep my mouth shut."

"Good," Pacey says, and Eli walks away, bringing the attention back to me. "So you talked to her last night? Did she get the furniture?"

"Yes, and yes," I answer.

"Did you swoon?" OC asks.

"What? No. Jesus. It was nothing like that. It was a solid text convo. We joked a bit, and she thanked me for the furniture with a picture today."

"She sent a picture?" Silas asks. "Let's see it."

"No, I'm not going to show you the picture."

"You have to show us the picture," Pacey says. "We have to see if there are any hints in it."

"Hints?" I ask.

"Oh yeah, hints." OC nods knowingly. "There are ways girls take pictures that can give us a good indication of their thoughts. Position, angle, clothes, expression. It all matters."

"That's absurd. It's just a regular picture."

"Says the guy who didn't know he should walk around with his shirt off to get the girl," Silas says. "Show us the picture."

"Yeah, show it to us." Pacey pokes my leg.

"It's the only way to figure out what's going on in her head," OC adds.

That's when I glance up at Posey, who's sitting in a pulled-up chair in front of me, slowly rubbing his hands together with a smirk on his face.

"What's with the silence?" I ask.

A maniacal smile crosses over his face. "Just pleased with myself. This is unfolding perfectly."

"I'm out of here. I need a shower." I go to stand, but Silas and OC grip one of my shoulders and sit my ass right back down.

"Sorry, boss," OC says. "But we're going to need to see that picture."

"Yup, you're not going anywhere until we see it." Silas glares at me, and everyone turns to Posey, who is sitting there, looking like the fucking Godfather, ready to give the nod to have someone's head blown off.

"The picture," he says in a terse voice. "Show it to us."

When I realize there's no way they'll let me escape without showing it to them, I mutter, "Jesus Christ," before reaching for my phone out of my locker and finding the picture in the text. I click on the picture so they can't see any of the text and show it.

Immediately, Posey grabs it, and the boys flock around him, checking it out.

"Hair is done. Makeup is on," Silas says.

"Casual clothes but not dressed up," OC adds.

"Not a sexy pose, just a selfie with a smile," Pacey calls out.

Posey rubs his chin, then sits back on his chair. After a few seconds of studying it, he looks up at me and says, "This is . . . not a 'please come between my legs' picture."

"Jesus fuck, Posey," I moan. "Of course it's not."

"Well from the way you were skating today, we thought that it was a nearly topless picture of her making a kissy face at you," Silas says. "This is just a normal picture."

"I know," I say, snagging the phone from him. "That's what I told you."

OC scratches his cheek as he says, "So if Holmes was skating that fast and possessed that much energy on the ice from just a simple thank-you picture, does that mean . . . ." He pauses, trying to put pieces together in his head. "Does that mean he really is in love with this girl?"

"No," I say as the collective group says yes.

"I don't love her," I reiterate. "I just have a little crush, okay?"

"Ha, little, that's funny," Silas says.

I peel off my socks and shin guards, then ask, "Are we done

here? Because you motherfuckers stink, and I don't want to be around you anymore."

Posey nods to everyone. "We're done, but I'm glad to see we're making progress. Remember to text her tonight, but keep it simple, nothing like sweet dreams, my little ball of angel glitter."

I cringe. "Who the fuck says that?"

"You'd be surprised by the things that come out of Silas's mouth when he speaks to Ollie." Posey grins.

"Fuck off," Silas says, taking the attention off me. Thank God. "I don't call Ollie a ball of angel glitter. She would fucking laugh in my face."

"I think I heard you call her your pet," Pacey says.

"Uh . . . no," Silas says. "It's just babe . . . and good girl."

"Fuck, do the girls love that," OC says.

"They do." Silas nudges me. "When you get to that point with Blakely, remember to call her a good girl whenever you can."

"I don't need your fucking suggestions when it comes to the bedroom."

"That's right," OC says with such conviction. "It's because he has the girth-o-nater. He doesn't have to say anything, just wield that thing like the goddamn orgasmic weapon that it is."

"Stop talking about my dick. It's getting weird."

"Dude, we're never going to stop talking about that canon," Pacey says, causing all the guys to laugh.

Chapter Eight

BLAKELY

"Welcome back," I yell as Penny walks into her fully decorated office that I coated in streamers, confetti, and a mini brunch for her and me. Virgin mimosas included—yes, that means it's just orange juice, but calling them virgin mimosas sounds fancier.

Hand clutched to her chest, clearly startled, she says, "Oh my God, I was not expecting that."

I walk up to her and pull her into a hug. "I'm so glad you're back. Was dropping Holden off at day care hard?"

When I pull away, Penny adjusts her dress and says, "A little. I'm glad they offer day care here at the arena so I can go check on him whenever I want."

"Yeah, I'm sure that gives you some relief."

"It does." She sighs. "God, do I look okay? I'm still not back to my pre-baby size, and I was feeling it today when I got dressed."

"Penny, you look beautiful. It takes time, and there shouldn't be a standard of when or if you reach your pre-baby figure. You're beautiful just as you are."

"Thank you." Her shoulders droop in relief. "Eli said the same thing to me this morning when I was FaceTiming him. He told me that I was easily the sexiest I've ever been. A part of me feels like he was just saying that."

"I believe him. That man is so in love with you."

Just then, her phone beeps with a text, and she quickly looks at her screen. "Sorry, the day care said they would text me with . . . oh, it's Eli." She takes a second to read it and smiles as she texts him back.

"What did he say?"

"The pervert took a screenshot of me while we were Face-Timing, and I was in my bra and underwear, and he just got done jacking off to it."

"Well, if you had your doubts, there's your answer."

Her smile is from ear to ear as she continues to text him. "God, I shouldn't be this happy about something like that." She looks up at me. "But I am."

"As you should be. I'd be so lucky if I could turn on a guy that much." I walk over to the virgin mimosas and hold up a glass for her. "To having you back at work."

She clinks her glass with mine. "I'm so excited to be back. I missed it." We both take a drink, and she sets her purse down only to take a picture frame out of it. She flashes me a picture of her, Eli, and Holden all together, a professional shot from her newborn photo shoot.

"God, I love your little family. It's adorable."

"I love it too," she says as she sets the picture down on her desk so she can look at it when she's working. "Are these cronuts?"

"Only the best for my bestie," I answer while we both sit in the chairs in front of her desk. We each take a cronut and bite into the flaky crunchiness at the same time. "Mmm, these are so good," she says.

"They really are. I got some for the apartment too. I thought Halsey might like some tomorrow morning. They return tonight, right?"

Penny nods. "Yes. I can't wait for Eli to get home. I will say this, parenting a newborn by yourself is hard. He's so great when he's home that I could use the break for a night."

"I can't even imagine."

"Also, I miss him holding me at night. Having a baby and going through this new experience is scary and alarming at times, so having Eli wrapped around me, comforting me, is really helpful. I feel so lost at night when he's gone."

"Well then, I'm glad they're coming home tonight." I take another bite of my cronut, a few flakes falling to my black trousers. I brush them off as I say, "You and Holden should come over for dinner tonight and have a meal out on the balcony with me."

"I'd love that, but I have a lot to do before Eli gets home tonight like laundry and cleaning."

"Do you want me to help?"

She shakes her head. "No, that's okay. I'm going to put on the game and get it done while watching it."

My phone dings with an email and I glance at it, spotting Huxley's name.

The job offer.

"What's that look for?" Penny asks.

I snap my head up and offer her a fake smile that barely reaches my cheeks. "Uh . . . nothing."

She tilts her head to the side, not believing me for a second. "Nice try. You had a scared look on your face." She nods at my phone. "What just came in?"

I sigh and lean back against my chair. "Ugh, I didn't want to tell you this on your first day back."

"Tell me what?" she asks.

"Well, Huxley Cane stopped by my office the other day and offered me a new job."

"Uh . . . what?" she asks. "Who is Huxley Cane, and why is he trying to take you away from me?"

A nervous chuckle falls past my lips. "Huxley Cane is the billionaire who owns Cane Enterprises with his brothers. They invested in The Jock Report and have many properties from coast to coast. They have many fixed-income housing for single moms and people who can't afford the expense of living in cities. They're one of the front runners for eco-friendly office buildings, revolutionizing how major corporations handle daily waste. They have a lot going on, and his wife is also cousins with my college roommate."

"Uh-huh, blah, blah, blah, why is he stealing you?"

I smile. "He offered me a job with their philanthropic side of The Jock Report. I don't know what the details are, but he did just email me, and that's what the look was. I've been both waiting on the email and nervous to get it."

"Nervous because I might murder you if you leave me, or nervous that you might like the job so much that you do leave me . . . in my time of need?"

"How is this your time of need?" I ask her.

"Uh, hello. I just had a baby, and I don't feel like myself."

"Your boyfriend just jacked off to a picture of you."

"Doesn't mean I don't feel insecure."

"You're right, sorry," I say. "I didn't mean to set aside your feelings like that."

"That's right, you're sorry. Now, to make me feel better, how about you just delete that email, and we can continue celebrating my return with these cronuts?" She holds hers up, examining it as if it's a piece of gold in her hand.

But I don't move. I think about the email.

What it says.

What the offer might be.

When she notices that I'm clearly focused on the email, she says, "Ugh . . . is this something you want?"

"I don't know," I say. "I really have no clue as I've been waiting to see what it's all about."

She gestures to my phone. "Well, open the email. Let's see."

I unlock my screen and open the email. I decide to read it out loud. "'Blakely, it was so nice seeing you the other night. Thank you for treating my family with kindness and thinking about the little things like a quiet suite for the babies. I appreciate it. As I said, below is the job description, and the offer we're making you is two hundred fifty' . . . holy shit."

"Wait, what?" Penny sits up and leans over. "Two hundred and fifty thousand dollars? For one job? What does it entail? Nudity?"

I chuckle and shake my head. "The company is thriving and has the best employee feedback. This is probably why. Look, two hundred and fifty thousand dollars a year with guaranteed bonuses based on goals. Full, paid-for benefits, and even a housing stipend. Is he joking with this?"

"Uh, I hope so."

"'The job would be VIP relations' . . . oh my God, with the athletes. I thought it would be with organizations or the public, but I'd still be able to work with the athletes, which is huge for me."

I can sense the worry in Penny's voice when she says, "Would you have to move?"

"I have no idea. I'm assuming yes. Kenzie told me they have an office in Los Angeles, and since I'd be head of the Pacific Coast, I'd assume they'd want me in the office."

"Doesn't Ollie work for The Jock Report?" Penny asks. "She lives here."

"I know, I thought about that, but her job is different. I feel like it can be remote. I'm not sure this could be."

"Does it say? Email him? Are you really considering this?"

I set my phone down. "I mean . . . I think I am. Look at the job, it's amazing. The pay is unlike anything I'll get here. The benefits . . ." I let out a deep breath. "It feels too good to be true. I probably wouldn't have to live in an apartment that floods, you know? With a stipend, I could afford something nicer."

"I guess so." Penny frowns as she sets her cronut down. "I

want to be happy for you, and I think in the depths of my best friend soul, I do feel happy for you, but I also hate Huxley Cane. And I hate that he came in with this amazing opportunity because I don't want you to leave me."

"I get it. I'd probably have the same reaction as you. When I first heard about the job, I was concerned about leaving you, leaving this job, leaving the guys I love working with, but I'm also extremely flattered to be considered. To be given the opportunity, you know? Not sure there is as much room for me to grow with the Agitators."

"Yeah, I know." She tips back her virgin mimosa. "God, I wish this had champagne in it."

"Me too."

We're silent for a moment, then she says, "I'm proud of you, you know. That's a huge opportunity, and if I weren't so sour about you possibly leaving, I'd be throwing my arms up in cele-bration."

"I appreciate it. We don't have to talk about it."

"Yeah, let's change the subject. Uh . . . how is it living with Halsey?"

I shrug. "He hasn't really been home, as you know. Oh, but . . . he did walk around the other morning with his shirt off."

"Wait, really?"

I nod. "Yeah, I was just as confused as you. He doesn't seem like that kind of guy, but there he was the other morning, drinking his coffee in nothing but a pair of shorts."

"Dear God, what did he look like?"

I smirk. "Let's just say I don't think I've ever seen a man that ripped in real life. I've never noticed his forearms until the moment he lifted his coffee to his lips. They were all so rippley that you could see them twitch under his skin. It was hot. He might be the silent, quiet one, but man, does he spend a lot of time in the gym. I was flummoxed at first."

"Oooooo," Penny coos. "Looks like someone is crushing on their new roommate."

"Oh my God, no, that is the furthest thing from the truth. Sure, he's attractive, but yeah, there's nothing romantic there. Although, he was joking a bit the other morning, and I thought that was nice. I think he needed to warm up to me, you know? Maybe trust me with his plant. I don't know, but he was texting me the other night and joking too."

"Joking with you in text? I'm not sure I've ever seen him joke. Interesting." She pauses for a second, almost as if she's thinking about something. "You know, these last two games, he's looked different on the ice. Faster, don't you think?"

"Haven't noticed." I shrug.

"Hmm, and you say nothing is going on?"

I shake my head. "Nothing. I wouldn't go there with him. He's just . . . different. Not my type emotionally or personality-wise. But he is nice to look at."

"Yeah, he is. He has that boy-next-door look."

"He does." I glance at the time and realize I have a meeting in ten minutes. "Ugh, I should get going. I have a meeting." We both stand, and I give Penny another hug. "I'm so glad you're back."

"Me too." When I pull away, she takes my hand in hers and says, "Seriously, I'm really happy for you, but please don't make a decision without consulting me. I can't possibly be blindsided. I need to prepare for your departure."

I chuckle. "I promise."

—————

BLAKELY: *[Picture] Sherman says good luck, Daddy.*

Halsey: *He does not call me Daddy.*

Blakely: *That's not what he told me.*

Halsey: *Then he's lying to you for attention.*

Blakely: *LOL. I bet that's it. Are you ready to score some more goals?*

Halsey: *Prepping my stick now.*

Blakely: *Well, go get them. Good luck.*

———

BLAKELY: *You won! Yay! Unsure of what the return to the apartment is like for you. Do you want me to get your bed ready or anything? Turnkey service?*

Halsey: *Uh, I'm good.*

Blakely: *Are you sure? Should I light up a pathway for you? I can stay awake and flag you in, in case you're so delirious from it being so late.*

Halsey: *Seriously, I'm good. I'll be quiet so I don't wake you.*

Blakely: *Feel free to bang pots. I don't care. I'm just a fly on the wall. This is your apartment, so do what you need to do.*

Halsey: *I'll be quiet.*

Blakely: *Okay, but if you need anything, just let me know. Also, a few things. I started putting a blanket around Sherman at night because I was nervous I wasn't doing enough. I tuck him in and play his sound machine that I got him. Ten solid minutes of birds chirping. Assumed that's what he wanted to hear. Don't be alarmed if you see a blanket around him. It keeps him warm.*

Halsey: *I'm sure he appreciates it.*

Blakely: *I think he does. He looks . . . perkier. Also, I restocked the fridge with some of those protein drinks you have and some other food, so help yourself. I spent the evening cleaning the apartment, not that it was dirty, but I felt like if I mopped, I'd feel better about staying here for free. I also put an envelope of cash on the counter with your name on it. It's for the phone. And there are cronuts waiting for your consumption in the morning whenever you wake up.*

Halsey: *You didn't have to clean, but thank you. I told you, you didn't have to pay me back, so take the envelope and put it in your purse. And thanks for the cronuts.*

Blakely: *I have a feeling the envelope is going to be a problem and will be passed back and forth. Challenge accepted. Safe flight.*

Halsey: *Thanks. Have a good night . . . and yes, challenge accepted.*

———

I TIPTOE across the concrete floor on bare feet, shoes in hand as I make my way to the kitchen. I made my lunch the night before as well as my coffee so all I have to do is put some ice into it when I get to work. Just need to grab some things, and then I'll be on my—

"Morning."

"Jesus fucking Christ," I say as I fly into the wall, clutching my shoes to my chest. I steady myself and then see Halsey lying on his couch with a book in hand. "Dear God, why are you up so early? I thought you'd be sleeping."

"Slept on the plane and couldn't sleep past six this morning." He sits up, shirtless once again, showing off that perfect stack of abs. "Sorry for scaring you."

As my heartbeat and fight or flight slowly starts to settle back to normal, I say, "Didn't sleep much, huh? Is that because you sleep on an air mattress?"

The look of shock on his face is almost comical.

I hold up my hand. "And before you say anything, I wasn't snooping. I was going into your room to put the envelope with money on your nightstand when I saw that your bed was sunken right in the middle. That's when I toed it carefully and realized it was an air mattress. I took the liberty of blowing it up for you before you got back."

"Oh . . . thanks." He lifts from the couch, avoiding eye contact as he moves into the kitchen and starts making coffee.

I set my shoes down on one of the island chairs and ask, "Do you always sleep on an air mattress?"

"Uh . . . no," he says, still avoiding eye contact.

Why is he being weird about it? Sure, I went into his room, but I wasn't trying to dig around for some dirt or anything. It was innocent, and the only reason I mentioned the air mattress is because . . . oh my God. It hits me all at once.

No.

There is no way.

Stepping closer, I say, "Halsey, did you give me your bed?"

He leans against the counter, hands propped up on the edge

as he says, "I didn't have time to grab you one, so yeah. No big deal."

"No big deal?" I ask. "Halsey, you gave me your bed, and you chose to sleep on an air mattress. Why on earth would you do that?"

He sifts his fingers through his hair, pulling on the strands. "Well, I didn't want you not to have a bed. I'd rather sleep on an air mattress than make you sleep on one. It was an easy solution."

"It was a solution that didn't need to happen. I could sleep on an air mattress no problem. I don't mind it at all. In fact, I'm going to switch beds right now." *Easy solution, my ass. It's ridiculous.*

I charge back to my room feeling guilty as shit that I took this man's bed, and I start pulling my blankets and sheets off. He shows up right behind me, gathering the blankets and trying to put them back on the bed.

"Stop that." I swat at his hand. "I'm giving you your bed back." I move to the corner, stick my hands under the mattress, and lift on three, only to barely make it budge. "My God, what is this thing made of? Lead?" I attempt again, but it's not going anywhere. "How can something so comfortable be so heavy?" I motion to him. "Here, give me a hand."

He stands there holding my blankets, shaking his head at me. "No, I'm not going to help you."

"Halsey, you can't possibly think that I'm going to sleep on this bed knowing it belongs to you. Come on, help me."

"We're not switching it. You're a guest, so you get the nice bed."

"You're the owner, so you get the nice bed," I shoot back.

"If I'm the owner, then I get the last say, and I say you get the nice bed. I get the air mattress and you get to keep your money. End of discussion."

I take a step back. "End of discussion?" I prop my hands on my hips. "Halsey Holmes, do you really think that kind of talk is going to go over well with me?"

He shrugs. "I hope it does because I'm not changing my

mind." And with that, he tosses the blankets back on the bed and walks out of my bedroom.

Well . . . I would not have expected that kind of attitude from him, but here we are.

Little does he know, I don't go down without a fight.

Chapter Nine

HALSEY

"Dude, she saw the air mattress."

"What?" Posey says as he picks up a water bottle while we lean against the boards after skating around to warm up our legs.

"She asked me why I was sleeping on an air mattress. She went into my room and saw it, then put the pieces together and figured out that I gave her my bed. She proceeded to strip her bed bare and attempt to drag the mattress to my room."

"Did she?"

"She couldn't even lift it off the frame."

"Did you help her?"

"No. I told her she was the guest, and I'm the owner of the apartment. Therefore, I decide who gets the bed. End of discussion."

Posey cringes in horror. "Dude, you said that?"

"I know." I grip my stick tighter. "Fuck, I felt my balls shrivel up as I walked away. The look on her face wasn't good. I proceeded to clam up after that and haven't talked to her since."

Posey shakes his head while the rest of the guys finish up and start filtering past us on their way back to the locker room. "That's a fucking setback. How could you tell her end of discussion?"

"I was embarrassed that she saw the half-dilapidated air mattress, and I didn't know what to say. She caught me off guard when she attempted to drag the regular mattress out of her room. It was a clusterfuck, and I wanted her to stop, so I said end of discussion."

"Who did you say that to?" Silas asks as he slides in next to us.

"Holmes said that to Blakely," Posey answers.

"Nooooooo," Silas says in a low voice. "Holmes, man, I know you're new to this, but you don't say that shit to women."

"I fucking know," I shout, which grabs the attention of our coach. "Shit, let's move this off the ice."

Together, we filter past the bench and down the hall toward the locker room.

"Wait up," Eli says, catching up to us. "Christ, I'm sore."

"From what?" Silas asks as we spot Penny at the end of the hallway with her tripod set up and a question for us to answer for social media.

"Uh . . . I'll tell you later," he says with a smirk. He leans into Penny and gives her a kiss. "Hey, babe."

"Hey," she says while pressing her hand to his chest. "Did you stop in to see Holden?"

"Yeah, he looked happy."

"He seems to be doing okay. I'm glad about it. Now, please answer my question so I can continue to soar as the best social media manager to ever exist."

I glance at the question and read it out loud. "What's your favorite Taylor Swift song?"

"Oh, that's easy," Posey says.

"Wait!" Penny holds up her hand and presses the record button. "Okay, go."

"Favorite Taylor Swift song has to be *Shake it Off*," Posey answers.

"*Are You Ready For It*," Silas says.

"Uh . . . that Romeo and Juliet one," Eli answers.

"*Love Story*," Posey says.

"Right, yeah, that one."

They turn to me and I say, "*The 1*."

Penny stops recording and clasps her hands together. "Perfect, boys, thank you." Then she turns to me and points her finger. "Now, I have to talk to you."

"Talk to me?" I point at my chest.

"Yeah, you." She glances over her back and steps forward. "Word on the street is, you like my friend."

My eyes flash to Eli who looks guilty as shit. He bites his lower lip and says, "Listen, things got a little crazy last night, and I might have said some things out loud to prevent myself from . . . finishing too early. I was just saying stuff off the top of my head."

"Jesus Christ," I mutter.

"Well, is it going to be the finger or the belly button?" Silas asks.

"The finger," Posey says, looking irate. "We aren't even going to test his ability to hold a hockey stick. For fuck's sake, man, it wasn't that hard to keep a secret."

"To be fair, I screamed like a girl when I said it out loud."

"How is that being fair?" I ask.

He shrugs. "Please don't chop off my finger."

"What the hell is going on?" Penny asks.

"Nothing you need to know." Posey grabs Eli by the shoulder and pushes him toward the locker room.

"Wait," Penny calls out. "I promise I won't tell her . . . I actually . . . I need your help."

Posey pauses. "What kind of help?"

Penny glances over her shoulder again, probably checking to make sure Blakely isn't around. "Blakely was offered a new job, and it's unmatched, like she would be stupid not to take it, but I don't want to lose her, and that might be selfish, but I just had a baby, and I'm still highly emotional and very erratic, so I need you to make my best friend fall in love with you so she stays here and never leaves me."

"Oooo, plot twist," Posey says as he lets go of Eli. He gives him a once-over and says, "Your fingers are safe for now, but you're currently on probation. Understood?"

Eli nods vehemently. "Understood."

"Now." Posey turns toward Penny. "Tell us more about this falling in love thing."

"Well, I think if it were the right guy, Blakely would stay here, you know? And she did say how attractive Halsey is. She said you had an amazing body—"

"Told you the no shirt would work," Posey says, swatting my shoulder.

"Wait, you did that on purpose?" Penny asks.

Posey leans in and says, "We have an entire plan that revolves around a shirtless Holmes attempting to get Blakely to fall for him, you know, since he loves her so much."

"I don't fucking love her. I just have a crush is all."

"Don't listen to him," Silas says. "He loves her."

"You have a plan? Why didn't you tell me?" she asks Eli.

Looking like a deer caught in headlights, he looks among all of us and says, "I didn't want to be in the middle. I didn't want to be subject to getting my finger chopped off. There was a lot of pressure, and I really don't want to be a part of this." With that, he leaves, not even looking back.

I don't blame him. I want to take off too.

"In his defense, the minute we told him what we were planning and that he couldn't tell you, he stepped out. He said he couldn't do that."

"Aw, look at him loving and respecting me."

"He does, a lot," Silas says.

"He's a good man." She turns her attention back on me. "Okay, enough about Eli. Let's figure out how you're going to make my friend fall for you. Going shirtless is not going to work.

And no offense, I'm sure you have an amazing body, but she's unfazed by that. You guys need to step up your game."

"Going shirtless was just one thing on a list of ways we were going to entice her," Posey says.

Penny folds her arms over her chest. "Uh-huh and what are the other ways you planned on enticing her?"

The boys fall silent, glancing back and forth between each other.

"Uh . . . showing her his penis?" Silas asks.

"No," I say so fucking fast. "We are not showing her my penis or even talking about my penis."

"Why? Do you have a nice penis?" Penny asks.

"An amazing penis," Posey answers while holding his hands up and forming an obnoxiously large circle.

"Stop that." I swat his hands down.

"What? I'm just being honest."

"We are not using my penis as an enticement. Hell, we're not enticing her at all, okay? This has gotten out of control. We are dropping it—"

"To hell you are," Penny says, coming right up to me with that pointy finger of hers. "You listen to me, Holmes, and you listen good. I did not exit a child out of my body to just sit here and raise it without a best friend by my side. Do you understand what a postpartum woman goes through?"

"Ehhh . . ."

"Underneath this pretty pink blouse I'm wearing are raw nipples. Yeah . . . raw. They are chapped and have been sucked on and tugged on and brutalized to the point that I'm not sure I even have feeling in them anymore. And my stomach." She clasps her hand to her stomach. "It is jiggly but not, but also . . . jiggly. Explain to me how that works? It's as if when I got pregnant, an extra layer of skin was added but never fully attached to the underneath layer so it just moves around freely. And my feet . . . they fit in nothing," she whispers in a scary tone, and I can feel the hairs on the back of my neck rise. "Nothing. All I can say is thank God for my generation creating the casual but professional look by incorporating sneakers with trousers because I wouldn't have anything to wear on my feet if it weren't for the fashion trends right now. And don't get me started on the underwear I have to wear now." She grips my jersey, coming in closer. "They are . . . enormous. I could wrap your head and Posey's head together in one pair. So you can understand I need my best friend. Therefore, find your balls, man, because you are going to make my friend fall for you so fucking hard that she won't know what to do with herself. Got it?"

I swallow hard, staring down at the maniacal eyes of Eli's girl, and I feel myself slowly nod.

She pats my cheek. "That's a good boy." She straightens out her blouse. "Now, what is the plan?"

Startled, Posey clears his throat. "Uh, what were you thinking?"

"Glad you asked."

PENNY: *Are you home yet?*

Halsey: *This doesn't feel right. I don't want to trick her.*

Penny: *Dear God, Holmes, didn't I tell you to grab your balls?*

Posey: *I witnessed the balls comment. My balls actually shriveled up from it.*

Silas: *I'm still trying to dig mine out of my asshole after she mentioned raw nipples.*

OC: *Uh . . . am I supposed to be on this text thread?*

Pacey: *What's happening?*

Posey: *Penny is part of the Frozen Fellas now.*

Silas: *Trust me, don't fight it. She has raw nipples.*

OC: *Is she taking Eli's place?*

Silas: *Consider Eli dead. I don't think he can stomach the pressure. He's softened since he's become a dad.*

Penny: *There is nothing soft about him!*

Posey: *Christ, Silas, don't anger it.*

Penny: *It?*

Posey: HER! I meant her! Don't anger her. That was my phone. Not me. I'd never call you it. Please God, don't make my nipples raw like yours.

OC: You know, I think this Frozen Fellas thing has become a bit too much for me. I was all for it until raw nipples were brought into the conversation.

Penny: Are you calling me raw nipples as a nickname, new guy?

Posey: Oh dear God. It's angered.

Posey: I mean she! She's angered.

Silas: Well, there go my balls again.

Pacey: I can't breathe, this is hilarious.

OC: NO! I didn't call you raw nipples. I meant the topic of raw nipples.

Penny: Does a woman's postpartum body offend you, new guy?

Posey: For the love of God, apologize and stop talking.

OC: Please forgive me. I will not say anything else. Just . . . don't kill me.

Penny: That's better. Now, Halsey. I'm telling you, make the dinner. She's going to love it. Perry never cooked for her. This is the perfect way to ease yourself into her good graces. And sloppy joes is one of her favorite meals. Follow the instructions, and nothing will go wrong. Now DO IT!

Posey: Listen to her.

Silas: Please . . . please, Holmes, just do it.

OC: Penny is the best, everything she says is correct and awesome, and she's so smart.

Pacey: LOLOLOLOL

Penny: Good boys . . . very good boys.

I PLACE the pan from the drawer on the stove.

You can do this. You can cook. It can't be that hard. The instructions are so simple a child could make it. Nothing can go wrong.

I turn on the burner, then pull the ground beef out of my grocery bag and set it on the counter along with my other ingredients, ketchup being one of them. Who fucking knew?

Not sure where Blakely is, but I don't bother looking for her while I open up the pre-chopped onions. It was a solid find for me because to hell if I was going to have Blakely find me in the kitchen crying while chopping.

I toss some oil in the pan, then throw the onions in the pan as well, taking a step back because fuck those things smell. I study the pan. See? Easy.

"Are you cooking?" Blakely asks, walking in from the balcony.

I had no clue she was out there but hope she really likes the furniture. I had her in mind with every piece I purchased. The table so she could work out there. The loungers so she could relax. And the loveseat so that maybe one day, we can sit in it together with an open fire.

"Yeah. Sloppy joes. I'm going to have extra if you want some."

"I love sloppy joes. Do you want me to help?"

"Nah, I'm good," I say.

"Are you sure?"

"Positive," I say as I grab a wooden spoon, pretending I know what I'm doing as I stir the onions around. "I have stuff to make a salad to go with it. Do you like salad?"

She smirks. "Yes, I love salad."

Of course she likes salad, you idiot. What kind of question is that?

I'm losing my confidence.

Between Penny scaring the literal crap out of me, the pressure of not fucking up my chances, and the insane conversation I had with Blakely earlier about the bed, I'm flustered.

"By the way, I moved your bed."

I pause stirring and look over at her. "What?"

"I found these things that helped me slide the bed through the apartment. The hardest part was getting the mattress on them, but once I did, it was smooth sailing from there. And moving the air mattress was a piece of cake."

"I told you I didn't want the bed."

I toss the ground beef into the pan, unsure if my timing is right, but hell, it'll all cook down together.

"Your lower back says differently." When my eyes narrow, she says, "Uh yeah, I looked up your injuries to prove a point. See, told you not to mess with me. The bed is yours. I'll be snuggling up on the comfort of air tonight."

"Blakely . . ."

"What?" She smiles proudly at me.

"You shouldn't have done that."

"Oh yeah, what are you going to do about it? Switch them back?"

"Yes," I say. And without even thinking about it, I charge toward my room to switch the beds right then and there.

Blakely chases after me. "Don't you dare!" she calls out, and when I reach the room, she charges past me and flops on the bed, arms and legs splayed out as if that will stop me from moving the bed.

"You realize I can lift you and the mattress together."

"You wouldn't dare shimmy me off this bed."

"You don't think I will?"

She shakes her head. "No, you're too kind."

"Watch me," I say as I grab the comforter in one hand and give it a quick tug, dragging her with it.

"Nooooo," she cries out as I wrap her up in the blanket and deposit her to the side. I quickly tear the sheets off and toss them her way, adding to her entanglement. "Stop that this very moment," she calls out.

Ignoring her, I lift the mattress and put it on its side, then I drag the heavy-ass thing toward the doorway, only for her to throw her body onto it, sending the mattress into the wall and right out of my hands.

"You are not taking this anywhere." She grips it like a spider, her expression determined.

I lift the mattress on its side again and wiggle it until she falls off to the floor. I regret it for a second, hoping I didn't hurt her, but when I see she's okay, I tug it again. I get it halfway out my bedroom door this time before she climbs on top of it. Only she doesn't cling to the side. Instead, she straddles the top, grips it with her thighs, and holds on to the top of the doorframe.

"Try me, Holmes."

"Let go of the door."

"Never," she hisses.

"Blakely, I'm not letting you sleep on the air mattress."

"Well, guess who is not in charge of me? You. That's who. So I suggest you put this mattress back on your bed and walk away. I have all freaking night and I will not give up, and the minute you leave this apartment, and you're skating your little heart around that ice, I will be moving this mattress back to your room. I'm relentless and stubborn and refuse to let you win this match." A smile passes over her lips. "End of discussion."

I don't know what it is—her sass, that smirk, or the reverberation of the words I used on her this morning—but it creates a sense of revenge inside me, bringing me to the stubborn motherfucker I've been known to be. Over my dead fucking body will she be sleeping on an air mattress.

"Fine," I say.

"Fine?" she asks, thinking she's won.

I move back into my room while she hops down from the mattress. I feel her eyes watching me walk into my attached bathroom. I reach into one of the drawers, grab a pair of scissors, and walk past her, headed right for her room.

"What are you doing?" she asks.

I remain silent, walking past Sherman, who now has a picture of a cat set up next to him. What the hell is that about?

I'll ask questions later. I have a mission to accomplish at the moment.

"Halsey, why are there scissors in your hand?" She runs up to me, tugging on my hand, but I keep moving forward. "I asked you why you have scissors in your hand." She tries to stop me from moving forward, but she's no match, and I walk right into her bedroom.

"Halsey Holmes, you put those scissors down this instant."

I step up to the air mattress, cock back my hand, and lean forward to jab just as she throws her body in front of me.

My hand stops just in time. "Jesus, Blakely, what the hell are you doing? I could have stabbed you."

"You're not popping this air mattress."

"Yes, I am." I move around her, but she moves with me, throwing her arms out and protecting the stupid thing.

Trying to outsmart her, I leap over her and cock my arm back again, only to be stopped by her climbing on my back and knocking the scissors out of my hand.

Because the air mattress is unsteady, and I'm surprised by her attack, I falter in my balance. I step to the side, missing the mattress completely, and fall to the floor, rolling my ankle in the process.

"Aw, fuck," I cry out as I land flat on top of her, knocking the wind out of her.

Pain shoots up my ankle. She remains lifeless beneath me, and the scissors land inches from me on the floor. On a grunt, I reach for them and bring the tip toward the air mattress, just as she wraps her arms around my shoulders, holding me back.

"No, don't."

"It's . . . happening," I call out just as I make one last attempt. I lift and stab the air mattress, popping it with one big burst of air.

Relieved, I roll to the side and catch my breath as she tends to the air mattress.

"I can't believe you did that." She attempts to stop the air from escaping by covering the hole with her hands, but it's pointless. "What did this mattress ever do to you other than provide you comfort?"

I wince as pain shoots up my leg. Fuck . . . that's not good.

I crawl past the deflating air mattress and use the wall to help me stand. When I put even slight pressure on my foot, pain radiates through my leg, causing me to crumple back to the floor.

"You realize I'm just going to sleep on the couch now, right?"

I feel her eyes fall on me. "Did you hear me? Couch? Wait . . . are you in pain?" She crawls toward me. "Are you crying?"

"No," I grunt out.

"Oh God, wait . . . you are in pain. Is it your back? Should I get you ice? A brace? Tiger balm? Do they even still make that? What can I do?" She presses her hand to my back. "It feels hot. Does that mean you snapped something inside it? I think I read that once, that hot muscles indicate an injured muscle. Is that right? Did you injure the back?"

"My . . . my ankle," I say.

"What?" she nearly yells. "Your ankle? Are you serious? I swear to God, if you're not serious, I'm going to murder—"

Beep. Beep. Beep. Beep.

The shrill sound blasts through the apartment, nearly curdling our ears.

"Jesus, what's . . ." She pops her head up like a prairie dog and sniffs the air. "Is something burning?"

"Burning?" I ask, totally out of it.

"Yeah, it smells like . . . oh no, is it the sloppy joes?" she yells as the fire alarm sounds off in the apartment.

"Fuck. It is." I go to stand again, but she pushes me back on the floor, landing me on my back.

"Shit, sorry, I didn't mean for that to be aggressive, but don't get up." She points at me. "Stay right there. I'll get the sloppy joes."

"I can—"

She plants her foot right on top of my chest, and in a demon voice, she says, "Get up and I will bring that pan over here and use your nut sac as a trivet. Got it?"

I hold my hands up in surrender. "Fine." I am just as terrified by Blakely's demon voice as I am of Penny's. Who taught who? Because surely, they weren't raised with that voice, right?

She takes off, and from where I lie on her bedroom floor, I hear her open the sliding glass doors to the balcony as well as a few other windows.

"Shit, this is torched," she says from the kitchen, causing me to shut my eyes in disappointment.

Yup, you idiot, good job. Not only did you burn dinner but you pissed her off. And you hurt your foot, right when we're on a goddamn winning roll. Pretty sure this is not what Penny and the boys envisioned for me tonight. But fuck, I didn't want her sleeping on a stupid air mattress. Is that too much to ask?

After a few seconds, she comes back into her bedroom, bringing the stench of burnt onions with her. Hands on her hips, she says, "I'm well aware the odor surrounding me is unpleasant so if you tell me right now you're faking this injury, I will lose it on you."

I shake my head. "I'm not faking it."

"Okay, so you're telling me you hurt your ankle?"

"Yes."

She stares at the wall and nods before throwing her arms up in the air. "Great, I just hurt the ankle of our number-one player, ruining the chances of the Agitators winning the Stanley Cup. Great." She leans against the wall and slides down it until she's sitting.

Her hands cover her eyes and I'm unsure if she's going to cry or if she's going to scream, but to avoid both, I say, "You think I'm the number-one player on the team?"

"Holmes, I've been with you guys for a year. A fan for years before that. Of course I know you are." She holds her hand up to me. "And I just jumped on your back without thinking about the consequences!" My ankle throbs, but I'm also riding a small high here. *Blakely thinks I'm the best on the Agitators.*

"Blakely. Look at me."

"I can't," she says through her hands, which has muffled her voice. I chuckle. I can't help it. She's adorable.

I sit up and pull her hands off her face.

"There she is." I lift her chin and find watery eyes staring back at me. "Blakely, I've rolled this ankle a million times. I've played with worse. I just need to see my trainer."

"Your trainer. Of course. I need to get you to your trainer. I'll drive you there. Come on, Holmes. Hop up, and I'll take you. Oh, but you can't hop up. Well, you might be able to hop, but not all the way to the arena—"

"Blakely?" She finally takes a breath and squints at me.

"Yes, Halsey?"

"There are crutches in the front hallway closet. You grab those, and I'm going to text my trainer to meet me at the arena."

"Right, on it." She bolts out of the room, and I pull my phone out of my pocket and text Grace, our trainer.

Make sloppy joes, she said. They're easy, she said. But no, it's easier for me to make a fool of myself than cook a simple dinner.

This was not what was supposed to happen . . . you dumbass.

BLAKELY DRIVES like she has precious cargo in the car. She refuses to go above the speed limit, and she asks if I'm okay every few seconds.

"Yes . . . I'm fine. Seriously, you don't have to keep asking," I say as my phone buzzes with a text.

Penny: *How's it going? I'm dying to know. Do we hear wedding bells?*

I roll my eyes. If only she fucking knew.

Posey: *How were the sloppy joes? I tried the recipe because I was curious. Really enjoyed the added onions.*

Silas: *Ha! I made them too. Fucking delicious.*

OC: *Is it weird that I cooked them as well, but only because I want to get on Penny's good side?*

Penny: *Very smart, new guy. Very smart.*

Knowing we have at least ten more minutes until we reach the arena by the way Blakely is driving, I text them back.

Halsey: *Burned the fuck out of the sloppy joes because I was wrestling a mattress. I rolled my ankle, so we're currently on the way to the arena to meet with Grace. I ended up popping the air mattress with scissors.*

Silas: ***BLINKS***

Posey: *Uh . . . I don't think that's what we planned.*

OC: *Wait, so you're hurt?*

Pacey: *Fuck, dude!*

Halsey: *Yeah, I'm hurt, and dinner was roasted.*

Penny: *This.*

Penny: *Is.*

Penny: *Perfect!!!*

Silas: *I say this with all the gentility that I can muster, but how is our center rolling his ankle perfect?*

OC: *Clearly, Penny knows all so we should just listen to her. Yay, you rolled your ankle!*

Posey: *Dude, have some nuts.*

Pacey: *I'm with Levi.*

OC: *I'm so confused!*

Penny: *Okay, it sucks for the team, but this is perfect for Halsey. He will be out for, what? A week or two? Blakely will be so distraught that she'll want to take care of him every chance she gets, leading to them falling in love! Can't you see, it's perfect!*

Posey: *She's right.*

Silas: *Huh, that does make sense.*

OC: *See, all hail Queen Penny.*

Penny: *Okay, pull it back, new guy.*

OC: *Sorry.*

Halsey: *She has a job. There is no way she will take care of me, and I don't need to be taken care of.*

Posey: *Don't be a stubborn motherfucker. Take this chance and go with it.*

Pacey: *Take it, dude.*

"Are you still doing okay?"

I glance over at her, and her worried lip. "Yes, Blakely. Seriously, I'm good."

"Okay." Her eyes fixate on the road in front of her, but I can see the tension in her shoulders and the sorrow in her expression.

"I shouldn't have tried to move the bed or pop it for that matter. Call me old-fashioned, but I just wanted to make sure you were comfortable. You're my guest."

"I know, and I'm sorry. I was being stubborn and trying not to get in the way and bother you, but I ended up making it worse. We burned dinner and popped an air mattress and made a mess of our rooms. And you won't be able to play hockey. Do you think it will be for the rest of the season? I really am sorry."

"It won't be the rest of the season, and it will be fine. Okay? I should have just left everything alone."

"No, I should have."

I sigh. "Listen, Blakely. We can go around in circles about this, or we can just apologize to each other and not bring it up anymore."

She stops at a red light and turns toward me, tears in her eyes. "I just feel really bad."

Shit.

I don't want to see her cry.

Ever.

Those tears about to pour over feel like tiny sharp knives digging into my chest.

I want to pull her into my chest, hug her, brush my hand over her hair, tell her everything is going to be okay, but I don't own that privilege, so instead, I say, "I know, Blakely. But I promise you, it will be fine. Okay?"

She nods as one single tear streams down her cheek. She wipes it away and says, "I'm sorry, Halsey."

"I'm sorry, too." I offer a comforting side smile, unsure of what else to do.

She wipes at her eye, and as the light turns green, she starts driving again.

Fuck . . .

If only.

If only I could tell her that I don't care about what happened, just that I care about her comfort, spending time with her, and making sure she's okay. I hate that she's upset. I hate that she's holding this guilt. That's the last fucking thing I want.

I want to see that shining smile of hers, those brilliant eyes full of joy. I don't want to be the source of her pain and discomfort.

Feeling sick about it, I text the group.

Halsey: *She feels so guilty. She's crying. I can't fucking take this. I don't want her upset and holding on to this guilt. What the fuck do I do? Because anything I say doesn't seem to penetrate her mind.*

I glance out the window and see the arena up ahead just as my phone buzzes.

Penny: *She will hold on to this guilt until she feels better. Let her feel her pain. Let her do what she can to make things right in her head. Accept her help.*

Pacey: *I don't know Blakely well, but I know if this was Winnie, she'd want to do everything she can so that, in her mind, she's rectifying the situation that she helped create. I agree with Penny. Let her work through this herself.*

Silas: *Same with Ollie.*

Posey: *And when she works through it, that's when you take advantage of the time with her.*

Penny: *Correct, boys. I'm proud of you.*

OC: *I'm still thinking about how you used the word penetrate. I keep thinking about your penis. I think there is something wrong with me.*

Halsey: *You've lost a lot of my respect.*

OC: *I accept this.*

Chapter Ten

BLAKELY

Hands full of two sandwiches, drinks, and potato salad, I push through the door leading to the ice baths in the training room where Halsey is icing his foot.

To say I want to crawl into a hole and never be seen again is an understatement. I can't believe I injured our star player. Not only injured him but took him out of the game. I saw how swollen his ankle was the moment he took his sock off. Yeah, it's not good. The trainer immediately started doing range of motion exercises with him, and with the pain searing through his face, I knew I had to get out of there, so I ran out to the deli next to the stadium for some food. It's the least I can do since dinner burned, and we won't be having sloppy joes anytime soon. It's a shame because he was trying hard to brown those onions.

Well . . . they browned.

"Hungry?" I ask as he looks up at me.

"Starving," he says.

I pull up a chair next to him and hand him a turkey and

provolone sandwich. "I hope you like turkey. I wasn't sure and it seemed like a safe option."

"Love turkey. Thank you."

"There's a pickle wrapped up in there as well."

"I can smell it," he says as he finds the pickle and takes a huge bite.

I scan for his foot in the ice bath that's swirling around, but I can't see anything. "How's the ankle?"

"Can't feel a goddamn thing." He lifts his sandwich to his mouth.

"I guess that's good," I say as I unravel my sandwich as well. "What are they saying about play time?" I know it's probably the last thing he wants to talk about, but I need to know. I need to know if he can play or if he's done for the season. How much did I mess up the Agitators season?

He wipes his mouth with a napkin he plucks off my leg. "Grace thinks I'll be good to go in two weeks and when she says good to go, she means heavily taped up and stabilized with everything I do, even walking around when I'm not on the ice."

"Wait . . . two weeks, that's it?"

He nods. "She said it's rolled, but not that bad. There will be a plan to follow consistently when I'm home and I'll have to come in here every day, but other than that, she thinks I'll be good to go in two weeks, which isn't ideal, but that's only six games. I think the boys can hold out for that."

"Okay . . ." I look down at my sandwich, my tears forming again. This time, they don't fall as Halsey places his hand on my leg and pulls my attention back to his eyes.

"Hey, like I said, it's all good. Okay? We apologized and we're moving forward, right?"

I nod and sniff back my tears. "Right."

"And if you're up for it, I'm going to need some help."

"Help?" I perk up. "I can do that. What do you need help with? I'm your girl, anything you need."

There's a soft smile to his lips but nothing that reaches his rare, full-capacity smile. "Well, I injured my driving foot, so I won't be able to drive back and forth to the arena. I could hire a car service—"

"No, I can drive you. I can drive you anywhere you need. I planned on emailing my manager today and letting her know the circumstances that I might need to work from home for a little bit and just come in on game days. I'm sure she won't mind, especially if she knows I'm helping you out."

"If she says no, it's no big deal."

"No, it's fine. I'll make it work. What else will you need?"

"Just some help around the apartment. I have to do a lot of exercises and ice and elevation."

"Got it. I can help with that. Will you need help showering? I can wash with my eyes closed."

He chuckles. "I think I can handle that."

"Yeah, probably don't want a stranger rubbing you down with their eyes closed."

He pauses for a moment and says, "I don't think you're a stranger at this point."

"I guess not. I did straddle your mattress tonight, which . . . oh God, I have to get that back into place."

"I texted Posey and Silas. They're working on it, don't worry."

"They are? Oh God, did you tell them what happened? Do they hate me?"

"They don't hate you and they know accidents happen. They were actually impressed with your ability to lift the mattress on your own. Posey and I struggled when we moved it to your room before you moved in."

"I struggled a lot," I say, handing him a fork for the potato salad and popping the lid. Together, we each scoop a forkful. "I almost knocked Sherman over, and you can imagine the heart attack that ensued."

His brows lift. "Almost knocked over Sherman. Not sure I'd have forgiven you for that."

"If I did, you wouldn't have ever seen my face ever again."

"Well, I'm glad you didn't . . . for multiple reasons." He

directs his attention at the potato salad and for a moment, my body heats from that response.

For multiple reasons . . .

Is he implying he would be sad if he didn't see my face again?

Doubtful.

"By the way, what was with the cat picture you put next to him?"

"Oh, that's Horace. He's my childhood cat. After I almost knocked Sherman over, I was horrified, and I think he was just as scared and shaken, so I thought Horace might keep him company. Honestly, it was all done in a panic and I meant to take the picture down before you got home but forgot."

"I bet Sherman liked it."

"It seemed like his little branches fluffed up, so I think he did."

"Might need to keep the picture there."

"I'm not opposed to the friendship if you aren't."

He chews on some potato salad and says, "Two inanimate objects forming the bond of a lifetime."

"Not sure anyone else would let me carry on such an asinine farce."

He cutely shrugs. "It's not harming anyone. Have at it. As long as they don't start dining together or anything like that."

"Damn, and here I was about to put out a bowl of milk for Horace while Sherman drank up his water."

"Not sure I'd have recovered after walking in on that."

"I'd have perished over the cuteness overload."

He smirks and takes another dip into the potato salad, easing my anxiety. If I were to hurt anyone and take them out for six games, it's best that it was Halsey, because I'm not sure any other player would be as nice as he is being.

PENNY: *Heard Halsey hurt himself.*

I watch over Grace and Halsey as they talk together while she wraps his ankle.

Blakely: *Yeah, thanks to me. I don't want to get into it, but if you think I'm feeling guilty, times that by one thousand.*

Penny: *Oof, I'm sorry. Is he okay?*

Blakely: *Out for two weeks, so if they end up losing their momentum, I'll have no other choice than to take the new job. There will be no way I can show my face around this arena again.*

Penny: *Stop. I'm sure the boys will keep winning. It will be fine. Silas and OC can pick it up and I think Rivers might be coming back soon.*

Blakely: *No, he's still out for a bit. I asked. I think they're bringing someone up to help out. All because of a stupid air mattress.*

Penny: *What about an air mattress?*

Blakely: *He was sleeping on one. Gave me his real bed. I found out and switched beds. He was mad because he wanted to be a good host and give me the nice bed. It was a huge thing, but now there is no air mattress and just one bed.*

Penny: *One bed . . . that sounds like fun.*

Blakely: *Oh, I'll be sleeping on the couch. That's where I belong after all.*

Penny: *Maybe you can share the bed.*

Blakely: *LOL! Okay.*

Penny: *What? You're both adults. And I've sat on that couch, it's not great. It's not like you're going to accidentally slip your hand down his pants. You said he isn't your type.*

Blakely: *Uh, I'm not sharing a bed with Halsey. Have you lost your mind?*

Penny: *No, but think about it, he didn't want you sleeping on an air mattress, do you really think he's going to want you sleeping on the couch? Wasn't arguing about sleeping arrangements what got you into this mess in the first place?*

Blakely: *Penny . . . we're not sharing a bed. That is insane.*

Penny: *Okay, good luck telling him that.*

Blakely: *There is no way he'll offer to share his bed. He has to keep his leg elevated anyway. I'm sure he doesn't want a propped-up leg with a* *stranger in his bed. There's sharing an apartment, and then there is sharing nighttime space. That's going too far.*

Penny: *Just a suggestion.*

Blakely: *Well thank you, but it's not going to happen. Oh, and it looks like he's done so I'm going to drive him back to his place. I'll let you know when I'm coming in tomorrow. My schedule will be wonky now because I'll be helping him out.*

Penny: *Sounds good. Happy sleeping . . . on the couch.*

━━

"YOU GOOD?" I ask as Halsey crutches through the door, only using one of the crutches. Grace wants him to use his ankle and keep it moving so it doesn't swell up even more so he's using one crutch for assistance. The grimace on his face the whole way down the hallway of his apartment building just brought on that massive amount of guilt all over again.

"Yup, good." He enters the apartment and goes straight to the couch where he sits on the arm and lets out a deep breath. "Fuck, I forgot how painful this is and I don't say that to make you feel bad."

"I know. You're allowed to gripe, I promise, I'm good now. I've transitioned to mending mode." I glance around the apartment. "It seems like the boys took care of the meat in the pan and cleaned up. That was nice of them."

"Yeah, they're good guys." Halsey yawns. "Shit, I'm tired."

"Right, okay. Let's get you to bed. I'm sure they put the sheets and covers back on your mattress. Do you want me to check?"

"Nah, just grab a sheet from the closet for me. I'll park it out here on the couch and you can take the bed."

How did I know he was going to say that?

Maybe because the whole reason we're in this situation is because he was mad about me sleeping on an air mattress. Penny is right, he's not going to let me sleep on the couch, but I can't possibly get any sleep knowing that he's out here with a hurt foot.

"Halsey, I don't want you sleeping on the couch."

"If you think you're going to sleep on the couch—"

I hold up my hand, stopping him. "I know what you're going to say and where this is going. Neither one of us wants the other sleeping on the couch. I get it. So . . ." I swallow hard, embarrassed that I'm even suggesting this, but I don't want to run around in circles all night about sleeping arrangements. "We're both adults. Why don't we just share your bed? It's a king. We won't fumble over each other, and then that way, we can figure out a bed situation later. It could be temporary."

"I don't want to make you uncomfortable," he says.

"It's not . . . for me, I mean if it is for you, I understand, but there is no way I'll be able to get any sleep knowing you're out here, and I'm sure you'd be the same way if I slept on the couch. So can we just share the bed, at least for tonight?"

"I mean . . . yeah, if you're cool with that."

"It's fine. Like I said, we're adults, the bed is big enough. It'll be okay."

"Okay, sure, that's fine with me."

"Thank you." I let out the breath I've been holding. "Okay, I'm going to go get dressed for bed, brush my teeth, and wash my face. Do you need help getting ready?"

He shakes his head. "Nah, I'm good." He stands again, leaning on one crutch.

"I'll grab the pillows from my room so we can prop up your ankle."

"That works." Awkwardly he shifts toward the hallway. "Uh . . . see you in a bit."

I smile. "Yup, call out if you need anything."

As we go our separate ways, I quickly type a text to Penny.

Blakely: *We're sharing a bed.*

Penny: *Ha! I knew that was going to happen.*

Blakely: *I was in no mood to argue. And he was already geared up to tell me every reason why I wasn't allowed on the couch.*

Penny: *That's Halsey. Eli was saying he's easily the sweetest on the team. Cares the most. He gave some of the best advice to him and Silas when*

141

they were struggling with their relationships. I'm not surprised at all that he didn't want you on the couch.

Blakely: *Yeah, he is the sweetest. I've actually been surprised by how he's taken this. And also at how well he's communicated things too. We were going back and forth about how he injured his leg and whose fault it was. He stopped us both and suggested we just apologize to each other and leave it at that. It felt so . . . grown-up.*

Penny: *He's a smart man. Maybe this one bed situation will lead to something else. **wiggles eyebrows***

Blakely: *You realize I'm only a few weeks out from breaking up with my longtime boyfriend and that by no means am I even close to ready to date someone else, let alone think about it.*

Penny: *I know . . . but he's so yummy.*

Blakely: *Do you tell that to Eli?*

Penny: *No way, his man ego isn't strong enough to handle such a sentence.*

Blakely: *Didn't think so. Okay, I'm exhausted, I'll see you tomorrow.*

Penny: *See you tomorrow.*

When I enter my room, I notice the deflated air mattress is gone and the sheets and blankets are folded nicely in the corner. God, the guys really are the best. Hard to believe these strong, intimidating hockey players have actual lives outside of the rink. Like I'd never expect just from the look of them that they would care this much about each other, and I know that's probably an awful thing to say. But they cleaned up this whole place while Halsey was getting treatment just so we didn't have to deal with it when we got back.

They aren't just teammates, they're a family.

Reminds me of my college days when Kenzie and I did pretty much anything for each other. These boys have the same kind of bond.

I move around my room, throwing on a pair of cotton shorts and a simple tank top before heading into the bathroom where I finish getting ready. I'd normally wear something else to bed, something silkier—I just like the way it feels when I'm sleeping—

but I don't want to show up for our sleepover looking like I'm ready for a dirty romp. Don't want to scare the man.

I brush my teeth extra long, not wanting to breathe potato salad on him, go to the bathroom and throw my hair up into a silk scrunchie before heading to his room where I find him sitting on the bed looking at his phone.

Extra pillows in hand and a bottle of nerves in my stomach, I step into his room and say, "All set?"

He looks up from his phone and nods. "Yup. Wasn't sure what side of the bed you wanted."

"Whatever side you don't want and, I swear to God, if you argue with me about it, I'll hurt your other ankle."

He smiles. "I'll take this side, closer to the bathroom in case I need to use it in the middle of the night."

"Probably smart." I look at his shorts and T-shirt and ask, "Is that what you normally wear to bed?"

"No," he answers, "but I also didn't want to make you uncomfortable."

"The only thing that will make me uncomfortable is if you're not comfortable, so strip down to whatever you sleep in."

He thinks about it for a second and just shrugs as he pulls his shirt from over his head—the only way men know how to take off a shirt—and shimmies out of his shorts, leaving him in nothing but a pair of black boxer briefs.

Okay . . . so Penny is very right about the whole yummy thing because . . . wow.

I know I've seen him without his shirt on before, but now that he's in nothing but a pair of boxer briefs, it brings our friendship to a whole new level.

I mean, look at those thighs.

I've never been a man-thigh kind of girl, but my God, his are thick and his calves and his knees and . . . oh my God, Blakely, stop looking at the man's legs.

Clearing my throat, I say, "Lean back and I'll get the pillows situated and drape the blankets over you. Does that work?"

"Yeah, that works," he says as he sets his phone on the night-stand, then leans back and moves his legs up onto the bed.

Because I'm apparently an absolute pervert, the first thing my eyes go to is his crotch where I catch an obvious bulge. It's not the kind of bulge where he's turned on, just his everyday package and . . . wow. It's there . . . a bulge of all bulges.

It's *really* there.

Like . . . I've never seen anything like it. I mean, Perry had a nice penis, but it wasn't really all that much to write home about. *Man, I feel so disloyal even thinking that.* But . . . he left me. So . . . let's be real here.

Halsey Holmes has a giant penis. *Something you'll never see in person, Blakely.*

I tear my eyes away and focus on the task at hand—no need to get sucked into those thoughts, not right before you share a bed with him. I situate the pillows under his ankle as he lifts his leg and I help him adjust until he's comfortable. "That good?" I ask.

"Yeah, I think so. Not sure it will stay the whole night, but we'll see."

"If they collapse or your legs fall off, just tell me and I'll help you adjust again."

"Okay," he answers, not putting up a fight.

I drape the blankets over him but he only brings them up to his stomach. It makes him look naked under the sheets . . . *which is not good.*

My ears go hot, my skin flushes, and I'm suddenly envisioning what it would be like to see this man naked. Completely naked. *What if he'd taken off his boxer briefs as well as his shorts? Good lord.* I move around the room quickly, plug my phone in to charge —one of the boys must have put my charger in here too—and get into bed.

There's a decent amount of space between us and when I say decent, I mean maybe a foot if we're lucky. Halsey takes up much more space than I was anticipating, but it's fine.

I turn toward him and look up at the ceiling. "Crap, I forgot to turn off the lights."

"I'd offer to do it myself, but I'm pretty sure getting up and needing you to readjust the pillows will be more annoying than you just turning them out yourself."

"Look at you learning." I laugh and hop out of bed, turning off the lights and jumping back into bed, bringing the covers all the way up to my neck.

"Are you cold?" he asks.

"No, I just like to be fully covered. I like the comfort of it. I'm going to assume you get too hot at night given you're nearly naked and don't have the blankets up to your chin."

"That would be correct," he says. He lets out a large sigh. "I have to be at the trainer tomorrow at eight. Do you think you could take me?"

"Yes, anything you need. I'll bring you over and work in my office until you're done. Does that work?"

"Yup," he answers. "Thank you. I appreciate it, Blakely."

"Of course."

"And if you're not busy, how about we watch the game here and grab pizza or something?"

"Oh, you don't have to watch it at the arena?"

"Nah, they'd rather me stay home and get better than shuffle around the arena."

"Okay, then yes, that would be fun. Let me see if Penny can cover my VIP suites. I'm sure she can."

"Great." He yawns. "Okay, I'm about to pass out. Good night, Blakely."

"Good night, Halsey."

MY ALARM GOES OFF, shooting me straight into a sitting position only to fumble around with it until I figure out how to turn it off through my blurry eyes.

"Goodness," I mutter as I rub my face. I need to get one of those hatch alarms that gently wake you up, not the blaring regimen that wakes me up every morning with a jump-start to my heart.

Not sure if I was super tired last night or having the comfort of someone next to me in bed again, but I slept soundly, so freaking soundly that when I look to the side, I realize I didn't hear Halsey get out of bed and crutch his way out of here.

Way to take care of him, Blakely.

I toss the covers off me, only to quickly make the bed, and I slide out of the bedroom and down the hall where I find Halsey dressed, showered, and sitting on the island drinking a cup of coffee.

When the hell did he do all of that?

"Good morning," he says.

This morning he's wearing a heather gray shirt that just says hockey and it makes me smile. It's something a non-fan would wear to their first sporting event, yet, he's a professional wearing it. He's also in a pair of athletic shorts.

"Good morning." I see his leg dangling off the counter and say, "Shouldn't you be elevating that?"

"Probably."

"Let me guess though, this is where you like drinking your coffee?"

He shrugs. "I like routine."

"Understandable." I pour myself a cup and mix some creamer into it before turning toward him. "How did you get ready without waking me up?"

"Don't know, honestly. I even tipped over into the dresser, crashing to the floor, and you didn't even move."

"Oh my God, you did?" I set my coffee down. "Are you okay? Why didn't you wake me up?"

He smiles. "Just kidding. I kept my balance the whole time."

My eyes narrow at him, and I swat at his good leg, causing him to chuckle. "Don't do that."

"Just teasing, I could have gone further with it."

"What do you mean?" I ask, bringing my coffee to my lips.

"Back in high school, Holden rolled his ankle and it wasn't too bad, but our mom was freaked out because it was a few weeks before a big showcase. She was worried he wouldn't be able to play. To be a dick, he pretended he fell down the stairs. He lay splayed across the floor at the base of the staircase while I ran down the stairs, hitting the walls, making the sound effects while he groaned with every slap to the wall. I hid in the hall closet while my mom came rushing in to see him bent and crooked at the base of the stairs, his crutches flung across the carpet."

"Oh my God," I say slowly. "Halsey Holmes, that's terrible."

"Yeah, it was." He smiles to himself. "But fuck did we laugh so hard about it, even when we were grounded in our room. We could not stop laughing."

I point my finger at him and say, "Don't you dare do anything like that to me, got it?"

"I would never. You scare me more than my mom."

"Good, keep it that way."

I take a large sip of my coffee and tilt my head back. "I don't think I've slept that deep in a long time. Here I am supposed to be taking care of you and instead, I'm out cold, hopefully not snoring . . ."

"There was no snoring."

"Thank God. Anyway, that was some deep sleep."

"Were you really tired?"

I shrug. "Probably, but also . . ." I pause, not sure I want to divulge the real reason.

"Also what?" he asks.

And just look at him, those eyes of his, intent on mine, ready to listen. The way he holds his mug—wrapping his fingers around the whole thing—and how the fabric of his shirt so effortlessly clings to his biceps. He really is a dreamy man.

Maybe that's why I find myself telling him the truth.

"I always sleep better with someone next to me. Kenzie and I shared a bed in college, especially when we were going through difficult times. And when I was with Perry, we obviously shared a bed. It's been a little tough since we broke up that I think I found comfort in being next to you last night." I wince. *Stop talking, B. He does not want to hear about you sleeping with Perry.* "Hopefully that doesn't sound weird. Or clingy."

"It doesn't," he says. "It actually makes me feel good, that I could provide you comfort. I know what it's like to lose someone important in your life, and finding comfort during those times of unease and uncertainty is what matters."

"Thank you. And I know you're probably ready to kick me out of the bed so I can find something today and have it delivered."

He's silent for a moment before he connects his eyes with mine. "Or . . . you don't have to."

"You want to share a bed with me?" I chuckle. "I doubt that."

He shrugs. "You didn't bother me and if it gave you comfort, then it's fine. And it's not like you're here for long, so there's no need to get another bed. I'm good with it if you are."

"I mean . . . sure. I just don't want to intrude."

"You're not."

"Okay." My cheeks blush for some reason. Maybe because your extremely attractive roommate just told you that you can continue to sleep next to him at night. "It feels awkward now."

He chuckles and slowly slides off the counter. "Then let me be the one to walk away . . . or crutch away. There's a bagel place on the way into the arena. Want to stop there for breakfast before we head in?"

"That would be perfect. Give me like twenty minutes and I'll be ready." I take one more sip of my coffee and then head down the hallway to my room, a smile on my face the whole time.

Chapter Eleven

HALSEY

"Fuck, man. I can't believe you're out for at least two weeks," Silas says as he sits next to me in the locker room.

I just got done with some painful treatment, thanks to Grace, and I figured I'd visit with the guys before letting Blakely know that I'm ready to go back home. I want to give her some time in her office before I pull her out.

"I know, but Grace thinks if I stick to my treatment plan and don't miss one thing, I'll be ready to come back."

"I don't want you to reinjure it."

"I won't," I say. "You know Grace, she tapes us up with what feels like steel rods."

"True," he says as he leans back on the bench. "Hell, tonight is going to be rough without you though. Are you staying to watch?"

"No, going to watch from my apartment. I actually asked Blakely to watch with me."

He slowly turns his head and faces me. Whispering, he asks, "Did you tell Posey this?"

"No, why?"

"He's going to be so fucking obnoxious that I don't think I can bear him knowing."

"What do you mean?" I ask.

"He's seemed really chill in the Frozen Fellas group, but he's been bragging up a storm in a separate text about how he's the best matchmaker to ever walk the goddamn planet. Of course, Pacey let him have it last night and said he shouldn't be celebrating while our center is laid up with a bad ankle. We haven't heard from him since but if he knows you have a date planned—"

"It's not a date."

"Oh, he'll call it that. Like Jesus, he's been insufferable. It's almost as if he's trying to avoid something in his life so he's incessantly involving himself in ours."

"That's probably the case," I say just as OC walks into the locker room.

"Oh shit, man, how are you doing?" he asks, coming up to me and taking a seat.

"Good. Slightly in pain, but just got done with treatment."

"I can't believe you rolled your ankle fighting over an air mattress."

"Yeah." I pull on my hair. "I need to come up with a better story, because it doesn't sound great."

"To me it does," Silas says with a smirk.

"How was everything last night?" OC asks.

"Good." I glance around the room. "Don't say this to Posey, because his head might explode, but I shared my bed with Blakely last night. Nothing happened but this morning, she said it was the best night's sleep she's had in a while. She said it was probably because she felt comfortable sleeping next to me."

"Dude." Silas slaps my chest. "That's huge."

"She really said that to you?" OC asks.

"Yeah." I can't hide my smile. "It was the first sign I've gotten from her where I thought . . . maybe there could be something there."

"There's definitely something there and, now that you get to spend all of this time with her, Posey was right, this is the perfect chance to make your move," Silas says.

"Yeah, I think it is, but I'm going to take it slow. Feel her out and then, maybe when the time is right, I'll ask her out."

OC shakes his head. "I swear, if this all works out and you end up marrying this girl, Posey will never, and I mean never let us live it down." Fuck, he's right. But if I were to end up with Blakely, *nothing* would overpower the utter happiness I'd feel. *I'd have my girl* . . . something I still can't even imagine.

"I think that's a risk I'm willing to take," I say.

⌐⌐

"THIS SMELLS AMAZING," Blakely says as she grabs a piece of cheese pizza and puts it on her plate. "I don't think I've ever ordered pizza from here before."

"It's my favorite," I answer before taking a bite of pepperoni. We ordered half cheese, half pepperoni and I don't know why, but I think it's fucking cute that she wanted just regular cheese.

The game is on in front of us, the announcers in the background talking about my absence from the game and how it might affect the team, but I tune them out.

"Do you always get cheese?" I ask her.

Her eyes are fixated on the TV, most likely listening in.

"Hey." I nudge her foot with mine, drawing her attention. "Ignore them. They're paid to talk, but they're not necessarily paid to state the facts. The boys reassured me that they will be fine without me."

"You're right. Sorry." She turns toward me. "Yes, I always get cheese, I love it. Perry hated that I wanted cheese and so he'd get pepperoni and make me pick them off and put them on his."

My brows draw together. "How is that fair to you?"

151

She shrugs. "I'm pretty chill. But this is true cheese and it's so good."

As long as this woman is in my life, I will make damn well sure that she always has just plain cheese pizza as an option. What a fucking douche.

When she's finished chewing, she swallows and says, "So tell me, what would be going through your mind right now if you were on the ice warming up?"

I glance over at the TV where the guys are skating around, doing some stretches. "Probably wondering if anyone is recording me while I stretch my inner thighs."

She laughs. "Oh, you mean the move where it looks like you're humping the ice? Uh yeah, people are recording you. Haven't you seen our social media?"

"I try to avoid it. You learn pretty quickly that social media is a blessing and a curse. There is so much love to drown yourself in, but there's also the negative. It might be few and far between, but the negative comments and posts, they're like freshly soiled seeds in your brain, planting themselves without even giving you a choice. And they grow and root themselves deep inside. That one negative comment becomes all you can think about—despite the love, despite the praise, despite the accomplishments."

"I guess I never thought about it that way since we're always posting positive things. Although, there are some comments on our posts that people will be sure to say how much the team sucks."

"Those comments are just rowdy fans from other teams," I say. "It's the other ones like . . . the wrong twin died." *Something I've never admitted to a living soul.*

"Stop." She sits taller. "Please don't tell me that's true."

"Unfortunately, it is," I say, unsure why I went from how good this pizza is to the dark thoughts that capture my mind daily. Because there are many times that I believe that narrative. *Holden was the better player. The better man. The more outgoing, likable man.* And when you read that someone else thinks that way, it's hard to ignore.

"That is such a shitty and awful thing to say." *Facts.*

"Confidence runs rampant when someone can hide behind a keyboard. It's why I ignore social media. I get my energy from the present fans, the ones I meet outside of the arena or at special events, because those are the ones that matter."

She shakes her head. "You're right, but how freaking disgusting. I'm so sorry people think it's okay to treat others with such disregard."

I just shrug. "Only makes us tougher."

"But you shouldn't have to put on a layer of armor to face the world."

"Some might say it's the price we pay for being in the spotlight."

"No." She sets her pizza down. "You might be in the spotlight, but you're a human first. Being treated like that is unacceptable."

"Thanks." I love how much she's defending me. It's very true, the spotlight can be a distant, dark place where loneliness quickly creeps into your soul. But no need to get into that. To lighten the mood, I say, "Maybe you should be my bodyguard and snap at the people who wrong me."

"Oh, I would. I can be a keyboard warrior. I can put people in their place no problem. Just direct me where to go."

"Why does it feel like if I unleashed you and Penny on the anti-fans that you would end up making them cry in minutes?"

"Because you're aware of our superpowers. No one messes with us or the people in our group."

"Am I in your group?" I ask.

"I mean . . . you and Sherman are for sure in the group. Maybe Sherman a little more than you."

"I want to say I'm insulted, but I also understand the connection."

"Is it weird that I was looking up plant clothes today? There was nothing, but I did find some bowties made for stuffies that could work for him. It would be adorable. A purple one for game days. He would be dressing up just like his daddy."

"What did I say about that? He doesn't call me Daddy."

"As far as you're aware." She takes a large bite of her pizza. The melted cheese extends out as she pulls the pizza away. I reach out and help her, snapping the cheese string in half. She smirks up at me and my heart seizes in my chest. It's the most beautiful smile . . . ever.

Her eyes light up.

Her lips are full of grease and cheese.

And there's a tiny dimple cutting into her right cheek.

I like this girl so fucking much. The more time I spend with her, the more I realize it.

She isn't just beautiful—on the outside—but on the inside, she has this uplifting spirit. Her warm personality makes you feel like you can be yourself without any passing judgment. It's easy to relax with her.

It's why I find myself letting my guard down and talking about Holden. I haven't wanted to search for a book to escape into. *The first time in years.*

"Do I have cheese on my face?" she asks.

"Huh?" I'm shuffled out of my thoughts.

"You're looking at me as if I have cheese on my face."

Shit, you're staring again, you moron.

"Oh sorry, no, I was just impressed with that bite."

"Oh yeah?" She wiggles her brows. "Well there's more where that came from." She opens her mouth wide and takes a giant bite of her pizza. Impressive. She can unhinge her jaw and shove the pizza in there.

"Impressive, but check this out," I say before attempting to shove the entire pizza into my mouth . . . but failing miserably when the pizza hits the back of my throat and my gag reflex kicks in, causing me to pull the whole thing out.

Mouth slightly full, she laughs, tears springing to her eyes. She takes deep breaths as she chews and then swallows. She washes it down with a lime La Croix and says, "Oh my God, you're such a man. That gag reflex is strong on you." She leans forward and elbows me like we're chums. "Not something I ever had to worry about."

Jesus.

Christ.

Didn't need to know that.

Because now that's all I'm going to think about.

That and the way she was able to unhinge her jaw.

"Ooo, was that TMI?" she asks.

"No." I shake my head. "Just surprised, as I haven't met a girl without a gag reflex." I pause and tilt my head. "Shit, that sounded bad."

She chuckles. "Ooo, tell me more."

"Yeah, I'd rather not."

"Damn." She smirks. "And the conversation was just about to get good."

<hr>

"DO you think if you played tonight, they would have scored more?" Blakely asks, turning toward me in bed.

The boys won but by the skin of their teeth. Pacey was working overtime in front of the net, not letting one goal pass, while Hornsby and Posey defended the goal well. Silas scored the one goal for the team, leaving it to a one to zero win.

I was pretty nervous there for a second.

"I don't know," I say. "The Yetis seemed like they were on their A game today. They're a quick team. I'm honestly surprised Posey and Hornsby were able to keep up." I consider it. "Probably would have scored a goal."

She chuckles. "Ooo, a little bit of cockiness. Didn't know you had it in you."

"There's still a lot you don't know about me that would probably surprise you," I reply.

"Is that a challenge to ask you a question?"

"Could be," I say.

"Hmm, okay. Well, I know that you like blueberry-flavored things. I know that you like to read and, despite liking to read, you don't have bookshelves for all of your books, which drives me a little nutty. I know that you somehow formed a bond with a plant named Sherman." If only she knew the truth about that. Although, when I pass by him, I do feel a kinship toward him now. "I know that you're protective and kind and care about your friends and was a bit of a hellion when you were younger. That seems like a lot."

"Only the tip of the iceberg," I say.

"Well, I will say this, you're not as shy as I initially thought you were. More just quiet, but it seems like when you're comfortable, you open up. Does that sound right?"

"Yeah, I think so."

"So that means you're comfortable with me?" she asks.

"I wouldn't let you in this bed or take care of Sherman if I wasn't comfortable with you."

"Makes sense." She shifts an inch or so and I can feel her body heat—it lights my skin on fire. "So tell me something I don't know."

"There are a lot of things you don't know. Be more specific."

"Okay." She pauses, giving it some thought. "What's your best memory?"

And here I thought she was going to ask something like what my favorite color is, but she's diving deeper. I like that.

"Best memory? Well, I have a few but they all revolve around the same thing. Playing hockey out on the frozen pond with my brothers Hayden and Holden."

"Oh right, you have an older brother. Do you see him much?"

I roll my teeth over my bottom lip. "No. I haven't seen him since Holden's funeral."

She sits up on her elbow. "Wait, really?"

"Yeah," I say, swallowing down the emotion traveling up my throat.

She's silent for a second and her hand connects with my arm. "Is this hard for you to talk about?"

"Yeah," I answer.

"Okay, well we don't have to talk about it," she says. "We can talk about something else or go to bed. Or I can tell you about my first period to defuse any uncomfortable feeling. I can make you feel even more awkward with a story about how I got it in the grocery store and what I thought was a melted strawberry popsicle on my pants . . . wasn't."

I lightly smile. "That's okay. I can talk about it." I turn my head so I can get a better look at her beautiful face in the moonlight. A shadow casts on the right side of her face, but the left is easy to make out. Her eyes are penetrating. It makes me lose every boundary, every wall I've ever erected around myself. "Losing Holden took a big toll on my family. My parents divorced after his death. Hayden and I haven't been able to speak to each other, let alone look at each other, and I can't remember the last time there was a family gathering. Well, I guess it was the funeral."

"I'm so sorry," she says, rubbing her thumb over my forearm.

"It was silent that day," I continue. "Not a sniffle, not a single moan of sadness. I think we were all still in shock. We went through the motions, receiving hugs and condolences. We didn't say a word to each other and once we lowered him into the ground, we went our separate ways. Nothing and no one has been strong enough to pull us back together because the person who could do that, is the person we lost."

"Halsey, I don't know what to say, I'm sorry."

"There's nothing really to say. That day will forever leave a mark on my life. I didn't just lose my brother, I lost my family. It's why my boys are so important to me now. And they get that. They understand that I need them more than they probably need me. It's why they let me be who I want to be when we're up at the cabin or when I'm in the locker room quietly reading. They know I need my space and I need my escape. There are times where they push me out of my comfort zone, but they also get me, and they know when they're pushing too hard."

"They know your limits."

"They do," I answer.

"Do you usually let new people into your life? Or are you afraid you might also lose anyone new?"

I look her in the eyes and say, "You're new and you're here. Does that answer your question?"

Her lips turn up. "I guess it does."

"I do fear the unknown though. I like to know where people are, the people who are closest to me. I like to make sure they're safe. It's why I've gone out with the guys, not because I want to, but because I feel more at peace if I know what they're doing, if I can make sure they're being safe."

"That makes sense. Are they aware of this fear?"

"Probably not." I stare up at the ceiling. "Hell, I think I've divulged more to you than any of them."

"Really?" she asks.

I look over at her. "Really. And maybe it's because I know you won't give me shit about what's on my mind."

"Ooo." She cringes. "That's where you're wrong. I very much will give you shit. I just need to find the right thing to give you shit about . . . like . . . the books. For the love of God, Halsey, get bookshelves."

I chuckle. "Maybe it will be a project I take on while I'm healing."

"As long as someone else is building them and anchoring them into the wall, then sure, sounds great. The last thing we need is Bob the not-so Builder putting up his own bookshelf and having it fall on top of him, breaking a wrist because you have no business putting together anything."

"I built the nightstands."

"Wow, where's your tool belt? We need to gild it in gold."

I let out a low laugh. "It's in the hall closet. Put it in a shadowbox while you're at it."

She pokes my side. "Okay, funny man."

"WANT me to bring dinner over to you since you're icing?" Blakely asks.

"Sure."

She made tacos tonight and I tried helping but she wouldn't let me, of course. I sat on the counter for a little bit, keeping her company, but my timer to ice went off, which put me on the couch. It's an off night for the boys so we decided to eat dinner and watch a movie . . . my choice.

I decided to make a very shocking—hear the sarcasm— choice and picked the movie, *Miracle*. She asked me the other night what my favorite hockey movie was and it was no contest. I get chills at the end of the movie every time.

Blakely walks over with a cookie tray full of plates, taco shells, beef, lettuce, salsa, and cheese, as well as drinks. I let her sort everything out and when I reach for a plate, she swats at my hand.

"Tell me what you want and I'll put together your tacos for you."

"You know, I can do it, right?"

"I know, but I do it best."

My brow raises in question. "Says who?"

She grins. "Me, of course. Now, tell me what you want."

Letting her win, I say, "I'll take the works."

"Ooo, just the way I like my tacos too." She starts with cheese on the bottom of the shell and then adds the meat, then the salsa, and finishes off with the lettuce.

"Smells amazing. Thank you, Blakely."

"Of course. I've been craving these for a while. Perry never really liked tacos so I'm excited to share these with someone else."

"He didn't like tacos?" I ask, confused. I feel like tacos are a universal food that everyone likes. I can't imagine one single person saying they don't like tacos.

"Well, he was more into a fancier taco. Like . . . he needs refried beans and rice and olives and fajita veggies."

"Isn't that more of a burrito?" I ask.

"That's what I told him." She hands me my plate. "But he'd try to shove it all into a taco shell and it would break. He'd then get so irritated and just start piling everything into a bowl and crunching the taco shell on top. At the end of the day, he wasn't eating a taco and it just . . . it irritated me. Sometimes simplicity is key."

"I agree," I say right before I take a bite, letting the flavors wash over my tongue. "These are really good."

"Thank you. My secret is freshly grated cheese. Other than that, there's nothing special about them."

We both laugh. "I knew it had to be the cheese. Truly elevates the meal."

"And elevation is key when eating tacos." She holds up her finger cutely, as if teaching a lesson.

"Besides adding fajita veggies and refried beans and all of that, right?" I eye her.

She smirks. "Exactly." After she takes a bite, chews, and swallows, she says, "I got an email today from Huxley."

"You did?" I ask, feeling my skin start to crawl. I almost forgot about the whole new job thing. Fuck that billionaire—can't he cool his jets? Jesus, let the girl breathe.

"Yeah, he was asking what I thought about the offer. I told him it was a great offer, but I was nervous about moving and also leaving my current job. He told me he understood and reassured me that the office was one of the best places to work and that all moving expenses would be paid. He'd also have someone on the team help me find a place to live."

And just like that, my anxiety rears its ugly head, making my skin break out into a sweat.

"That's, uh . . . nice of him," I say, trying to stay calm, even though panic is racing so fucking hard in my chest.

"I do think it's a little odd that he'd want me to relocate. Then again, if he gave me the option to work remotely, I feel like I'd let the team down. Like I don't want to be that one asshole that doesn't work in the office, you know? Employees are bound to resent that person."

"I think times have changed," I say. "I think technology has allowed us to expand what working in an office really means."

"Yeah, I guess so. Anyway, I asked him when he needed to know by and he said I had some time, but that he was just checking in to see if I needed more money. I laughed and told him more money is always good and he came back with a salary of three hundred thousand dollars."

What the fuck, Cane?

What is his game?

Sure, Blakely is amazing at what she does, but three hundred thousand? That has to be life-changing money for her.

"Wow, really?" I ask, feeling dread consume me.

"Yeah. I feel like that's unheard of for a position he's trying to fill, and I'll never see that kind of money with the Agitators, but I don't know, I still have to think about it."

Yeah, think long and hard.

Take your time.

Let me figure out how the hell I'm going to convince you taking a job of a lifetime is not worth it and that staying here with me is what you really want to do.

"Probably smart," I say, trying to sound as understanding as possible and not like the one-sided asshole that's firing off in my head. "Take your time, think it over. And hey, if you don't think you want to take the job, that's fine. It's really about what you want. I know you like living here."

"I love it here. One of the reasons I didn't follow Perry to Australia is because of how much I like it here. And because of my job. I feel like it would be weird if I left Vancouver for a new job."

Even though it pains me, I say, "You can't think about it that way. You have to look at the job, at the living conditions, and figure out what will make you the happiest."

"You're right," she says on a sigh. "At least I have some time to decide. But boy is he making it harder and harder to say no."

"Seems like a great opportunity," I say, despite knowing I'd fucking miss her if she left, if she moved. I'd be irritated and gloomy. Mad and angered. Sad that I didn't shoot my shot.

Maybe that means I need to expedite this process a lot quicker than expected.

I've made progress with her, I can feel our bond growing, but I wouldn't say it's anything that would hold her in place.

"We shall see." She wipes her mouth with a napkin. "Hey, did you see that new cookie place opened up around the corner from your apartment?"

"No," I answer. "What was it?"

"Pie Cookies, something like that. They looked so good."

"Yeah?" I ask, pulling out my phone and typing it in. Pie Cookies comes up immediately and I see that they deliver. "Want Frederick Garrlo to order some and have them delivered?"

She chuckles. "Do they deliver?"

"They do."

She sets her plate down and immediately scoots in close to me so she's leaning on my arm. "What flavors do they have?"

I chuckle and open up the menu for us both.

"Ah, Halsey, they have a blueberry cream cheese cookie. You love blueberry."

"Adding that to the cart," I say as I click on the plus sign.

"Hmmm . . . oh look, rocky road with a marshmallow center. Yes please. Add."

"Should we each pick one more?"

"I don't think we'd be doing the cookies justice if we didn't."

"I think you're right." I scroll slowly and end up adding a strawberry cheesecake, sticking with a theme, and she grabs one that's labeled chocolate desire, giving me the heads-up that this girl really likes chocolate.

Once they're ordered, we go back to our tacos while noting how excited we are about the cookies and that they better be good. It's casual, fun, and feels so right, like I've been sharing meals and conversations with this girl forever. And as we talk about stupid things like why the Smurfs are blue and is it because they eat too many blue things and will that happen to me because I like blueberry flavored things, I think to myself . . . Holden would fucking love her.

He would be sitting back, legs propped up on the coffee table with one crossed over the other and a giant smile on his face, watching me interact with Blakely, knowing deep down that she's perfect for me.

I knew it the day I first met her.

The moment I looked her in the eyes.

And with every day that I spend with her, I'm just confirming that feeling. She's everything I could ever want.

But will she ever believe she's meant for me?

Chapter Twelve

BLAKELY

"Thank you for covering the suites for me," I say as I hand Penny a box of cookies from Pie Cookies. I stopped by briefly before coming into work. I helped Halsey to the trainer and came straight to her office.

"What are these?" she asks.

"The best cookies ever. Halsey and I got some delivered the other night. They're so freaking good."

"You and Halsey?" she asks with a lifted brow.

I roll my eyes. "Nothing like that. Since he's home and not on the ice, we've been spending our nights together eating meals and watching the games. It's been nice."

"Nice? And nothing's going on?" she asks.

I shake my head. "No. Nothing."

"Not even . . . at night?" Her brows lift to her hairline now. "Because you're sharing a bed, right?"

"Oh my God, Penny. We are two mature adults who don't immediately become horndogs the moment we have to share a bed. I promise you, nothing romantic is happening between us."

"Nothing?" she asks, looking disappointed.

"Nothing. If anything, he's more like a brother to me."

"A brother?" she shouts.

"Yeah. I feel like I can talk to him about anything without judgment and he feels the same way. He even said he has a self-made family and I think I'm a part of that. It's a good relationship."

"Wow, that's . . . that's great," she says before picking up a cookie without even looking at it and shoving it in her mouth.

"Uh, that's the apple pie." I point at the half-eaten cookie in her hand.

"Yeah, fine." She sets it down. "So you don't have even the slightest bit of interest in Halsey?"

"No . . . why . . . why do you keep pushing this?"

Her eyes go wide. "I'm not pushing anything. I'm just . . . curious, because you know, I kind of went through the same thing."

I take a seat in front of her desk and cross one leg over the other. "What do you mean you went through the same thing?"

"With Eli. We were forced to live with each other and slowly, over time, we started to fall for one another."

"Yeah, but you also had a wild night of fucking prior to that, had a baby on the way, and were both very attracted to each other. Halsey and I have never had a wild night, probably the wildest night being the death of the air mattress, there is absolutely no baby on the way, and as much as I like to convince myself I'm in that man's league, I'm not even close to it. He doesn't see me that way. I'm pretty sure he sees me as a friend and that's cool. Different circumstance."

"I guess so," she says softly.

"Why the push for more?" I ask her.

"I don't know, I just . . . you know, don't want you to be alone. I know losing Perry was hard, and I think Halsey could be a good guy for you."

Losing Perry has been hard. I miss him. It's the longest we've gone without talking to each other. Yet, I haven't felt as devastated as I thought I would. Maybe that's because I've found a new friend to spend time with. Maybe if I was still living in our apartment, his loss would be so evident. I'd feel his absence daily. Yet, new place, new roommate . . . and it hasn't been that bad. Especially now I'm sharing a bed with Halsey. That has definitely helped with the end-of-the-day sadness. Yet, I'm still not in any dire need to find someone else. Or mourn Perry. Things are just . . . smooth. Easy. And Halsey? *He's still quiet.* But I couldn't imagine dating someone so high-profile. And hot. And built . . . and with a smile that's far too dangerous.

"Like I said, he's way out of my league and, even though I've gotten to know him better, I still don't think he's the kind of guy for me. That's it."

She slowly nods. "Well, I guess that's it."

"Why do you look so upset? It's my love life, not yours."

"Correct, but it's hard being a partner to a professional hockey player. It would have been nice if you joined the club."

"Well, there's always Posey."

Penny's nose turns up. "No, you are not the girl who will fit into Posey's bologna-loving life. Not a match, putting that out there now. Don't even consider it."

I chuckle. "What about OC?"

"Ehh . . . isn't he more like a brother to you than Halsey?"

"Yeah, he is, just testing to make sure you're looking out for my best interests and not just trying to hook me up with anyone."

"If that were the case, I would have thrown a party over the suggestion of Posey. That man is desperate for love."

"You seem desperate to find me love."

She shrugs. "Isn't that always the case with people who are in love, they want everyone around them to be in love as well?"

"I guess so." I stand from my chair. "But I'm good for now. Thank you."

"Are you leaving?"

"Yeah, I need to take care of a few things while I have the time here."

"Okay. Thank you for the cookies."

"Thank you for all of the help."

"You know I'm here for you, always. Remember that as you start . . . making decisions."

I roll my eyes. "Subtle much?"

"I thought it was. I could have said something like if you moved to a new job you wouldn't have the same unconditional support that you get from me." She gives me a cheeky grin. "See, I was subtle."

"Very." She lifts up from her chair and I give her a hug. "I adore you."

"Just remember how much."

HALSEY

PENNY: *SHE CONSIDERS YOU HER BROTHER!!*

I stare down at the text, my mind barely processing the words in front of me as my foot soaks in the ice bath.

What?

Why the hell would she say that?

I quickly type Penny back.

Halsey: *What?*

Posey: *Wait . . . hold on . . . do not fucking tell me we've been friend-zoned. I will chuck my bologna sandwich across the room right now!*

Pacey: *Please chuck it into the trash, it smells disgusting.*

Posey: *Your face smells disgusting!*

Silas: *How is that productive?*

OC: *I would say it's not, but you know, just stepping in here. Anything Penny says is correct because she is queen.*

Posey: *Seriously, dude, pull your head out of her ass before I tell Hornsby you're hitting on her.*

Penny: *He would not be happy.*

OC: *Jesus, I'm not! I swear. I'm just trying to be liked here and not chewed apart by a mama bear with scary fangs.*

Halsey: *For the love of God, can we bring it back to the brother thing? Did she say that to you?*

Penny: *Yes! I was talking about you, you know suggesting how great and hot you are, and she went and said that you're like a brother to her.*

Silas: *Not going to lie, that's a fucking blow.*

Pacey: *Can't see us bouncing back from that.*

OC: *Not that my opinion matters, but fuck, man, that's harsh.*

Posey: *I am dead now.*

Halsey: *Why would she say that? We've been getting along great. I haven't been giving off brotherly vibes.*

Penny: *Have you been giving off boyfriend vibes?*

Halsey: *Yeah, I got us cookies the other night.*

Posey: *That's it? Have you been doing the no shirt thing? Have you accidentally let her walk in on you naked? You're sharing a goddamn bed, have you scooted in close and aroused her with your morning erection?*

Silas: *The erection thing is a bit much.*

Pacey: *And the naked thing isn't?*

OC: *You know, in my experience, girls like guys that listen.*

Posey: *For the LOVE OF GOD exit the chat, OC.*

Halsey: *I'm not letting her see me naked or poking her with my erection. What is wrong with you?*

Silas: *If I were you, I'd use the girth-o-nater to my advantage. I did it with my piercings with Ollie.*

Penny: *Umm . . . piercings, let's talk about that some more. Halsey, what are your thoughts on piercing your penis?*

Halsey: *Not good.*

Posey: *I think this is a drastic move we might have to make.*

OC: *Oh, I have an idea. Why don't you ask her about piercings and see if she likes them? Maybe see if she'll accompany you to get one.*

Posey: *Okay, that's a great idea. You're back in the convo.*

OC: *Yes! *Fist pump**

Halsey: *I'm not talking to her about dick piercings.*

Silas: *Might get you out of the friend zone. You need to bring attention to the sexual part of the relationship. So talk about your dick.*

Pacey: *I'm really here for the entertainment, but I can't see how this could go wrong.*

Penny: *Do it, Halsey, or I'll take this into my own hands and I don't think you want that to happen. Talk to her about the dick piercings!*

———

BLAKELY

"YOU SEEM A LITTLE STIFF. Is everything okay?" I ask Halsey as we drive back to the apartment. He took longer with his treatment today, which was good for me because I got some things accomplished that I've put on hold.

And good news, he doesn't have to use his crutches anymore, but Grace asked if I'd still drive him, just to be safe.

I didn't have a problem with that at all.

"Yeah, everything is good," he answers while rubbing his palms over his thighs.

"Are you sure? Because you're not acting like your normal self. You seem nervous."

"Nervous, heh . . . no, not nervous," he says, looking out the window now. "What uh, what would my normal self be?"

"Well, you just finished training, therefore you'd normally tell me about how it went and talk about the boys and maybe something stupid Posey did or said. Of course, this is because I ask you, not because you initiate it. Even though you can hold a proper conversation, you're more subdued and quieter than others."

Jeez, I hope that didn't sound too creepy. Two weeks with this guy and I already know him like the back of my hand.

"Just thinking about something," he says.

"Care to share?"

From the corner of my eye I notice the tight set of his jaw, which only makes me more curious. What is going on in that head of his? It has to be good, whatever it is.

"Eh, you don't want to hear about it."

Little does he know.

"Actually, you have me incredibly intrigued. Tell me what's on your mind."

He shifts uncomfortably, his jittery motions making this so much more intriguing. Does it have to do with me? Maybe something I said? Maybe something that happened while he was getting his ankle worked on? Maybe . . . oooo, maybe there was a fan that he ran into and she's obsessive and turned into a stalker and he saw her.

The imagination is running wild.

Finally, he clears his throat and says, "Uh . . . ever hear about"—he clears his throat again—"piercings on a guy's . . . uh, penis?"

Blinks

Errr, what?

Well, that was not what I was expecting, not even in the slightest.

I'm actually so caught off guard that the corners of my lips twitch upward, a laugh wanting to escape my throat, because . . . penis piercings? That's what has him all in a tizzy?

What the hell happened while he was icing his foot?

I thought maybe he was worrying over something that happened while he was doing his exercises, like . . . maybe he blasted a fart right in Grace's face while she was stretching him. That would warrant the tight jaw and the uncomfortable shifting. But a dick piercing? Never in my wildest dreams would I have expected him to say that . . . which of course sends my brain into a tailspin.

Because Halsey Holmes is nervous about talking about penis piercings.

It's so cute. So adorable. And so unmistakably hilarious.

Keeping my composure, I say, "Yes, I've heard of penis piercings. Why do you ask?"

I can visibly see him gulp. "The guys, they thought that I, uh . . . that I should, you know, get one."

Oh dear God, what goes on in that locker room?

Okay.

Stay calm.

Do not laugh.

BLAKELY! Do not freaking laugh right now.

He's clearly distraught. This is a moment for him, and you need to be a supportive friend.

DO NOT LAUGH!

"Do they now?" I ask, my smile not holding back. "What are your thoughts on the idea?"

"I have none."

"Well, not to throw you off, but it seems like you do have some if you're not yourself at the moment. Are you considering it?"

He lets out a sigh and shifts again. "Sure," he says, almost as if he's giving up.

"Sure you're considering it? Do you know what kind of penis piercing you want?"

He rubs his hand over his thigh again, avoiding all eye contact with me as I drive us back to the apartment. "No, not really."

"Is there a reason you want one? Is it more for pleasure for others or is it like a decorative thing for you? Like . . . hanging up ornaments on the Christmas tree?"

"What? Uh, no." He shakes his head. "I mean . . . not decorative."

"So pleasure then. I have heard that having sex with a man who is pierced is a whole new experience. Is that what you want to offer to the ladies?"

"Fucking hell," he mutters. "I, uh . . . sure, I guess."

My cheeks flush from the thought. "Well . . . that could be . . . fun. Women like to be pleasured."

"They do." He nods, then as if he thinks of something really quick, he says, "I pleasure them just fine. Like, I don't need this piercing to give them a better time, if that's what you're thinking. I don't need the piercing like another guy might need it. I'm perfectly capable in that regard."

I'd assume he is from the bulge I've seen.

He drags his hand over his face. "What I'm trying to say is that I'm good at sex, and I don't mean that in a narcissistic way."

"I'm not thinking that. It's nice to have confidence in your sexual capabilities. Glad to hear you can rock a girl's world." I pat him on the shoulder. "Well done."

"It's just, I don't want you thinking I need this piercing for anything other than just . . . wanting one, I guess."

No, Halsey, I never would have guessed that you're the type of guy who'd want to strap his dick down and get it pierced. I wouldn't even think a tattoo would be of interest. That's how bland of a man I consider him.

"Well, if you're into that kind of pain, it might be great for you. A real step forward. Let me ask, do you like penis pain, Halsey?"

"Jesus Christ," he mutters as he turns his attention back to the window.

"Well . . ." I push.

"You know, forget I even said anything."

Probably for the best.

HALSEY

HALSEY: *That was a fucking disaster.*

Posey: *What do you mean? Are you ruining this for us?*

Halsey: *No! You are!*

Silas: *What did you say? Did you say it right?*

Penny: *Yes, please regale us with what you said, because we did nothing wrong. This is all on you.*

Halsey: *All you told me to do was talk about dick piercings with no guidance. And then you threatened me if I didn't talk about it.*

Pacey: *In Halsey's defense, that's exactly what happened.*

Halsey: *Thank you!*

Posey: *But what did you say?*

Halsey: *I just said that the guys were talking about how I should get a dick piercing, and it was so awkward and uncomfortable that I ended the conversation when she asked if I was into dick pain.*

Silas: *She asked you about dick pain?*

OC: *Are you into dick pain?*

Halsey: *NO! Like I said, a fucking disaster.*

Penny: *Disaster? I call that a SUCCESS!*

Posey: *I was just about to say the same thing.*

Halsey: *How the hell was that a success?*

Penny: *Take it from the only lady in the group, she's now thinking about your penis and that is step one.*

Posey: *^^^ Correct. There is penis thinking now.*

Silas: *Yeah, I can see the validity in that.*

OC: *I know it's worked on me. **winces***

Pacey: *I like you more and more every day, OC.*

OC: *I feel that hard.*

Halsey: *So now she's thinking about her brother's penis? Is that what we wanted?*

Penny: *Precisely. On to stage two.*

Posey: *Onward ho!*

Pacey: *Oh I can't wait to fucking see what stage two is.*

Penny: *The first touch.*

Halsey: *What?*

Penny: *Listen closely . . . lean in. Are you ready?*

Halsey: *Jesus Christ.*

Posey: *I think that's his way of saying he's listening.*

Penny: *Good. So she's thinking of the penis. Now, we need to lean into the first touch, and it needs to be in bed.*

Halsey: *No fucking way.*

Penny: *Remember the threat? It applies to stage two as well.*

Halsey: *I'm not going to touch her in bed. That's completely uncalled* *for. And what kind of touching are we talking about?*

OC: *GRAB HER TIT!*

Pacey: *Dude.*

OC: *Right, sorry. I charged to that rather quickly. Please disregard.*

Penny: *Just a light graze, like an oopsie-daisy touch. And if you can't nut up and do it in the bed, then maybe in the kitchen while getting dinner, but it has to be a graze with an impact.*

Halsey: *What does that even mean?*

Posey: *Dude, you act like you've never touched a girl before. You know the zones . . . lower back, back of the neck, side right below the boob . . . stomach if you're feeling risky.*

Silas: *Go for lower back, that's safe.*

Pacey: *Definitely not side boob.*

OC: *I personally think the neck might be good. Ladies are into that whole hand necklace thing.*

Silas: *Shit, yeah. Ollie loves that.*

Penny: *Yes to all. Stage two commence!*

<hr>

BLAKELY

"DO YOU WANT A SMOOTHIE?" I ask as Halsey walks into the kitchen, not a limp in his step, which gives me hope. I think he's healing well and will be able to play soon. I don't ask about his timeline for two reasons.

One, I don't want to put pressure on him. He'll be ready when he's ready, and the team has been holding on without him. They lost the last two games, but they could afford them.

And the second reason is because I've enjoyed having him around. I know I probably shouldn't be selfish like that especially since this situation isn't permanent, but it's been nice to have the company. I didn't realize how lonely I was since Perry's been gone.

Halsey in his typical shorts and nothing else leans against the counter next to me and says, "What kind are you making?"

Fresh from the shower, he smells amazing, like he dipped himself in soap and didn't rinse it off.

"Chocolate, banana, and peanut butter with some oats."

"Sounds good. I'll take one if you don't mind."

I smirk at him. "It's why I offered."

"Do you need help?"

"Can you peel the bananas for me?" I ask.

"Yeah, I can handle that." I hand him two bananas and toss some ice into the blender.

"This is my favorite breakfast smoothie ever. Back in college, Kenzie and I tried different combinations and recipes, looking for the perfect smoothie. We tried some doozies until we found the best combo or ingredients."

"Oh yeah?" he asks. "What were some of the doozies?" He sticks one of the bananas in the blender as I measure the protein powder for two.

"Kenzie thought it would be a good idea to try to mix tapioca pudding with grapes and ice."

"Ew," he says with a sneer. "Why did she think that would be good?"

"She was attempting to be creative. It did not work out." I stick the other banana in the blender, and he tosses the peels in his compost bin on the counter. I've never composted before, but his building composts, so I've learned, and I've decided when my apartment is finally ready, I'm going to try it as well. "Okay, we just need the oats." He hands me the canister and I pour about half a cup into the blender.

He takes a step closer to me and fidgets as he looks into the blender.

"You okay?" I ask.

"Huh? Oh yeah. Just interested in how it's all mixed. Blenders are fascinating."

I chuckle. "They are, aren't they?"

God, he's so strange sometimes. Confident and sure of himself.

Then completely awkward and aloof.

Funny and charming.

Dark and distant.

He's put me through a roller coaster of emotions, yet for some odd reason, each of those emotions seems to fit him perfectly.

I turn the blender on and together, we watch the ingredients mix.

Yup, blenders sure are fascinating.

He steps in another inch until we're next to each other. He keeps his eyes trained on the blender, but when I glance up at him, I catch his teeth pulling on the corner of his mouth as if he's nervous.

"Worried about what it's going to taste like?" I ask.

"Oh no, it smells good."

"Okay. I promise I wouldn't feed you sludge."

He nervously smiles. "I trust you."

What is with him?

I turn off the blender and detach the pitcher from the base. "This is seriously the best you'll ever have." He leans in closer while I pick up a glass. I hold it up to pour just as he lifts his arm. Assuming he's trying to help, I turn toward him while saying, "I've got this."

But as I turn toward him, his hand that was about to touch what I assume is my upper back, slides right over my shoulder and to my breast.

Exactly . . . on my breast.

Palm to nipple.

Eyes wide, I stare up at him and catch the realization cross over his face. His expression runs from interested to absolutely mortified.

"Oh fuck," he says, lifting his hand off my breast as if my nipple just burned his palm. He then shakes his hand, attempting to what I can only assume is shake the cooties off.

But of course, because Halsey is Halsey, in the midst of his shaking, he slams my hand, sending the pitcher right out of my hand and straight to the ground between us, where it shatters, sending smoothie in every direction.

"Jesus fuck, I'm sorry." He quickly grabs the paper towels and starts cleaning as I stare down at him, watching.

Did Halsey just touch my boob?

I think . . . I think he did.

═══

HALSEY

HALSEY: *Abort. Abort. This is not going well. I fucking touched her tit! I violated her very being.*

Silas: *How the fuck did you manage that?*

Pacey: *Dude, that was NOT one of the zones we talked about.*

Posey: *HER TIT??*

Halsey: *Yes. Her fucking tit!*

OC: *Why was your hand that high? I mean, understandable if you were reaching for my grandma's lower back or stomach and accidentally touched a boob since my grandma's hang low, but Blakely?*

Silas: *Are you really calling your grandma's boobs low-hanging? Dude, show a little respect.*

Pacey: *Ninety-five percent of the grandma population has breasts that are neighbors with their belly buttons, but we don't talk about it. Those boobs have seen things . . . respect their journey.*

OC: *Sorry.*

Posey: *How did you touch her tit?*

Penny: *Wait, hold on. I'm catching up. You touched her boob? THIS IS AMAZING!!! How did it happen?*

Halsey: *This is not amazing. She was humiliated. I was humiliated. And then the smoothie we were making splattered all over the floor. It was a gigantic mess. Nothing about it was great.*

Posey: *Not even the boob?*

Halsey: *I didn't have time to even register what her boob felt like.*

Penny: *She has great boobs.*

Silas: *But how did it happen?*

Halsey: *I scooted in close and attempted to touch her like you said, I aimed for her upper back, thinking that was the safest zone, and she turned at the same time, and I touched her boob.*

Posey: *The upper back? Dude, that's just putting you right back into the friend zone.*

OC: *Yeah, that's like a "Hey pal, how you doing?" zone. Not a "come sit on my face" zone.*

Pacey: *He's right.*

Silas: *Thank GOD she turned.*

Posey: *I was just about to say that. Her turn saved this entire mission.*

Penny: *Boob touch is perfection. Could not have gone any better. Think about it . . . she's thought of your penis, and now you've touched her breast. You might as well let her catch you caressing yourself. Then we would have hit the jackpot.*

Halsey: *You have lost your goddamn mind if you think I'm going to let that happen.*

Posey: *You know I'm all for these stages, but I think him pleasuring himself in front of her is a touch too much.*

Silas: *He's already semi-messed up every stage, the last thing we need is him prematurely coming and hitting her in the eye.*

OC: *Ahh, the old pirate . . .*

Silas: *Ehh, not quite. Isn't that when the giver is doing the blowing, and the receiver blows one in the eye?*

Pacey: *And then the receiver also kicks the giver in the leg?*

Posey: *And the giver then says Arghhhh like a pirate?*

Penny: *I'm about to disown all of you.*

Posey: *That's fair.*

Halsey: *Can we get back to the boob! I don't think this is working. We didn't talk the rest of the day. I'm failing!*

Penny: *You're not failing, we just need to think of something . . . something drastic. Like a real curveball. Let me think on this. I can come up with something great.*

Chapter Thirteen

BLAKELY

"You don't mind stopping here real quick?" I ask Halsey as I pull up to my apartment.

To say things have been awkward is an understatement. I worked the whole day at the office so Oden took him home yesterday, but now that the guys are out of town, I'm back to driving Halsey.

I don't mind.

But it seems like it's extremely painful for him.

And sure . . . he touched my boob.

It was an honest mistake. Not quite sure where he was going with the whole proximity thing, but it's not like he set out to touch my breast. He apologized profusely, even stuck a Post-it Note on my door for when I got home that said *I'm sorry*. He holed up in his room for the night, which made things even more awkward.

So when I came into his room for our good night slumber

party, he was stiff as a board, apologized once more, then turned away from me and went to sleep.

This morning, I made the smoothie that sprayed across his entire apartment and tried to make a joke about it, but I could see just how uncomfortable he was, even though he attempted to smile.

I am hoping it was the fact that he didn't mean to touch me that has made him so miserable. And *not* the fact that my boob was so disgusting that it sent him into this catatonic tailspin where I am made of sludge and cooties. Because I know I have great boobs, but now I'm starting to doubt that with every minute that goes by that he doesn't talk to me.

"No, it's cool. I can stay in the car. Give you some privacy."

This guy . . . the number of times he's offered me privacy since the boob touch.

I don't want privacy. I just want things the way they were.

Getting slightly irritated because I miss the fun Halsey, I turn in the car and say, "You touched my boob."

His frantic expression would make me laugh if I wasn't so frustrated.

I press my hand to his and smile. "Halsey, it's okay. I don't feel like you violated me or whatever horrific thoughts are running through your head. It was an honest mistake."

"I would never violate you, Blakely," he says while his hand eclipses mine.

His large . . . callousy hand.

"I know." I look him in the eyes. "But you're acting like you did, and it's weird. I don't want it to be weird."

"I'm sorry." His thumb rubs over my knuckles, and for the first time in a really long time, a wave of butterflies hits me—like they were unleashed with the short, tight stroke, erupting an influx of lust through my veins.

Where the heck did that come from?

"Um, yeah, I know you're sorry," I say, me now taking the awkward role. "It was an accident, no need to apologize anymore. I wasn't offended. Honestly, it was the most action I've gotten in a while. So I should be thanking you."

That brings the smallest of smirks to his lips.

"Yeah, it was the most action I've gotten in a while as well."

I raise an eyebrow. "So that means you didn't get that penis piercing?"

It's his turn to give me a brow raise. "Think I'd be walking normally if I did?"

I laugh out loud and shake my head. "Guess not. Plus, I'd probably have to drive you to get it. What an adventure that would be."

"I'd never be able to look you in the eyes again."

I squeeze his hand and say, "I'm glad we had this talk about you touching my boob."

"Yeah, it's been a real thrill for me."

I laugh some more, loving how in the right moments, he can be so funny.

"Okay, now that things are not awkward anymore, do you want to come up to my apartment and see where all the water damage is? If you thought the conversation we just had was a thrill, wait until I give you a water damage tour. You'll barely be able to go to bed tonight from all the excitement you experience."

His smile stretches across his face. "Can't wait."

We both get out of the car, and when I round it to join Halsey, I take a chance and lean into him, putting my arms around his waist and pulling him into a hug. I half expect him to stiffen, but he doesn't. Instead, he wraps his arms around me and pulls me in tight. It feels so . . . *natural. Weird.*

"If you accidentally touch my boob again, please don't let it be weird."

"Promise," he says softly. His arms feel like two giant security blankets wrapped around me.

We stand there for a few more seconds before I let go of him and then lead the way up to my apartment. He's quiet for the most part, just taking it all in. We reach the second floor via stairs that we took slowly for his sake. He said we didn't have to go slowly, but I told him if he injures that ankle again on my watch I'll never be able to forgive myself.

When we reach my front door, I take out my key and unlock it.

"The place I had with Perry was much nicer than this, but I don't mind this building, and it's close-ish to work. Just sucks that it flooded on day three."

He doesn't say much, just takes it in. And I know he's not judging me. For someone so wealthy, he's not an elitist. *So different from Perry, now that I think about it.* Which makes me wonder why I feel I have to justify this apartment . . .

When I push open the door to my apartment, I'm greeted with clear duty tarps, construction materials, and tools. And an odd, funky smell. No clue what that is.

"And this is home," I say on a sigh.

"I like what you've done with the place." He glances around, and I can see some worry etched in his brow as he takes in the size of my tiny kitchen and the lackluster living room space that barely fits a loveseat.

I shut the door behind us and say, "My other place was much bigger, but since it's just me, I thought this would do. Although, after being at your place for a few weeks, this feels like a cardboard box compared to your luxury apartment. There isn't even a doorman in this building or a parking garage. Man, I should have never stayed with you." I laugh it off, but I don't think he finds it funny.

"You can stay with me for as long as you want," he says, turning back to me. "Seriously. I don't use that second room, which is obvious from the lack of bed in it, so you can occupy it as long as you want."

"That's really nice, Halsey, but this place isn't bad, plus, if I take that job, who knows if I'll be moving or not."

"Right." He stuffs his hands in his pockets. "Are you here to grab something?"

"Yes," I say, walking toward my bedroom with Halsey following. "I have a wedding to attend this Friday, and I need to grab the dress and shoes I planned on wearing."

"A wedding, that's cool," he says.

"You'll be all alone on an off night with the boys out of town. What are you going to do without me?"

I glance over my shoulder to catch him twist his lips to the side. "I guess read."

"Living on the edge." I open the door to my bedroom where the most foul and mildewy smell swirls around us. "Oh my God, what is that?" I lift my shirt over my nose, but the smell is so pungent, my shirt does nothing to block it.

Halsey's face nearly goes green as he lifts his shirt up too and covers his nose, giving me the smallest view of the patch of skin below his belly button.

"Fuck, that's bad."

"Bad? It's atrocious. What is that?"

"Smells like death," he says.

"All my clothes are in here, so they probably smell too," I say, moving to my closet where I open the door and find a dead rat, right in the middle.

The most blood-curdling scream flies out of my mouth as I jump back and run right into the brick wall behind me—the brick wall being Halsey. His arm goes around me as I squirm against his rock-hard chest.

"What's going on?" he asks, his voice full of concern.

"A dead rat, a dead rat, there's a dead rat." I run in place. "A half-massacred, dead rat in my closet!"

"Really?" He leans over my shoulder for a look. "You've got to be fucking kidding me," he says in a menacing tone.

"Oh God, I'm going to puke it smells so bad in here."

He quickly shuts the door behind me and places his arm around me. I squeeze in tight as the vision of rat guts dance precariously through my head. Holding me close, he leads me out of my bedroom and toward the front door. "We're leaving. Now."

"But I need to talk to the landlord because a rat is stinking up my clothes. Something needs to be done."

"You're not talking to the landlord—"

"Halsey—"

"You're not talking to him . . . I am."

And with that, he moves me out of the apartment, helps me lock up, since my hands are shaking, and then he takes my hand in his and walks me down the stairs, taking one at a time to make sure he doesn't hurt his ankle again.

"Where is the office?" he asks.

"Halsey, you don't—"

"Where is the office, Blakely?" he asks, his voice sterner this time.

Shocked, I answer, "In the back, last door on the right."

Hand still in mine, he leads me back to the landlord's apartment where he raises his fist and bangs on the door—not only startling me nearly out of my shoes but most likely the landlord as well.

While we wait, he turns toward me and quietly asks, "Are you okay?"

"Y-yes," I answer, my mind whirling with the fact there is a dead rat in the closet . . . alongside the realization that Halsey has another side of him I've never seen before.

Protective.

It's an asset I've always admired but never experienced until this moment.

He studies me, his hazel eyes examining me as if the rat himself came out and bit me. His hold on my hand grows tighter as he pulls me in closer to his side, and I allow it.

Not because I'm so terrified about a rat that if I don't lean in I might faint, but because Halsey's providing a form of comfort I want to lean into. *He's put me at ease.*

You can hear my landlord rumbling around on the other side of the door. Halsey patiently waits, but I can see his fist gearing up to pound again for another knock. It takes about a minute, but when the landlord, Mr. Gorman, opens the door, I'm privileged to watch his face morph from utter annoyance to complete awe.

Look who's a huge fan? It's written all over his face. Too bad Halsey is not going to let the man fanboy.

"Halsey Holmes. Holy shit. Is it really you?"

Mr. Gorman pays no attention to me while he fumbles to sweep his hair to the side and straighten out his pizza sauce-stained shirt.

In a calm, but firm tone, Halsey says, "My girlfriend is renting 2B from you, the one that got flooded." Girlfriend? Um . . . okay. Wasn't expecting that, but I have no problem going along with it if it means this problem will be fixed, so I snuggle in close, playing the part.

"Oh yes, 2B." Mr. Gorman straightens up. "I'm sorry it's taken so long. We've had some minor setbacks."

"Seems like you've had a lot of setbacks. Are you aware of the dead rat that's in her closet, stinking up her entire bedroom as well as the clothes she has hanging in there?"

"A dead rat?" He swipes his finger under his nose, fidgeting beneath the glare of Halsey Holmes. "I was quite unaware. I'm sorry—"

"Look at her, not me. Blakely is the one you should be apologizing to." The snap of his voice actually makes my nipples hard.

"Right. Right." Mr. Gorman looks at me and says, "I'm sorry, Miss . . ."

"White," Halsey says in such a dark, menacing tone that I'm slightly scared and also, God, I hate to admit it, but turned on.

"Miss White, that's right. I'm sorry about the dead rat."

"So what are you going to do about it?" Halsey asks, challenging him, something I probably would have never done.

"Uh." Mr. Gorman scratches the top of his head, the sound of his nails scraping across his dry scalp a complete wet blanket on the excitement rolling through me from Halsey's take-charge behavior. "Well, I guess I can remove the rat."

"You guess?" Halsey asks, brows raised.

"I mean, I will. I'll be removing the rat because that's unacceptable. And I'll, uh, I'll have the apartment cleaned."

"Fumigated," Halsey says.

"What?" Mr. Gorman asks.

"You will have the apartment fumigated."

Mr. Gorman raises his hands as if he's trying to calm Halsey down. "Now that's not necessary."

"Oh, you don't think it's necessary?" Halsey's shoulders grow tense. I don't think I've ever seen him this angry. Maybe on the ice before, but that's different. That's adrenaline. This is . . . this is outrage. He's truly upset for me. And I disturbingly find it so hot. "So what do you think is happening to the dead rat in her closet? It's already been chewed apart by God knows what, which means there are probably fucking maggots everywhere. In her clothes, around the bedroom. This is a severe health risk and you're going to subject her to that? My girl?" Halsey points at his chest. "Over my dead fucking body. So you either get her apartment fumigated and disinfected, as well as every last possession she owns in there, or I'll be speaking with my lawyer and, when I say I have no problem spending the money to teach you a lesson, I'm not fucking kidding."

Mr. Gorman backs away, his expression completely stunned. "Is that a threat?"

"Yes," Halsey answers with a sneer to his lip. "Fix it." And with that, Halsey guides me down the hall and out of the apartment building. "You're not fucking living here."

"What?" I ask.

"There is no way in hell you're going back there."

"But . . . you told him to fix it," I say, confused. Why make a big deal over fumigation if I'm not even going to stay there?

"Only because you need your things cleaned and disinfected. I'll have my lawyer get you out of your lease and you can stay with me until you find a better place. No way in fuck are you going to live here. The guy is a fucking slumlord, the building is dilapidated, and you're too fucking good to be caught dead in an apartment like that. Not happening."

Umm . . . okay. Hard to fight with him when he says it like that.

When we get to my car, he's shaking with adrenaline as he moves to the driver's side and opens the car door for me. I don't get in right away. I *can't*. Instead I turn toward him. *I want to calm him down.* At least put an end to the tension in his shoulders. "Halsey, I appreciate you protecting me back there, but I do want you to know that it wasn't that bad."

"Wasn't that bad?" he asks. "Blakely. The moment I walked into the building, I knew you didn't belong there. It's old, dirty, uneven, and doesn't even have a lock on the front door. Anyone could walk into the building. Not to mention, I don't trust that fucker to have a key to your place. Do you know what men like him do? They walk into your apartment whenever they want, waving the landlord card. I don't trust the safety of the building, and I don't believe any of the construction he'll do will be up to code. He's a cheat, a sleaze, and cuts corners, it's evident by the quality of his building."

"But it's all I can afford right now."

"My place is free. You can afford that."

"Halsey," I sigh. "I'm not going to overstay my welcome."

His index finger slides under my chin, forcing my eyes on his. "Listen to me when I say, you will not be overstaying your welcome. I wouldn't offer if I didn't mean it." He takes a deep breath and the anger slowly begins to slide away as he says, "Please just consider it."

When he looks at me with those pleading eyes, I feel myself bending to his will. "I'll consider it."

"Thank you," he says before pulling me into a hug, a hug I was not expecting but I'll take. And as he wraps his arms around my shoulders, and I bury my head against his chest, I realize that this man has quickly wormed his way into my life. When I moved in with Halsey—temporarily of course—I never would have imagined that scenario turning into this, where Halsey hugs me on the side of the road after threatening my landlord.

Even though Perry was a very good boyfriend, I don't believe he would have given Mr. Gorman the same trouble, nor would he have laid out a set of demands attached to a threat. Not that Halsey is my boyfriend or even romantically involved with me, but the mere fact that this . . . friend—I think that's what I can call him—is more protective than my boyfriend ever was, surprises me. It's astonishing how . . . *safe* I feel. Cared for. *Did I not feel that way with Perry?*

He cups the back of my head, keeping me close as he quietly says, "I'm not sorry for what I said and did."

"I know," I reply.

He gives me one more squeeze and says, "I'll never be sorry for sticking up for you, Blakely."

He gradually pulls away, his eyes on mine as his fingers slowly glide down my arm until he's not touching me anymore—but the feel of his hand touching mine remains embedded in my skin as I stare up at him.

Calm passes over us both, an understanding of our friendship. He's drawing a line in the sand, at this moment, letting me know that I am a part of his life now and no matter what, he'll never let anything happen to me.

It makes me feel special.

Like I have more than just Penny to rely on, like my roots here in Vancouver might have been disturbed when Perry left, but they're growing back with Halsey's presence.

With his hand pulling on the back of his neck, he studies me before saying, "Okay . . . well, now we need to go shopping."

Okay, that was a change of subject. "What do you mean?"

"For a dress. We need to find you a dress for the wedding."

"Oh . . . you don't have to go. I'm sure that's the last thing you want to do."

"No, I do," he says. "I'm not doing anything, and I want to help."

"Really? In all the years I was with my boyfriend, he never

wanted to go shopping with me. I doubt you'd want to do that as just my friend."

"I'm saying I do," he says with conviction. "So take me."

Is he for real?

From the expression on his face and the seriousness in his tone, I'm going to have to say yes. It might be nice to have someone with me, someone who could tell me what looks good and what doesn't. And he's right, I need a dress. I'm not about to put any rat-maggot dress on, so a new one is in order.

"Okay," I say. "But I'm buying dinner. Understood?" I point at him.

"We'll see about that," he says as he rounds the car and moves to his side.

Of course he'd say that. The man has chivalry tattooed to his heart.

⸺

I STARE at myself in the mirror, feeling slightly nervous. This is the first dress I've tried on after we spent about half an hour with the boutique owner of Luxe Closet, one of my favorite stores, walking around and pulling everything I thought might look good on me. And to my surprise, Halsey pulled a few too, ones I never would have thought to try on.

He's now sitting outside on a red velvet couch, waiting for me to show him, and that's where I stand with the nerves.

The first is a black polka-dotted dress. With a spaghetti strap, V neckline, and a ruffle skirt that's short in the front but long in the back, I thought it might be cute. It shows off my legs while still being elegant. My first choice.

Stepping outside of the dressing room, I hold my breath as I show off the first dress. I stand there, feeling slightly exposed as Halsey's eyes travel up my frame, starting at my feet and moving all the way up to my face.

My assumption is he's going to tell me I look good in every single one of these dresses because he's the kind of guy who'd never want to make me feel bad. Also known as the pleaser, I don't think he'd ruffle feathers, so I need to watch his face closely to see if he truly thinks the dress is pretty on me or not.

"What do you think?" I ask.

He shakes his head. "Not for you."

Oh . . . not, uh, not what I was expecting him to say, obviously.

I laugh. "Not for me?"

"Nope. Next." He shoos me away with his hand, making me laugh some more.

"Oh, okay, fashionista." I head back into the dressing room and strip out of the dress, a smile on my face. This just got a whole lot more interesting. I thought that dress was pretty, but now . . . now I'm invested in seeing what Halsey thinks is pretty.

I hang the polka-dotted dress back up and shift it to the "no" hook. Next, I try on a yellow tier ruffle dress with a scoop neckline. I have a feeling he's not going to like this one either, but since I'm invested in his opinion now, I want to hear what he has to say.

I step out of the dressing room and in front of Halsey, who is already shaking his head.

"You don't like it?"

"I didn't like it when you pulled it and I don't like it now."

"I see. Is it the ruffles?"

"Yes. They do nothing for you."

"Good to know." I nod and then say, "I do want you to know that I'm my own woman, and I'll be making this decision based on how I feel, but I appreciate your feedback."

"Uh-huh, now try on something else." He leans back on the couch and stretches his arms out along the top of the cushions, manspreading and making himself at home. I don't want to admit it because the man is far too attractive for his own good, but God is he owning that couch . . .

Just like he owned you in front of your landlord.

No, don't get started with that. The last thing I need is to start having thoughts other than friendship about Halsey.

I change into a blue velvet dress that he said was okay but I can do better. A black dress with a long slit that I witness him stare at for longer than I expected but he passed. And a rose dress that had an overlay of lace he claimed to look like a table-cloth his grandma owned.

Now I'm wearing my last pick, which is a short red dress with a halter neckline and a tulle skirt.

"No," he says before I can fully step out of the dressing room.

I rest my hands on my hips and say, "You didn't even give it a chance."

"Because it's not for you." He nods toward the dressing room. "Try on the light-blue one I chose."

"The flowy one?"

"Yes, the flowy one."

"Don't you think that one is a little much?" I ask.

"For you? No. Try it on."

I don't know why, but that response makes me blush.

I go back into the dressing room, strip out of the red dress—which in all honesty I didn't like either—and take the light blue gown off the hanger. The fabric is incredibly lightweight, gauzy almost with a hint of a sparkle. I fit it over my body and curse inwardly because I can already see that the bodice was made for me with its structured boning and beautifully draped, off-the-shoulder sleeve. It has a Grecian feel about it with a high slit on the right that reaches my upper thigh. And because of the tight, low bodice, it lifts my breasts, but I can't quite reach the zipper.

"Might need help with this one," I say as I stare at myself in the mirror.

It's so beautiful. I hate that he was right that I should have tried this on in the first place. I thought maybe it was going to be a touch too fancy but it's not at all. It's just perfect.

"Help with what?" Halsey asks.

"The zipper," I say as I poke my head out past the curtain. He lifts from the couch and walks toward me. When he parts the curtain and steps into the dressing room with me, I catch the way his brows raise while a slow smile tips up his lips.

I beat him to it before he can even say anything. "I know . . . I know. You were right."

He stays silent as he moves behind me. From the reflection in the mirror I watch as he dips his head and grips the tiny metal zipper while his other hand holds the bottom of the zipper. With one tug up, I'm all closed in. That's when he looks into the mirror as well from over my shoulder, staring at me in the confined space of the dressing room. He wets his lips, his expression morphing from cocky to pleased. Those eyes rake over me like they're an X-ray, able to see right through me, leaving me feeling exposed, raw . . . and beautiful at the same time.

He steps back after a second and scratches the side of his jaw. I turn around to face him and in the small confines of the dressing room, I hold out the dress and ask, "What do you think?"

"I think you look beautiful," he says, his voice low, gruff. "Made me speechless."

Once again, my cheeks flame.

"Thank you," I say, suddenly feeling shy. "And I hate that I'm going to have to give you credit, but I think this is the one."

His eyes travel down my body and then back up again. "Your choice, but yeah, you look really fucking good, Blakely."

"Thank you. Okay, I'll get this one."

"Good," he answers, not moving, just staring at me, keeping his eyes fixed on mine. I feel my body shiver under the strength of his gaze.

What is happening?

This is not the Halsey I know. I'm used to the guy who's quiet, maybe a joke here and there, but remains neutral most of the time. This Halsey, he's unwavering, he's demanding, he's bone-chilling with those expressive eyes that he usually hides behind.

"Um, can you unzip it for me?"

"Of course," he answers as he rests one hand on my hip,

then slowly unzips the back, letting each zipper tong pop before the next one. It's so slow that the energy between us grows, the tension becoming thick. My pulse picks up, my breath, my awareness that there is an extremely attractive man behind me, unzipping my dress, and if I were to turn around, he'd get more of a glimpse than he was probably looking for.

"There you go," he says, breaking through my thoughts.

I hold on tightly to the bodice, keeping it close to my chest, then turn around to look up at him one more time. "Thank you."

"Any time." He moves his hand over the back of his neck before offering me the tiniest of smiles. It's the most adorable thing I've ever seen. "Knew that dress was going to be the one. Should have tried it on first."

"Where's the fun in that?"

"Very true," he says while casually wetting his lips. "The sweet feeling of knowing I was right all along is better with the upfront denial."

"Cheeky."

He smirks and then retreats to the couch where he drapes his arm over the back.

Yup, this is a different side of him for sure, and I'm feeling slightly out of breath. From his expressions, the subtle way he wet his lips, and his delicate touch as he zipped and unzipped my dress.

I offer him a quick smile before I shut the curtain to the dressing room and then lean against the wall, taking a few deep breaths.

You're fine, Blakely.

Nothing to worry about over here.

Halsey just happened to defend your rights with your landlord, while holding your hand, and then state that you weren't living in that apartment.

That's fine, just a protective friend.

And sure, he took you dress shopping and patiently sat there while you tried on dresses and just so happened to pick the right dress for you. *Because he knew what would look amazing on me.* And maybe feeling his hand on your hip, unzipping your dress was a nice feeling, but that's all it was, a nice feeling.

And the way he looked at you, that's . . . that's fine. It was just an expression. Nothing to it.

There is nothing to it at all . . .

Then how come I want to go back out there and have him hold my hand again? Or better yet, have his hands on me —*because hell did that feel incredible.*

Chapter Fourteen

HALSEY

Halsey: *I'm fucking this up. I honestly don't think I have a chance with her.*

Posey: *What? Why do you say that? That's not the positive thinking we're looking for.*

OC: *He's right. We need to manifest this.*

Silas: *How are you fucking it up?*

Pacey: *Penny, has Blakely said anything to you?*

Penny: *I'm texting her right now. I'll ask her how it's been going living with Halsey.*

Halsey: *BE SUBTLE!*

Penny: *Don't worry, I will. She hasn't said anything to me, but we haven't really talked about it other than the whole brother thing. But I've been nervous to give my position away, so I don't press that much.*

OC: *Ooo, she's being stealth about it. I like that.*

Silas: *I'm going to start telling Eli about how you're sucking Penny's ass.*

OC: *I'm NOT SUCKING HER ASS! Jesus.*

Penny: *It feels like a light sucking.*

Posey: *As much as I love the banter in these texts, we need to get to the point at hand. Why does Halsey think he doesn't have a chance? What happened?*

Silas: *Great question.*

Halsey: *I was an overprotective asshole who told her she wasn't allowed to stay in her apartment because it wasn't good enough for her. I proceeded to hold her hand and yell at her landlord.*

Posey: *Explain to me how that's bad? Seems like a white knight situation.*

Silas: *Ollie would probably hump my face if I did that for her, not that I need to since we're living together, but you get the idea.*

Pacey: *Winnie too. How is this bad?*

Halsey: *She hasn't really spoken to me since. I took her dress shopping, because she's going to a wedding and needed a dress. And that was okay, a little awkward, but that was right after the landlord thing. We usually hang out in the living room, but she's been in her room. I just think I fucked it up. Should I apologize?*

Posey: *NO. Don't apologize. You can't be sorry for standing up for her.*

Silas: *He's right. If she's mad at you for standing up for her, then so be it, but you can't take that back because you meant it, right?*

Halsey: *Every fucking word.*

Pacey: *Then stand by it. Penny, any info on your end?*

Penny: *She's just saying everything's fine. She might be onto me. Or protecting the situation because if things are weird, that's usually something she'd tell me. Then again, if she thinks I'm too close to Halsey by being with Eli, she might not want to tell the truth, if that makes sense.*

Posey: *Yeah, that makes sense. **Scratches chin** What do we do now?*

Halsey: *Drop it. I don't want to put more distance between us.*

Penny: *I don't think we can drop it. We're so close. This is a minor setback, although I don't even think it's a setback. I think . . . it probably made her think.*

Halsey: *What do you mean?*

Penny: *You have to understand Blakely. She just got out of a long-term relationship, and it was a good one. Perry was a good guy and loved her. She* *loved him, but that love wasn't strong enough. Your display of "affection" when telling off her landlord probably freaked her out because that's the kind of love she was missing with Perry. That guttural instinct to lay everything down for her. He didn't when he left, and the fact that you didn't even blink an eye about taking the sword for her probably freaked her out.*

Posey: *So what you're saying is that we've made progress?*

Penny: *I'm saying that we might need something monumental to really shift her frame of mind, because I know for a fact she's said Halsey isn't for her.*

Halsey: *Fuck, she said that?*

OC: *Ouch, why does that make me physically ill?*

Posey: *When the hell did she say that?*

Penny: *I didn't want to say anything at first, but yeah, she's said it. I just don't think she sees you as someone she could be with. Like I said before, more of a brother.*

Silas: *This doesn't bode well for us.*

Pacey: *He did something monumental, and it freaked her out. So what the hell is he supposed to do? Fuck her?*

Halsey: *I'm not fucking her.*

Penny: *That actually might work.*

Posey: *I'm all for Halsey fucking her.*

OC: *I know I'm not supposed to mention the penis, but dude, give her the good stuff and she'll come back for more.*

Silas: *It's risky, but I say fuck her too.*

Halsey: *You are all useless. You've created a situation where I've failed time after time and sure, some of it has been my fault, but this advice has been asinine. If anything, the only accomplishment I've made when it comes to Blakely is being friend-zoned. So thank you. Also, I'm not fucking her!*

OC: *Even though I read that as a nice thank you, I think this is a situation where we're not supposed to say you're welcome.*

Posey: *You're going to be removed again.*

OC: *Understood.*

"DO YOU MISS IT?"

"Miss what?" I ask as I casually lean back on the couch, electrolyte drink in hand. Even though I'm not playing right now, I still adhere to no drinking before a game—or during for that matter in my situation. Blakely has asked me why I don't drink a beer while watching the game, and I tell her because I wouldn't be able to drink one during the game if I was playing. She thought it was funny.

That's me, the fucking funny brother.

The funny brother drinking the electrolytes like a goddamn geek, wearing an Agitators shirt while trying to fixate on the tied game in front of me—rather than look at Blakely—because I might say something stupid like . . . do you want to go fuck?

Yup.

That's what those stupid texts have done to me. They've made me think about fucking her way too much and now it's in my brain, ready to be unleashed by my stupidity.

Another reason I'm not drinking any alcohol. Because one too many might lead me to say something stupid.

"Do you miss playing?"

"Yeah," I answer. "Watching them and being unable to help is way more painful than this ankle injury."

"Would you rather play injured?"

"Yeah." I move my thumb over my jaw, and from the corner of my eye, I catch her watching the small movement. "But I know it would be stupid. If I played injured, it would hurt the team more than help them."

"Because you could possibly reinjure it?"

Wow, this is the most she's talked to me since the dress shop.

"That and because I wouldn't be on top of my game. I'd probably be slow, and that's not helpful to anyone."

"Do you think you'll be ready in a few days?"

"I hope so. Feeling pretty strong." I rub my hands over my pants as the game goes to a commercial. "Thanks by the way, Blakely."

"Thanks for what?"

"For all of the help you've given me. I know it probably

hasn't been easy moving your schedule around, but I appreciate you making the effort."

"Of course. We created this mess together, so we're fixing it together."

Yup . . . friend-zoned.

That is such a friend response.

Nothing has felt more awful.

"So does this mean this is our last game together, Halsey?"

"It is," I answer. "We should have celebrated."

She's about to respond when her phone dings with a text message. Trying to give her privacy, but also curious if it's Penny looking for more information, I glance in her direction just in time to catch her face fall, her expression turning ghostly.

Uh-oh, that can't be good.

"Hey, is everything okay?" I ask.

She looks up from her phone and shakes her head. "No. I just got a text from Perry."

Perry as in the ex-boyfriend Perry?

What the hell does that fucker want?

If he's asking her to take him back, I'm going to kick my leg right through my concrete wall.

Because fuck!

I'm trying to remain neutral despite the anger that shot right through my body. Muscles are tense. Jaw is clenched. Sphincter is tight. Yeah, I said sphincter. We're going there.

"What does the text say?" I ask.

Please don't say he wants you again.

For the love of God, don't let that be my shit luck.

Shakily, she stares down at the text and reads it out loud. "'Hey B, hope you're doing well. Probably not the person you expected to hear from but wanted to see if you're still going to Arlene's wedding. I'm actually flying back for the wedding and wondered if you wanted to hang out.'" She looks up at me, her expression neutral.

Well . . . what does she think of that?

Is she annoyed? Because I'm annoyed.

Because I know exactly what Perry wants when he says *hang out.* It's basically a *"let's get naked"* text. Does she want *that?* Does she want to fuck him again?

Is she glad he's going to the wedding so he can be her plus-one and post-wedding fuck?

Because I want to rip his nuts off for even considering flying across the world for a goddamn wedding.

The game comes back on the TV, but my attention remains on her and what is going on in that beautiful head of hers.

Finally after what feels like minutes of silence, she says, "Why . . . why is he going to the wedding?" Her eyes start to water, and her lips grow tight. "I don't want to see him."

Treading lightly, because I don't want to show just how fucking gleeful that response made me, I ask, "Would Arlene and Marco be upset if you didn't go?"

"Yes, and I'd hate to miss it." She lets out an irritated sigh and leans back on the couch. "This is stupid. Why would he come all the way back from Australia for a wedding? I was the one who introduced him to Arlene and Marco. Technically, they belong to me. And now he's going to fly across the world just to make me uncomfortable? Who does that?"

A dick, that's who.

"When is the wedding again?"

"This Friday. There's no game so I'm free for the night. It's why I said yes." She groans. "God, of course he'd do this. He was never a vindictive man, and he never played mind games. He was very loyal, so this is why he's going. Because he's so loyal." She starts to tremble, her voice shaking and her eyes welling up with more tears, but she won't allow them to fall. I can see the panic bubbling up, and I don't fucking like it.

I don't like the tears welling in her eyes.

I don't like the shakiness in her voice.

The trembling of her lip.

I like nothing about it.

And I feel this need to correct the situation.

To make it better for her, just like her apartment.

I'm itching to make this better, to remove the frown from her face. My mind starts racing with how I can find a solution, anything to make sure she's no longer sad.

"Like, dude, everyone knows you're in Australia. Just stay there. Enjoy your new life with your new job and your new apartment and possibly your new wenches that you have crawling at your feet. And why even text me? He wants to meet up? Hang out? As if I don't have a life of my own? Like is he trying to—"

"Take me," I say before I can stop myself. It's the first solution that pops into my mind, and as Blakely stares at me in shock, I realize this actually might be a good idea.

Yeah, she should take me.

I could protect her.

Be there for her.

Hold her hand . . .

Although from the look of shock and confusion that passes over her face, I'm gathering that maybe she's not on the same wavelength as I am.

Quietly, she says, "What?"

Yup, you did it now. You said it. Now you have to follow through.

You wanted your chance.

Here it is.

Take it.

My eyes stay connected with hers so she knows how serious I am. "Take me to the wedding."

"Wh-why would I do that?" she asks.

Yeah, Halsey, why would you do that?

Maybe because I'm practically in love with you.

Because I can't get enough of you.

Because if I don't take you to the wedding, you might fall for your ex again, and I don't think I can handle that.

Because I want my goddamn chance at holding you for a night.

"You can pretend I'm your boyfriend and won't have to worry about Perry at all," I say, the words flying out of me before I can stop them.

She doesn't answer.

Instead, she sits there, stunned.

Unmoving.

And I start to panic that my opportunity to take a chance will wildly backfire on me.

But what could really happen? *She says no and you deal with rejection?* Well, guess what? *She considers you as her brother.* Can't get any more rock bottom than that.

Finally she asks, "You want to pretend to be my boyfriend?"

"Yes." I say it with such certainty that she can't decipher if I'm being serious or not. When she doesn't say anything, I add, "This way, you can go to the wedding, enjoy it, and not worry about Perry. I'll make sure he doesn't go near you, and you don't have to be alone."

Her eyes lift, and through those thick lashes, she asks, "You'd do that for me?"

Oh shit . . . is she going to say yes?

My entire body tingles with anticipation.

Please fucking say yes.

Give me one night, Blakely.

I'll prove to you how much I deserve you.

"Of course," I answer. I want to hold her hand. I want to tell her I'd do anything for her . . . fucking anything, but I don't want to show all of my cards. I think the desperation is already thick in my voice.

Her teeth run over her bottom lip as she looks away. "Marco would die if you were at the wedding. He's a huge Agitators fan. I'm sure they'd have no problem making room for you if I told them we were dating." She winces. "But would that look bad? That I started dating someone new right after Perry and I broke up?"

"Who fucking cares," I say. Fuck, she's so close to saying yes. "You're allowed to move on as quickly as you want without judgment. And if there is judgment, then those people shouldn't be in your life anyway."

She slowly nods. "You're right." She brings her legs up to her chest and rests her chin on her knees. "You really wouldn't mind? I feel bad asking you to go with me. I know it's your day off, but . . . you've already done so much for me. I'd feel like I'm asking too much."

"You're not asking me to do anything. I'm telling you to take me."

"Yeah, I guess you are." She blows out a heavy breath. "Okay, let me see what Arlene and Marco say."

The biggest fucking smile wants to cross over my face, but I hold back. Instead, I turn back toward the game with a nonchalant reply. "Cool."

HALSEY: *I did something big. Astronomical actually.*

Posey: After the loss we suffered tonight, I'm hoping this astronomical thing is good.

Pacey: I let three goals go by, better be fucking amazing news.

OC: Silas is currently abusing the wall we share in the hotel room. I believe kicking, maybe punching. Either way, I don't foresee him on his phone.

Penny: Eli has not texted me back. Is he okay? The fight he got in didn't look good.

Posey: He's good. Letting steam off with a beer. I'm sure he'll get back to you soon.

Halsey: Maybe not the best time to text. Fuck. Sorry, guys.

Pacey: No, we need the distraction. Please just tell us you're going to be back with us soon.

OC: Silas and I miss you.

Halsey: There's a great possibility I'll be playing soon. If anything, maybe just to get out there for a few minutes. We'll see what Grace says.

Posey: Is that the good news? Because I'd be glad if it was.

OC: We all would.

Halsey: That's not the news.

Penny: Eli just texted me. Did you know he got punched in the nuts?

Pacey: Yeah, he had to readjust his cup in the penalty box, which was awkward for everyone.

Penny: Who punches the cup?

OC: Someone who wants to be a dick.

Posey: I've done it a few times. You shift the cup to the side and force your opponent to readjust, and I'll tell you right now, that shit never sits the same.

OC: Really fucking annoying.

Penny: So he wasn't hurt, more inconvenienced?

Pacey: Exactly. Anyway, Halsey, what's the news?

Halsey: Perry is coming back for a wedding that they're both going to.

Penny: WHAT?! Why? Ew, did he say he wanted to get back together with Blakely? I will riot!

Posey: You'll riot? I'll throw a goddamn tantrum right in front of her.

Halsey: No, he said he wanted to "hang out." So it was a "DTF?" IMHO. She looked really panicked, which I took as a good sign. So I told her to take me as her date, and I'd pretend to be her boyfriend.

Posey: You did?!?

OC: Is it weird that my nipples just got hard?

Penny: You're pulling a Silas! Oh my God, this is amazing. What did she say?

Halsey: She said yes.

Posey: Boner . . . I have a fucking BONER! She fucking said yes? Slap me in the ass because I need to be woken up from this dream.

OC: Should I be concerned that I didn't get a boner but my nipples are hard?

Pacey: Both of you are fucking idiots.

Penny: I approve of hard nipples and the boner because this is HUGE, Halsey. This is it. This is your in! Now you'll have a chance to make your move.

Posey: I agree. This is it. This is monumental. You get to protect her from the ex she doesn't want to talk to, and while pretending to be her boyfriend. You get to touch her, hold her . . . maybe even kiss her.

Halsey: I'm not kissing her.

Silas: Just catching up despite being in a shit mood. Kiss her. Touch her just like if she was yours. You get one chance, don't fuck it up. Take it from me who went through this.

OC: I need to learn more about this fake dating thing.

Penny: *Trust me when I say, this is where you move in.*

Halsey: *But things are already strained. What if I make a move and fuck it all up?*

Posey: *I'd treat this as the championships, man. You have to be all in, no matter what's going on between you two. You either show her the man, the boyfriend you can be, or you let her go.*

Pacey: *I agree with everyone.*

OC: ***Eats popcorn** Just here for the storyline.*

Silas: *Is he kicked out again?*

Posey: *Yes.*

Penny: *Yes.*

Pacey: *I don't know . . . I think he brings charm.*

Chapter Fifteen

BLAKELY

"Hello?"

"Blakely, it's Huxley Cane."

Sitting on a chair in my bedroom since there's no bed, I try not to sound nervous. "Huxley, it's so nice to hear from you." Especially since I've been avoiding you.

"I'm going to get to the point. I want to know if my offer is of interest to you or if I should move on to finding someone else. As far as I'm concerned, you're who I want for the job, but I don't want to force you into anything."

"I appreciate that," I say as I stare at myself in the mirror across from me. I'm sitting in my robe with my hair and makeup done for the wedding. Just need to slip on my dress. "And I don't mean to hold you up, but I guess I'm just trying to figure out what I want to do with my career. The direction I want to take."

"Can I help in any way? I'd like to remain neutral. If anything, I can appreciate your ability not to jump headfirst into a new career."

"Well, I do have a few questions."

"Ask away."

I play with the tie on my robe as I ask, "The moving thing. I don't know if I want to leave Vancouver. That's been a big holdup for me."

"What if I said you could work remotely?"

My interest piques, but doubt also creeps in. "I don't want coworkers to resent me if I don't move to Los Angeles."

"I'll say this. We have people who work remotely as well as in the office. It's really their preference. We run our business with the notion that not everyone can work productively in an office and not everyone can work productively at home. Would it be nice to have you in the office? Of course, but we offer both options for a reason, to see what best suits each employee. You being in Canada won't be any different from someone else who lives in LA and works remotely. The great thing about technology now is that with a click of a button, you're transported into the conference room whenever we need you."

Relief fills me as I lean back in my chair. "And you mean that?"

"One thing you need to know about my brothers and me is that we're not going to bullshit you, Blakely. If I say it, I mean it."

"Of course, I'm sorry for even questioning you."

"Don't apologize. It's a fair question. What else?"

I cross one leg over the other. "Will I be working directly with the athletes? Because right now, I work more with the VIP customers. It's like seventy-thirty. I'd prefer to work more one-on-one with the athletes. It's what I find the most fun. I wanted to get into player relations but slipped into VIP sales and marketing. I've learned a lot, and I've loved this job, but if I rotate to something new, I want to rotate into a direction that brings me the joy I'm looking for."

"The only people you'll be working with are the athletes signed up with The Jock Report and their appointed staff. It's all about interacting with the players, ensuring their voice is heard and portrayed. There will be occasional travel requirements, but nothing that takes you away from Vancouver for long periods of time. A lot of the job can be done through online conferences." He pauses, and I take a moment to think about that. It sounds ideal. *It sounds surreal.* "I chose you, Blakely, because you're composed, professional, intuitive, and dynamic, and I know our athletes would thrive under your care. You're what I've been looking for."

"Thank you," I say as I consider his words. *"You're composed, professional, intuitive, and dynamic. You're exactly what I've been looking for."* I've held off answering for too long. Any other person would have moved on, but Huxley Cane sees something in me, something he likes. And honestly? I'm already thriving from that confidence *in me.* Imagine what it would do for me if I worked for him? If I had that level of professional guidance and encouragement daily? I like the idea of working more with the athletes. And I can't beat the money and the financed housing. Not to mention, it might be fun working from home . . .

I close my eyes and before I can stop myself, I say, "I'll take the job."

"Good," Huxley says, not even bothering to make sure I mean it. Probably because he knows it's an offer I'd be stupid to refuse. "I'll have HR send over the official letter. If you sign by Monday, we'll include a signing bonus. I look forward to working with you. I'll be in touch."

And then he hangs up, leaving me feeling stupefied.

I slowly lower my phone and stare at myself in the mirror.

Holy shit, did I just accept a new job?

I bite down on the corner of my lip. What was I thinking?

I know what I was thinking . . . the job was too good to turn down but, God, now I have to tell Penny. I have to tell my boss. I have to tell Halsey. Not that . . . not that I'm sure he'd care. It's not like I work directly with him. Still.

Just the thought of Halsey, though, makes my stomach churn with nerves.

The past few days have been slightly eye-opening for me.

Halsey has been different. And not in a bad way, just, for lack of a better word, different. I know that makes no sense, but I thought I was getting used to his quiet spirit. That was until he spoke to my landlord and helped me pick out a dress. Now I don't know how to act around him. I feel awkward because I liked it.

I liked the way he protected me.

The way he stood up for me.

The way he treated me like I was precious.

And what does that say about me?

As a woman in the sports industry, fighting and clawing my way through it, I've felt very strongly about lifting women up, protecting our fight for equal opportunity, and here I am, mildly swooning over him standing up for me.

There's a light rap on my door. "Blakely, you okay?"

Speak of the devil.

I stand from the chair and open the door, poking my head out. That's when I see him in a dark blue suit with a black lapel, black button-up shirt, and black shoes. His pants cling to his thighs and then stop just below his ankles, showing a touch of skin. His shirt isn't fully buttoned, as the top two are left open, giving me a slight view of the impressive chest beneath his clothes. He's left his scruff on his face but has cleaned it up, and his hair is gelled, faded on the sides with a thick tuft styled in a messy way, making him look so incredibly adorable . . . but also lickable at the same time.

"Hey, do you need help with your dress?"

His deep voice crests over me like a warm shower, heating the blood in my veins.

What the hell is happening to me with this man?

"Uh, yeah, do you mind?"

"Not at all," he says as I open the door.

I give him another once-over, this time, lingering on that little patch of skin over his chest. Clearing my throat, I say, "You look nice."

My palms start to sweat, which is insane because I've seen

this man in a suit many times. So many times that I think I've seen him in a suit more than in a hockey jersey. So what's different now?

I've said he's attractive before.

I've noticed how hot he is when he takes his helmet off on the ice and his hair is wet from sweat, his eyes zoning in on his competitors.

And I've clearly lived with this man to know that he smells like a freaking dream fresh from a shower of aphrodisiacs.

So what's changed? *Is it because I'm no longer looking at him from behind my very clear I-have-a-boyfriend glasses?*

He presses his hand to the buttons on his suit jacket and looks down at himself. "Thank you. I tried to pick something that would go with your dress but not be too matchy. I can change if this doesn't work for you."

"No, it works." I wet my lips as I give him another scan. Oh, it works on so many levels.

"Good."

And then silence falls over us.

Because I'm awkward. And now I'm thinking about him on another level.

A level I shouldn't even consider.

I've said it before, and I'll say it again—Halsey is not my type. I've never thought of him as someone who checks the boxes. However, I'm learning that maybe my boxes have changed.

He's . . . protective. Charming. Attentive. Engaged. Genuine. I don't feel as though I'm competing with him like I did with Perry. He's thoughtful. Contained. Generous. Handsome. *And sexy.*

It's as though he's got everything I never knew I wanted. Which means he currently checks *all* my boxes.

We stare at each other for a few seconds before he shifts uncomfortably and says, "Uh, your dress?"

"Right." *Shit, come on, Blakely.*

Spinning on my heel, I grab it from the hanger that's hanging on my closet door. I step into the bathroom and barely shut the door before tearing off my robe and tossing it over the sink counter. I slip into my dress, deciding to go without a bra, since the boned bodice does all of the work, and I zip the dress up as much as I can before I head into the bedroom again, where I find Halsey standing in my room, hands in his pockets, staring at the floor.

When he notices I exit the bathroom, his eyes slowly rise until they find me and then . . . they roam.

They roam from my feet, up my legs to where the slit stops at my upper thigh, to the waist of the dress, and then the bodice that clings so expertly to me. I catch his Adam's apple bob before he steps up to me.

"Turn around," he says in a low, dark voice.

My mouth goes dry as I turn around and then shift my hair to the side.

His hands find the zipper, and he slowly pulls it up until it's fully secure. To my surprise, he takes my hair from my hand and drapes it back over my shoulders.

My eyes connect with his when I turn around, and I quietly say, "Thank you."

He moves his hand over his jaw. "You look gorgeous, Blakely."

My cheeks flame. "Thank you. I, uh . . . I just need to slip on my shoes."

"Need help?" he asks.

"Oh no, I'm good," I say, fumbling to move around him and get to my nude-colored pumps. "Oh, sorry, just need to reach those."

"These?" he asks, bending at the waist to pick up the shoes.

"Yup, those. Plan on wearing them unless you want to wear them." I look up at him and swallow hard when I see his brow is raised in a cute, quizzical way. "Do you?"

"Do I want to wear your shoes?"

I laugh because, Jesus, am I nervous now. "I mean, of course you don't. You would be at a high risk of rolling your ankle again if you did."

"Yeah, rolling an ankle is the reason I don't want to wear your shoes," he says in a joking tone.

"Right . . ." I slip my shoes on and meet his eyes. *Pull it together, Blakely.* But I can't. I'm all shaky and jittery inside and can't stop myself from blurting out, "I'm nervous."

His brow pinches. "Nervous. Why?"

I shake my hands out. "I don't know." Actually I do know. *It's you, you're the reason I'm nervous.* But I know I can't say that to him. "I've never done this before. This fake dating thing. I'm nervous about seeing Perry. I don't want him cornering me to talk. I don't want people asking me questions. I don't—"

His fingers fall on my lips, silencing me. And as the room goes quiet, our eyes connect, his hazels to my greens.

Slowly, he lowers his fingers. The air around us feels thick like it's trying to pull us together.

Gently, he says, "Let me worry about Perry, and you worry about enjoying your friends getting married." He entwines our hands together. "As far as the fake dating, that's easy, just pretend you're into me." Pretty sure I don't have to pretend that. "Hold my hand, lean into me, dance with me. Unless you find me so repulsive you can't do those things."

"I d-don't find you repulsive," I say. Quite the opposite actually.

"Then you should be good." He tugs me toward the living room, but I pause to pick up my phone and put it in my clutch before we keep heading toward the front door. "You ready . . . *babe?*"

And goosebumps just broke over my skin . . .

He winks and, dear God in heaven, *help me get through this night.*

We move past the couch and because I've clearly lost all faculties, I call out, "Bye, Sherman." The plant now has a permanent scarf around the base of his pot and a picture of my dead cat next to him. I think it's cute that Halsey rolls with it and doesn't mind the new additions.

Halsey pauses to glance at me with a humorous twitch to his lips. "Do you always say goodbye to him?"

I press my hand to my chest. "Of course. Don't you?"

He peeks over his shoulder at the plant and then back at me. "No."

"Well, looks like the nanny has become more of a mom. Maybe I need to take custody."

"If he starts wilting when you're gone, then maybe you will."

I smirk and let Halsey guide me out the door. This man's dry sense of humor. Interestingly, the nerves slip from my shoulders.

The job.

The stress of Perry.

The awkwardness.

It all slides away as Halsey takes my hand and leads me to his car. *He really is a wonderful man.*

Maybe this will be a fantastic night after all.

<hr />

"OH GOD, THERE HE IS," I say as I spot Perry out of the corner of my eye.

The wedding was breathtaking. The venue is an old, renovated warehouse with the original brick painted white. All the ducts are exposed, giving more height to the ceiling, but they've been painted black and have scattered bulbed lights under them. The dim lighting and original hardwood floors give it a romantic feel.

Arlene and Marco easily spent around one hundred thousand dollars on flowers because rows and rows of pink peonies are draped everywhere. Down the wall, from the ceiling, gathered into vases surrounded by votive candles floating in water, and strung together in rows draped over every doorway.

Never in my life have I ever been to a wedding like this, so romantic, intimate, but also large with so many guests.

And of course, Marco had to meet Halsey right away, and when I say right away, I mean before the wedding. Slipping him in as a guest was no big deal. Guess it pays to be one of the best hockey players in the game.

Now that the ceremony is over, I sit on a stool in front of a high-top table while Halsey stands next to me. He slips his arm around my waist and leans in close to my ear, the move once again creating a wave of goosebumps. That's how it's been through the whole ceremony.

He's put his arm over my shoulder, held my hand, and spoken closely to my ear as if it's just the two of us in this room. He's invaded my senses with his touch, his mouthwatering scent, and his whispers.

He's pretended to be madly in love with me.

He's protected me.

Paid attention to me.

He's claimed me.

"Where's Perry?" he asks, his lips almost touching my ear.

I compose myself and say, "Brown suit by the bar. Brown hair."

Subtly, Halsey looks over my shoulder, and I know the minute he spots him because his hold on me tightens. It's as if he's warning all men in the building that I'm not to be touched, let alone looked at. "He's headed over here."

"What?" I panic. "Seriously?"

He smooths his thumb over my hip. "Blakely . . . I've got you," Halsey says as if this is no big deal. He lifts his beer to his lips and takes a larger gulp than what he's been nursing. When I asked him if he was going to drink tonight, he said since it wasn't a game night, he thought that he would . . . despite possibly having a game tomorrow. He's not sure if he'll play, but we'll see. I don't blame him for the liquid encouragement. I need it too.

"Hey, Blakely," that familiar voice says from behind.

Here we go.

I plaster on a smile and turn toward Perry.

In the month or so I haven't seen him, his hair is longer, his beard is shaved, and he's tanner. Probably that Australian sun he's been soaking up. Whereas Halsey has sharper, more precise features with his carved jaw and sinful eyes, Perry is the boy next door with a rounder nose and youthful cheeks. Comparing the two side by side, I can see Perry's appeal—he's a good-looking man—but Halsey has the face and body of a man you'd find on a magazine cover.

"Hey, Perry," I say. Just as he goes to lean in for a hug, Halsey steps in and holds his hand out for a shake.

"Halsey, nice to meet you." Perry abruptly steps back and looks Halsey up and down. Perry's six foot wilts under Halsey's six foot four.

He stumbles for a second, but Perry takes Halsey's hand and shakes it.

"You must be Perry," Halsey says as I watch his grip grow tighter on Perry's hand.

Perry's jaw firms up as he nods. "And you're . . . you're . . ."

"Her boyfriend," Halsey says, the title sending a chill up my spine.

Perry's brows rise as he looks at me, and I know what he must be thinking.

Wow, that was fast.

That or . . . *was she cheating on me, and that's why she didn't move with me?*

I'm about to set the record straight when Halsey says, "New boyfriend. Still fresh."

"Oh, I see." Perry releases Halsey's hand. "Well, I guess congrats. You've got a good one." Perry gestures toward me as Halsey moves to my side and wraps his arm around my waist again. And then he does something unexpected, he leans into me and presses a kiss to the top of my head as he squeezes me tight.

"A really good one."

Perry clears his throat, obviously caught off guard by this new development. Well, I was caught off guard too. Looks like we're both feeling the same way. "Hey, boss, think I can talk to Blakely for a second by myself?"

Halsey shakes his head. "Nah, we're good."

The shock on Perry's face almost makes me burst out in laughter. There's no way he expected that response.

"We're actually going to dance, so if you'll excuse us . . ." Halsey helps me off the stool and connects our palms, hand in hand, but Perry steps in front of us.

"Only for a minute."

"I'm sorry, but what did you not understand when I said we're good?" Halsey asks, his voice turning menacing.

Perry's eyes narrow. "I'm not trying to start a scene. I just want to fucking talk to her."

Keeping his expression neutral, Halsey replies, "And I said we're good. Whatever you have to say, you can say in front of me."

"Blakely, surely you won't let this asshole stop you from talking for yourself? When have you ever accepted that?"

He's got a point, but I can't help but love the freedom of not having to deal with this, of leaning on someone else to protect me, to keep me safe from whatever Perry has to say. Because I don't want to hear it. I don't want to know what's on his mind because, whatever it is, it can't be good for me mentally. *And Halsey seems to get this without me saying a thing.* Strange as it seems, I feel like I've already mourned losing Perry. Seeing him feels uncomfortable, but I'm certainly not pining for him. *Which I'm glad to know about myself. I'm okay without him, after all.* Something he didn't think I would be. Interesting. *Yay for me.*

Halsey steps in close to Perry and says in a dark voice, "Calling me an asshole is not going to guarantee you leave this wedding unharmed. She asked me to speak for her tonight because she's mine, so like I said, whatever you have to say, you can say to us both."

Mine.

That one word vibrates through me as the tension between Perry and Halsey grows.

Perry would never have taken this tact. He would have told me to talk to the guy so we don't create a scene. Not Halsey. He said he'd shield me, and he's keeping to his word.

"Fine," Perry says before looking me in the eyes. "Blakely, I'm moving back to Canada and want you back. I made a huge mistake, and as we speak, my things are being shipped here. I got our apartment back, and now I need to find a way to earn your forgiveness."

I blink.

A few times.

I was not expecting him to say that.

Maybe a *sorry for moving to Australia* or possibly wishing me the best of luck.

But he's coming home, and he wants my forgiveness? Wow, just wow.

Halsey grows more tense as he steps in even closer.

While I'm reeling with this new information, Halsey mutters, "Too little, too late. Leave her the fuck alone."

And then he pulls me out onto the dance floor.

He tugs me in close, rests his hand on my hip, and grips my hand tight as he slowly starts moving us to the music. My heart races as he leans in close to my ear and says, "If you want him back, tell me right now and I'll step aside. If not . . . then I'm going to make sure I spend the rest of the night showing him exactly who you belong to."

Do I want him back?

I . . . don't know.

I wasn't expecting Perry to ever stake claim over me again. Not after the way we left things.

And when he left, I wasn't entirely heartbroken, more confused . . . maybe slightly relieved.

But relieved from what?

That's what I don't understand.

Did I not love him?

Because I thought I did.

I thought we were going to be married.

So why did I think losing him wasn't a heartache? The music plays and we move together, almost as if we've danced together a thousand times before. *It's nice.* And it's giving me space to be with my thoughts for a little longer.

Halsey's finger slips under my chin, forcing me to look him in the eyes. "Do you want him?" he asks, his expression soft as he speaks to me, nothing like the hard stone Perry had to face.

Do I want Perry?

I don't think I want him the way I want the man right in front of me.

The desire isn't there.

I don't get goosebumps when he's around.

And I sure as hell don't feel weak-kneed whenever he speaks to me.

I bite the corner of my lip as I swallow. "I . . . I don't think so."

"I need a solid answer, Blakely. Do you want him?"

From the way Halsey holds his breath and grips my waist so tightly, it almost feels like my answer rests heavily on his heart.

I wet my lips delicately, then say, "I don't want him."

He slowly nods and whispers, "Then you're mine for the night."

And before I can ask him what that means, he leans down, closing the space between us. To my utter shock and surprise, he gently presses a kiss to my lips.

It's so faint, so featherlike, that I almost feel like I'm imagining it until a bolt of lust spikes through me, awakening a sleepy sexual beast that's been in a slumber for quite some time.

Oh my God . . .

He pulls away and whispers, "Let's get drinks."

Yes . . . drinks.

Please drinks.

"WOOOOOO!" I shout as Arlene and Marco kiss, thanks to Arlene's aunt clinking her wineglass for the tenth time during dinner.

Not sure who is more drunk at this moment, Aunt Glass Clinker . . . me . . . or Halsey.

Perry sent us both into a tailspin, well, Perry and the kiss. The kiss heard around the world!

Maybe not around the world, but that's what it felt like, a smack of all lip smackers. Does that make sense? Either way, Halsey kissed me, and I swear I could hear a pin drop at that moment.

I could actually feel the pulse between my legs.

Yup . . . this girl, your girl, she was turned on.

And it was such a simple kiss. Barely a kiss. A peck. I've had more intimate kisses with an ice cream cone.

But after the kiss, we headed to the bar, took two tequila shots, courtesy of my order, and then I grabbed a special wedding cocktail designed for the bride and groom while Halsey grabbed another beer.

With empty glasses now in front of us, our plates have just been delivered, and we're feeling good.

Really good.

I turn toward Halsey, my knees pressing against the side of his leg, and I say, "He's scowling again."

With a goofy grin, Halsey places his hand on my thigh and says, "Good. Let him fucking scowl."

Perry sits across from us at the same table, something I know Arlene probably couldn't avoid. I'm okay with it; this was all last minute, so I'm not going to complain. Thankfully, the peonies are giving us an ounce of privacy.

"Want some more mashed potatoes?" Halsey lifts his fork to my mouth.

"I have some on my plate."

"Yeah, but eating it off my fork is better."

"Is your fork magic?" I ask.

He nods. "Yup."

"Then put the magic in my mouth."

He smirks and slides his fork past my lips. I wrap my mouth

around the tines, and as he pulls the fork away, I suck on it, hollowing out my cheeks.

His brows raise as he says, "That was fucking suggestive."

"Well, you can't be the only actor between the two of us. I've got to throw in some moves for at least the supporting actress nomination. I feel like you're carrying the team on your back right now."

"I'm glad you see it that way." He takes a mouthful of his mashed potatoes. "Because that's exactly what's happening. About time you carry some weight around here."

"Are you saying I'm not holding up my end of the bargain?"

"I'm saying you can pretend you like me more." He takes a sip of water from the glass in front of him and sets it down.

"My body language is pointed toward you, and that's a good sign. What more can I do without making a scene . . . like dry-humping your lap?"

"Dry-humping at a wedding? Class, Blakely. Show some fucking class."

That makes us both laugh.

"My apologies. How about this." Bringing my hand to the back of his neck, I lightly play with the small hairs at his nape. "Does this work?"

"It's a start," he says as he places his hand on my exposed thigh from my slit and then slides it high, making my entire body twitch with anticipation. "This is better."

"Oh, I see," I say as I move in closer, causing his hand to move higher, almost to the juncture of my thigh. I move my other hand to his chest, where I undo another button and slide my hand along his exposed skin. "God, you're so muscular," I say, loving how his heated skin warms my palm. When our eyes connect, I ask, "This better?"

"Much," he says, his thumb sliding over my thigh.

No one can see his hand—it's blocked by the chair and the table—and nor can they see his thumb moving back and forth, but it feels right, like that minor stroke is playing the part.

And that's what we're doing, right? We're playing a part.

We're acting.

Yet when he looks into my eyes, it doesn't feel like he's acting. It feels like he's seeing straight into my soul.

"I bet he's watching," I say.

"How could he not?" Halsey says. "You're breathtaking."

Butterflies erupt in my stomach because, oh my God, he's playing with my freaking heart.

Does he mean that? Is he just saying that in the hopes that Perry can read lips? Because he can't, not that I know of at least.

Unsure of what to say, I reply, "*You're* breathtaking."

He chuckles. "Yeah? You think so?"

I smooth my hand over his rock-hard chest. "Yes, just feel this, it's so strong. Who knew a chest could be like this?"

"Perry wasn't much of a weightlifter?" he asks.

I glance over at Perry who's speaking with the older woman next to him. I shake my head. "More of a runner. He kept in shape, but he didn't lift or anything like that."

"What do you prefer?"

"This," I say, running my thumb over his chest.

"Good." He turns toward me and interlocks our legs so one of mine is between his. He keeps his hand on my thigh as he says, "What else do you prefer?"

"What do you mean?" I ask, wondering if this intimate conversation is part of the show. Is he trying to make me blush, make me swoon for the show of it, or is this real?

Why am I even thinking it's real?

He's way out of my league. No way would someone like Halsey even consider me for anything intimate.

Yet . . .

The dressing room.

Him zipping me up.

That kiss.

It feels so real.

Then again, I've been drinking. Maybe that's all this is, my drunk mind wandering on me.

I'm exposed right now and slightly raw from my ex being in

the same room and his announcement that he's moving back here. It's been an attack on all fronts. So maybe I'm just clinging to any feeling I can grasp . . . including Halsey's heady caresses.

"What else do you prefer in a man?" he repeats as his thumb runs across my exposed skin.

A thrumming erupts between my legs when his eyes connect with mine. His hand moves up another inch, and I can feel everything twitch inside me with anticipation.

"Umm . . ." I wet my lips. "I prefer someone attentive. Someone who likes to have fun. Someone who cares about me and our relationship."

He nods. "What else? Be more specific."

"More specific?" I ask. "Umm . . . I guess someone who'll challenge me but also go along with me when I need it."

"Like ordering cheese pizza because you love it and don't want to pick off the pepperoni?"

I smile. "Exactly. I also want someone who isn't afraid to show me who they really are and what they really want in all aspects in life . . . including the bedroom."

His eyes turn dark, and I know that reaction isn't acting. There is no way.

"And what do you like in the bedroom?" he asks, his hand moving up another inch.

My heart rate kicks up as I quietly say, "Everything."

One of his brows lifts. "Everything?"

I slowly nod. "Everything."

The smallest of smirks falls over his face before he pulls away and lifts from his chair. Confused, I'm about to ask him where he's going, but he holds his hand out to me. I take it, ready to walk away with him anywhere.

The dance floor has started to fill as people have finished their meals. The lights have dimmed, and the music has grown louder. Halsey walks me over to the bar, pressing his hand to my lower back and leaning into my ear. "Want another drink?"

"Yes," I answer without even thinking about it.

And I want him to have another drink, because I like this looser side of him.

"Mind if I order for you?" His hand rests above my ass now.

"Please do," I say, my voice coming out breathless.

He turns toward the bartender while keeping his hand possessively on me and holds up two fingers. "Two shots. Tequila with lime."

He releases me for a moment while he pulls a twenty out of his wallet and sticks it in the tip jar, then he moves us to the end of the bar, where he leans against it and pulls me between his legs and holds me there at the hip.

"Tequila shots?" I ask with a raised brow.

He grins. "Can you handle it?"

"I can, but can you? You're the one who doesn't drink as much."

"Consider it my last drink of the night."

"Are we headed home after those?"

He shakes his head. "Nope."

"No? What do you have planned?" I ask as he brings my hands to his chest, where I keep them and lean into him. I catch him glancing over at our table for a moment, and then he returns his attention to me.

"We have an ex to make jealous," he says before he thanks the bartender for our shots.

He holds one out to me, and I take it despite the weird sensation spiking through me from his comment.

We have an ex to make jealous.

I know that's why Halsey's here with me. I'm well aware of his purpose, but . . . I don't know, a small part of me thought that the touches, the grazes, and the kiss were all maybe something a little more.

But his comment brings me back to reality.

He's here for a reason, and if Halsey's anything, he's a man of his word. We will make Perry jealous.

Hiding my sigh of disappointment, I clink my shot glass with

Halsey and take the shot down before biting on the lime, skipping the salt altogether.

When I set the glass down, he says, "Want to dance?"

I shiver as the burning liquid flows down my throat. "I need to go to the bathroom first."

"Hurry up." He winks before releasing me.

On steady yet slightly wobbly legs, I move away from him, only to glance over my shoulder once to find him watching me walk away, those soulful eyes fixated on me and me alone.

God!

He's good.

He's really freaking good.

He's truly making me feel like I'm the one who matters the most in this room. Not the newly wedded couple, not the single girls bouncing around looking for his attention, or the guys, for that matter, but me.

Just me.

Too bad it's not real.

I head into the bathroom, move by a few girls fixing their makeup, and take care of business, being extra careful with my dress so it doesn't fall in the toilet somehow. Once finished, I stand in front of the mirror, where I wash my hands and look at my reflection.

My cheeks are flushed.

I have a slight smirk to my lips.

And I look . . . happy.

Not sure the last time I sported this kind of grin, even when I was dating Perry.

Maybe I wasn't in love with him the way I thought I was. Perhaps his moving was a blessing I didn't know I needed.

Yet he's back . . .

He's back, and I feel nothing toward him.

After so many years of being together, you'd think there would be a twinge of emotion from seeing him, but . . . nothing.

And that right there says everything.

I exit the bathroom and head down the hallway just as a tall figure steps in front of me. Startled, I let out a squeak as my eyes lift and find Perry standing in my way.

Ahh, of course. He couldn't make it easy, could he?

"Sorry, did I startle you?" he asks.

"Yes," I answer, hand to chest.

"Excuse me," a lady says from behind. Perry grips my arms and moves me to the side so I'm up against the wall, and he's in front of me.

"What are you doing?" I ask.

"I wanted to talk to you without your bodyguard."

"He's not my bodyguard, Perry," I say with an eye roll, even though he kind of is.

"He can't be your boyfriend. There's no way you moved on that quickly unless you were cheating on me."

My eyes narrow. "I would never, and the fact that you're even accusing me of that is proof that you didn't know me as well as I thought you did."

He pushes his hand through his hair in distress. "You're right, that was uncalled for. I'm sorry. I'm just . . . fuck, Blakely, I'm confused."

"What are you confused about?"

"What am I confused about?" he asks as if it's not so blatantly obvious. "How about how you could move on so fucking quickly?"

"Did you expect me to sit back and mourn while you lived your life in Australia? Perry, you were the one who decided to leave. You were the one who wanted to break up."

"I didn't want to break up. I wanted you to want to be with me."

"And I did," I say, keeping my voice low so as not to cause a scene. "But I told you, I didn't want to move. My life and job are here."

"Which are more important than I am."

"Perry, you chose a job and a new country over me . . . how is that any different from me choosing my job and my comfort? It's not. And now you're coming back, so was it worth it?"

"It wasn't," he says, moving in on me. "I realized that the fucking moment I arrived in Australia. I thought that maybe I was just nervous, but the more time I spent there without you, I knew I made a goddamn mistake. That's why I'm back." He smooths his hand up my arm. "It's why I want you—"

"I suggest you remove your hand from my girl before I fucking do it for you," Halsey says just as he comes into view. And oh my God, does he look furious.

Perry looks over his shoulder but doesn't stop touching me. "I was with her ever since college. I reserve the right to talk to her alone."

"You reserve the right to talk to her," Halsey says right before pushing Perry's hand off me. "But you sure as fuck don't reserve the right to touch her." Halsey approaches, towering over Perry and me, and pulls me into his side. "Especially when she belongs to me."

Perry shakes his head and takes a step back. He then gestures to Halsey and says, "You like this? You like this sort of asshole behavior? Jesus fuck, Blakely. What happened to you? I leave for just over a month, and you lose your goddamn—"

Before Perry can finish, Halsey has him by the collar of his shirt, pressing him against the wall, which startles the few people heading to the bathrooms.

"Halsey," I say, startled and scared at the same time.

"Watch what you fucking say to her," Halsey seethes. "Nothing is wrong with her. She's perfect, and you're the douche who didn't realize it. So leave her the fuck alone, or next time, this isn't going to end with you only walking away with some broken pride."

Halsey releases him, then grabs my hand and tugs me toward the dining room. We head straight to our table, where he picks up my clutch and hands it to me.

He pulls me in close and speaks directly to my ear. "I can't fucking stay here with him lurking. If you want to leave, I'm leaving now. If you want to stay, you can stay. But . . . I . . . I can't."

I can feel him shaking with anger, and I'm not sure what has gotten into him or made him this charged up, but I do know I don't want to stay here without him.

"Let's go," I say.

And with that, he leads me out of the venue and straight to a taxi.

Chapter Sixteen

HALSEY

I can barely fucking breathe.

The city of Vancouver races by me as I stare out the window, telling myself to calm the fuck down, but I can't seem to flip the switch.

Seeing Perry pressing Blakely up against the wall fucking did me in.

My entire being went black, and before I knew what I was doing, I pressed him up against a wall, ready to plow my fist into his stupid fucking face.

And there is no reasoning behind it other than I was jealous.

I couldn't stand the idea of him being near her. Of him being able to reconcile any sort of feelings with her.

Because he left.

He was the idiot who decided to take a new job that took him *away* from her.

He was the one who fucked up and left the door open for me to slip in.

A door I've struggled getting through.

I've faltered. I've made mistakes. And I've put myself so far into the friend zone that I can do very little to get myself out of it.

Tonight was supposed to be that night.

And there he was, attempting to tell her how much he missed her.

Fuck off, Perry. You had your chance; tonight was mine.

But . . . I think I screwed it up even more. Blakely has been staring out the window beside me, probably regretting she had to leave her friend's wedding since I couldn't keep my emotions in check.

She should be snuggling into me. Holding my hand. Letting me touch her and kiss her. Listening to how I truly feel about her.

Instead, I'm an angry fucking asshole thrumming with the need to do something reckless, something to distract me from the regret beating through me.

When we pull up to the apartment, I thank the driver and open the door. Blakely does the same, not letting me do it for her.

I can't be sure what she's feeling right now, what she's thinking.

Whatever it is, it can't be anything positive about me.

In silence, I open the apartment building door for her and then follow close behind, resting my hand on her lower back as I guide her toward the elevator.

Fuck, I hate myself.

I hate myself for not being able to control my anger.

For not being able to ignore Perry and enjoy Blakely.

My time was cut short because I cut it short. I could be dancing with her right now—her body pressed against mine and her hands roaming my chest, something she did a few times tonight.

Instead, we're as cold as stone toward each other as we ride the elevator up to the apartment.

And I don't know how to bridge the gap between us.

I don't know how to apologize. I don't know how to express

my feelings to her—that I've liked her for so goddamn long that I lost my shit when I saw her with Perry and couldn't stomach the idea of her giving him a second glance.

The elevator comes to a stop, and with my hand on her back, I move her down the hall to our apartment.

Yes . . . our apartment.

That's how I've come to think of it now. Just me and her . . . and Sherman, sharing this living space. Sharing dinners together.

Jokes.

Stories.

And now it feels like it was all for nothing. I had one chance for her to see me differently—*to want me*—and I blew it.

I shut the door once Blakely is inside and set my wallet and keys on the side table. Blakely remains next to the door, her hands clutching her purse in front of her.

I slowly raise my eyes to hers and when hers meet mine, indescribable need for this woman hits me so fucking hard that the air is sucked right out of my lungs, leaving me breathless . . . needy . . . erratic.

Just from one look, from those eyes, the eyes that captivated me from day fucking one.

And they haven't stopped. They've held my attention. They've gripped me by the heart and have held me close. They've made me realize that there truly isn't anyone else on this earth that I want in my arms.

It's Blakely.

It's always been Blakely.

It will always be Blakely.

And as I stare back at her, I wonder, *why isn't she moving?* Why isn't she attempting to get ready for bed? Why is she just standing there, looking slightly nervous but also hopeful at the same time?

Her gaze dips to my mouth and then quickly back to my eyes.

Did I imagine that?

Surely not.

She looked at my mouth.

The universal signal that she's interested.

I return the gaze, checking out her mouth as her little pink tongue peeks out and wets her delicious lips.

My heart beats erratically as hope springs in my chest.

Please . . . please let her want this as much as I want it.

I take a step forward, and I watch her chest rise and fall more rapidly.

Nerves rip through me, making my stomach tumble and slip with each breath.

I close the space between us, and when she doesn't move or say anything, I realize this is it. This is the fucking moment I've been waiting for. If I want to make something happen, this is the time.

I take a deep breath and scan her beautiful face. Those lips wet and ready, those eyes looking hungry and willing.

I'm going to take what I want and face the consequences after because if I don't, I'll regret it forever.

Before I can stop myself, I close the last of the space, grip her face with both hands, and crash my mouth down on hers.

I don't have to wait for her to reciprocate. It's immediate. She drops her clutch to the ground and throws her arms around me, kissing me back with such force.

She's . . . she's fucking kissing me back.

Fuck.

I push her against the door and plant my body along hers, not letting her escape now that I have her. From the way she clings to me and submits to my mouth, I'm guessing she doesn't want to go anywhere.

I slide my mouth over hers, opening our lips together, and then slip my tongue against hers. She reciprocates the movement, and I fucking melt.

My nerves.

My reservations.

My regrets.

They all fucking melt out of me. Pure, alpha confidence replaces everything as I move her hands above her head, pinning them against the door as I drive my tongue deeper into her mouth.

She tastes so damn amazing.

Better than all the times I've imagined owning this mouth.

And when she gasps from what I demand from her with my tongue, sheer need pulses up my spine.

"You taste so fucking good," I say as I pull away, kissing across her jaw and down her neck. Her chest continues to rise and fall as I hold her in place, but she practices deeper breaths now as I move my mouth to her collarbone and across her shoulder. "Your skin is so soft, like fucking velvet, Blakely." I move back up to her neck and ear, where I whisper, "Tell me you want this. That you want me."

She takes a deep breath and wraps her fingers around my hand, clasping them together against the door. "I want you, Halsey."

"Good," I whisper right before turning her around. She turns her head so her cheek rests against the wood. "If this is too much, tell me to stop." I kiss down her neck, across her shoulder while my hand rests on her hip. My pelvis presses against her backside, showing her exactly what she does to me. How fucking hard she makes me.

A gasp falls past her lips, and I catch the sound on my mouth before kissing her again, claiming that mouth of hers and making it mine.

"I'm taking what I want," I say into her ear. "I won't stop until you tell me." I release her hands and clasp the zipper of her dress. "I won't fucking stop until you say, understood?"

She nods.

"No, I want to hear your verbal agreement. Do you understand that I'm taking what I want, Blakely? I'm taking your mouth, your body, and I'm marking it as mine until you tell me to stop."

"Yes, I understand," she says, sending euphoria through me.

She just gave me the green light. *Thank. Fuck.*

I pull down her zipper until it's completely undone. That's

when I notice she's not wearing a bra, something I didn't pick up on when I zipped her into her dress earlier this evening.

I slide my hands down her arms, dragging the fabric of her dress with me until it falls to the floor, pooling at her feet. Her ass is encased by white lace underwear, giving me a sneak peek of her perky ass. Her back is smooth, free of any mark besides one tattoo under her shoulder blade. A few starbursts that I'm sure have specific meaning.

I don't touch her right away. Instead, I shrug out of my jacket, unbutton my shirt, and remove my shoes and socks. The entire time I take her in, I soak up this moment that I've dreamed of for so fucking long.

When I'm ready, I step up behind her, my front to her back, and slowly slide my hands up until my fingers are just below her breasts. I let my thumbs caress the soft, plush underside of her boobs, which causes her to lean her head back against my shoulder.

"What do you like, Blakely?"

"Everything," she says.

"I know that," I answer. "But specifically, what do you want from me? From tonight?"

"Pleasure," she answers as I move my thumbs upward, just below her nipples. She moans and grabs the back of my neck. "I want to feel all of you, every last inch. I want to scream. I want to feel so out of control that I black out from the pleasure."

A smirk tugs on my lips. "That I can do," I say as I lean forward to get my first view of her breasts right before I pinch her nipples.

Fuck, her tits are big. I knew they were, but they're real and soft, and her nipples are so goddamn hard. They feel like little pebbles, begging to be played with.

"God, yes," she says as she moves her ass against my crotch. "Oh my God, Halsey," she says as her hand moves between us, and she discovers my length and size. That small caress nearly makes me come in my goddamn pants. "You're huge."

"Good thing since you want to scream tonight," I say right

before I spin her back around and bring my mouth to hers. Our lips collide, and I lift her by the ass to pin her against the door. Her legs wrap around my waist in just the right spot that her center smooths along my length. "Feel that, baby? That's how you make me feel. That's how much you turn me on." I pulse into her, and she groans into my mouth. "Think you can take all of this?"

My lips move along her jaw, nipping at her skin as she glides against my cock. "You're . . . you're so big. I don't . . ." She moans when I nip at her neck. "God, I don't know."

"You're going to take all of me, Blakely, even if it takes hours. Your pussy will take every last fucking inch of me."

And then I walk her back to the bedroom, keeping my mouth on hers the entire time until I hit the bed and lay her down carefully. Those hypnotic eyes stare up at me as I take off my shirt and toss it to the ground.

Her gaze roams over my chest, she wets her lips, her entire expression making it clear how much she wants this. That gives me all the motivation to continue taking what *I've* always wanted since the moment I met her.

I undo my pants and push them down, leaving me only in a pair of black boxer briefs. She scoots back on the bed, and I move over her. I lean down and bring my mouth to hers as my hand slides up her side to her breast, where I squeeze it in my palm. Her back arches against me as she moans with satisfaction.

"Do you like your nipples to be played with?" I ask while I move my mouth down her neck again. Pausing at the juncture of her shoulder to suck on her skin, I know damn well it will leave a mark and don't give two fucks about it. Because I want her waking up tomorrow knowing who owned her the night before.

"Yes," she says as I move to her breasts.

"Good," I say right before I tug on one of her nipples with my teeth.

"Fuck," she says as she lifts her back, arching so high that her breast slams into my mouth. I open wide and suck hard, taking in her nipple and swirling my tongue around it while my hand plays with her other breast. "Don't stop."

Is she insane? The only way this is ending is if she tells me to end it.

I can't get enough of her. I can't move fast enough. I want everything from her.

I move to her other breast and squeeze it while sucking her nipple, pulling and tugging. Offering a little nibble that drives her nuts.

"How fucking wet are you?" I ask as I bring her breasts together and kiss between them and then move to her stomach, where I kiss down to her belly button. I spread her legs, giving me room, and then feel her grow uncomfortable for a moment, so I pause. "I want that pussy on my tongue."

"Halsey . . . I . . ."

"Tell me to stop. That's the only way I won't bury my face between your legs." I pause for a second, giving her a moment to decide, and when she doesn't say anything, I tear off her underwear and marvel at how bare she is before I settle between her legs, spread her open, and press my tongue against her clit.

Her legs shoot up to her chest where she grips them as she shifts her pelvis forward. "Oh my God," she cries out as I flick my tongue across her clit rapidly.

If I wasn't so desperate to hear her come, I'd take my time with long, languid strokes, but fuck it, I need this. I need to see her lose herself with me in control.

"You taste so fucking good. Fuck, I could spend hours between your legs." I dive my tongue against her while my hands travel up her body to her breasts where I play with her nipples.

Rolling.

Teasing.

Tugging.

She moans even louder as her body starts to tense.

"I want you coming on my tongue. I want you coming all over my goddamn face." I bury my mouth even more between her legs, lapping up every ounce of her pleasure, while her orgasm builds and builds.

"Oh fuck, Halsey. Oh God. I'm . . . I'm right there."

I bear down, flicking my tongue so rapidly that I can barely breathe, and when she's just about to come, I pull away and press two fingers inside her.

"Oh . . . God," she groans as I scoop my fingers inside and against her G-spot. Her eyes fly open. Her legs shoot out as her hands grip the sheets. "Fuck . . . ahhhh," she yells, and it's the most gorgeous fucking thing I've ever seen.

I move her legs open again, continue to scoop upward, and finish her off with my tongue, licking her until she screams my name in ecstasy and falls over the edge, her orgasm ripping through her entire body and making her convulse beneath me.

"What a fucking greedy pussy you have," I say as I move my fingers against her inner walls, feeling her squeeze them tight. "You better squeeze my cock like that." I remove my fingers, and with my eyes on her heady ones, I slip them inside my mouth and suck every last drop of her off me. "You're fucking delicious."

While she floats down from her orgasm, I remove my boxer briefs, my erection so fucking hard that it's painful. I grip it and start pumping, moving some of the pre-cum over my length to help. As I stare down at her, I say, "I'm going to fuck you so hard tonight that you're going to forget your name."

Then I flip her over to her stomach and prop her ass up in the air. I smooth my hand over the smooth skin right before spanking her, leaving a red mark right where I like it.

"Oh fuck, Halsey."

I pause before doing it again and lean forward. Speaking close to her ear, I ask, "Did that hurt?"

"Yes."

"Do you want it again?"

She takes a second, swallows, and then nods. "Yes."

I smile and then place a kiss between her shoulder blades, down her spine, right on her ass, and then lift and spank her again.

"Fuck," she groans. This time, it's a pleasurable sound. "Oh my God, why do I like that?"

"Because you're my good girl who likes to be punished." I spank her again, and she groans into the mattress.

I smooth my hand over the red spot and lean down, pressing more kisses along her back.

"Are you on birth control?" I ask her.

"Yes," she says.

"Good, because I want this cunt bare. Tell me if you don't want that."

She doesn't answer.

"Tell me, Blakely."

"I want you bare," she says, her voice wavering.

Nervous she might be second-guessing that choice, I flip her back over and look her in the eyes. Her dazed, dreamy eyes.

"Are you nervous?"

Her eyes find my cock, and I watch them widen as she takes me all in. "Halsey," she whispers.

I don't want her to be scared, so I take her hand, and I bring it to my cock. "Feel me," I say. "Explore me."

Tentatively, her hand smooths around my length before squeezing it. She then sits up and pushes me down on the bed. I lie down and sift my hands behind my head, giving her full access as my erection strains up my stomach.

"Jesus," she says as she straddles my legs.

And at this moment, I've never felt luckier. Because I have Blakely, my dream girl, naked and on top of me, touching my cock like it's the most magnificent thing she's ever seen. I couldn't have dreamed this, never in my wildest dreams, yet here I am, experiencing it, feeling it, being with her.

"You're gorgeous," I say as she slides her hand up my length. "So fucking beautiful, Blakely."

Her eyes meet mine.

She wets her lips.

And then she lowers down on top of me and presses her mouth to mine. I roll on top of her, and she spreads her legs, making room for me as I run my length along her slit while my mouth takes control of hers.

"You're so fucking sexy," I say between kisses. "I want to own this body." I grip her breast. "I want to fuck every inch of it. Come all over you, inside you." I kiss her jaw as her legs spread even more. "I want your voice hoarse from screaming. I want you waking up tomorrow with the feel of me still between your legs." I move to her neck. "I want to ruin you, fuck you so hard that you'll never think of another cock."

She groans, and I press the head of my erection against her entrance. She tenses, so I bring her hand to her pussy and whisper, "Play with yourself. Relax and show me how you give yourself pleasure."

I sit back just enough to see two fingers making slow circles over her clit.

"Is that how you masturbate?" She nods. "Good."

And as she slowly starts to relax, I push myself inside her.

"This tight hole, fuck, it will be the death of me." I roll her nipple between my fingers. "Relax, baby. I need you to relax."

She lets out a deep breath, and I allow myself another inch.

"Fuck," she says, her head thrashing to the side. "You're so big."

"You made me this hard. The taste of your cunt on my tongue, the sound of your cries in my ear. I want more. I'm going to fuck you so hard, Blakely. Relax so I can make us both come. Keep playing with yourself."

Her hand moves faster, and I lean down and start making bite marks along her collarbone, only to soothe it with kisses. She sighs again, and I press in another inch. Halfway there. But she's so tight, I feel like I could come, just like this, half in.

"Baby, please, I'm fucking dying here."

"Just . . . just press in."

"No," I say as I kiss her neck, sweat starting to form on my lower back as I exercise an immense amount of control. "I'll go slow and savor every moment of this."

She sucks in a sharp breath of air. "I just need you in."

Understanding where she's coming from, I say, "Let out a deep breath." She exhales, and at the same time, I thrust my hips all the way until I bottom out. The sensation of being wrapped so tightly by her makes my eyes roll in the back of my head. "Fuck, this tight cunt is going to make me pass the fuck out."

I grip the blankets beneath us, my knuckles going white as I feel like I'm stuck in a vise grip. She's so tight it's almost borderline uncomfortable, threading between pain and absolute pleasure.

Needing to do something, I start moving my hips in and out. It's slow at first because, Jesus Christ, I can barely pull out, but once she starts twisting and turning beneath me while still playing with herself, her arousal makes it that much easier.

"That's it, you good fucking girl. Keep lubing my cock." I descend over her breasts again, and this time, I don't suck, I nibble. I tug. I pull on her hard nipples. I mark my way around the orbs, leaving bite marks, sucking over them, increasing the color, the claim I have on them.

"I . . . I'm close." She starts to clench, but I'm not there yet. I don't want her coming yet, so to my dismay, I pull out of her only for her sweet protest to fill the room. "Halsey."

"You're coming on my cock when I tell you." I bring my body closer to her face and say, "Open up that pretty little mouth for me."

Eyes wide, she pauses for a moment, but then she slowly opens up. I slide just the tip past her lips, where she sucks on it, her tongue swirling around the opening.

"Yes, baby. Just like that. Fuck, your mouth is so hot." I sit taller on my knees and grip the headboard as I angle my cock better for her. I dip it into her mouth, and she opens it wider, letting me sink farther. "Stroke me. Make me desperate to come."

I can tell by her hesitation that she's never done this before. This is all new, and even though I want to take it easy on her, I also don't want her to think it would be any different. This is what it's like to be with me. This is how I need it.

I want her to hear me. Know what I want, what I think about her, how she makes me so fucking needy for her goddamn touch.

Her hand creeps between my legs, and she cups my balls gently.

"Harder, Blakely. Don't be too gentle."

She sucks my tip with more force and squeezes my balls tighter, and my legs nearly give out on me.

"Ahhh, fuck yes, baby. Again."

She repeats the suck and the squeeze a few more times until my legs are shaking, and I can feel my balls start to tighten with my orgasm.

I pull away from her, flip her on her stomach again, and then prop her ass up. Before she can even think about what's happening, I slap her ass right before I press the head of my cock at her entrance. The combination of surprise and spanking makes her unaware of my cock so I can slide right in without her nerves holding us off.

This position helps me go deeper, and then I touch her in just the right spot, her cries of pleasure searing my ears. I wrap her hair around my hand and tug her head back while I hold her hip with my other hand.

"Oh my God," she whispers as I tug tighter and thrust into her. She claws the bed, trying to stay in place, but there's no use. My hips start moving her until she presses against the headboard. She steadies herself as I pound into her from behind, not letting up, not letting her catch her breath.

Because I need to come.

I need to come so fucking bad inside her that I can feel it light up my entire body.

"Take my cock. Squeeze it, baby. I want to feel that tight cunt spasming around it."

"Fuck . . . me," she whispers as her body tenses even more, and she cries out in pleasure. "Halsey," she screams, and then she convulses around me, tightening around my cock so much that everything around me fades to black.

"I'm going to ruin this pretty little pussy."

I let go of her hair.

I grip both of her hips.

And I rock into her until my stomach bottoms out, a burst of pleasure shoots through my veins, and a tidal wave of white-hot pleasure tears through me.

"Motherfucker," I cry out as I pulse into her, coming over and over until nothing is left inside me.

I slow my hips down as her pussy continues to convulse around my cock, causing it to twitch inside her. We both collapse on the bed, me on top of her.

I kiss her shoulder.

Her neck.

Her cheek.

And when she turns just enough so I can find her mouth, I kiss her there too.

"Fuck," I whisper as I slowly pull out of her and catch some of my cum as well.

I've never come that hard in my life. Never.

I walk over to the bathroom, where I clean up and wash my hands, and when I'm about to bring her a washcloth, she appears at the bathroom door wearing my button-up shirt and looking so thoroughly fucked and mine that I lean toward her, tip her chin up with my finger, and press a kiss to her lips.

And to my delight, she kisses me back.

Knowing she probably wants to take care of her own business, I give her space in the bathroom as I lie back down on the bed, staring up at the ceiling in utter disbelief.

Blakely and I just had sex.

No, we didn't just have sex. We had mind-blowing, life-altering sex. If I wasn't sure that Blakely was the girl for me before, I sure as fuck can confirm it now.

She's it for me.

She's mine.

And I'll spend every waking hour making sure she knows that.

After a few minutes, she reappears in the bedroom, turning

off the bathroom light behind her. She hasn't buttoned up my shirt, just used it as a covering, so I'm pleased when she takes it off before getting into bed. I don't give her one second to think she's sleeping alone tonight. I wrap my arm around her and pull her into my chest so she's spooned against me.

I kiss her shoulder. "You okay?"

"Yes," she whispers.

"You sure?"

"Positive," she says as she curls into the pillow we're sharing.

Leaving it at that, I bury my head in her hair and close my eyes, joy settling my heartbeat and allowing me to drift into a deep sleep.

THAT FEELS SO GOOD.

I groan as I turn to my back, sleep still consuming me as I feel a warm body crawl on top of me.

My hard cock is stroked, and a smile passes over my lips as I envision Blakely on top of me, playing with my dick.

Yes . . . fuck, it feels so good.

So goddamn good.

And then, when I think my cock will be stroked one more time, instead, it's sheathed in warmth . . . tight warmth.

My eyes part open, and I find Blakely on top of me, riding my cock as she plays with her tits.

"Holy shit," I whisper as she glances down at me, her hair falling over her face before she pushes it behind her ear.

"I need to come," she says as she rocks over me.

I bring my hands behind my head as my dick grows harder inside her. "Then use me as your fuck toy," I say.

Her hands fall to my abs, and she grips them with her nails as she grinds harder on my cock. "Halsey . . ." She takes a deep breath.

"What, baby?" I ask as I pulse up into her, helping her out.

"I love your cock. Oh my God, it's so good."

That makes me smile. "Well, I love your tight cunt. So grip those fucking tits of yours and come for me."

She tilts her head back and rocks her hips faster while she plays with her nipples. I take her hips and help her rock faster over me. It's so sexy, so unexpected, and the best way to be woken up in the middle of the night that I'm lost with euphoria. The moment she starts tightening around me, her orgasm building a tremor deep within her, my cock swells. I surge up inside her as my cum spills out of me.

"Holy shit, I'm coming," I say as she cries out in ecstasy, her head thrashing as she orgasms.

She rocks over me for a minute more before she collapses on my chest and wraps her arms around me, my cock still inside her.

Her breathing slows down, and she starts to drift off to sleep on top of me. If I wasn't so afraid of getting her cleaned up, then I'd let her sleep there, but I don't want anything bad to happen to her, so I lift her and bring her to the bathroom, where I help clean her up as well as myself.

Then I carry her back to the bed and lay her down. I lie next to her, but this time, she curls into my chest right into my side, making me the happiest motherfucker ever to live.

———

"YOU DIRTY FUCKING GIRL," I say as I spank her again and again and again.

With every slap to her ass, her pussy gets wetter and wetter as I lap at her clit.

Her hot mouth slides over my cock while we're in the sixty-nine position, something she climbed into. While she sucks on the tip of my cock, she reaches between my legs and plays with my balls, something I love so goddamn much.

"Has anyone ever played with you here?" I ask as I move my finger over her other hole.

She gasps and clenches.

I take that as a no.

"Don't worry, baby. This tight hole will be mine too." And then I spank her again as I flick at her clit. The combination sends her over the edge, and she's coming all over my goddamn face just the way I like it. When she finishes, I flip her over on her back, hover over her, and pump at my cock with such ferocity that I'm coming in seconds, all over her perfect tits.

She smirks up at me when I'm done, and I can't take that look. I fall back on the bed and drape my hand over my face.

She doesn't say anything. She just kisses my cheek and goes to the bathroom again.

Fuck . . . me.

I don't think I can have her wake me up one more goddamn time.

This night might be the death of me.

At least I'll die a happy man.

▭

"HALSEY, oh my God . . . oh my God," Blakely cries out as I slam into her, her legs draped over my shoulders, her tits bouncing with every thrust.

Just when I thought she was the one who would be the death of me, it turns out it's my cock.

I woke up again with the biggest erection of my life, and she felt it because she woke up too. It took me seconds to get her primed, and now that I'm inside her, I can't stop.

"You like that, baby? Then make me come," I say through clenched teeth as I feel another wave of pleasure start to tip me over the edge.

She squeezes around me, and just like that, I'm fucking gone.

I lose control and pulse into her so hard that her head bangs against the headboard. I'm so gone that I can't stop, and as she comes, her body trembling in my arms, I join her with a roar of an orgasm.

We ride it out until we're both spent, and I fall onto the bed with her.

After a few seconds of catching my breath, I turn toward her and brush my hand over her head. "You okay?"

She nods. "I'm good."

"I'm sorry." I caress her cheek. "I didn't mean to slam you against the headboard."

The corner of her mouth tilts up. "It's okay."

And then she gets up and goes to the bathroom—without a shirt over her this time. Comfortable in her own skin, I watch her perfect ass sway away from me, and I sigh against the bed.

Fuck . . . how did I get so lucky?

Chapter Seventeen

BLAKELY

I stare at the daylight starting to creep past the curtains.

I'm sore. Without even moving, I know I'm sore.

Between my legs.

Along my back.

My head.

My arms.

Everything.

Everything in my body is sore because I had the most out-of-body experience of my entire life.

It's why I'm off to the side, not curled into Halsey, trying to figure out what the hell happened last night. I had sex with the man four different times, and every time, I came multiple times.

I . . . I had no clue sex could be like that, and it's throwing me into a tailspin.

I had nice sex with Perry.

It was fun.

We had a good time.

But last night, that was . . . that was confusing. Gratifying. Beyond comprehension.

I have so many mixed feelings and thoughts that I actually feel sick to my stomach. What the hell did I do?

I glance over at Halsey whose hair is flopped over his forehead, his five o'clock shadow thicker, and his strong, muscular chest out in the open for me to stare at.

Touch.

Kiss if I want.

And that's exactly what's freaking me out. He gave himself over to me last night.

The man who would barely talk to me, who likes to have his nose stuck in a book, had the dirtiest mouth I've ever heard.

The things he said to me.

The things he did to me.

I'm still trying to wrap my head around it.

I glance back at him and know that I need a second to breathe after everything that happened last night, to let my brain process it. *I thought he was pretending.* But the moment his lips touched mine in the apartment, I knew he wasn't acting. I could feel that kiss all the way down to my toes, and there was nothing fake about it. *And man, can he kiss.*

I slip out of the bed and tiptoe toward the door. Thankfully, he's sound asleep, so I slip past the door and head to my room, picking up my dress in the entryway in the process. When I reach my room, I shut the door and lean against the wood as I stare up at the ceiling.

"Oh my God," I whisper as I press my hands to my beating heart.

I need a warm shower to ease the pain in my body and then I need to get to work. I need . . . I need to talk to Penny.

I slip into the shower and let the warm water fall over me as I wash my body gently, making sure to focus between my legs where Halsey's beard burn has rubbed me nearly raw. My mind runs over the number of times that man licked me—sucked me down there—and did it with so much pleasure, like it was his own personal feast.

No one has ever feasted on me the way he did.

I move my soap over my breasts where he controlled me so effortlessly with a pinch to my nipple, a nibble, a bite.

And when I wash my chest and neck, I can feel certain sore spots I know I'll have to cover up when I get a good look at them.

I wash my hair, my face, and let the warm water rinse over me for a few more minutes before I turn it off and step out of the shower. That's when I look in the mirror for the first time and feel my jaw nearly drop to the floor.

Holy.

Shit.

I look like a leopard, spotted and marked all along my neck, my collarbone, my chest, my breasts. Deep purple bite marks. Hickeys scattered all over me.

I approach the mirror, towel in hand, and examine the markings. "Oh my God," I say as my fingers pass over them, one by one, examining every single way he claimed me.

And I know he meant to claim me because he said it. He gave me the play-by-play of what he was doing, what he was feeling, what he wanted me to do.

His dirty voice still rings through my head, his words sending a chill down my spine.

I want my cum on your face.

This greedy cunt wants more, doesn't it?

Use me as your fuck toy.

My cheeks flame, and I look away from the mirror, embarrassment and satisfaction hitting me at the same time.

Trying to block out the night, I dry myself off and make work of getting ready. Every once in a while, Halsey's voice passes through my thoughts and makes me pause, but I keep moving forward.

I don't bother drying my hair. I just put it in a low, tight bun, and because I'm so sore, I opt for business-casual joggers, a simple white shirt tucked in the front, and sandals. I dress up the outfit with a necklace, earrings, and some bracelets.

Given the tornado my body went through last night, I don't have to worry about walking in heels or feeling uncomfortable.

I spritz some perfume on my neck, and then on a deep breath—and a hope and a prayer that Halsey's still sleeping—I open the door to my bedroom and walk out . . . only to find Halsey leaning against the counter with a cup of coffee in hand.

Of course.

Dressed in a pair of athletic shorts and nothing else, he looks positively gorgeous with his messy hair, scratch marks across his chest—*did I do that?*—and a sleepy daze in his eyes.

"Morning," he says as I steel myself and try not to be awkward.

I lift my hand in a short, concise wave and say, "Morning."

Yup, not awkward at all.

His brow knits as he sets down his coffee. "Everything okay?" He starts to approach, but I move around the couch in the other direction so he can't get too close.

"Oh, yup, everything is great. Just . . . have to get into work."

"It's six fifteen," he says.

"Yeah, early day. Lots of emails and stuff like that. You know how those VIPs are. Oh God, did I say VIPs? I mean V-I-Ps. I don't want to refer to them as VIPs, as that seems douchey. Anyway, early morning so I better get started." I move toward the door, where I find my clutch from the night before. That will do. I tuck it under my arm and grab my keys from the side table.

"Blakely, wait," he says, trying to close the gap between us.

"Those emails won't answer themselves," I say as I tug on the door. But it doesn't open. He comes closer. Dear God, if I smell him, I might not leave this apartment. My legs are already trembling from the way he's approaching me . . . with determination in his eyes. I tug on the door again, but it's not budging. "What is this, some sort of trick door?" I ask with a nervous laugh. "Does it need a command?" I use my index finger as a wand and say, "Blakely says open now."

Halsey walks up right behind me, reaches around me, and unlocks the door.

I can feel the heat of his chest at my back.

The feel of his breath on my neck.

The slide of his hand over my hip.

"There, you can escape now," he says, knowing exactly what I'm doing.

I glance over my shoulder and say, "Not escaping, just, work, you know?"

"Yeah, I get it," he says, rocking back on his heels with a hurt look in his expression.

Dammit.

I don't want to hurt him. But I also . . . fuck, I don't know what's going on.

Sex isn't supposed to be like that!

I want to scream it at him.

Pound him on the chest.

Tell him that it was the best and worst night of my life.

But instead, I slide the door open and say, "Well, have a good day. See you at the arena."

"Yeah, see you there."

And then I'm out of the apartment and regretting everything I just did.

HALSEY

"I FUCKED UP," I say as I take a seat in the locker room after spending an hour in treatment early this morning. Luckily Grace was in there early, ready for me.

She didn't entirely clear me for the game, but I'm going to at least suit up and warm up with the boys.

"Please," Posey says as he presses his fingers into his brow.

"That's not what I wanted to fucking hear from your mouth. How the hell did you mess up this time?"

"He messed up?" Silas asks as he walks into the locker room, a towel over his shoulder. "Jesus Christ. How?"

"What's happening?" Eli says, joining us as well.

"Halsey fucked up." Posey gestures his hand in my direction.

"Does this have to do with Blakely?" he asks.

"Yes," Posey says, stepping in with all the information. "Blakely had to go to a wedding last night, and her ex was going to be there, so Halsey told her to take him as her date and pretend to be her boyfriend. She agreed, they went, and apparently, he blew the one chance he had of escaping the friend zone he put himself in."

Eli winces. "Sounds brutal. What did you do that fucked everything up?"

"I slept with her last night."

The boys stop everything they're doing and slowly turn toward me.

A naked man could come flying in here, do the helicopter with his wiener, and they wouldn't even blink an eye as silence falls around us.

And from their expressions, I can tell that's not what they were expecting to hear.

Silas has a giant smirk.

Eli looks shocked.

And Posey . . . well, his jaw drags across the floor.

"You . . . you slept with her?" Posey asks.

I nod. "Yeah, and not only did we sleep together, but we fucked." I lean my head against the wood of the locker. "Several times."

So many fucking times.

And every time felt like the goddamn first.

Mind-blowing.

Earth-shattering.

Nearly blacked out every goddamn time.

"Uh, explain to me how that's fucking up because, in my book, that's success," Silas says.

You would think.

"Because this morning, she couldn't get away from me fast enough. She snuck out of bed and said she had to get to work. It was just past six in the morning. She's avoiding me." I can still feel how uncomfortable and awkward she was. Hell, she could barely look me in the eyes.

"Huh." Posey rubs his jaw. "That seems like an unusual response. Let me ask you this . . . did she find completion?"

"Christ, why did you have to say it like that?" I ask as I rub my hand over my face.

"I'm trying to be polite," Posey answers. "So did she?"

"Yes. Multiple times and I'm leaving it at that."

"Are you sure?" Silas asks.

I look him dead in the eyes and say, "I can still taste her on my tongue."

Silas smirks and then leans back, happy with my answer.

"Okay, so she found completion," Eli says. "So maybe she just doesn't know how to react the next day." He shrugs. "Simple as that."

Posey snaps his finger at Eli and nods. "Yes, the awkward *she doesn't know what to say to you the morning after* routine. That's easily fixable."

"How is that fixable?" I ask.

Posey holds out his hand. "Let me see your phone."

Silas slaps his hand to my chest, holding me back. "Don't. Don't you let him touch your fucking phone. He'll text her and make an ass of you."

"I'm an expert at texting," Posey says.

"I don't know about that . . ." Eli replies.

Posey gives Eli the side-eye. "Coming from the man who texted Penny about eating a fucking apple. I saved that relationship for you." He looks at Silas and says, "And the reason you got sexy pictures from Ollie was because of me."

"You texted her, *oye my dick*," Silas says.

"And guess who has a live-in girlfriend now." Posey points at Silas. "You're fucking welcome." He holds his hand out to me again. "Now let me fix this for you. Trust me. I know what I'm doing."

⊏⊐

BLAKELY

"FINALLY," I say as I practically spring into Penny's office and close the door behind me.

If it had a lock, I'd flip that as well.

"What took you so long to get to work today?"

She looks up from her computer at my frazzled state. "Holden had some separation issues this morning."

"Holden did, or you did?"

"Maybe a little bit of both," she answers before picking up her to-go cup of coffee and taking a sip. "Now what's going on?"

I glance over my shoulder just to double-check that the door is shut, and when I turn back to her, I say, "Halsey and I had sex last night."

She clamps her hand over her mouth, blocking the coffee that flies out. The brown liquid dribbles over her fingers and straight to her desk.

"Jesus," she says, trying to clean it up.

I help her with some napkins, and once she's relatively clean, her eyes find mine again, shock registered across her features.

"You had sex with Halsey?"

I nod. "Yup." I twist my hands together. "Several times." And then I grip the neckline of my shirt and pull it to the side to the bite marks that I didn't bother covering up.

"Holy. Shit," she whispers.

I release my shirt and take a deep breath. "Penny, I need you to look me in the eye and promise me on Holden that you won't utter this to another living human."

She holds her hand up. "Promise."

Knowing she's true to her word, I lean closer to her desk, press my palm to the surface, and glance down at the floor. "Halsey Holmes has the biggest dick I've ever seen."

When I look up, I watch a slow smile creep over Penny's lips. She whispers back, "How big?"

I wet my lips and say, "I stopped breathing for a second when he started . . . slipping it in. Took a good minute or so for him to, you know, fully get in there."

She leans back in her chair and stares up at the ceiling. "Wow, that's great. Good for you."

"No, not good for me."

Her smile disappears as she brings her gaze back to me. "What do you mean not good for you? Did he hurt you? Is that why you walked in here weird?"

"He didn't hurt me, but yes, I'm walking weird because I sat on a light post several times last night." She chuckles. "Penny, this isn't funny."

"I'm sorry, but I don't understand the panic. It seems like you had a good night last night."

"It wasn't just good, Penny," I whisper again. "It was life-altering."

"Explain to me how that's bad."

I lean back in my chair and say, "I don't know how to explain this other than . . . I feel like the world lied to me."

"What do you mean?"

"Penny, I had no idea sex could be like that. That I could experience that much pleasure in a matter of like . . . seven hours. It was unlike anything I've ever experienced and not just because of his penis." Penny smirks. "He was . . . God, it was like he knew everything about my body that I didn't even know. He knew exactly what I needed before I could even consider where I wanted him or what I wanted him to do. And then . . ." I bite on my bottom lip. "He had this voice, this deep, dirty-talking, filthy voice that was relentless."

"Wait." Penny holds up her hand. "Halsey Holmes is a dirty talker?"

"That's putting it mildly," I say. "The things he said to me, the way he said it, I still can feel my body tremble from the memory of it. When I say last night was life-altering, I'm not kidding, and it's really freaking me out."

"But why?"

"Because," I say, feeling exhausted just thinking about it. "I was with Perry since college. Before him, I had a few interactions with men, but he was truly a first for a lot. I was—what I thought—madly in love with him. I thought we were going to get married. He was good to me. Sweet and funny. He taught me what love was. And we had great sex together. I was satisfied. He was what I knew up until last night. And the fact that I could have a mind-blowing, spectacular night with a man who I've . . . well, who I've become friends with, it's throwing me for a loop. The things we did, they were ungodly." I press my hand to my forehead. "For God's sake, Penny, I woke him up in the middle of the night by sitting on his lap and helping myself. I've never done that, but I was insatiable. He was my drug last night that I became fully addicted to after one orgasm." I shake my head and blow out a deep breath before looking Penny in the eyes and saying, "I was cock-shocked, and I don't know how to handle it."

Penny snorts so hard that I see a droplet of snot fly out of her nose and right onto her desk.

She picks up a tissue and wipes at her nose—*and the desk, thank God*—while she laughs.

"This isn't funny," I groan.

"Blakely." She dabs at her eyes. "You just said you were cock-shocked."

"Because I was!"

My phone dings with a text message, and I quickly glance at the screen. When I see it's from Halsey, I gasp.

"What?" Penny asks. "Is that him?"

I nod. "He's probably going to call me out for leaving so abruptly this morning."

"Read it."

I swipe my phone open and click on the text message.

Halsey: *Thanks for letting me use your main hole last night.*

My brow knits together as I stare down at the text.

Main hole?

As in my vagina?

Who freaking says that?

"What did he say? Is it sexy?"

"No." I cringe. I hold the phone up to her so she can read it.

"Thanks for letting me use your main hole?" She pauses for a moment and then throws her head back and laughs so hard that she starts to cough. "Oh my God . . ." She waves her hands in front of her face as actual tears of laughter spring to her eyes.

"Why would he say that? That is the unsexiest thing he could have said, especially after the things he said to me last night." I place my hand on the desk and say, "Penny, he told me to use him as my sex toy."

I watch her cheeks turn a shade of pink. "He said that?" she whispers.

"Yes, that's what I'm talking about. It was an unreal experience. So why would he send this text message?"

Penny leans back in her chair and rocks in it for a few seconds before I see realization hit her. "Oh my God."

"What?" I ask.

She shakes her head. "I bet you anything he's talking to the boys. That text wasn't from him. Guarantee it was from Posey."

"Posey? Why would he text me?"

"No, it's not from Posey. I mean Posey wrote it, but it's supposed to be from Halsey. Posey is acting as Halsey."

"Why would Halsey let him do that? Halsey is clearly much better at saying sexy things than Posey."

"Probably nervous. Posey did the same thing with Eli and Silas. I remember Eli telling me all about it. When he did it for Silas, Eli found Silas naked on the floor of the locker room with

Posey twisted over him, fighting for his phone. Apparently, Posey said something stupid like *oye my dick* to Ollie."

"Oye my dick?" I chuckle. "Wow."

"Yup." She points at my phone. "That has Posey written all over it."

"So why would he have Posey help him?" I ask.

"Isn't it obvious? You freaked him out by leaving and now he doesn't know what to do. He's desperate and is leaning on Posey to help him." She glances at her nails. "Wrong move if you ask me, but you pushed him to this point."

"Well, he freaked me out with his giant cock and dirty talking." I toss my hands up in the air. "What the hell was I supposed to do?"

"Fair trade." She smirks and nods at me. "Text him back."

"What the hell do I say? You're welcome?"

"That's a good start. But I have a better idea."

HALSEY

"MAIN HOLE?" I yell as I look up at Posey who seems very satisfied with himself. "You called her vagina her main hole? What the fuck is wrong with you?"

"Told you not to let him have your phone," Silas says. "This is *oye my dick* all over again."

"You know, when he helped me, it actually went pretty well now that I think about it," Eli says, scratching his chin.

"It went well for both of you," Posey says and looks at me. "And this will go well for you too. Just watch."

Through a clenched jaw I say, "How the fuck is this going to go well for me?"

"Because you brought up sex and that will bring her back to last night. Knowing you and what you have in your pants, she'll be transported back into a beautiful moment of ecstasy, so when she sees you, she'll be reminded of that. It's called subliminal messaging."

I punch him dead in the arm and say, "It's called being a fucking moron. Jesus Christ." I stand from my seat and move toward the center of the locker room while Posey rubs his arm with a hurt expression. "I have to fix this."

"Or maybe you don't," Eli says.

"What do you mean?" I ask, looking to him for advice since he's the one person who isn't invested like the rest of the idiots I've involved.

"If there's one thing I know, it's that you keep pressing forward. You ignore the awkward tension and keep taking what you want, then it will work out for you."

"You want him to just . . . keep doing her?" Silas asks.

"Yup." Eli shrugs. "Keep moving forward. Keep giving her what she was taking last night. At some point, she's going to break. Until then, show her how you have ruined her for any other man."

Just then, my phone dings with a text back.

Silence falls over the locker room as I look down at the text.

Blakely: *Thanks for impaling me with your giant stick.*

My mouth goes dry as I slowly look up at the boys.

Posey smiles and says, "From the look on your face, I bet you owe me a thank-you. Go ahead, I'm all ears. Lay it on me."

"Fuck off," I say as I sit back down on the bench.

Keep moving forward? Keep fucking her? *Is that even a question? Of course, I want to keep fucking her.* I've never had a better night than last night. Hands down, sex with Blakely is mind-blowing. The noises she makes. Her insatiable greed. *Her mouth. Her body.*

Keep fucking Blakely? Yes. Please. That's something I can do, something I want to do. Only question is, will *she* want that?

Chapter Eighteen

BLAKELY

This is so awkward.

Here I am, slipping into Halsey's bed without him, after we were so sinful in it the night before. But he's on my mind. Once my responsibilities at the game were done, I booked it out of there and came straight home where I took a bath and soaked in my feelings.

Halsey played for a grand total of one minute. I believe they wanted to see how he was out on the ice, and from what I saw, he was really good. How he can skate with a rolled ankle, I have no idea, but then again, the training staff are miracle workers.

And I hate to admit it, but when he was on the ice, I couldn't take my eyes off him and how he effortlessly glided around the rink, passing the puck and avoiding being slammed into the wall.

He's so good at hockey, it's why he's so mesmerizing to watch. I wonder what he was like out on the ice with his brother. They were probably magic.

But now that I slipped into my silk pajama set—yup, it's all I had left that was clean—sleep eludes me as I'm turned away from the door and on the far edge of my side. I could not be more obvious.

I told myself I was going to be asleep by the time he got home, but from my mind racing over what's transpired between us, I can't seem to find that natural sleep I'm looking for.

It's why I'm getting up to grab some of my melatonin when the front door opens and shuts.

Oh God, he's home.

I slink back under the blankets and curl into my pillow where I pretend to sleep. Besides the entryway, the lights are off in the apartment, so when he turns that one off, the entire room is drenched in darkness. The only light is from the sliver of the moon peeking through the curtains.

His feet pad down the hallway and into the bedroom where I hear him set his phone on his nightstand and plug it in.

Be cool.

You're asleep.

For all he knows, you've been sleeping for a long time.

He moves into the bathroom where I hear him brush his teeth and remove his suit that he's required to wear to and from the arena.

Everything is fine. No need to worry about what's going on. *He thinks you're asleep. Just stay still and everything will be okay.*

I let out a slow breath, not wanting to be detected but wanting to calm my racing nerves and, when he leaves the bathroom and comes into the bedroom, I mentally prepare myself.

This is it.

As still as still can be.

Maybe add a little snore to make it believable . . . wait no, don't do that.

He slips into the bed and then to my utter surprise and shock, he places his arm around me, his palm to my stomach, and he drags me across the bed and right into his chest.

His mouth falls to my ear as he lightly whispers, "You belong here."

My breath catches in my chest as his hand slides under my shirt and his warm palm presses against my stomach.

Okay, was not expecting that.

Well, that's okay, we can work with this. So he likes to spoon. The man probably—

Oh God, did he just swipe at my boob with his thumb?

I hold my breath as I wait in anticipation to see if he does it again.

When he doesn't, I realize I was imagining it.

There was no swipe.

It must have been the fabric of my shirt—

His thumb drags across my breast again and this time, I know it was intentional because he pulls me in even closer, his erection pressing against my ass.

And that's all it takes.

A wave of arousal pulses through me as his mouth finds my ear and he asks, "Why are you wearing clothes?"

Because I'm the fool who thinks that we can forget about what happened last night. In reality, we can't forget about it at all.

His hand moves out from under my shirt, which makes me want to protest, but then, his dexterous fingers start unbuttoning my silk top.

"This should not be on you," he says as he makes his way up to the top. I don't even think I can unbutton my shirt that fast yet, he does it with one hand.

When he's done, he parts the shirt open, exposing my breasts, and he cups one of them in his rough, calloused hand. I try to hold back, but I groan as I press my ass into his erection.

"Mmm, that's it, baby. I knew you weren't sleeping."

Of course I wasn't, how could I, knowing he was going to slip into bed with me?

He circles my nipple lightly with his fingers while he kisses my neck, and the combination of the two has me throbbing between my legs—something I now know this devilish man has over me. I know how amazing he can make me feel and, even though I'm out of my mind with confusion, there is one thing I know for sure. I want him to make me come again.

Once he circles my nipple a few more times until it's completely hard, he pinches it with his index finger and thumb, rolling the sensitive nub and causing me to gasp.

"I fucking love your tits," he says as he moves to the other one. I roll to my back an inch, giving him better access. "I could play with them for hours."

I could come from him just playing with them.

"But I have other plans," he says as he moves his hand down my stomach to the waistband of my shorts. He pauses for a second and says, "If you don't want to come on my cock tonight, tell me right now, or else, I plan on destroying this pussy."

I squeeze my eyes shut as my bare chest rises and falls into the night air.

There's no way I'm stopping him, and he knows it because he doesn't give me much time to react. He pushes my shorts down, and I kick them to the side right before he props my top leg up into a figure four position, opening me up more.

"Now let me see how wet you are." His lips skim over my ear, sending chills down my arm as he slips his hand between my legs. His fingers drag along my center and when he feels how drenched I am, he groans in satisfaction. "Such a good fucking girl," he says before bringing his fingers to his mouth and sucking on them. "I've been craving this pussy all goddamn day. Have you been craving my cock?"

He shifts behind me, pulling down his briefs and pushing them all the way off so his cock is now lined up against my ass.

"Y-yes," I answer.

"Yes, what?" he asks as his hand floats back up to my breasts where he grips and massages them, letting the air hit my pussy. It turns me on even more.

"Yes, I've been craving your cock."

"Good girl," he says as he releases my breasts and positions his penis at my entrance. I take a deep breath and then let it out as he pushes inside.

It's sore at first, but once he's fully in, all I feel is satisfaction.

"The sounds you made last night, I couldn't stop thinking about them." He pumps into me, cupping my breast with one hand while his other now grips my neck. He presses down carefully, making me aware that he has me by the neck, but not too much to scare me. And it only throws fuel to the flame of my arousal. The possession, it's so sexy. "I'm obsessed with hearing the way you come and feeling the way you squeeze my thick cock." He pumps again. "I've wanted to touch you all goddamn day." He pinches my nipple and I groan loud enough for him to do it again. "I craved this cunt." He presses his head against mine. "Fuck, I need more."

He wraps his arm around my stomach and then rolls us so he's lying on his back, propped up by a pillow, and I'm lying on top of him, my back to his chest. My top flies open, exposing my breasts and with both hands, he grips my nipples and pinches them as he whispers, "Fuck my cock, Blakely."

"God," I groan as I move my hips up and down along his body.

This position, it's new, it's different, and it feels so fucking amazing. I've noticed quickly that I like him behind me, taking me from behind in any way. This being one of them.

"Fuck, Halsey," I whisper as I move my hips faster.

"You close, baby?" he asks.

I nod. "Really close."

"Good." He kisses the side of my head. "Me too."

And then he pinches my nipples harder, rolling them and pulling on them, making me so goddamn ready that it only takes a few more pumps of my hips before my stomach bottoms out, my entire body goes numb, and my orgasm hits me so hard that I cry out his name into the dark of the night.

"That greedy fucking cunt," he says right before his cock swells inside me and he's coming, wave after wave until his body goes slack and we're completely sated.

He loops his arm around my waist, holding me still as he stays inside me. He kisses my shoulder, my head, and then he taps my chin, forcing me to turn so he can kiss my lips momentarily.

But even though the kiss is brief, it feels far more intimate than what we just did.

After a few more seconds of making out, he releases me and helps me to the bathroom where we both clean up. When we're done, he takes me back to the bed, but removes my shirt, and leaves me naked with him. He slips in behind me, spoons me to his chest, and he whispers, "This is where you belong. Don't fucking forget it."

Talk about being fucked into a dream-filled slumber.

———

OKAY, so yeah, he told me I belonged in his arms last night. No big deal. But that didn't prevent me from slipping out of them this morning, taking a shower, and getting ready for work. *And I'm still walking funny because I needed to ride his light post again throughout the night. Who am I?*

I might be cock-shocked, but I have things to do today, like give the team my notice and try to figure out an action plan to stop thinking about Halsey's penis between my legs.

Good luck to me.

After I finish my hair and makeup, which I feel slightly ashamed to say I spend more time on than I normally do, I prepare to leave my room. I convince myself the effort's because I was feeling glamorous this morning, but deep down, I know it's because when I walk out of this room, I'm going to see Halsey and I want him to look at me with dark, sinister eyes.

It's also why I chose the dress that was hanging on the back of my door.

Deep red, it hits me mid-thigh, has sleeves to lend toward the professional side, but with the square neckline, it makes my boobs look amazing. The same boobs Halsey said he could play with for hours. I painted my lips in the same red color, and I paired the outfit with three-inch heels that I know will make my legs look amazing.

So . . . yeah . . .

I finish getting dressed, and when I look at myself in the mirror, I feel . . . gorgeous.

I turn to the side, checking out my ass in the dress, and then turn to the other side. It took me longer than I wanted to cover up all of Halsey's bite marks, but I think I did a pretty good job. My hair flows down my back in soft waves, and my eyes stand out from my thick coat of mascara. I can't remember the last time I felt this pretty.

Oh wait, I can . . . when Halsey looked at me when we were trying on dresses.

I close my eyes and take a deep breath.

How?

How can one man completely change my way of thinking? My way of feeling? It boggles my mind. Perry wasn't a bad guy, so how can Halsey make me feel exponentially more than Perry ever made me feel?

May be something I might never understand.

I grab my purse for the day and then on a deep breath, open my door, and sure enough, Halsey is waiting in the kitchen, watching my door with a cup of coffee in hand. Disheveled and fresh from bed, I've never seen a sexier sight.

"Morning," he says, staring at me, his eyes trailing from my heels up to my breasts, and then my face.

"Morning," I say slightly awkwardly as I make my way toward the front door.

But he doesn't let me walk past him as he puts his hand out and stops me. "Leaving so soon?"

"Early morning again," I say.

He nods and sets his coffee mug down.

Whereas yesterday he seemed confused, this morning he seems sure of himself. He moves in close and then walks behind me. He slips his hand around my waist, pushes my hair to the side, and presses a kiss to my neck. "I don't like that you cover up my marks."

"I . . . I can't walk around with them."

"Afraid people will know you've been fucking me?" he asks. "Or are you afraid they'll think you're a dirty fucking girl?"

I swallow as his hand comes up to my neck, the exact place where he held it last night. "The latter," I answer.

"Good answer," he says as his other hand travels to the hem of my dress. "Is this for me? Or someone else?"

"For me," I answer.

His lips smile against my neck. "Liar." He pulls the hem up, exposing my thong, and then he tugs on my underwear, pulling it down my legs until they're completely off. He then adjusts my skirt back and moves around to the front of me. "You don't need this." He holds up my thong and then sticks it in the waistband of his shorts. He reaches for his coffee, leans against the counter, and says, "Have a good day."

Uh . . . he wants me to just walk out of here without underwear?

I'm all for some kink, but this dress is short.

"Halsey, I need my underwear."

"As far as I'm concerned, you don't," he says and then moves into the kitchen where he pulls the carton of eggs from the fridge, almost as if he's dismissing me.

What is happening?

Who is this man and what has he done with the Halsey I *thought* I knew?

Because the quiet, understated man I've lived with for a few weeks is nowhere to be seen. He's an alpha male with my thong hanging over the waistband of his shorts, and there has to be a reason for that.

THERE . . . sent.

I sit back in my chair and shut my eyes. I spoke with my

manager first thing this morning when she arrived, telling her about the opportunity I've been handed. I told her I'd have stayed with the Agitators, but the opportunity was too good to pass up. She agreed with me and told me she wished me the best of luck and asked me to send my formal resignation through email, which I just did.

Now . . . to find a way to tell Penny.

Knock. Knock.

Oh God, is that her?

I open my eyes just in time to see Halsey walk into my office wearing a pair of joggers and a tight-fitting T-shirt. When his eyes meet mine, my body immediately builds with lust. He shuts the door behind him, locks it, and then walks toward me with one thing on his mind . . . me.

"Wh-what are you doing here?" I ask as he comes around my desk.

He doesn't answer me. He tugs me up from my chair, moves it to the side, and then hikes up my skirt before sitting me on the desk.

"Halsey," I say breathlessly as he moves to his knees and places my feet on his shoulders. My hands fall behind me to prevent me from scooting back, and his eyes meet mine.

"I need to fucking taste you," he says right before burying his head between my legs and pressing his tongue along my slit.

"Holy fuck," I say as my head falls back.

"Jesus Christ, Blakely," he says as he makes long, languid strokes with his tongue. "You taste so fucking good." He grips my ass, holding me in place, his fingers digging into my skin as he picks up the pace of his tongue.

It's pathetic how quickly my body tightens, and my world starts to darken around me, my muscles tensing and building toward my impending orgasm whenever he pleasures me.

"You're close, aren't you?" he asks as my legs tremble next to his head.

All I can do is nod as he slips two fingers inside me and presses that spot that will make me scream.

I bite down on my bottom lip as his tongue flicks rapidly against my clit, bringing me so much pleasure that I don't think I'll be able to stay quiet.

"Oh God," I quietly groan as my body tenses.

His fingers move faster.

His tongue presses harder.

And within seconds, I'm clamping my hand over my mouth and moaning as my body convulses from a very quick and intense orgasm.

Halsey laps up every second of it, too, continuing to run his tongue over my clit until I have nothing left inside me. He kisses my inner thigh, then the other, and then kisses my pussy before pulling back. Staring down at me, he says, "You're so fucking hot when you come."

Then he shoves his joggers and briefs down, exposing his large erection, and sits on my office chair.

"I want you on your knees, and I want that red lipstick all over my goddamn cock."

I blink a few times, still catching my breath, but when I see him staring at me, stroking himself, jealousy rocks through me.

I stand on my wobbly legs, push my skirt down, and then kneel before him. I take his heavy cock in my hand and bring the tip to my mouth.

"Fuck yes," he says as he slouches in the chair and grips my hair in his fist.

His encouragement empowers me, so I take him deeper, stretching my mouth wide but also letting my teeth scrape along the veins of his length.

"Your fucking mouth, Blakely," he says. "It's so fucking perfect. Just like that. Take me as far as you can."

I bring him into my mouth as far as I can go and then pull back, giving myself a chance to breathe. I grip the base of his cock and start pumping him as I suck the tip, swirling my tongue around and around until I feel him shake.

He groans, the heavenly sound hitting me all the way down

to my toes, and when he tugs on my hair, I know he's growing closer and closer.

"You're so damn hot, your mouth. Fuck, Blakely. Make me come on your tongue."

I bring him into my mouth again, this time sucking harder, hollowing my cheeks, and he groans even louder, almost too loud. He starts assisting me, helping me move my head up and down as he squirms beneath me.

Wanting to push him over the edge, I move my other hand between his legs and cup his balls while moving my fingers behind them and pressing against his sensitive flesh.

"Fuck . . . me," he says as he tenses, his hand gripping the armrest.

Knowing he's close, I bring him to the back of my throat, causing me to gag for a moment, but that must do the trick, because his hand grips tighter in my hair, his quads tense and he says, "Swallow my cum," right before he falls over the edge.

And I listen.

I swallow every last drop before pulling him out of my mouth and licking up his length until he's clean.

His grip on my hair loosens, and his hand falls to my face, where he brushes his thumb over my cheek tenderly.

He helps me to my feet before putting himself back into his pants. When he stands, his hand goes to my face again, and his thumb swipes under my mouth.

"Might need to touch up your lipstick." Then he leans forward and presses a kiss to my neck.

My jaw.

My cheek.

And then right on my mouth before he steps aside and moves toward my office door.

I want to call out to him, ask him what the hell is going on, but before I can muster the courage, he's gone.

"I'M SO glad you could make it to dinner," I say to Ollie as she pierces her steak salad with her fork.

"Me too. It's been a while since I've been able to meet up with you ladies."

After the blow job in my office, I realized there was no way I'd be able to go back to the apartment tonight knowing damn well that the guys have an off day. I don't know what I'd do with Halsey with that much spare time. So I worked late and arranged a dinner with Winnie, Pacey's girl, and Ollie. Penny wanted some family time with Eli and the baby, I completely understood. And I was quietly relieved she wasn't coming as I hadn't told her about the new job. Yet. *Was not looking forward to that conversation.*

"I asked you guys here for a reason."

Winnie and Ollie both look up at me, momentarily pausing their forks. "What's going on?" Winnie asks.

"First of all, this is a vault, right? We won't go home and tell our men what we talked about?"

"Those gossiping hens?" Winnie asks. "No, I'm good. I don't need Pacey inserting himself in whatever you're about to say. He'd probably never shut up about it."

"Same," Ollie adds. "I have enough on my plate with work. I won't be saying anything to Silas."

"Thank you." I let out a deep breath and say, "Halsey and I had sex."

"What?" Ollie and Winnie say at the same time.

"Holy crap. When?" Winnie asks.

"Two days ago, and then last night, and then today in my office."

"In the office." Ollie smiles. "That's hot."

"It was." My cheeks turn red. "He . . . uh . . . sent me to work with no underwear on. And then he showed me why."

Winnie shakes her head. "Halsey Holmes. Now, that surprises me. Ever since I've known him, I was under the impression that he didn't care for anything other than books and hockey. I didn't even think he knew what sex was."

"Oh . . . he knows," I say. "He knows really well."

"Wow, I had no idea." Winnie shakes her head. "So this is a good thing?"

"I don't know," I say. "I've been staying at his place because my apartment flooded. And well, in all honesty, I invited you to dinner because I didn't want to be alone with him for so long tonight. I was afraid of what might happen."

"How could you be afraid?" Ollie asks. "Clearly, he would have stripped you down to nothing and had fun."

"Exactly."

Winnie and Ollie exchange glances. "Why is that a bad thing?" Winnie asks. "I know the moment I get home, Pacey will do the same thing, and I can't wait."

"Same with Silas," Ollie says.

I stir my fork around my salad and say, "We haven't really talked about what has happened between us. One moment, we were friends and I wasn't thinking about him in that way at all, and then the next he's telling me that I'm a good girl right before he spanks me."

"Ooo, he spanks you?" Ollie asks. "That is one of my favorite things. Sometimes, Silas will just insert himself from behind and spank me until I come. He gets off so hard from that."

Wow . . . yeah, I guess I'd expect that from Silas.

"But," Ollie adds, "I see where you're coming from. Maybe you need to have a conversation with him."

"And say what?" I ask. "Oh hey, Halsey, I've noticed that you like sticking your penis inside me lately. Want to have a conversation as to why?"

"I think it's a great opening line," Winnie says with a smile. "But also, Halsey seems like the type of guy who'd slow down if you asked him to."

"But I don't want him to slow down."

"Then what do you want?" Ollie asks.

"That's the thing, I don't know. I've never been more confused, and I'm using you two to avoid the situation."

Winnie chuckles. "Well, I do love being a decoy, so why don't we focus on something else."

"Great idea," Ollie says. "Tell us . . . is Halsey pierced like Silas?"

I give her some serious side-eye. "Not helping."

She laughs. "Sorry. How about this . . . I heard you might be taking a new job with a certain company."

"What?" Winnie asks. "You're leaving the Agitators?"

Shit, how could I forget about Ollie working for The Jock Report?

"Remember when I said this was all in the vault? Well, I mean it. I haven't told Penny yet. I'm just trying to find the right way to inform her."

"Yeah, she's going to be upset. Wait." Winnie looks up. "Are you moving?"

I shake my head. "No, I don't want to, and Huxley said I could work remotely."

"They really are the best," Ollie says. "I report more closely with Ryot Bisley than the Cane brothers, but they are seriously amazing. There's a reason they're one of the top corporations to work for."

"I'm really excited about it, but I haven't told anyone besides my boss."

"Not even Halsey?" Winnie asks.

"Remember, they don't talk," Ollie says with a wink.

"Do you know when you're going to tell everyone?"

"Soon. Penny is the one I have to break the news to first. I think I might go to her place for dinner when the boys are out of town next."

"And Halsey . . ." Ollie asks.

"That I don't know."

Chapter Nineteen

HALSEY

"How does the ankle feel?" OC asks as he comes up to me in the training room.

"Good," I answer while I wait for Grace to come over and wrap it.

"Think you can play more tonight?"

"I'm hoping for it. Up to this one." I nod at Grace, who walks up with some pre-wrap in her hand.

OC smiles. "Hey, Grace. How are you?"

She glances over at him and gives him a curt smile. "Good." She then turns to me and taps the edge of the table. "Scoot down."

"Yeah, okay. I'll catch you later," OC says. I watch him wait for Grace to say something, but she doesn't.

Interesting.

When he's out of sight, I say, "What was that about?"

"What was what about?" she asks.

"It seemed like there was some tension there."

"No tension." She smiles up at me but then gets back to work.

Okay, I'm not buying it. I tuck away the information for now, though, because I don't want to make her uncomfortable, especially when she holds the right to tell me to sit my ass on the bench tonight. And I don't want to do that. I need to fucking play.

I have all of this pent-up adrenaline inside me that I need to take out on the ice.

And where is the adrenaline coming from? Blakely, that's where.

Last night, when she came home from dinner, she took a while getting ready for bed, and when she finally came over to sleep with me, she was wearing pajama pants and a T-shirt. I told her it was unacceptable, stripped her out of it, and then proceeded to fuck her three times.

Each time, she asked for more.

In all of my life, I've never had sex like this.

Ever.

Point-blank, this is the most and best sex of my goddamn life.

And the thing about it is I can't get enough of her. I can't satiate this feeling I have inside every time I see her, and she's the same way. We don't talk . . . we just fuck.

I know that will come back and hurt me at some point because I have so much to say to her—so fucking much—but I feel like I'm on borrowed time. She's still awkward. She's still a flight risk. And I'm scared that with one wrong move, she'll take off without warning.

So I'll keep doing what I'm doing until she's comfortable.

"So what do you think?" I ask Grace. "Think I can play more tonight?"

"I think so," she says as she tears a piece of tape with her teeth and then lines it along my ankle. She looks me in the eye and adds, "But if you reinjure this because you're going too hard, I'm going to be very upset with you."

I chuckle. "You and everyone else."

"Then you know what's at stake. Good." She finishes taping and then sets her things to the side. "Be careful, but you should be good. If it hurts even remotely, you come off that ice. Understood?"

I nod. "Understood."

With that, I hop off the table and head to the locker room.

This is exactly what I need: a place to dispense all of this energy pulsing through me.

———

"THEY'RE TRYING TO HURT YOU," Silas says as he tilts his helmet back on his head, the game playing out in front of us.

"You don't think I fucking know that?" I say as I watch our second string take the puck down the ice. I squirt some water into my mouth and take a deep breath. "Every chance they get, they're trying to slam me into the boards."

"Posey is getting pissed," Silas says. "He's going to unleash soon."

"Let him," I reply. "This is fucking ridiculous."

"Get up, boys," our coach says, indicating we're about to switch up the lines.

Silas and I both pull our helmets down and snap them into place.

"Change it up," Coach calls out, and Silas and I are out on the ice immediately. I fall behind Pacey at the goal, grabbing the puck from him. Silas, OC, and I head toward our goal, shooting the puck back and forth and driving it forward.

It's the third period, we're tied one to one, and I know it's because I'm not at peak performance. I'm good enough to be able to push it these last five minutes.

I flick the puck to the right, where Silas grabs it and then passes it to OC. I move toward the middle, slice to the right, and wait for the puck, only to be slammed right into the boards, the move knocking the air right from my lungs.

I crumple to the ice while the whistle is blown, and a commotion breaks out on the ice. I glance up just in time to catch Posey uppercutting someone in the ribs.

Fuck . . .

Silas comes over to me while the fight breaks out, and he places his gloved hand on my back. "You good?"

"Yeah," I answer as I slowly come to a stand.

"How's the ankle?"

"Fine," I say as I rest my hands on my thighs and bend over. "Just got the wind knocked out of me."

"Well, Posey is taking care of it."

Under any other circumstances, I'd probably join him, but I don't want to injure myself even more, so instead, I watch from a distance, planning my attack for when game is in play again. *But fuck, is it awesome to be out on the ice again.*

THE APARTMENT IS DARK AGAIN.

No surprise there.

The question is, what will she be wearing tonight?

After Posey was put in the penalty box, along with Rhodes from the other team, Silas, OC, and I drove the puck up the ice again. We missed a few shots, but with one minute remaining, we were able to score. An assist from me, a goal from OC.

Thank fuck we won because I would not have enjoyed losing that game.

I toss my keys on the end table and walk toward the bedroom. Blakely's not curled up on the bed. Confused, I set my phone on the nightstand to charge it and go to the bathroom where I quickly strip out of my suit and brush my teeth. When I'm ready for bed, I check the bed again, and when I don't see her, I head into the living room. She emerges from her bedroom, wearing a pair of black lace underwear and a lingerie top tied together just at her cleavage.

Jesus.

Fuck.

I wet my lips and ask, "That for me?"

She walks right past me and replies, "It's for me."

I follow closely behind, and just as she reaches the bedroom, I step up behind her and loop my arm around her waist, pulling her into my chest.

When her ass rubs against my growing cock, I whisper, "Wearing that was a bad idea if it was for you because my dick seems to think differently."

I glide my hands up her stomach to her breasts and cup them. Her head falls back on my shoulder, and that's all the indication I need. Green light.

I tug on the tie of her top until it loosens and her tits spring free. Then from over her shoulder, I stare down at her hardened nipples and start playing with them, loving the way she rocks against me as I play with her.

She's so fucking responsive to everything I do to her. I never have to question if she likes how I play with her because she *shows* me.

"How do you want my cock tonight, Blakely?"

"I . . . I don't know," she answers breathlessly.

"I want to play," I say as I leave her top on but keep it open. I sit her on the bed and then reach into my nightstand to pull out two vibrators and some lube. I toss them on the bed and watch her look them over, a curious gaze in her eyes.

I shed my boxer briefs and then bring my cock to her mouth where I run the tip along her lips. Being the good girl she is, she parts her lips and swirls her tongue around the head before moving to the underside and dragging her tongue up and down my length.

Christ, that feels so good.

"Sinful fucking mouth," I say as I pull away from her and then lie on the bed. "Ready to play?"

I pick up the thinner vibrator and put some lube on it, then hand it to her and say, "Play with me."

Her eyes light up when she realizes what I want.

"Really?" she asks, her breath picking up.

"Do whatever the fuck you want to me, just make me come."

She switches the vibrator on, straddles one of my legs, and then she drags the vibrator over just the tip of my cock and across my balls. I spread my legs for her and place my hands behind my head. I see her swallow right before she moves the vibrator down lower. Smiling, I watch as she finds her way, and when she reaches my ass, I groan in anticipation.

Her unsure eyes flash to mine, and I give her a nod. "Give it to me, Blakely."

Fuck, I can't remember the last time I did this, but hell, do I want it more than ever, especially with her. I want her to know she can play with me any way that she wants. I'm open to every-thing, and she never has to be shy around me. Showing her this vulnerability is a step in that direction.

She slowly inserts the vibrator inside me, and I mentally relax, letting the vibrations calm me as she pushes it in.

"That's it, baby, make me so fucking hard."

When she lets go of the vibrator, leaving it where it is, she sits back on her heels as her eyes transfix on my cock, which is grow-ing, twitching, and seeking satisfaction as it stretches up my stomach.

"I love your cock so much," she says as she leans forward and presses her tongue along the length.

"Your mouth is going to make me come." I take deep breaths. "I want you to come with me."

"How?" she asks.

"Grab the other vibrator," I say through gritted teeth as my entire body starts firing off with pleasure. Fuck, it feels so damn good.

So.

Fucking.

Good.

She placed it in just the right spot and there's no way I'm going to last long.

When she grabs the vibrator, I say, "Straddle my cock."

She moves over me, her tits swaying with her every movement. And when she's settled and lowers her wet pussy along my length, I feel full satisfaction. *She's turned on by me being turned on.* Not sure anything is sexier than that.

I take the vibrator from her and slide it along my length, directly under her clit so we sandwich it between us and experience the vibration together as I turn it on.

Immediately, her hands fall to my chest as her head dips forward.

"Oh God, Halsey."

Her fingers dig into my pecs. I grip her breasts as she starts to slowly and carefully rock over the vibrator. Between the vibrator and the friction, I'm seconds away.

I squeeze her breasts, loving how she's so urgently seeking her pleasure.

"Oh my God," she moans, her nails now digging deep into my skin. "Oh fuck, Halsey. It's . . . it's too much."

"It's so hot when you're on top of me."

She sucks in a sharp breath of air. "I . . . I'm going to come." That was quick.

I toss the vibrator to the side and witness her anger as her eyes widen.

"I want that drenched pussy squeezing my cock when you come. Sit up." She lifts just enough for me to position her over my cock, and then I slam her down.

"Oh my God," she screams, her head falling back, her tits pressed up.

"Fuck me, Blakely. Fuck me hard."

And she does.

She lifts up and slams down on me, rocking her hips, twisting them, swirling, going absolutely feral. *Fuck, she's breathtaking.*

"Harder," I say through clenched teeth as a bolt of pleasure shoots up my spine thanks to the vibrator. My cock begins to swell, and I'm right on the precipice. "Jesus fucking . . . Christ," I shout as my cock explodes inside her. I shoot my cum so hard that I black out. Everything around me fades into nothing as I hear her cry of pleasure in the distance, followed by my favorite feeling in the entire world—her pussy clenching around my cock.

"Fuck!" I yell as I feel myself double down, my orgasm still ripping through me.

"It's too much," she says as she rocks her hips hard. "Oh fuck. Oh God. Ohhhhhhh . . . fuck," she cries as her nails break my skin.

My God, her passion. Her fire. Nothing is better than this. Nothing will ever beat this feeling of euphoria. *She's mine. Fucking mine.*

When she collapses on top of me, I roll her to the mattress and then pull the vibrator out of me and toss it on the ground. I then spread her legs and bring my mouth to her pussy where I start lapping at her clit, tasting every last bit of her until she's writhing again, her head flailing back and forth, and her voice hoarse from screaming.

"Fuck," she says softly, almost as if she's on the verge of tears. When she slowly opens her eyes and stares up at me, a look of wonderment in her expression, I know at this very moment that there's no way in hell I'm ever letting this woman walk away from me.

Never.

———

"MORNING," I say as Blakely emerges from her room, fully dressed, ready to avoid me this morning, just like every other morning.

And just like every other morning, she takes my breath away as she tentatively walks toward the kitchen.

This morning, she's wearing high-waisted, wide-legged black trousers and a long-sleeved crop top that shows off about an inch of her stomach. Her hair is tied back into a ponytail, and she's wearing that red fucking lipstick again.

"Good morning," she says as she walks into the kitchen, avoiding eye contact.

Either she's completely embarrassed by what we've been doing, or she has no idea how to react to it. Either way, I need those eyes to look at me. I need them to see me for who I am, not just this man who keeps fucking her over and over again.

I don't want to scare her away, but I also don't want her thinking I'm a sex freak who's only using her for that.

I have to leave today for a short away trip, and the last thing I want to do is leave with this awkward tension between us.

But breaking that tension is going to be tough.

"This is for you," I say to her as she grabs a protein shake from the fridge.

She turns around and takes in the folded-up shirt in my hand.

"What's that?" she asks.

I set my coffee down and unfold it. "To wear to bed when I'm gone."

Her eyes meet mine as she says, "You're giving me one of your shirts to wear at night?"

"Yes," I say and take a step forward. I tilt her chin up with my finger and say, "You better wear it."

Her eyes search mine for a moment before she says, "I will."

"Good." I close the little space between us and press a light kiss to her lips before pulling away. Like I said, baby steps. I want her to know I'm thinking ahead, but I'm not pushing her too much, too hard. "You look absolutely beautiful today, Blakely."

"Thank you." She glances at her outfit. "I'm glad I grabbed a number of work outfits before I left my apartment."

That's a good reminder to check if her landlord has actually fumigated her apartment. *Not that I want her going back there. I don't want her going anywhere.*

"Me too. I have to pack. Have a good day, Blakely."

"Safe flight." I start to walk away when she calls out, "Halsey?"

I look over my shoulder to find her holding my shirt close to her chest. "Yeah?"

"Thank you for this."

"You're welcome," I answer before I walk back to my bedroom with a huge smile.

Maybe I'm doing everything right after all.

———

"I THINK I ate some bad bologna," Posey says as he clutches his stomach on the plane. "Not feeling too great."

"Maybe you should stop eating bologna," Silas says.

"I second that idea," Pacey adds.

We're sitting at a table for four. Silas, Posey, Pacey, and me. Across the aisle is Hornsby and OC. We're attempting to play cards, but Posey keeps stopping to take deep breaths.

"Dude, if you're going to puke, can you not sit across from me?" Silas asks. "Maybe go hang out by the bathroom or something."

"I second that idea," Pacey repeats.

A sweat breaks out across Posey's forehead. "Yeah, maybe not a bad idea." He stands from the table and shoots back to the bathroom.

"He's an idiot," Silas mutters as Hornsby shifts into the seat where Posey was sitting.

I glance over at OC, whose head leans against the side of the plane, his eyes closed.

Hornsby whispers, "Did you guys see this?"

He flips his phone toward us so we can see the screen.

"What is it?" Silas asks.

"A job posting," Hornsby replies. "For Blakely's job. A friend just asked me if it was a good job or not."

"What?" I say as I snap the phone from his hands and read the posting.

My eyes scan it so fast that I barely process what it says.

My heart hammers in my chest as I realize that, yes, it's a posting for her job.

"What the fuck . . ." I whisper.

"She didn't say anything to you?" Hornsby asks.

"Does it look like she said something to me?" I ask as I set his phone down and lean my head back, my mind swirling with every thought conceivable.

How long has she known?

Did she know at the wedding?

Is she only fucking me, knowing that she's leaving?

Is that why she's grown detached? Why she leaves every morning before we can actually talk? Because she's fucking leaving for a new job?

"Dude, are you okay?" Pacey asks.

"No," I shout. "I'm not fucking okay." I pinch the bridge of my nose. "She took another job and didn't tell me. Is she moving? Is that why . . ." I clench my jaw. "Is that why she's been so emotionally distant?"

"She's still avoiding you in the morning?" Hornsby asks.

"Yes, and I did what you told me to do. I kept fucking her. What I thought was good advice. Now, I'm fucking a girl who's probably leaving. No wonder she's not talking—she doesn't want to grow attached. I'm dispensable to her."

"You don't know that," Pacey says softly.

"Then explain to me what's going on."

The boys all exchange glances, silence falling among us.

"That's what I thought," I say as I stand. "Fuck . . . this."

I walk to the back of the plane where I can be alone.

BLAKELY

"WAIT, have we really drank a bottle and a half of wine?" I ask Penny as I reach for the bottle to refill our glasses.

She scans my apartment, taking in the empty to-go boxes from The Garbanzo Bean, the one empty bottle, and the child-free space, thanks to Penny's parents who are watching Holden.

"I think we did." She wiggles her glass at me. "Fill 'er up."

I chuckle and finish off the bottle, filling our glasses for us both.

"So is there a reason you lured me into your sex-pad with wine and good food?" Penny asks.

"Can't a girl just hang out with her friend?"

"She can," Penny replies. "But you also have this look on your face like you need to tell me something. Are you in love with Halsey? Because I approve."

I shake my head. "No."

"Shame." She sighs heavily. "He's perfect for you."

"I don't want to talk about Halsey right now."

"Well, that seems loaded, but I'll put that on hold. What did you want to talk to me about?"

Here goes nothing.

I take her hand in mine and lift her glass of wine to her lips. "Take a sip, and then I'll tell you."

Her brow creases.

She stares for a moment.

And then her eyes widen.

"Did you take that job?" I wince, and that's all the confirmation she needs. "No, seriously?" Her eyes start to well up with tears. "Are you leaving me? Moving away? I can't be a mom with a baby daddy who is in and out on away trips. I need you."

I squeeze her hand to calm her panic. "I took the job, but I'm staying here."

"Wait . . . like, you're not moving?"

I shake my head. "No. I don't want to move, and I told Huxley that. I want to stay here. I like it here. I'm comfortable here. And how could I leave you, Penny?"

"That's what I'm saying, how could you possibly leave me?" She tips back her glass and slugs it all back before lowering it and huffing. "Jesus, don't scare me like that."

I chuckle and take a sip of my wine. "I thought you were going to be mad that I was leaving my job, you know, since I won't be at the arena with you."

"I mean, that sucks, sure, but I care more that you stay here. And from what you've told me, the job seems amazing, so I don't blame you for wanting to make a change."

"Yeah, Huxley made it hard to turn down."

"Yeah, he seems like a man who gets what he wants. I wonder what it would be like to be married to him."

"I'm sure he demands a lot in the bedroom like Halsey."

Penny's eyes widen again with intrigue. "Oh yes, tell me more about that."

"I thought we were talking about the job."

Penny waves her hand in dismissal. "You took the job, and you're not moving. We covered that. Now . . . let's talk about Halsey." She wiggles her brows.

"I told you—"

"Do you really think I'm going to sit here with wine in my hand—well, an empty glass of wine in hand—and no baby and not talk about the man you've been fucking?"

"No, but I was going to put up an effort to avoid it."

"Nice try. Now, tell me why you're just having sex but nothing else. I thought you guys were getting close. Wasn't he your pretend boyfriend for the wedding?"

"He was," I say, "but ever since then, I don't know what to say to him. He's different in my eyes."

"How so?" Penny asks.

"I told you," I groan. "He shook me. I can't look at him the same. He's a completely different man, all alpha and demanding. It's like one night unleashed an entirely different human."

"Yeah, but have you even given him the chance to talk to you? Aren't you avoiding him?"

"Yes," I answer before tipping back the rest of my wine. We're going to need to open another bottle.

"Then how do you know what it would be like with him if you're just fucking each other and not talking? You need to talk to him."

"How do I even do that? I can barely look at him when we aren't in the bedroom."

Penny thinks about it for a second, then when her eyes land on my phone, she says, "Text him."

"Come on." I roll my eyes.

"I'm serious. This is a great way to break down that awkward boundary."

"Uh-huh, and what do I say to him?"

"I don't know, maybe be direct. Ask him if it's always going to be awkward with him."

I'm about to tell her that's the most ridiculous suggestion I've ever heard, but then I think about it for a second. The idea has merit. Just ask him. No beating around the bush, no small talk, get straight to the point.

Then again, is that what I want? What happens when we do talk? Where do I want this to lead?

"I don't even know where I want this to go with him."

"Valid." Penny nods her head. "Do you like him?"

I roll my teeth over my bottom lip as I avoid eye contact. "I mean, I think there's always been a small piece of me that liked Halsey, even when I first met him. I always thought he was sweet and kind and not ruggedly stupid like the other guys. He was soft-spoken, which I found fascinating for a hockey player. More subdued. And of course, it's hard not to look past how handsome he is."

I pull my legs into my chest and rest my arms on my knees. "And then when I started living with him, I found out that he has a great sense of humor. We joked around a lot, and he became a good friend. So yeah, I think I've always liked him." *As a person. Never thought I'd want to date the guy.*

"Then the sex should be the cherry on top of the cake."

"But . . . I don't think I know him."

"What do you mean?"

"Sure, I've gotten to know him while living with him, and he's talked about his brother, but a side of him comes out when we're intimate, a side I never expected. I think about what the boys have said, what you have said, that he used to be more lively, more energetic before his brother passed. Makes me wonder, do I actually like the real guy? Or do I like a veil of the man he portrays himself as?"

"Wow," Penny says. "I guess I never thought about it that way. Eli has mentioned how different Halsey used to be."

"And with this change I've seen in him when we're intimate, it just makes me believe there is so much more to him that he's not showing. I'm nervous it won't be the man I like."

Penny slowly nods her head. "Well, I guess there's only one way to find out." She picks up my phone and hands it over to me. "Text him. Worst-case scenario, he's not the man you started to like, and you can move on. But you can't keep fucking and not talking. If you like him, find out if you like all of him."

She's right.

The sex is amazing, but I can't keep avoiding him. There are only so many times I can go into work early, and when I start the new job, there will be no escape, not until I find a new place at least.

Might as well text him . . .

HALSEY

I TOSS my bag on my bed, then flop backward, my hands covering my face as I feel the need to scream.

She took the fucking job.

I can't believe it.

After everything we've done together. It wasn't enough.

It wasn't enough for her to stay.

I'm not fucking enough.

And isn't that a tough fucking pill to swallow?

Knock. Knock.

One hundred bucks says that's Pacey checking in on me.

I lift from my bed, open my hotel room door, and sure enough, it's Pacey.

"Not now, dude," I say, shaking my head.

"Posey wanted me to check on you. He's still nursing his stomach."

"Tell him I'm fine." I go to shut the door, but Pacey puts his hand out, stopping me.

"I know you're not fine."

"Okay, how about this? I want to be left the fuck alone."

Pacey nods. "Yup, that works."

And then I shut the door, moving back into the room just as a text dings on my phone.

"Jesus fucking Christ," I mutter, knowing it's probably Posey.

Wanting to shut them all up, I grab my phone to text the group but pause when I see Blakely's name.

Immediately, my stomach flips, and I sit up on my bed as I open it.

Blakely: *Will it always be this awkward between us?*

Okay, not what I was expecting to read. Then again, I don't know what I expected her to say. We haven't said anything to each other since we started having sex.

For a brief second, I consider asking the boys for help on this, but in all honesty, I think I'm in this goddamn mess because I've been doing this whole thing their way. Far too many cooks have been in the kitchen, and I think it's time I handle this relationship with Blakely on my own.

No more "main hole" comments.

No more advice on how to make her fall for me.

And no more group texts that give me more anxiety than help me.

If I want Blakely, then I'm going to do this on my own.

Halsey: *No. I don't want it to be awkward.*

I kick off my shoes and sit back against the headboard, waiting for her to text back.

Blakely: *I don't want it to be awkward either. I miss talking to you.*

"Fuck," I mutter as I rub my eyes. I should have been talking to her this whole time, but this is also not something I want to discuss over texts.

Halsey: *I miss talking to you too, Blakely.*

Blakely: *Then maybe we can have a conversation about . . . everything.*

Halsey: *I'd like that, but not like this. Not over text. When I get back, we'll talk.*

Blakely: *Okay.*

Halsey: *But have you had a good day?*

Blakely: *Yeah, it's been good. Penny's over tonight. Child free. Someone opened a few bottles of wine.*

Halsey: *Someone might have a headache come tomorrow morning when her baby wakes her up.*

Blakely: *Ha ha. Most likely the someone who supplied the glasses too.*

Halsey: *That would be my guess as well. I'll be thinking of you wearing my shirt tonight. I'll miss having you next to me.*

Blakely: *Same. I look forward to when you come back. Until then . . . I'll take care of Sherman.*

Halsey: *Thank you. Have a good night.*

Blakely: *You too, and good luck tomorrow.*

I toss my phone to the side and drag my hands over my face.

Fuck . . . this will easily be the worst away trip ever because now I have to wait. Thank God it's only one game. If this was a longer road trip, I'm not sure I'd be able to wait that long to talk.

Now I have to figure out what I want to say to her.

First things first, she's going to find out how I feel.

Second thing, ask her out on a real date.

Third thing . . . get her to stay somehow.

———

"DRIVE SAFE," Posey calls out to me as I get into my car and slam the door.

I've never loved a five thirty game time more now than ever. After crushing our neighbor team, the Beavers, we were able to take showers, hop on the plane, and take the quick one-hour flight, giving us plenty of time to get home, which is exactly what I'm doing.

I'm racing home.

The adrenaline from the game still pumps through me, and I want nothing more than to go up to Blakely and tell her exactly how I feel.

Especially after the game we had. A win of four to two, I don't think I've ever skated better, even with my ankle feeling slightly sore. I tore around the ice, tracking the puck, feeling the presence of my teammates, and connecting with them harmoniously on the ice.

It felt good, and I'll play off that feeling and take what I want.

The boys—especially Posey—have tried to talk to me about Blakely but I've shut it down. All of it. I've buried myself in my book, ignored the outside world and chatter, and I've remained composed as I've planned what I'm going to say to Blakely when I see her.

My hands grip the steering wheel tightly as I pull out onto the main road. It's not that far from the private airport to my apartment, but it's long enough for me to feel itchy with anticipation.

I just hope she's still awake. *If she's not, I plan on waking her up.* What I have to say can't wait. I can only hope that once she knows how I feel, that she'll see why I've tried so hard to win her. I've fucked up time and time again, but I hope she'll see past those blunders, see past my awkwardness, and know that she means the world to me.

And that I hope she feels something similar for me too. And that she'll stay . . . with me.

As I drive through the empty roads, the streetlights casting over me like a spotlight, I feel the presence of Holden fall over me.

He'd think I was such an idiot, the way I've handled this entire situation. He would have told me from the beginning to ask her out. From the moment I first laid eyes on her, he would have told me to wiggle myself into her life, even if she did have a boyfriend. Not the best advice, but I know right now he'd be saying, "I told you so. Should have been honest with her from the beginning."

And it's times like this, where I feel so disconnected, that I miss him more than ever. He was the guy who'd help me pull it all together. He grounded me.

I love my guys, and I know I wouldn't be here today if it weren't for them, but sometimes, it isn't the same as having my twin brother . . . or my big brother, Hayden. Or my parents.

My throat grows tight thinking about the loss our family has suffered. Not just from losing Holden, but the disconnect between my family after he passed. Holden and I were so close with Hayden, and now that he's in California with his wife and their kid, I'm . . . I'm so far removed that I don't even know how old my nephew is. I know nothing about him. Is he playing hockey?

If Holden were alive, he'd be ashamed of all of us.

He wouldn't want it like this.

"Fuck," I grumble as tears spring to my eyes. "Not now." I wipe them away, and I take a deep breath.

I can't focus on my family, and its pitiful demise. I need to focus on Blakely.

And that's what I do. I set my mind on her and her alone, blocking out the rest of the noise.

When I pull into my parking spot at the apartment, I barely put the car in park before I'm out the door. I grab my duffel bag, sling it over my shoulder, then head straight up to the apartment, thankful there's an elevator ready for me.

Nerves pulse through me as I reach my floor and walk to my door.

You can do this.

She deserves to know how you feel, and she doesn't want it to be awkward anymore, so this is it.

Take your shot.

I open the door to a dimly lit apartment. Blakely is curled on the couch with the TV on. When she sees me, she lifts to a more seated position.

"Oh . . . wow, you're back fast."

I shut the door behind me and set my bag on the ground. "Short trip," I answer.

"I can see that." She rubs her eyes, then turns off the TV. "I guess I didn't realize what time it was. I had a cup of coffee because I slept during the game and wanted to stay awake. I think it's done its job."

I nod but don't move because fuck, I feel frozen. Now that she's here, right in front of me, I've lost all of my words, everything I've prepared to say to her.

She looks me up and down and says, "Well, I guess I should get to bed." She stands from the couch and folds her blanket before draping it over the couch's armrest.

Say something, Halsey.

Tell her how you feel.

Don't let her walk away to get ready for bed when this sits heavily on your chest.

But as she starts to head toward her room, I know I'm losing it.

The moment is slipping from me.

And panic starts to set in.

"I like you," I call out, pausing her retreat.

Slowly, she turns around, her hair floating over her shoulder as her surprised eyes connect with mine. "What?" she asks.

Jesus Christ, Halsey, be softer.

I let out a heavy breath and take a step forward. "I like you, Blakely. I've liked you for a very long fucking time. Since the day I first met you. And I, fuck . . ." I pull on the back of my neck. "I never made a move because I respected the fact that you had a boyfriend, even though it pained me, so I kept to myself." I take another step forward, keeping my gaze on hers, trying to read her neutral expression. She's giving me nothing to work with. "But that entire time you were with Perry, I felt like you belonged with me. And when you broke up, I felt like I had a chance, but I didn't handle it properly." I push my hand through my hair. "I actually handled it in all the wrong ways. I should have just asked you out on a date, but instead, I tried . . . I tried to show you that I have potential to be someone you could like and, Jesus, it was stupid."

"Is that what you want?" she asks. "To ask me out on a date?"

"Yes," I say, feeling the desperation in my voice. "I want to take you out, Blakely. I want to talk. I want to have a relationship more than what we do in the bedroom. When you said you missed talking to me, I felt the same thing, deep in my soul. And I know I should have said this sooner, but fuck . . . I want you to give me a chance. Desperately. I want to see where this connection between us could go." I close the space between us, growing so close that if I reach out I could take her hand in mine. I could press my palm to her cheek. I could hold her close to my chest. "And I know that you took a new job, that you'll be leaving, but I would—"

"I'm not leaving."

"What?" I ask.

"I took the job, but I'm not moving. I'm staying here."

"R-really?" I ask, hope surging through my chest.

She nods. "I'm not going anywhere other than trying to figure out where to set up a home office. I didn't want to leave Vancouver. I love it here."

"Fuck, seriously?" I ask as I drag my hand over my hair.

"Seriously." She smiles.

"Jesus." I let out a heavy breath.

"Does that change anything that you said?"

My eyes snap up to hers. "No," I say quickly. "It changes nothing. It only makes it easier on me. I was trying to figure out how to do this long distance."

She smiles that gorgeous smile that I fell for the first day I met her. "Well, no need to worry about that. I'm not going anywhere."

I'm a little shocked and having a hard time processing everything. Relief floods through me, but there is one thing I know, and it's that I want to date this woman. I want to show her that we're perfect for each other.

So I reach out and take her hand in mine. Looking her in the eyes, I say, "Then can I take you out on a date tomorrow night?"

Her fingers tighten around mine. "I'd like that."

A euphoric feeling beats through me. *She said yes.* I had the fucking courage to ask her out, to take my chance with this amazing woman, and she said yes, which means the opportunity is there.

The opportunity to make her mine.

I lift her hand to my lips, and I press a soft kiss to her knuckles. "Then it's a date."

She smirks and then leans in. Standing on her toes, she kisses my lips softly before pulling away. "It's a date."

She releases my hand, and she walks off to her bedroom, where she shuts the door.

I grip my hands together on the top of my head and let out another deep breath.

Fuck, I did it.

A large smile spreads across my lips.

I fucking did it.

Turning away from her, I grab my duffel bag and head into my bedroom, where I strip down and get ready for bed, thinking how proud Holden would be. If he were here right now, I'd text him that she said yes, and he'd probably say something like, "Finally, you dickhead. Took you long enough."

Just the thought of it makes me chuckle as I finish brushing my teeth.

I turn off the light to the bathroom just as Blakely walks into my bedroom wearing the shirt I gave her to wear.

My mouth goes dry as I take in how the fabric nearly swallows her up, draping well past her elbows on the sleeves, and the hem hits her mid-thigh.

I move my hand over my mouth, looking her up and down with a slight shake of my head.

"That looks amazing on you."

"It's my favorite shirt to wear."

"Good," I answer as I take her hand and lead her to her side of the bed. I pull back the sheets and comforter and help her into bed. That makes her smile.

I lean down and kiss her head before moving to my side of the bed and slipping under the covers. I turn off the light and roll toward her. I wrap my arm around her waist and pull her into my chest, where I nuzzle my head against her neck.

"Is this okay?" I ask her.

"Why wouldn't it be?" she asks.

"I don't know the limits now that I'm taking you out. I feel like the paradigm has shifted. I want to make sure I'm not doing anything that's crossing the line."

She chuckles. "Halsey, your face has been buried between my legs, so snuggling is not crossing a line."

I laugh and kiss the side of her neck. "I don't want to assume I can touch you."

"Touch me all you want," she whispers as she brings my hand under her shirt. "I love feeling you against me."

Fuck, and I love feeling her. Every inch of her.

But I'm also afraid that if I have access to her body, we'll be in the same position we were before, when all we did was fuck and not talk. And even though that was so goddamn amazing, I know that there's so much more to us than that.

"I think I want to take it slow with you."

That makes her laugh again. "Slow? I'd be interested to see what your fast is, if this has been slow."

"What we were doing was feral desperation to feel what I've wanted to feel for over a year. But I don't want our intimacy to define who we are as a couple. I want to talk, date, and get to know you on a deeper level."

She turns so she's on her back and looking up at me. "So do you want me to sleep on the couch then?" My brows pinch together, which causes her to laugh. "Just kidding. I don't want to have that argument again." She cups my cheek, and her thumb rubs over my scruff. "I can be good with slow. As long as this cuddling doesn't stop."

"Do you think I could have you in my bed and not hold you?"

"I'm thinking no," she answers.

"Exactly."

Her hand falls to my chest as she says, "This feels so surreal."

"What do you mean?" I ask.

"I was just talking to Penny about you and how I've missed talking, and I know it's been my fault. I haven't even given you a chance to talk to me before I've bolted out of here."

"And why were you bolting?" I ask.

Her eyes bounce back and forth between mine. "You changed me in a way I wasn't expecting." She wets her lips. "God, this feels embarrassing to talk about."

"You don't need to say it," I say.

She shakes her head. "No, I want to be honest with you. I said I wanted to talk, so I'm going to talk." Her fingers dance along my bare chest as she says, "I didn't know sex could be like that. It was shocking to me and, I know it seems stupid, but I was under the impression that I was madly in love with a man I thought I was going to marry. The love I shared with Perry is what I thought was the precipice of what I could feel. The intimacy we shared had felt like it was . . . *enough*. I didn't think it could be any different, but then . . . then we shared the night of the wedding, and it flipped my entire idea of sex upside down. It was confusing to me and hard to process, which is why I bolted the first morning. I needed to catch my breath. And then when I came home, and it happened all over again, I felt like my brain was short-circuiting, and it seemed easier to leave than to tell you how you altered everything I ever knew."

I lightly stroke my thumb over her jaw. "You weren't the only one altered that night. I understand the feeling, Blakely. I wish you would have talked to me because I could have told you it felt the same for me."

"Why didn't you say anything?" she asks.

"I was nervous that I'd scare you away if I said something. You were already fleeing the scene, so I thought that if I could keep fucking you, you'd continue to come back, and that's how I could hold on to you. I see that was a very stupid idea now."

"Well . . . the sex wasn't stupid," she says with such a beautiful smile.

"The sex was the best I've ever had," I say.

"Same," she says shyly, which just makes me like this woman that much more.

I lean down and press a kiss to her forehead as I continue to stroke her jaw.

When I pull away, she says, "So basically we were both altered that night and didn't know how to handle it."

"Yeah, sounds like it," I answer. "Sorry that I handled it so poorly."

"You didn't." She shakes her head. "I was the one who didn't handle it well."

"Maybe we both could have handled it better."

"Maybe more me than you."

I shake my head. "That's not who I am, Blakely. I'm not cold like that. I'm not the kind of man who just fucks, and that's it. Sure, I was rabid to have you, but after, I wanted so much more than to just hold you before you fell asleep. I wanted to talk, I wanted to kiss you until you were so comfortable that you could pass out in my arms. I wanted to cherish you, but instead, I was a cold, demanding man." My stomach seizes from the thought of it. "I'm sorry."

"Don't apologize," she says. "Please, Halsey, don't apologize. Okay? I wasn't hurt by it. I was so turned on every moment you whispered into my ear and demanded what you wanted from me. If that isn't how you normally—"

"That part of our intimacy was true," I say, wanting to make that clear. "It's the after and between I wasn't proud of."

"Oh." She bites her lower lip. "So . . . all of the command in the bed, all of the ways you twisted me and fucked me, that was real?"

The corners of my lips tilt up. "Yes, Blakely, that was real."

She glances away before saying, "Well, good to know."

I chuckle and lean down, pressing a kiss to her neck, and then work my way up to her jawline. "You good with that?"

"Very good with that." She shifts under me and wraps her arms around my neck. I lift my head and press my lips to hers. She parts her lips and swipes at my mouth with her tongue.

I groan against her. "Blakely."

"Hmm?" she asks.

"Slow, remember?"

"Yes, I remember. Slow sex, I'm all for it."

I laugh and pull away. "Not slow sex, slow pace with intimacy."

"Coming from the guy who told me to use him like a sex toy."

Laughing some more, I flip her to her side and pull her into my chest. "I can't be held accountable for what I say when you ride me."

"If you were, I'm pretty sure you'd be arrested from that filthy mouth."

I nuzzle into her. "You like it."

"I do," she says softly while holding on to my arm that's holding her.

I kiss her ear and situate my head next to hers. "I'm glad you texted me and that you're staying here, Blakely. I like you a lot, and I want to prove to you that I'm serious about dating you. Worth your time." *You mean everything to me.*

She's silent for a second. "From the first day I met you, Halsey, I knew deep in my soul you were worth my time."

———

POSEY: *Listen, I'm starting to get nervous. You've sunk back into old habits of not talking, and I don't want to lose you to books again.*

Pacey: *I'm leaning toward feeling nervous about it as well. I know the new job isn't what you were expecting, but dude, we can figure something out.*

OC: *I don't have much to contribute other than I'm here for you.*

Eli: *Is this a new text thread? Has Penny been removed?*

Silas: *Do you want to get together tonight? We can figure something out, come up with a new plan.*

Halsey: *Can't tonight. I have a date.*

Posey: *Lord, fucking help me. Are you going out with someone random? I swear to God, Holmes, I can't take this shit.*

Silas: *He wouldn't do that.*

Posey: *Oh really? Because I've seen him do it. You were too busy with Ollie when he started feeding his yearning with random women at bars.*

Pacey: *Yeah, I remember that. It was Ollie's birthday, right?*

Posey: *It was a disaster. I can't go through that again.*

Silas: *Oh yeah, I recall something like that.*

Eli: *Was I there?*

Halsey: *The date is with Blakely, you fucking idiots.*

Pacey: *Really?*

Posey: *Wait . . . seriously?*

Silas: *Dude, you asked her out?*

OC: *Okay, is it weird that I just got butterflies?*

Halsey: *She's not moving. She's staying here. I told her how I felt last night, that I've been pining after her for over a year. And I asked her out. She said yes, then she fell asleep in my arms.*

Posey: ***Jaw drops to the ground***

Silas: *Holy shit.*

Pacey: *Well, that's a fucking 180.*

Eli: *Oh yeah, Penny told me she wasn't moving this morning. I was too busy with Holden to relay.*

Posey: *Jesus, Eli!*

OC: *Okay, the butterflies have now turned into shivers of joy.*

Pacey: *Do we need to go over date options?*

Halsey: *No, I'm good. Taking it from here . . . on my own.*

Posey: *Uh, what?*

Silas: *Dude, that's harsh. You're just going to cut us out like that?*

OC: *You seriously can't do that to me. I've become invested in this.*

Eli: *It seems like he has a handle on it.*

Posey: *Shut up, Hornsby, no one asked you.*

Pacey: *Eli is right.*

Posey: *Or you, Pacey!*

OC: *Is this how it always is in this group? You reel us in and then hang us out to dry? If so, I don't think I can handle it.*

Eli: *Nah, we just shift focus. So . . . how are things with Grace, OC?*

Posey: *WHAT? Grace, our trainer? Dude . . .*

OC: *You're a dick, Hornsby.*

Silas: *And . . . the focus has shifted. Enjoy your date, Holmes.*

Halsey: *Thanks, I will.*

OC: *Uh, I did not sign up for this. How about we talk about Posey and the girl he's been crushing on?*

Silas: *He's not crushing on anyone.*

Pacey: *Do you mean his bologna?*

Eli: *Lady Bologna and her mistress mustard. Yup, let's discuss.*

OC: *He hasn't told you about his girl? Interesting . . .*

Silas: *Posey, what the hell is he talking about?*

Eli: *If you're seeing someone, I'm going to set your bologna stash on fire.*

Pacey: *There's no fucking way.*

Halsey: *Who is she, Posey?*

Levi Posey has left the conversation.

Silas: *The motherfucker.*

━━━

I STAND in the entryway of the apartment, rubbing my hands together in a nervous tic while I wait for Blakely to emerge from her bedroom.

I planned the whole evening out, wanting to make sure I gave us time to talk and enjoy each other rather than take her to a movie or show, which limits our ability to converse. I told her it was a casual evening, so nothing too fancy and to wear shoes she was comfortable walking in.

I opted for a pair of worn black jeans, a white shirt, and a denim button-up with the sleeves rolled up to my elbows. I considered wearing a hat to somewhat disguise myself, but I don't like how I look in a baseball cap, so I styled my hair and stuck a pair of sunglasses in my shirt pocket—hoping for the best.

The door to Blakely's bedroom opens, and she steps out into the main living room. She looks so fucking beautiful.

She chose a pair of white skinny jeans that fall just at her ankle. She paired them with matching white shoes, a tan shirt that's tucked into the front of her jeans, and a black faux-leather jacket. Her hair is curled into waves and half up, half down so there aren't any strands in her face. Her lips are painted in a neutral color, and her captivating eyes are more pronounced from the makeup she applied.

When she looks up and sees me waiting, her eyes briefly scan over me before she smiles and walks up to me, placing her hand on my chest. I wrap my arm around her lower back and pull her in tight as she presses a kiss to my lips.

Fuck, she smells amazing.

She smiles against my mouth, then pulls away just enough to look me in the eyes. "I'm nervous."

I take her hand in mine. "No need to be nervous. We're going to have fun." I step away and force her to spin around. When she faces me again, I say, "You look beautiful, Blakely."

"I'm pretty sure I've worn better."

"Yeah, well, I like casual. You look really good."

Her cheeks blush as she curls into my chest. "You look really good too."

"Thanks." I move toward the door. "You ready?"

"Yeah, ready."

We head out of the apartment, and I lock up before putting my keys in my pocket and walking her toward the elevator. "What I'm about to say is going to come off very douchey, but I have to say it."

"Ooo, I can't wait to hear it."

We step onto the elevator, and I turn toward her. "I was going to wear a hat to try to disguise myself, but I don't like wearing hats all that much, so I brought sunglasses. I'm sorry if people recognize me and take up a piece of our night."

"Because you're so famous," she coos in a joking tone, which causes me to roll my eyes.

"Yeah, something like that."

"Something like that? Uh, you're like the crowned prince of Vancouver. People fall at your feet, and frankly, I'm here for the show. I'm excited to witness Halsey in public."

"We've been in public together before."

"Hmm, I guess we have. Well then, why the warning?"

"We're going to a more public space."

"Okay then, bring it on. I'm excited. Think grown men will cry? I hope they do."

"I hope they don't."

———

"WAIT, are we going to Granville Island on the aquabus?" Blakely asks as we walk down the dock toward a brightly lined boat.

"We are."

"Aw, I've always wanted to do this. Perry gets seasick very quickly, so we never got to experience the aquabus, and I don't know why I just mentioned my ex-boyfriend on our date. Please forget I said anything about him, and let's move on from this comment."

I laugh. "It's okay."

"I know he's not your favorite human."

I flash our tickets to the boat captain and lead Blakely to the head of the boat where we sit on one of the benches. It's small so we don't have a lot of room to work with, but thankfully, we're the only ones on board for the moment.

"Would I be friends with Perry? Probably not," I say as I place my arm behind Blakely on the bench. "But I don't hate the guy. I think he's a moron and, fuck was I a jealous asshole when you were with him, but I'm sure he has good qualities. I just don't care to find them out."

She chuckles. "That's a very honest answer."

"That's the point of this, Blakely. Getting to know you, being honest, and not holding back on anything."

"I appreciate that," she says and turns toward me. "So then, tell me about the first time you met me. What were your thoughts?"

"My thoughts?" I ask. "As in what did I think when I first saw you?"

"Yes," she answers.

I tug on a strand of her hair and twist it around my finger as I say, "Well, I thought 'holy fuck, this woman is gorgeous.'"

She gives me a get real look. "Seriously, Halsey."

"I'm being fucking serious. You stunned me. It was your eyes that captivated me first. And then you smiled, and I was fucking gone. I honestly don't think I heard one thing the entire time you talked to me. I was so caught up in the fact that I was feeling something for someone. I hadn't felt anything since my brother died."

She sits taller. "Really?"

"Yes," I answer. "I was pretty dead inside, Blakely. I shut down after Holden passed, and when I met you, I felt this sudden zap of life inside me. Like this fog had momentarily parted and let me see something, someone outside of my dreary life. You rocked me, and I knew I needed to learn about you. I didn't talk that much that day, but what I did say, I know it was more than I'd said to a stranger since losing Holden."

"Oh my God, Halsey, I had no idea."

"How would you know? It's not like I told you. And when I was signing all those things for you, I just kept thinking, how can I ask this girl out? I was fucking nervous, but I felt this deep need inside me not to part without giving it a shot. That was until you mentioned you had a boyfriend."

"No, stop, I did?"

I nod. "You don't remember?" When she shakes her head, I continue. "You were talking about how you were playing fuck, chuck, and marry with Perry, and you chucked me and felt bad about it since you met me."

"Why the hell would I say that to you?"

I laugh as the boat starts, and we pull into the water.

"I don't know," I answer. "But it was the subtle hint that I needed that you were off limits. I swallowed my crush, and I sat on it. The boys found out at one point, and once they did, they started dropping hints like . . . asking how I thought you looked that day, in front of you."

"Really?" she asks with such a cute smile. "I don't remember any of this. What would you say?"

"That you looked beautiful. That the color you were wearing looked really good on you. Just little things here and there."

"I hate that I never picked up on it."

"You had a boyfriend, so why would you?" I shrug. "Either way, when Posey found out you were single, he practically did a backflip into the locker room to spread the news. From there, it was a giant mess of the boys trying to get me to ask you out and figure out ways to get you to look in my direction. That's when Posey said I had a spare room for you to stay in."

"Wait, did he say that so you could get closer to me?"

Feeling shy about it, I smooth my hand over my forehead. "Yeah, and I know it sounds pathetic, so don't hold it against me."

"I think it's sweet," she says as she plays with the buttons on my undone shirt. "Also kind of funny that Posey did that."

"He loves inserting himself into our lives."

"So when I came over that morning and the curtains were wrinkled . . . was that because you tried to straighten up your apartment for me?"

"Yeah. Posey helped me make your room look presentable, or at least we tried. Unfortunately we had a mishap when moving the beds."

"What happened?" she asks as the boat picks up speed.

"I don't think I can say this to you. You might be heartbroken."

She taps her finger on my chest. "Remember what you said. You were going to be honest."

"You're right," I say. "So you know how Posey said it would be a great solution to move in with me because you'd have a place to stay and Sherman wouldn't be alone?"

"Yes . . ." she drags out.

"Well, Sherman wasn't a thing. I didn't have a plant. That morning before you came over, I went to the store and picked one up."

"No . . . stop, that's not true."

"Sorry." I shrug. "It is."

She clutches her heart. "But that was one of the things I liked about you. You had a plant, and I thought that was so cute."

"Well, I have a plant, and I do care about him. I think I know more about bonsai trees than I ever wanted to know. And I do have feelings for him now, but at first, he wasn't real."

"That is damaging." She shakes her head. "I've lived a lie."

I chuckle. "Well then, you might not want to know that's the second Sherman, not the first."

"What happened to the first?"

"When Posey and I switched the beds, the mattress slipped from our hands and knocked the original Sherman over. It was a fucking disaster. I had to call in reinforcements to clean up, get a new plant, and help set up the rest of the apartment. It's why the curtains and bed sheets were wrinkled. We were in a mad dash to make the apartment nice before you got there, and soil from a dead Sherman wasn't going to look good."

"Poor original Sherman. He never even had a chance."

"Sorry, he didn't."

"Wow, so is there anything else you deceived me about?"

I shake my head. "That was it. Anything that happened has been bad advice from the group, which . . . Penny was a part of."

Her eyes widen. "What?"

"She was trying to help me get close to you." I feel guilty saying that since they're friends, and I'm sure that betrays Penny's trust, but like I said, I want to be honest with Blakely. I don't want any secrets or anything to ruin my chances of being with her.

"She was helping you?" I slowly nod, and she looks away. I can't tell if she's angry, upset, or happy. "Wow," she says, shaking her head. Fuck, she's angry. When she brings her eyes back to mine, she adds, "You would think my best friend would have been a better help. Goes to show how much she knows me." She smirks and leans in to press a kiss to my lips.

Another wave of relief floods through me.

"You're not mad?"

"How could I be mad?" she asks. "I am speechless. Halsey . . . you have no idea how complimented I feel right now. To think that you've had feelings for me for so long . . . that you pursued me so decisively. I don't think anyone has ever treated me with so much devotion and respect. I'm in awe. If I'm mad about that, then something is wrong with me. I'm just sorry you had to suffer through bad advice."

"Trust me . . . so am I."

"THIS PLACE IS SO ADORABLE," Blakely says as she holds my hand, taking in the public market. "I've always wanted to come here."

"I'm glad you like it," I say just as I'm tapped on the arm. I turn around to find a father and daughter duo, both wearing Agitators shirts.

The little girl stares up at me with wide eyes. "Are you Halsey Holmes?"

I release Blakely's hand and squat down so I'm eye level with her. "I am," I say. "What's your name?"

"Annabelle Markey."

I smile and take her hand. "Annabelle, it's very nice to meet you. I see that you're an Agitators fan." I point at her shirt.

She nods. "You-you're my favorite player."

"Am I?" I ask. "That's such an honor. Thank you. Can I ask why I'm your favorite?"

"Because as Daddy says, you leave those sons of bitches in the dust."

"Annabelle," the father scolds, looking mortified.

I chuckle, and so does Blakely. "They're pretty slow compared to me, huh?"

Annabelle nods her head. "Yeah, you're so fast."

"Well, thank you." I then glance back at Blakely. "I'm on a date. Think we can take a picture real quick so I can go back to trying to impress this girl?"

Annabelle glances at Blakely, then back at me. "She's pretty."

"I know. Very pretty. I'm lucky, don't you think?"

Annabelle shakes her head. "She's lucky."

That makes me smile, and I stand. "Want a pic?" I ask the dad.

He nods, and Blakely steps in to take the dad's phone. We take a quick picture, I give Annabelle a hug, and then shake the dad's hand, and we part ways.

Blakely rubs up against me as she says, "That was really sexy, Halsey."

"Sexy?" I ask.

She loops her arm through mine and holds me close. "Really sexy, seeing you interact with that little girl. Made me all weak in the knees. You're a good man."

"Keep that in mind when you're considering a second date."

"I can pretty much guarantee you there'll be a second one."

Chapter Twenty

BLAKELY

"Be back," I say as I head toward the Sandbar restaurant's bathroom.

We walked around the island for a while, taking in the view, before Halsey brought me to the Sandbar where we have reservations. Of course we have one of the best seats in the place, overlooking the harbor and the skyline. We put in our order, and I had to excuse myself because . . . I'm feeling overwhelmed.

Overwhelmed in a *good* way.

I step off to the side in a small corridor in the hallway and pull my phone from my pocket, where I call Penny. I bring the phone to my ear, and she answers on the second ring.

"Hey, what's up?"

"I have like five minutes," I say quickly. "I'm out on a date with Halsey right now, and he told me that you were in on the whole plan to get me to like him."

"Uhh . . . he did?" she asks, sounding nervous.

"I'm not mad. I actually think it's cute that he was looking for help. Anyway, he took me to Granville Island for our date. We took the aquabus to get here, and we're eating at the Sandbar. I need to know if you had any input on this date or if this was all him."

"Okay, that's a lot of information. I didn't even know he was going out with you. I know Eli mentioned something about Halsey cutting everyone off from the details between you two because he was sick of all the input."

"So this was all his idea?"

"Seems like it. Are you having fun?"

"Penny," I say, swallowing hard.

"Yes?" she asks.

"I really like him. Like, I'm so overwhelmed with how much I like him that I had to take a step back. Right now, he's acting like the man I first started living with. It feels effortless being near him now that the awkwardness has faded and we started talking again. It's kind of scary how much I like him, and I needed to call you because I didn't want to freak out. This is too soon, right? I'm having feelings for a man, and it's too soon. I shouldn't have these strong feelings for someone else when I just got out of a long relationship."

"Yes, you did just get out of a long relationship. But I also think that if you and Perry had still been in love with each other —*actively dating each other*—then the breakup would have shattered you. I wonder if your relationship had already fizzled out by the time you 'broke up'. It may be that Halsey came into your life at just the right time. Exactly when you *were* ready for someone new." *Hmmm. I hadn't thought about it like that.* "You need to listen to your heart and follow that, not what people might think. If you like him, then you like him. Plain and simple. And take it from someone who waited a long time to be with the person they wanted to be with. If you like him, just accept it." I mull that over and then quietly say, "He likes me, Penny. He's liked me for a long time."

"We know. We've known. It's been torture for him. I don't think he's going anywhere. He's set in what he wants, and what he wants is you, so . . . enjoy this time. Get to know him. I think this could be something special between you two."

"You do?" I ask.

"I do. He's a good guy. And I know you're nervous about who he really is. I'd just keep asking him questions, keep pulling him out of his shell. I will say this, and so will the boys, we have never seen him so lively. He's changed since he's met you, and he's changed a lot since you broke up with Perry."

"Yeah, I know." I take a deep breath. "Okay. Thanks, Penny."

"You're welcome. Now go have fun. Don't overthink it."

"I won't."

I hang up the phone and stuff it back into my pocket before I head back to the table where Halsey sits, staring out the window. He isn't looking at his phone or trying to distract himself while I'm gone. Instead, he's enjoying the scenery while sipping some water.

Just makes me like him that much more. He's connected to the moment, not trying to distract himself with the outside world.

I walk up to the table, place my hand on his back, and rub it before taking a seat.

"Hey," he says, his eyes lighting up when he sees me.

How could I not have seen this before? The way he looks at me when I walk into a room. The subtle bounce of his Adam's apple. The shift in his posture or the soft acknowledgement in his voice.

It's been right in front of me this entire time, and I've been so blind not to notice. Here I thought that he was out of my league, when he's been inviting me into his world for a long time now.

"This is so beautiful," I say as I look out over the water.

"I'm glad you like it," he replies.

I look across the table at him and notice how his eyes are set on me, his interest pulled toward me. Even his body language is directed at me.

"I'm sorry," I say before I can stop myself.

His brow cinches together. "Sorry for what?" he asks.

"That I didn't know about your crush, that you had to watch me with someone else. That you had to wait so long."

"You don't need to apologize. You were worth the wait, Blakely."

And with that, it's solidified. I can see myself falling fast and hard for this man if I haven't started already.

———

"SO YOU WEREN'T a big hockey fan before you started working for the Agitators?" Halsey asks.

I shake my head. "I obviously followed it and knew about the sport because I was trying to get a job in sports, so I kept up on the top ones, but I wasn't a huge fan until I started watching all the games. Well, was forced to watch the games. The more I learned, the more I became invested in the sport and the team. I'd say I'm a huge fan now."

Halsey takes a mouthful of his roasted veggies, then asks, "Am I your favorite player?"

"What kind of question is that?" I ask with a tilt of my head.

"A fair one."

"Of course you're my favorite."

"Are you just saying that because you're technically my roommate who shares a bed with me?"

"No." I roll my eyes. "I'm saying that because you're the best sex I've ever had."

The smallest of grins passes over his lips. "Good answer."

"Thought you might like that."

"Do you have a second favorite player?"

I wipe my mouth with my napkin and set it on the table. "Um . . . I honestly think Pacey gets lost in the mix. The announcers are always saying that his job is easy because Hornsby and Posey are so good at what they do that it's hard to penetrate their wall, but I've watched Pacey score shutout after shutout and not earn the credit for it."

"I agree with you," Halsey says. "Ever since his head injury, he hasn't been given the credit he deserves, which is weird to me. You would think that with the way he performs, he'd get more praise."

"Do you think he'll be around much longer? I know he's getting older, and I'm sure Winnie can't be too happy he still plays when he continues to get migraines every now and again."

"I don't know," Halsey says. "Surprisingly, we don't talk about it. I don't think any of us want to consider playing without Pacey in front of the goal."

"Denial. I've spent time with it, and it's nice until it's not."

"Yeah, I've had my fair share of time with denial," Halsey says.

I can only imagine he's referencing his brother, and since we're being honest and getting to know each other, I decide to ask.

"You mean with your brother?"

He nods. "The stages of grief are a real thing. I lived in denial for a long time."

"Would you say you're at acceptance?" I ask.

He sets his fork down and sits back in his chair. He looks out toward the ocean, and to my surprise, he shakes his head. "No. I think I'm still at anger."

"Oh, I'm sorry," I say.

His eyes return to mine. "Don't apologize." He reaches across the table and takes my hand. "There's nothing to apologize about."

"I just assumed you were at acceptance."

"I would have assumed that too," he says softly. "But I'm not going to lie to myself. There's a lot I haven't taken care of when it comes to the loss of my brother, and until I do, I can't move on to the other stages."

"I can always help you if you need the help."

He shakes his head. "No, I don't want to worry you with that." He offers me a sad smile. "That's something I need to work at on my own."

He lifts his water and takes another sip. I watch as his lips touch the glass and suck in the water only to flow down his throat. *God, he's gorgeous.*

I'm still coming to terms with how long he's liked me. Is it just that Perry and I had been together for so long that we'd forgotten what first attracted us to each other? Is that why it's so nice to hear what Halsey first thought of me?

"You stunned me. It was your eyes that captivated me first. And then you smiled, and I was fucking gone. I honestly don't think I heard one thing the entire time you talked to me. I was so caught up in the fact that I was feeling something for someone. I hadn't felt anything since my brother died."

He's essentially waited for me. But what he's noted about his stages of grief does concern me, if I'm honest.

"I was pretty dead inside, Blakely. I shut down after Holden passed, and when I met you, I felt this zap of life inside me. Like this fog had momentarily parted and let me see something, someone outside of my dreary life. You rocked me, and I knew I needed to learn about you."

Does this mean he'll always process things internally? Because Perry was a little like that. And I realize now that it's probably what helped us drift apart. We became so good at simply problem-solving internally.

Halsey is such a different, complex man from what I thought initially. He's shy and quiet. There's his alpha, overprotective male side—which still gets me hot. The sex god. The swoon-worthy man. But I've always sensed his deeper, angry side, suggesting that terrible things have happened, and he's never really dealt with them.

If he doesn't address them, that can't bode well for our relationship. It's textbook. Should I be worried that he doesn't want me to be involved in that?

"Would you like dessert?" the server asks, breaking through our short bout of silence.

"Just the check," Halsey says, which makes me worried from his curt tone.

"Not a problem. Be right back."

The server takes off, and I'm about to apologize again for

making things so awkward that he wants to cut the date short, but then he says, "I wanted to walk around the public market and grab some dessert from a vendor. Does that work for you?"

"Oh yeah, that would be great."

"You sure?" he asks. "Because if you like something on the menu here, we can get it."

God, he's so sweet.

I shake my head. "No, grabbing something from a vendor sounds like fun."

⸺

"THESE ARE SO PRETTY," I say as I check out the thin gold bracelets that caught my eye at one of the jewelers. "Did you make these?" I ask the vendor.

"I did," the woman says. "It's one of my favorite sets."

"Can she see them?" Halsey asks.

"Of course," the woman says as she pulls them out of the case.

Halsey reaches for the bracelets and unclasps them one by one, only to nod for me to lift my wrist.

I give him a look, but he doesn't let up, so I lift my wrist and he puts them on.

They're so delicate and beautiful.

"Do you like them?" Halsey asks.

I look up at him. "I know that look, and you're not getting them for me."

He retrieves his wallet and fishes out his card. "Too late." He hands the card over to the vendor, and she turns away, not wanting to be part of this argument. Smart lady, take the money and run.

"Halsey, they're too much."

"They're not," he says as he lifts my chin and presses a kiss to my lips.

"Here you go," the vendor says as she hands back Halsey's card and a receipt to sign. He scribbles his signature, then the vendor hands him a bag with the jewelry boxes in them, but he shakes his head.

"She's wearing them out of here. Thank you, though."

"Are you sure?"

"Positive," I answer. "I don't plan on taking them off. Thank you. They're beautiful."

"They're perfect for you," the vendor says.

Halsey takes my hand and kisses my knuckles. "She's right, they're perfect on you."

I tug him to the side so we're out of the flowing traffic and place my hands on his chest. "You didn't have to do that."

"I wanted to get them for you."

I'm not going to put up a fight because it would seem ungrateful, so instead, I soak in this sweet moment.

"Thank you for my bracelets, Halsey. I really do love them."

"Of course," he says as he cups my cheek. I watch as a large smile breaks across his lips as he stares down at me.

"What?" I ask.

He lightly shakes his head. "Still in disbelief that I get to hold you like this. I convinced myself this would never happen, that I could only admire you from afar."

"Well, it's real, Halsey." I smooth my fingers over his chest. "This is so real."

"Feels like a dream. Afraid I might wake up and it will all be over."

I bring my hand to his side, and with my index finger and thumb, I pinch his side.

"Hey!" he shouts, moving away from me. "What the hell was that for?"

I chuckle. "See? Not a dream." I hold up my pinching fingers. "Pinchy fingers and all."

"You could have just stuck your tongue in my mouth. You didn't have to pinch me."

"No, this really seals the deal on what we have going on." I kiss his jaw. "But if you want me to stick my tongue in your mouth, I'd be more than happy to later."

He wraps his arms around my shoulders and brings me in close to his chest. He presses a kiss to the top of my head before saying, "If you stick your tongue in my mouth, I won't be able to not stick my dick in your . . . main hole."

I snort against his shirt and look up at him. "Please . . . for the love of God, confirm that was Posey and not you."

"That was one hundred percent Posey," he says. "A mistake I'll never make again."

"That man needs help."

Halsey nods his head. "More than you know." He takes my hand, and together, we continue through the market. "Word on the street is he's crushing on someone."

"Really?" I ask, looking up at him. "Tell me more."

―――

"WILL you be okay that there are no blueberries in this dessert?" I ask Halsey as he hands me a wooden fork—one for him, one for me.

"I think I'll survive. This looks good, though. I'm excited to try it."

"I never would have pegged you for a lemon-loving guy. Then again, I never would have thought you liked blueberry-flavored food so much, either."

"And what would you expect me to like?"

I lean back, giving him a slow once-over, and then tap my fork to my lips. "Hmm . . . if I had to choose, I'd say you like the taste of paper, oats, and marmalade."

"What?" he asks on a snort. "What kind of answer is that? Paper? Marmalade? Am I an eighty-year-old with xylophagia?"

"What's that?" I ask as he pops open the lemon coconut square we purchased to share.

"A person who consumes paper."

"How the hell do you know that word off the top of your head?"

He smirks. "It's called reading, baby. Maybe give it a try."

"Oh, with that sort of attitude, you won't be invited into my main hole for a while."

"Good." He tips my chin up. "Since we're taking it slow and all."

"Ohhh, nice try." I shake my head. "Fine, when we get back to the apartment, I'll make it my job to force you into coming somehow tonight."

"Oh no, please don't," he says, his voice full of sarcasm. "I'd hate every second of that."

I dip my fork into the corner of the lemon bar and lift it to my lips. "You know, you're really snarky for the guy who likes to play the quiet, shy card."

"I'm not playing any card," he says while he takes a bite of the lemon square as well. It's so freaking good. We should have purchased two. "Just been living in a fog until you came around."

I tilt my head to the side. "You can't say those things to me."

"Why not?" he asks.

"Because . . ." I look up at him through my lashes. "Makes me fall harder."

"Good," he says. "Then I'm doing my job."

⸺

I LOOK at myself in the mirror as I brush my teeth. The bite marks from the other night are fading, but still obvious.

My cheeks are still flushed from the way Halsey held me close while we floated back on the aquabus, telling me how lucky he was and how beautiful I am.

My heart is freaking full, and I'm trying not to be over-whelmed, but how could I not be? In the matter of weeks . . . WEEKS . . . I've found an unexpected man in my life that I just thought was an acquaintance. I've watched him morph and change, and I'm growing very attached to this man. I've developed such strong feelings for him.

It's insane.

So crazy to even try to comprehend.

I

MEGHAN QUINN

I thought I was in love, yet here I am with Halsey, feeling something entirely different, something deeper, something that beats through me all the way to the marrow of my bones.

How is that possible? Is Penny right? Had things between Perry and me fizzled to the point that we weren't really *dating* by the time we broke up? It does have merit. Yes, we had sex, but it seemed more like habit rather than lovemaking near the end. Definitely wasn't fucking. *How did I not see that?*

I spit into the sink and rinse my mouth with some water before I turn off the light to my bathroom and head into my bedroom. I glance at myself in the full-length mirror and adjust the lingerie set I decided to wear to bed.

It's a variation of the one I wore the other night where it's held together by a tie at my breasts. But this one is forest-green, see-through lace. It really does nothing other than entice the person you're trying to entice.

And even if he only holds me tonight, at least I'll feel beautiful while he does it.

On a deep breath, I head over to his bedroom, thinking about how weird it is that we're roommates who are dating and sleep in the same bed but still technically have different bedrooms. Probably best to give us both space. Not to mention, I don't think I'm in a position where I'm ready for him to watch me floss just yet. The only thing more intimate than flossing in front of your partner is going number two. Number one, no big deal, but number two, that edges out flossing by a hair.

The light on his bedside table is on, casting the room in a warm glow. He isn't on the bed yet, but he walks out of his bathroom as I approach, only to look to the side and catch me en route.

That's when he pauses, and his eyes unapologetically roam my body, fixating on my chest. He drags his hand over his mouth and says, "Blakely . . ."

"Yes?" I smile.

"What are you doing?"

318

"Getting into bed, why?" I glance at the bed. "Do you want me to sleep somewhere else?"

"You know damn well I don't," he growls.

"Okay, then what's the problem?"

He motions to my outfit. "That's the problem."

"Oh, right, sorry." I tug on the string that holds the top together, and when it pops open, showing off my bare breasts, I say, "You want me naked, don't you?"

"Jesus Christ," he huffs.

And I don't wait for him, I walk over to my side of the bed, drop my top to the floor but keep the bottoms up, and slip under the covers, casually picking up the lotion I keep on my nightstand and massaging a drop into my hands.

He remains standing by the bathroom.

Finally, I glance at him and ask, "Are you going to join me?"

He mutters something under his breath that I can't quite make out, then walks over to the bed, flipping off the switch to the light and blanketing us into the dark. Then he slips under the covers, but instead of grabbing me by the waist and pulling me into him like he always does, he remains on his side of the bed, stiff as a board, looking up toward the ceiling.

Aw, it's so cute how he's trying to avoid me. Little does he know.

I roll to my side, scoot in close, and press my body against him as I smooth my hand over his stomach.

He stiffens even more.

"Thank you for tonight, Halsey. I don't think I've had that much fun in a while." I kiss his chest. "And thank you for my bracelets. I love them so much."

"You're welcome," he answers tersely.

"We should have totally purchased another lemon square and put it in the fridge for later. It was so good. Didn't you like it?"

"Yup," he says as I shift, my nipples rubbing against his side.

"And that dinner was amazing too. I've always heard such great things about the Sandbar. I'm so glad we were able to go."

"Yeah, good," he answers. His clipped responses make me chuckle.

I smooth my hand over his chest, running my fingers along the ridges of his muscles. "Honestly, it was one of the best nights I've ever had. What about you?"

"Great night," he says on a sigh as my finger travels over his abs and around his belly button.

"That's all? Just a great night?"

I move my hand to the waistband of his boxer briefs, and just as I start to slip my fingers underneath, he grips my wrist and then rolls me to my back, pinning my hand to the mattress as he hovers over me. His erection presses against my thigh as my eyes connect with his frustrated ones.

"It was the best night I've had in a really fucking long time," he says through clenched teeth. "I've dreamed of the day that I could hold your hand and walk around, knowing you were the girl I could claim as mine. The night wasn't just great, Blakely, it was a fucking awesome reality that stemmed from many lonely nights dreaming."

And this is why I need this man. Right here. Why I need him to not block me off from being intimate. When he says things like that, I want to savor them and make them last longer. Feel him so deep inside me that I can't think of anything but him and me.

"Halsey," I whisper, but he continues.

"You're my dream girl, Blakely. Everything I ever fucking wanted. So never second-guess that."

"If that's the case, then why hold back with me?" I ask as I slide my hand not pinned down between us and grip his large bulge. His head falls forward as he sucks in a sharp breath. "Intimacy is not going to hurt us. Let's play. Let us have fun. Let's get to know each other on all levels."

His eyes connect with mine as he says, "I'll keep taking what I want from you, Blakely. Doesn't that scare you? Because it sure as shit scares me."

I shake my head. "It just makes me want you that much

more. To be desired is never a bad thing, Halsey. It actually makes me feel that much more powerful."

His grip on my wrist loosens as his body starts to melt against mine, his cock pushing into my palm.

"I'm going to want you every night," he says softly as he squeezes my bare breast. "I'm going to want you in every position. I'll want to own you, make sure you never leave this bed unsatisfied. I want you coming on my face every night. Coming on my cock every chance I can get. And I want that sinful mouth sucking me until nothing is left to give."

My legs spread as I start to throb with the possibility of what he's offering.

"You say that like it's a bad thing, Halsey."

"Isn't it?" he asks as he continues to massage my breast, but now lowering his lips to my neck.

"No." I sigh as he nibbles on the juncture of my neck and shoulder. "It's what I want too."

"I'm going to be too rough."

"I hope you are," I respond as I slip my hand into his briefs and grip his cock, slowly pumping him.

"Fuck," he whispers as he blows out a heavy breath against my skin, his hips pumping with my hand. "I want you to want me for me."

That makes me pause as I force him to look at me. "Are you afraid I'll only want you because of this? What we do in the bedroom?"

He nods.

I shake my head. "I want you for so much more than that, Halsey. But this connection is important too. You can have both equally."

"I want both," he says, sounding like a man of desperation.

"Then take both," I reply.

He hesitates, his mouth just hovering over my collarbone now, and as he slowly starts to lift, I grow disheartened, thinking he won't take what he wants. But then he crashes his mouth to mine and I'm instantly consumed by him.

All my blood rushes to my core, sending a tingling sensation out to the tips of my limbs as his mouth parts mine and his tongue dances along my tongue. Tangling, stroking, enticing me more and more with what I know he can sinfully do to me.

While his mouth takes charge, I grip the waistband of his briefs and push them down. Then I use my feet to push them all the way off until he's free of them. Next, I slip my underwear off, tossing them to the side. Then I spread my legs, *showing* him that I'm more than ready.

His hand squeezing my breast travels down my stomach to between my legs, where he methodically rubs two fingers over my clit.

"Fuck," he whispers as he makes small, concentric circles with his fingers. "This cunt will never stop wanting me, will it?"

"Never," I say as I bring my knees up to my chest, loving being so exposed to him and anything he wants to do to me.

"I'll never stop craving you." I rock my hips against his hand, bringing this sensation in my stomach to a heightened awareness. "I'll never stop wanting this pussy," he mutters as his mouth lifts back to mine.

He brings one of my legs down and starts rocking against it, rubbing his erection along my thigh, and it feels so naughty, so erotic to know that this man is so turned on that he needs to use my leg to ease the tension building inside him.

"I want to come all over your cock," I say.

"Promise?" He releases his hand from between my legs and then smooths it up my thigh. He lifts up and flips me over to my stomach. "This sight," he says as he runs his hand over my ass. "The most beautiful fucking thing I've ever seen."

He spreads my cheeks with both hands and then brings his mouth to my back hole, where he licks, and I nearly fly off the bed.

"Halsey," I gasp, only making him chuckle.

"Not ready for that, baby?"

I gulp, thinking about the kind of pleasure he could bring me. "I . . . I don't." I swallow hard. "I don't know."

"How about this . . ." He moves toward the nightstand and removes one of his slender vibrators. He lubes it up and then brings it back over to me. While teasing the tip along my ass, he asks, "Can I use this?"

Once again, I swallow hard and then slowly nod.

"Jesus, you're going to make me come so hard tonight." He gently massages my butt with one hand. "Tilt your ass in the air for me, baby," he says, and I do so, angling up and feeling more exposed than ever.

I feel him sit on his knees behind me while he continues to massage me, relaxing the tension that's building in my stomach. And then when I'm least expecting it, he inserts the already vibrating vibrator inside my ass.

"Breathe out," he says as I tense. "Come on, baby, take this for me."

I let out a deep breath, and he inserts it the rest of the way, hitting me in a place I didn't even know existed. I grip the comforter tightly as he tilts the vibrator toward my belly button.

"Oh my . . . fuck," I whisper as my back dips.

"Deep breaths," he whispers softly as his hands lovingly stroke over my body. He begins by smoothing over my butt, down to the dip in my back, up my spine, and around to my front, where he gently cups my breast. His normal rough relationship with my nipples remains calm, and he carefully rubs them in his fingers, bringing them to a hardened point.

There's no urgency.

There's no desire, burning a hole into his meticulous plan.

There's just him, taking his time and making me feel so good that my legs start to knock together as an intense pleasure builds deep at the base of my spine. A pleasure so different that it's actually startling.

"One day," he whispers as he trails his fingertips over my heated skin. "This ass will be mine. My cock will claim it, but we'll work up to that, baby. Right now, I want you to see how fucking good it feels."

He's right . . . this feels . . . incredible. Unlike anything I've ever felt before.

"Tell me you like it," he says as his hand trails over my shoulder and back to my breasts again.

"I love it," I say, feeling out of breath.

"Fuck . . . yes," he says as he lowers his head and starts lapping at my exposed clit.

I immediately clench but then relax as his thumb slips inside me, and he pleasures me on all ends.

"Halsey," I gasp as he switches his thumb for his fingers. "Oh my God."

My hips rock against him.

My stomach starts to tense.

And my legs go completely numb.

"You're close, aren't you?" he asks.

I nod, my voice completely lost now.

"I want to hear it, Blakely."

"I'm . . . oh fuck." I dip my head down, a bolt of lust shooting straight up my spine. "Fuck, Halsey . . . oh fuck," I cry as my body screams toward the precipice now. His tongue flicking against my clit, the vibrations against the sensitive nerves, spurs me into a tailspin of euphoria. "I'm going to . . . oh fuck!" I yell as my body tips over the edge and I start convulsing under his touch.

The inner walls of my ass constrict around the vibrator, a sensation I've never felt before.

The throbbing between my legs is so exponentially intense that I feel a wave of arousal seep down my legs.

And the short laps of his tongue make me buck my hips against his head, seeking out every last part of this delicious, earth-shattering orgasm.

When I finally catch my breath, Halsey removes the vibrator and turns me so I'm on my back. He straddles my stomach, and while holding his painfully large erection, he says, "Squeeze your tits together."

I don't even give it a second thought. I bring my boobs

together, and he immediately slips his dick between them. He grips the headboard and then starts fucking my cleavage so hard that he almost seems like a blur above me.

"These fucking tits, they're so goddamn sexy." He blows out a breath. "Jesus Christ." I release my breasts and open my mouth, bringing his cock straight to my lips. "Fuck, baby."

I suck his tip hard as I move my hand under him and start playing with his balls.

"Won't last long," he says as I squeeze. "Nope . . . won't last fucking long." He moves his hips, and his dick grows larger in my mouth. But at this angle, I can't take him very far. He knows this, so he sits back, lifts my leg onto his shoulder, and then positions himself against my entrance.

His movements are erratic, and desperation for him to come falls over us both as he plunges inside me and groans.

I look up at him and say, "Fill me with your cum."

His eyes roll to the back of his head as he pounds into me.

There's nothing slow about it.

He's demanding.

He's relentless.

He seeks out his pleasure and his pleasure alone, and it's so goddamn sexy that my body grows with need as well. To get me there quicker, I find the vibrator to the side, turn it on, and bring it to my clit where I let it vibrate against us both.

"My dirty, fucking girl," he says, gripping my hips. The angle of my leg adds to the pleasure. "You want another one, don't you?"

"Please make me come again, Halsey."

He grunts and moves even faster.

The bed shakes.

Our moans mix in the air.

And the slapping of our skin sets the rhythm as our pleasure builds and builds and builds until he shouts out my name, the sound echoing through the room as he pauses and shoots his cum inside me.

"Fuck . . . me," he cries just as I tip over the edge too, my pussy contracting around his throbbing cock, prolonging his orgasm.

He moans, I groan, and we shift together, taking every last drop until we're sated.

That's when he drops down and lies on top of me, feeling like the best weighted blanket ever.

I turn off the vibrator and toss it to the side before wrapping my arms around him and kissing his shoulder.

"Blakely," he whispers quietly.

"Hmm?" I ask as I keep him in place by wrapping my legs around him. I don't want him to move. I don't want him to go anywhere. He's mine, all of him. It's not too soon. I know that now. This man was meant for me. *How did I not see him?*

"I like you so fucking much."

A smile tilts my lips up as I continue to kiss his shoulder. "I like you so much, too."

He brings his lips to my neck, sending goosebumps along my skin.

"Please give me a chance to prove to you that I'm the man you need."

What is he talking about?

"You've already proven that."

He rises up just enough for me to see the scared look in his eyes. "I have baggage, Blakely. I don't want that to hurt us. I'm going to work on it, I promise."

"Halsey," I say while cupping his cheek. "I like you as you are. I think you're amazing." And that's not a lie. He's been so much more transparent since he started opening up. He acknowledges he's not far along the path of grieving, but that's okay too. *He wants me.* He waited for me. And he's so generous with his heart.

"I want to work on things now," he says. "Holden would want me to."

Very confused about where this is all coming from, I stroke his cheek and search his eyes for any explanation, but all I see is determination.

"Halsey, where is this coming from? This insecurity?"

With a sigh, he shifts off me and rolls to his back. I press a kiss to his chest and quickly head to the bathroom to clean up because I feel like whatever he has to say will be more than just a few seconds.

He follows me in and cleans up as well. Every once in a while, I catch him staring at me, and I can't help but swoon at the way his expression changes whenever our eyes connect.

Once we're done, we climb back into bed, and as he lies down on his back again, I move on top of him so our chests are pressed together, and I'm staring down at him.

"So . . ." I continue. "Where is this all coming from, Halsey?"

Chapter Twenty-One

HALSEY

She's so beautiful.

Just look at her face. Those eyes, they fucking slice right through me. The light freckles on her nose give her a look of whimsy. Those lips, they're so sweet and innocent but also sinful and dangerous.

And she's mine.

Even though it's all I've wanted from the moment I met her, it's settling in and now I'm terrified.

Why, you ask?

Because I wanted to share this night with someone. I wanted to tell my parents about how goddamn lucky I am to have taken Blakely out. I wanted to send them the picture Blakely and I took on the aquabus. I wanted to be able to brag about the girl in my arms. I wish I could call Holden, Hayden, or my parents, and find a time for them to meet my girl.

And sure, I have my boys, and they'd be ecstatic for me, but there's the pain that I feel deep in my soul that reminds me every day that I don't have the one person in my life I could have shared every detail with. And he'd have sat there and listened. He'd have called me a douche at times or made fun of me for liking a fucking lemon square, but in the end, he would have been proud of me and smiled.

I don't have that, and knowing I don't have that has messed with my head.

It's reminded me that having a shred of that comfort back is a possibility, but someone has to break the tension. Someone has to make that first move and, despite feeling so fucking sick over it, I know it needs to be me.

"Halsey." Blakely runs her finger over my jaw. "Talk to me."

I run my hand over her lower back, rounding her ass, then up her spine. It's slow, and it's comforting. It confirms she's here with me now, and she has no intention of leaving.

"Tonight was everything I could have asked for," I say. "When I say I've dreamed of this night for so long, I'm not fucking kidding. I'd lie here in my bed and think about what I'd do with you. Where I'd take you on our first date. What I'd say. And then it happened, and I feel so fucking euphoric, like I'm soaking in a high that I never want to end."

"You say that like it's a bad thing."

I shake my head. "It's not. Nothing about tonight was bad. It was perfect. You're perfect." I smooth her hair behind her ear. "And that's what's killing me because I want to shout to everyone that I'm the luckiest motherfucker ever." I pause and then say, "When we got home, do you know what my initial instinct was?"

"What?" she asks.

"To call Holden. When you went to your room, I sat and stared at my phone, wondering if I texted him if he'd respond. I wanted to tell him that I took out my dream girl, and how it was so fucking perfect. But I knew he wouldn't respond. That's when I thought about my parents and Hayden. I would have texted them in the past, but I knew that wasn't an option and it made me realize, I need to mend those relationships. If I don't, it will sit on my chest and then at some point, it might hurt our relationship, and I will not let that happen."

I press my hand to her cheek.

"You're it for me, Blakely. This is it. I want nothing else and I want to do everything I can to make sure this relationship goes the distance."

She gently smiles as she leans down and presses a soft, whisper-like kiss to my lips.

"No one has ever talked to me like that before," she says.

"Does it overwhelm you?" I ask.

She shakes her head. "It doesn't. It makes me feel secure, cherished, and wanted. And not to bring up Perry, but I think that's where the difference is when it came to my feelings for him. In some senses, we were so young when we first got together. Everything was fun, and then over time, it wasn't. We didn't grow with the relationship. I've thought a lot about this since he left. It wasn't actually that hard to let him go. And that showed me that our relationship wasn't as strong as I had thought it was. We wouldn't have gone the distance."

She smooths her palm over my heart. I can't say I'm sorry to hear that. I've wondered if I was a rebound, but I don't think I am now.

"But the connection we have? It's why I was so scared at first to be with you. This bond we have seemed so innate. Intense. It's real and it's honest, and it's so much more than just a fuck at night. Does that make sense?"

"It does," I say. "Because I feel the same way."

"Then don't feel immediate pressure to make things right with your family. You do that when you're ready. Remember that it's a two-way street here. It's not just up to you. But also, don't think you need to do it because of me or that you won't be healthy enough to be with me until you do. I care about you, Halsey. I want you as is, right now, in this very moment."

I wet my lips as my eyes stay connected on hers. "Thank you, Blakely."

She presses a kiss to my lips before saying, "No need to thank me, just keep holding me."

"Easy," I say as I roll her to her back and shift her legs open with my knee. She raises a brow right before I kiss down her body and keep going south so I can show her exactly how much she means to me.

———

"PENNY, YOU'RE STARING AGAIN," Blakely says.

"What? No, I'm not." She lifts her menu in front of her face, blocking us from view.

Blakely reaches across the table and tugs down the menu to reveal her friend. "Yes, you are."

Penny tosses her hands up in the air and says, "Fine, okay, I was staring, but how can I not? Eli is staring too."

"No, I'm not," he says. "I'm trying to decide whether I want soup and a salad or a hearty sandwich."

"Go with the sandwich, man," I say as I drape my arm over Blakely and she leans into me.

Blakely asked me this morning if I'd go to lunch with Penny and Eli because Penny was—as she put it—"frothing at the mouth" to see us together. It was an easy yes for me because any time spent with Blakely is a win, even if that means it feels like we're sitting in a fishbowl as her best friend watches our every move.

"Can't a girl just be excited for her friend?" Penny asks.

"A girl can be excited for her friend, but a friend can also be a creepy stalker who won't stop staring."

"Uh, because I'm in awe," Penny replies. "I've never seen anyone manifest anything as hard as Halsey did. I mean, look at you both. He has his arm wrapped around you, you're all cuddled in close, you both have smiles on your faces, and there's a tiny bite mark on your neck that you forgot to cover up." Blakely presses her hand to her neck. I saw the bite mark before we left and said nothing because I like people to know that she's taken. "It's so sweet and so amazing that I'm just sitting here in wonderment. So yeah, I'm going to stare. And Eli is going to stare."

"But I'm not staring."

Penny swats at her man. "Eli, stare."

"Oh, right." He clears his throat and looks up at us. He knits his brows together as he stares hard.

"Dude, she means look at us, not try to blow us up with the force."

Penny glances up at Eli and then smooths out his brow. "Don't be a creep about it, Eli."

"I don't know how to stare. This is weird."

"What's weird is that you're not as fascinated as I am about this development. You were there for the journey." She motions to us. "Marvel at the result."

Eli looks between us and Penny, utter confusion written all over him. "I don't know what to do here. I'm extremely uncomfortable. Do you want me to clap?"

"Yes," I say before Penny can say anything. "Clap for us, Eli."

He lifts his hands above the table, hesitant, only for Penny to swat his hands down. "Don't clap for them, that would make this weird."

"Jesus fuck, this whole thing is weird." Eli pulls on his hair. When he hears me chuckle, he points and says, "You're an asshole."

"How about this," Blakely says. "We start a conversation that doesn't make anyone uncomfortable? How about how the season is going?"

Eli shakes his head. "Nah, the last thing I want to do is talk about hockey. How about we discuss Valentine's Day."

"Very subtle," Penny says with an eye roll. "You mean your birthday?"

"Well, can't a guy discuss what he wants to do? We have the night off."

"Do you want a party?" Blakely asks.

He shakes his head. "No, I want Penny's parents to take Holden and Penny to take me in—"

Penny clamps her hand over Eli's mouth and says, "Say that out loud and I won't be taking you anywhere."

He smiles against her hand and in a muffled voice, he says, "Good to know."

Penny then turns to us and folds her hands together as she asks, "Are you two going to be each other's valentines?"

"Yes," I answer as Blakely says, "We haven't discussed it."

Question in my brow, I look at her and ask, "Planning on being someone else's valentine?"

"No," she answers. "Just didn't want to put any pressure on you. Perry often worked on Valentine's Day. He'd always escape early so we did something, but I never pressured him to do anything."

"Pressure me all you want," I say. "I want to know what you want, how you want it, and when you want it. If you desire a valentine's celebration, it's yours, baby."

"Oh my God." Penny clutches her chest. "He calls you baby." She swats at Eli. "Did you hear that? He calls her baby."

"Ouch," Eli says, rubbing his arm. "I have ears, Penny."

Ignoring them, I say, "Then let's celebrate. I'd love to be your valentine."

I lift her chin and press a delicate kiss to her lips. "Good."

"HOW'S THE ANKLE?" Posey asks as he comes into the ice room where I'm nursing my ankle in an ice bath.

"Good," I say, studying the heavy set in his shoulders and the irritated pull in his expression. "How's everything with you?"

"Great," he says, offering me a fake smile.

"You sure? Because it seems like—"

"I said everything is great," he grunts before taking his shirt off as well as his shorts, leaving him in nothing but his boxer briefs. He submerges himself up to the neck into one of the ice baths and breathes heavily as he lets his body adjust to the cold.

"Sore?" I ask him.

"Something like that."

I think back to the text conversation we had and I wonder if the girl OC was talking about has anything to do with his mood. Because he's been so invasive with my personal life, I decide to insert myself into his.

"Want to tell me about the girl?"

"There is no girl," he says.

"Says the guy icing his dick."

He glances over at me. "I'm not icing my dick."

"Then what are you icing?"

"My ego," he mutters.

"Care to share?"

"No," he says as he blows out a heavy breath. "I'm assuming everything's great with you and Blakely? You're welcome by the way."

Seeing that he's riding the bitter train, I decide to throw him a bone. "Thank you, Posey. Yes, everything's good with us."

"Better be your best man at your wedding. If it's Eli, I'm going to fucking scream."

"You're getting ahead of yourself."

"You're telling me you haven't thought about buying that girl a ring?" he asks, a knowing tilt to his head.

"I thought about buying her a ring the day I met her," I answer. "But I need to make sure she's ready, so cool it on the marriage talk."

"Well, someone needs to get fucking married. All of you have girls but no one's set a date."

"Why the rush?" I ask.

"Because . . . good things happen at weddings. Look at you. You started hitting it off with Blakely at a wedding. I need a fucking wedding."

"Dude—"

He holds up his hand. "I don't want to talk about it."

"Okay . . ." I pause and then ask, "Do you have a valentine?"

His eyes narrow. "I really hate you."

———

"DOES IT HURT?" Blakely asks as she sits on my lap while she gently traces the gash I took to the head tonight.

"Not too bad," I say.

Despite wearing a helmet, I took an elbow to the head, right above my eye. The hit was so hard, it split the skin and I had to get two stitches during the game.

"It looks disgusting."

I chuckle. "Thanks."

"Anytime." She looks me in the eyes. "I didn't like seeing you bleed. It made me sick to my stomach."

I stroke her thigh with my warm palm. "I was okay."

"I know, but it still sucks seeing it, you know?"

"Yeah, I get it. It's a hazard of my job."

"I guess so. Although, the black eye is kind of hot."

"I don't know what to think about that."

She laughs. "Neither do I." She rests her head to my shoulder and I hold her closely as we snuggle on my couch. "I hate that you're leaving tomorrow."

"Me too," I say as I kiss the top of her head.

"Penny was telling me that she and Eli have FaceTime sex all the time." She lifts up to meet my eyes. "Is that something you're interested in?"

"I'm interested in anything you want to do," I say.

"So . . . if I answered the phone wearing that lingerie you like so much, what would you do?"

"Start rubbing myself immediately," I answer.

She smirks. "I like that answer. Can I ask you another thing?"

"You can ask me whatever you want," I say as I pick up a strand of her hair and start twirling it.

"Do you ever watch porn?"

"What do you think the answer to that is?"

Mischievously she dances her fingers over my chest. "Yes."

"You would be right. At the moment though, since you've been around, I haven't needed it."

"What did you like to watch?" she asks.

I shrug. "Didn't matter. I don't have a specific kink. Anything that would get me hard, really. Why . . . do you have something you like watching?"

She shakes her head, but I can tell she's lying.

"We're honest, right?" I ask her and she nods. "So tell me."

"It's embarrassing."

"No, it's not," I say. "There is nothing embarrassing about getting turned on, it's natural."

She moves her teeth over her bottom lip before she says, "I really like watching guy-on-guy porn."

"Really?" I ask, surprised. "Huh, I wouldn't have guessed that."

"There's just something about it. I don't know. Two dicks are better than one."

My brow raises. "Well, just so you know, I don't share. There will only be one dick in this relationship."

She laughs. "Trust me, Halsey, you have enough dick in your pants for four men."

"Good answer."

She plays with the collar of my shirt. "Would you ever watch it with me?"

"Sure," I say.

"Really?" she asks with a look of surprise.

"Yeah, why not? If you're into that, then sure, babe."

She shakes her head almost in disbelief. "Perry would never."

"Good fucking thing I'm not Perry."

"You certainly are not."

⊏⊐

HALSEY: *I hate that I'm not there on your last day. I'd take you out to dinner to celebrate, then I'd eat you for dessert.*

Blakely: Don't freaking tease me, not after last night.

Halsey: Still thinking about it?

Blakely: Halsey Holmes, I will never stop thinking about it. My pussy is actually throbbing from thinking about it.

Halsey: Don't make me hard on the plane.

Blakely: Don't make me wet at work.

Halsey: If you're wet, then slip two fingers against the delicious clit for me and taste yourself.

Blakely: Can you NOT sext me right now? I'm trying to write a wrap-up email for my boss to give to the new hire so they know everything they have to take over.

Halsey: You started it.

Blakely: How about this. I go to the bathroom and you go to the bathroom and we FaceTime so we can masturbate to each other?

Halsey: I'm in if you're in.

Blakely: Oh my God, Halsey, I was kidding.

Halsey: Baby, don't play with me. You know I'm up for anything. Last night proved that.

Blakely: Stop talking about LAST NIGHT!

Halsey: LOL. Never.

Blakely: Then I'm going to have to end this conversation.

Halsey: Is that what you really want to do?

Blakely: No.

Halsey: That's what I thought. Is Penny doing anything special for your last day?

Blakely: Uh . . . why is there a bonsai tree being delivered to my office?

Halsey: Right on time.

Blakely: OMG, Halsey.

Halsey: Do you like her?

Blakely: There's a bow in her leaves! Halsey, you did this for me?

Halsey: Just a little decoration for your home office. Probably not smart delivering it to work because you have to cart her home, but I wanted something special for you on your last day.

Blakely: I love her. Oh she's a Chinese Elm bonsai. She's so beautiful. Does she have a name?

Halsey: That's up to you.

Blakely: Why am I getting so emotional over a freaking tree?

Halsey: Because you have the best fucking heart I know, and you care about things . . . even if they're mini trees.

Blakely: I love her so much. I want to put her next to Sherman. Ooo, I should name her with an S name, you know, so they feel cool together. Kind of like how you and Holden did that.

Halsey: That brought a smile to my face. So let's pick an S name. How about . . . Shonda after Shonda Rhimes. I know how much you loved Queen Charlotte.

Blakely: True, true, but I kind of want this little girl to be her own person, you know? To not have to live up to the name. Shonda gives her some big shoes to fill.

Halsey: I see that we're going to overthink this. How about you toss out some names?

Blakely: Let's see . . . Sylvie, Susanna, Shirley.

Halsey: Shirley is cute.

Blakely: Yeah, I agree and it goes so well with Sherman. OMG, they're going to be the best of friends. Halsey, this was such a wonderful gift. Thank you.

Halsey: Hell, if I knew you were going to like Shirley so much, I would have waited to give her to you in person to see your reaction.

Blakely: [picture] Here's a picture of me and her so you can at least have a sneak peek.

Halsey: Fuck, Blakely. You're so beautiful.

Blakely: You SPOIL me.

Halsey: I just state the facts. Glad you're mine.

Blakely: Glad you're mine, too.

━━

"HEY, YOU," Blakely sleepily says into the phone.

I lie down on the hotel bed while I hold the phone up to my ear. "Were you sleeping?"

"Maybe a little."

"Shit, I'm sorry."

"Don't be. I'm on the couch. I should move into the bed, but I just hate when you're not there. It's so empty and cold."

"You wearing my shirt?"

"Yes, but it doesn't replace you."

A smile tugs on my lips. "I miss you, too."

She yawns into the phone and then asks, "Did you win?"

"We did. It was a good game, so you shouldn't have fallen asleep."

"I've struggled sleeping, and I think my energy is drained from trying to make sure I'm doing everything right with the new job. I have to go to the office sometime next week when you're there for away games."

"Yeah?" I ask. "Maybe we can share a room?"

"Perhaps." I can hear the smile in her voice.

"If we're in the same city, we're sharing a damn room."

She chuckles. "Yeah, I agree with that. I didn't know I've become so dependent on you. How did you make that happen?"

"Just slowly needled my way in over a year and a half."

"Well done, sir. Now I don't sleep well without you. Look what you did to me."

"Trust me, I don't sleep well without you either."

She sighs over the phone. "We've become that nauseating couple."

"Best news I've ever heard," I say.

She chuckles. "So were you asked any stupid questions after the game?"

"Like what?" I ask.

"Like . . . what cup size do you wear?"

"What?" I laugh. "I don't think that's ever asked."

"Maybe not yet."

"All right, Blakely, your fatigue is showing."

"You might be right, but I don't want to get off the phone, not yet."

"Then get ready for bed and tell me about your day, but don't ask me if reporters asked me my cup size."

She laughs. "Why not? It's an interesting question. The women want to know."

"There should only be one woman who cares."

"Oh Halsey, trust me when I say, there is more than one woman who cares. You should see the comments Penny has to filter through every time she posts about you."

"Well, I only care about one woman."

"This I know." I sit up from the bed and go to the bathroom where I turn the phone on speaker and set it on the counter. "Are you getting ready for bed too?" she asks.

"Yeah. I'm fucking beat."

"I should have given you a pair of my underwear to cuddle and sleep with."

I chuckle as I line my toothbrush with toothpaste. "And with my luck, Posey comes charging into my room only to see me with your underwear around my head."

"I'm sure he's seen worse."

Together we brush our teeth. After I spit and rinse, I say, "So tell me about your day. Anything fun happen?"

"No. Just training and learning about The Jock Report. I was thinking that I could play around on your profile a bit to learn it better."

"I don't have one."

"You will tomorrow. I hope that's okay."

"Whatever you need, babe," I say as I switch off the light and go into the bedroom where I lie down. "Just pick a good picture."

"I have the perfect one in mind. It's from that game where you won in the last second against The Freeze. The Agitators use it all the time. Very recognizable, great for branding."

"Or maybe we don't use that picture," I say.

"Oh, you want to do a shirtless one? Maybe garner more donations?"

"No," I say as I drag my hand over my face. "That, uh picture, the one that the Agitators use all the time? I hate it."

"Why?" she asks in a curious tone.

"It's from the night we lost Holden. Every time I see it, I'm reminded of what happened after that game."

"Oh my God, Halsey, I had no idea. Does the team know that?"

"Obviously not. It's an epic shot for Agitators' history so I understand why they use it. It's like the Bobbies using the picture of Carson Stone jumping on Knox Gentry's back when they won the World Series. It's iconic."

"But if it causes you such difficult thoughts, maybe it's something we can talk to Penny about."

"Nah, it's okay," I say. "But for my personal stuff, I'd like to avoid it."

"We will." And to lighten the mood, she says, "I'm almost tempted to use a picture of you and me as the profile, you know, to make all the thirsty fans out there know that you're off the market."

"I'm cool with that."

"I'm kidding," she says. "Shirtless is what we have to do. Maybe a picture of you wiping the sweat from your forehead while you're in your gear, you know, showing off some of your stacked abs. That would be hot."

"I thought The Jock Report was a place where athletes can reach out to fans and tell their own stories."

"It is. And the story I'd like to tell when it comes to you is that you're extremely hot, have a god-like body, and are currently unavailable because you're all mine."

"Quite the story, I'll buy into it."

"And just another reason I like you so much. You go along with my craziness."

"Anything to keep you happy."

"Is that so?" she asks. "So what if I decided that I wanted to revisit the conversation we had a while back? You know, about the dick piercing. What if I said I wanted you to do that?"

"Get my dick pierced?" I ask. "If you want me to, I will."

"Stop it. No, you wouldn't."

"Baby, you've seen how open I can be. What makes you think a dick piercing would stop me?"

"Oh my God, I'm wet all over again."

"If that's the case . . ." In a deep voice, I say, "Take off your clothes."

"They're already off."

I smile as I move my hand down to my cock. "Mmm, such a good girl."

"IS it crazy that I missed you this much?" Blakely's straddling my lap on the balcony loveseat that I specifically picked out with the hopes that we'd use it together.

"No," I answer as I smooth my hands over her ass.

"I shouldn't be attached to you this quickly."

"Why not?" I ask.

She sits back and plays with the hem of my shirt. "Because it just seems so sudden, doesn't it?"

"For you, probably," I answer. "For me?" I shake my head. "I've been attracted to you for a while, Blakely. But I understand where it might feel weird for you."

"It's not weird," she says. "Just surprising. You always hear about people breaking up with their long-term boyfriend or girlfriend and how they needed to take like a year off from dating, and here I am, feeling so much more than I think I ever have only a couple months later." I bet she has no idea how relieved I am to hear that.

"Just means I was made for you, and he wasn't."

She smiles at that. "I guess so." She tugs on my shirt and I lift so she can take it off. She lays it on the couch next to me and brings her hands to my chest.

"Trying to make me hard?" I ask as the subtle music she chose plays in the background.

"Trying to get closer to you." She chuckles and shakes her head.

"What?" I ask.

"Ugh, I'm such a harlot. I can't get enough of your body."

"Same," I say as I slide my hands under her cotton shorts and grip her bare ass.

"But I don't want to have sex right now. I want to ask you stupid questions."

"Stupid questions?" I raise a brow.

"Yes, like . . . I want to know the benign things about you. I feel like I know you on a deeper level from the conversations we've had, but what about the stuff you'd put in your dating profile? I don't know those things."

"Well, *I love having sex with Blakely* would be something on my profile."

She gives me a look. "If you like having sex with me there better not be a dating profile."

"I've told you before, Blakely. I found what I'm looking for. I'm good."

That brings a smile to her face as she leans forward and lightly kisses me.

When she pulls away, I continue, "But if you want to know the—as you call it—stupid stuff, I'd be more than happy to tell you whatever you want to know."

"Okay . . . how about this? Why don't we ask questions and for every question answered, we get to remove a piece of clothing."

"I'm down," I say. "You took my shirt off so I think I owe you an answer."

"Good point." She sits back on my lap as she asks, "What's your favorite color?"

"Agitators purple," I answer.

"Are you just saying that?"

I shake my head. "No. I really like the color. And I think I've seen it so much that I've become accustomed to it now."

"Oh, that's cute then. Okay, your turn. Ask me a question."

"Who's your celebrity crush . . . besides me?"

She rolls her eyes. "Uh, well, depends on the kind of mood

I'm in. If I want someone big and burly, I really have a thing for The Rock."

"Solid choice," I say.

"But if I'm looking for someone on the smaller side but could still carry me around if I needed to be shuffled through a jungle like Tarzan and Jane—"

"A circumstance that happens quite often."

"Obviously." She taps her chin. "I think it would have to be Tom Hiddleston."

"Do you think he could Tarzan you around the jungle?"

She nods her head. "I truly do."

"Okay, then Tom and The Rock it is." I tug on her shirt and bring it over her head, revealing a see-through lace bra. "Christ, Blakely," I mutter as my hands find her breasts, her hard nipples pressing against the thin fabric.

"You're growing hard."

"Your fault," I reply.

She plants her hands on my chest and starts to rock over me.

"Keep doing that and you won't get all your questions answered."

"Try having some patience, Halsey."

"When it involves your wet pussy, I have zero patience."

"Question time. Focus. If you weren't playing hockey, what would you be doing?"

"Melting away into nothing," I answer.

She pokes my chest. "Be serious."

She continues to rub over me, making it hard to think, so I try to concentrate on my answer and not the friction building between us. "My answer probably would have been different out of college. I probably would have said something like coaching, but now . . . if I didn't have hockey, I think I'd want to be a librarian of some sort, maybe a book blogger. Something that involves reading."

She pauses and tilts her head to the side. "Why is that the most attractive answer ever?"

"Because you seem to have a penchant for nerds."

She chuckles. "Probably."

Then she lifts off my lap and helps me with my shorts, revealing my large bulge in my briefs. She wets her lips, her eyes meet mine, and then she sits back down on my lap where she slowly rubs over me in long strokes. "Tell me about your family. I feel like I know nothing about them."

"Seems strange that you don't know them. Well, there's my mom and dad, Heather and Adrian, and I have a younger brother named Elliott. He's working as a mechanical engineer in a big firm in Chicago. I'm close with my parents, but they live in Toronto, so I don't get to see them very often. We'll have to go visit them soon." *I'd love that. I think . . . but would they like me? I'm so different to her ex.* Best not to worry about that one for now.

"Well, I'm glad you've had Penny as your bestie here in Vancouver."

"Yeah, me too."

"Did you have a stuffed animal or blanket that you had to sleep with every night?" I ask, wanting to get her out of her clothes as soon as possible.

"A stuffed animal," she answers. "He was an alligator named Chompy."

"Fuck, that's cute," I say. "Do you still have him?"

"I do. He's in a box of things from my childhood that I've kept. Sometimes I feel like he's Woody from *Toy Story* with actual feelings, and he must hate me because he's stuffed in a box somewhere. I had him out in my apartment when I was living with Perry, but Chompy isn't the fella he used to be, and well, he creeped Perry out, so I put him away."

"Fuck that," I say, anger billowing inside me. "You can put Chompy out on display at our place. Hell, put him next to Sherman and Shirley."

She leans back again and this time, there's a softer look on her face as her hips stop moving. "You said our place."

Huh . . . I did.

"Well, that's because that's how I see it," I answer honestly. "To me, it's our place. Is that how you see it?"

"I did get a desk for my bedroom where I've set up a place for me to temporarily work." She swallows hard and her eyes meet mine. "I could make that a little more permanent if you wanted."

"Yeah, I fucking want that," I say.

"Really?" she asks.

"Blakely," I sigh. "What don't you understand?" I grip her chin and hold her steady so her eyes are forced to look into mine. "When I said I found what I wanted, I mean it. I'm just waiting for you to catch up to the feelings I have for you. If you want to make that second bedroom an office, I'll fucking help you pick out wallpaper. If you want to set up a dresser in our bedroom and move your clothes in there, tell me how I can help and what dresser you want. You're it for me. I'm sold. So whatever you want, you can have it."

She brings her hands to her back where she undoes her bra and lets it slide off her before she leans forward and presses her bare breasts against my chest. *Talk about a reward.* I suck in a sharp breath as her lips find my neck and she kisses up the column until she reaches my jaw. "Then help me pick out some wallpaper," she whispers.

Jesus . . .

How can I be this lucky? How is this actually happening right now? This woman who has had my heart, my mind, my fucking soul since the moment I met her, how did I possibly get her to fall for me? I'll never know, but I'll spend the rest of my life making sure she will always be mine.

"We also need some bookshelves for the living room for your books to make room for a dresser for me."

"Done," I say as her lips work down to my mouth.

"And we need a rug for the living room."

"Take me shopping, show me what you like, and it's all yours," I answer.

"And I have some things from my old apartment that could work here."

"I'll have the guys help me move them," I say as her lips find mine but instead of demanding kisses, she lightly pecks along my lips.

"And I want to iron the curtains."

I chuckle. "I'll help you."

"And we need to take the tag off the whisk."

"We can cut it off together as a symbolic gesture."

She laughs and then sits up again. I massage her breasts and play with her perfect nipples. "Are we really going to live together?" she asks.

"Baby, we've been living together for a while now."

"As roommates," she clarifies. "This'll be different."

"Yeah, it'll be so much better," I say. "Because you'll be my girlfriend."

"Exactly. So this is happening?"

"If you're looking for someone to debate whether you should do it or not, you're looking at the wrong person. If it were up to me, you would have been living with me as my girlfriend a year ago." I lean forward and lick the tip of her nipple, which causes her to moan.

When her head falls back and her chest moves forward, I slip my hand under her shorts and between her legs where I find her soaking and ready.

"This game is over," I announce as I lift her up and carry her over to a lounger. I strip off her shorts, loving that she's not wearing underwear, and I tear my briefs off. I move between her legs, position my cock at her entrance, and I sink into her deep warmth. "I need to fuck you hard now."

I grip the sides of the lounger and pump hard until we're both coming.

Chapter Twenty-Two

BLAKELY

"We could do this when we both get back from California," I say as Halsey walks, keeping one arm draped over my shoulders while he pushes the cart in front of us.

We've already picked out some furniture for my office and the bedroom, as well as bookshelves, a rug for the living room, and a rug for my office so we can make it *our* place—still so crazy that I'm saying that—and now we're at Target, looking through simple home goods. Halsey suggested a higher-end place, which I'd never shop at, but I told him the furniture is where we put real money into. The little things like a candle can be bought at Target.

"Nah, we need to get a head start on your office to make sure it's as comfortable as you want it to be. You already picked out the wallpaper, so why not the rest?"

"You're sure you liked the wallpaper I picked out and you're okay with actually having a wall with wallpaper on it?"

He pauses and turns to me. "Blakely, what makes you think I'm going to change my mind?"

"I don't know, I just don't want you thinking I'm taking advantage or anything."

"The thought would never cross my mind, okay? I want you to be comfortable and I want you to be with me, therefore, we're putting wallpaper up on the wall, we've bought furniture, and now we're purchasing the trinkets that will make the place more homey."

And this is why I can't help but fall for this man, because he cares about me, about us, about going the distance. He's one of the top paid players in the league, he has all the fame, all the glory, yet, he's the most down-to-earth man I've ever met. You'd never know he was one of the best hockey players currently playing because he doesn't flaunt it. He doesn't act like the world revolves around him. He puts me first.

He puts us first.

"Thank you," I say as I press a kiss to his jaw.

"Anything for you, Blakely," he says as he moves us toward the kitchen aisles. "Do we need another whisk?"

I chuckle. "No, we haven't used the one that we have."

"Can you tell that to Posey please? Because when we were panic shopping before you arrived at the apartment, he insisted I needed the whisk and I told him you wouldn't use it."

"I'll make him a card with a he-told-you-so mention for you."

"And that's why you're my girl," he says while pressing a kiss to the side of my head.

"Hey, do we need a waffle maker?" he asks, stopping in front of one.

I chuckle. "Are you domesticating yourself today, Halsey?"

He looks me up and down and then back at the waffle maker. "What if I am, do you have a problem with that?"

"Not even a little." I walk up behind him and put my arm around his waist while he inspects the waffle maker. "If you get one, we can get some of those Kodiak Cakes mixes that have extra protein in them."

"Then it's sold, we're getting a waffle maker." He scratches his chin. "Now the question is, which one? Two plates or four?"

"Four," I say. "That way we can eat together rather than me eating my two while you wait for two more to cook."

His eyes meet mine as he says, "Fuck, you're so smart," and then he plants a huge kiss on my lips, which only makes me smile.

"YOU DIDN'T HAVE to get these pre-built," Halsey says as he stares at the bookshelves we purchased. We bought an L-shaped bookcase that fits perfectly in the nook of the living room. I also surprised him with a reading chair and lamp that I bought on my own. Something he wouldn't buy for himself, but that he absolutely loves. He's also mentioned it will be perfect to fuck me on as well.

Not mad about that either.

"You weren't going to build this by yourself."

"You would have helped me," he says.

I shake my head. "No, that's where you're wrong. I would not have helped you. I'm not into building or getting frustrated with each other over the assembly of furniture. Now let's load your books on the shelves. The only thing we need to talk about is how you want them organized."

"I don't care." He shrugs. "Just stick them on there."

I clutch my hand to my chest. "Dear God, Halsey. I'm not even a big reader and I know that's sacrilege. You can't just stick the books up there. There needs to be purpose to it."

"Why though? I don't care."

"Clearly, given where you've been storing all of your books, but now that they're going to have a new home, let's treat them with some decency. Now your choices are as follows: we can group them by author, or genre, or by color."

"What do you mean by color?" he asks.

"Well, don't let me influence you, but it might be fun to do what the Home Edit does."

"What the hell is that?" he asks.

I roll my eyes. "I should have known, given the state of your apartment when I arrived. The Home Edit are two ladies that have revolutionized the way we organize our houses. Their claim to fame is turning everything into a rainbow. So if you have a bunch of crayons, you organize them into rainbow order. Or books . . . you group them by color and put them in rainbow order."

"Huh." He glances down at the books. "Yeah, that might be nice. Although, there are a lot of black spines."

"That's okay, we can stack those up high and hopefully the more colorful ones will be at eye level."

"That works for me," he says as he starts picking up books and sorting them by color.

I start helping him but he stops me and says, "You're not doing that right."

"What do you mean?" I look down at my small piles.

"You're not doing it with your shirt off."

I roll my eyes and swat him away. "Don't be a pervert."

"Baby, when you have a girl like mine, it's hard not to be a pervert. Now take off that top and those shorts. I want to see the goods."

I look him up and down. "Only if you do."

Eyes on me, he reaches behind his head and pulls his shirt off. Then he pushes his shorts down, leaving him in just his boxer briefs.

So . . . to match him, I take off my top and remove my shorts, leaving me in a thong and another see-through bra. I bought more once I saw how crazy they made him.

"Fuck . . . me," he says as his eyes immediately go to my breasts.

I hold my hand out as he takes a step forward. "Books first, sex on the new chair after."

"Promise?" he asks.

"Promise," I say.

"Then get to work, you dirty girl. I need that pussy in my mouth now." He slaps my ass and as a squeal comes out of me, he smirks and starts moving faster with the books.

Ugh . . . this man.

It's crazy to say, but . . . I love him.

I know I do. I did love Perry, but this feels so different. There were . . . boundaries with Perry. Limits. And it's not just that Halsey spoils me with *whatever I want*. It's more about his attitude toward me. I'm his world, which I've seen in Eli with Penny too. These guys have so much riding on their careers, so much pressure not to be distracted by anything other than hockey, but they're so sacrificial when it comes to how they love. And let me tell you, it's incredible to be the recipient of such devotion. I've always wanted what my parents have. They just complement each other in so many ways. They're different, just like Halsey and I are different, yet those differences make them better as a couple. *And I think I've finally found that too. I could imagine spending the rest of my life with this man.* More so than I ever felt with Perry.

These heavy feelings I have for him. It's love.

It's true, deep, real love.

Once-in-a-lifetime all-consuming love.

And I'm almost positive he feels the same way about me.

———

"YOU'RE QUIET," I say to Halsey as I stroke my fingers over his bare chest.

We're lying in bed, our breath still slightly labored from how Halsey took me against the wall, and I can feel him thinking. How do I know? Because he's the same after every time we have sex—he strokes my bare skin, telling me how soft it is. He's reminding me how beautiful he thinks I am, and he's kissing me carefully until I fall asleep.

But he's not doing any of those things, which means he's thinking about something.

Something is on his mind.

"Sorry," he says as he drags his fingers up and down my back.

"Don't be sorry. Is there something you want to talk about that might be occupying your mind at the moment?"

He turns his head and kisses me on the forehead. "Got caught up in how much I like you. Moments like these, I wish I could share this with people."

"What do you mean?" I ask.

"With Holden," he says softly. "He'd like you so much. He'd immediately see how perfect you are for me and I don't know, just sad that I haven't been able to share this with him."

"Oh, I understand."

He's silent again but then says, "I've been thinking."

"Yeah?" I say as I play with his trimmed chest hair, letting the short, stubby strands run against my nails. "What are you thinking about?"

"I was thinking about contacting my parents."

"Really?" I ask while I sit up so I can look at him.

He nods. "Yeah. There's been too much time that's passed where we haven't kept in touch, and I don't think that should continue. Hell, I don't know anything that's going on in their lives and that's scary. What if they need help or what if they're struggling? I don't know. I should at least try to contact them."

"Would you message them together? Because didn't you say they were divorced?"

"Yeah," he says. "I think I'd try messaging my dad first. He and I had a better relationship and my mom was closest with Holden so, I think if I approach my dad first, maybe that would be better."

"I agree," I say. "What about Hayden?" I bring my hand to his hair and smooth down the stray pieces. Beads of sweat still lay at his crown from how much he exerted himself.

"He'd be next on the list. I think he'd be the hardest to talk to."

"Why?" I ask.

"Because we said some shit things to each other. Things that

353

are hard to apologize for, so . . . yeah. I have to find the courage to talk to him."

"Can I help you find that courage?"

He smiles softly. "Just keep being with me."

"I'm not going anywhere, Halsey."

"Good." He sighs as he looks up at me. He plays with a strand of my hair for a moment and then says, "I'm so glad you're here with me. Still feels like I'm living in a dream despite it being reality."

"Feels like a dream to me at times as well."

He lifts up and rolls me to my back where he leans down and softly kisses me.

And those kisses turn into more kisses.

And before I know it, he's moving between my legs again.

I SIT on the edge of the couch, my hands clasped in front of me as I watch Halsey move the puck down the ice. He shoots it over to OC who passes it rapidly to Silas. Silas flies behind the net and flicks the puck back to Halsey. He twists to the side and backhands the puck to OC just as Halsey breaks free from the defense and cuts in front of the goal. OC delivers a precise pass and Halsey backhands it into the goal.

The siren sounds off and I leap into the air and silently cheer because Holden is sleeping on Penny's chest.

She lightly chuckles while I sit back down. Whispering, she says, "Your nipples are hard."

"Are they?" I glance down and sure enough, there they are, standing to a point. "Would you look at that, even when we're not in the same room he can make them hard."

Penny laughs and I recline on the couch with her. "You know, I'm really happy for you," she says. "You seem so genuinely filled with joy."

I turn toward her as the game cuts to a commercial. "I am. I'm really happy."

"I can tell. I don't think that smile has left your face since you two started dating."

I shrug. "I could say the same about you and Eli. I think when you meet the right person, they change everything about you. How you feel inside and out."

Penny nods. "I agree. Even though my pregnancy was hard on me, and Holden has been troublesome at times, just like any baby, whenever Eli walks into the room, I feel at peace." Her eyes meet mine. "I'm guessing it wasn't like that with Perry." That's an interesting observation Penny has made. She never said anything negative about my relationship with Perry, but I could tell she didn't think we really . . . fit. And although it felt easy with Perry—after all, we were together for many years—I feel such a soul-deep connection with Halsey. I'm just so happy.

"Not to the extent that I feel with Halsey. Perry and I got along fine. It's not as if we fought. But I do feel we'd both stopped giving each other our all. It feels insane. I nearly didn't get this." I shake my head. "Like, what if he never decided to move to Australia? I would have married him, and I wouldn't have known this feeling I have any time I think of Halsey. I would have missed out on so much."

"Have you heard from Perry at all since the wedding?"

I shake my head. "No. I did speak to Arlene, though, because I know some people saw the interaction, and I wanted to make sure it didn't negatively impact her wedding. She said she didn't even know until the next day when her family was gossiping about it at brunch. Apparently, Perry came off as an ass and Halsey a hero."

"I mean, that's how I saw it."

I smirk. "Hard not to side with the hot, overprotective hockey player. But Marco did connect with Perry to make sure he was okay. Apparently, he threw in the towel and went back to Australia, so, I think that chapter of my life is officially closed."

"How do you feel about that?"

"Fine," I say. "Like I said, the feelings I have for Halsey severely outweigh the ones I had for Perry, it's an easy choice.

Now, if Halsey was the one who left I'd fight. I don't think there's a bone in my body that would let him go. There is no scenario where that would ever occur."

"Sooo . . ." Penny drags out. "Does that mean you love him?"

I nod. "Yeah, I do."

"Oh . . . my . . . God," she whispers, then closes her eyes. "I still can't believe we were able to make this happen."

"Are you really taking credit?" I ask, brow raised.

"Uh, yeah. Maybe our suggestions aren't what won you over in the end, but it kept Halsey involved, and if we weren't pushing him, then I don't think he would have ever made a move."

"Which is so strange to me," I say. "He's such a confident man. You'd think he would have tried to get me on his own."

"Not when playing with his heart," Penny says. "He protects that carefully."

"I guess you're right about that."

"So what's next? You guys are officially living together, the place looks amazing, much better than the sterile four walls you originally moved into. Are you going to get married?"

"Hey . . . if anyone is getting married first, it's you and Eli."

"I know, we're working on it. We want to take our time. Maybe when Holden is a little older, he can be the ring bearer. We talked about it the other night. We want him to have a part in the wedding, and it would be adorable seeing him waddle down the aisle."

I move my hand to my heart. "My God, that would be so cute."

"Yeah, so it might be a while, but we're okay with that. What about you?"

"I think I just want to relax and enjoy the time with Halsey. Make it through the season, go up to the famous cabin in Banff during the summer, and see where it takes us. I know he's committed to me, though. He's said it several times."

"That's the one thing you have to love about these boys. They're loyal to their core."

"They are," I say as the game comes back on, and they show

a replay of Halsey's goal. He makes it seem so effortless as he handles the puck and glides along the ice. And I can vouch for the fact that this man is good at using his hands. "Also, Halsey has mentioned wanting to get in touch with his family again. He talked about it the other night."

"What did he say?"

"Just that he thinks it's time."

"Are you worried about it?" Penny asks just as Holden lifts his head but then slams it back down on her chest. She lightly grunts and rubs his back, soothing him.

"No, not really. I mean, I'm worried that maybe Halsey might not get what he wants from it, but I'll be there for him the entire time. He's mentioned wishing his family was closer. I think the more intense our relationship becomes, the more he wants to share it."

"You think because he wants to marry you?"

"Well, we haven't said I love you yet, but from the way he speaks about me, it sounds like he'd want to head in that direction. I can't imagine what it would be like to get married without your family, you know?"

"Yeah, so he probably wants to mend those relationships for what he has planned."

"I think so," I say.

She nods. "Well, I hope everything turns out the way he wants it to. He deserves happiness, and he's found it with you. I truly hope that's all he needs."

———

"YOU LOOK HOT," Halsey says as I walk into the kitchen wearing a black pencil skirt, navy-blue top, black tailored suit jacket, and black high heels.

"Thank you," I say as I walk up to him where he's sitting on the counter, drinking his coffee. I cup his cheek and kiss him, only quickly though before I pull away.

"Are you sure you don't want me to drive you to the airport?" he asks.

"Positive. You have to pack and get on the road soon yourself."

"I'd make it work for you."

I grab a protein bar—this almond coconut one that Halsey got me into—and stuff it into my carry-on before grabbing a premade iced coffee from the fridge as well.

"I know you would, but I don't want you stressing," I say. "Anyway, you have some important games to concentrate on."

"I'm not worried." He sets his coffee down and hops off the counter. My brilliantly handsome and muscular man walks right up to me and loops his arm around my waist. "We're taking the title this year, Blakely. I can feel it in my bones."

"All the more reason you shouldn't worry about me. Focus on what you need to do, and I'll see you in California."

He kisses up my neck. "What time do you have to leave?"

"Now," I say as I chuckle. "There's no time for that. Plus, you already had me twice this morning, hence why I have no time."

"Twice is not enough. It will never be enough," he says, bringing his lips to mine.

I let him kiss me, deep and hard, so I feel his love for me all the way to the tips of my toes, and I feel myself falling into his grasp, into this hold he seems to have on me.

His hold grows stronger.

His kiss lasts longer.

And I drop my bag to the ground as I wrap my arms around him.

He groans against me, then lifts me onto the counter. He pushes my legs to the side, twists my torso so I'm facing him better, and kisses me more, his tongue diving deep, his hands sifting through my hair. This man and his incredible kisses. *He's amazing. And I'm addicted.*

"Fuck, Blakely," he whispers just as he pulls away and leans his head against mine. "I know you need to leave. I'm not trying to be a dick here." When his eyes meet mine, I see the desperation. I can see that he wants to say something, and it's on the tip of his tongue.

"You're not being a dick," I say. "I will always love the way you want me."

"And I want you, so bad, every fucking second of my life." He takes a deep breath. "I can't stop thinking about you. And I hate this, when I have to leave. And I hate even more that you have to leave. I like knowing you're here in our apartment, safe."

That last word hits me hard because I know exactly what it pertains to.

This clinginess.

The need for him to hold me.

Touch me.

Be near me.

He's scared something might happen to me.

"Halsey," I say, looking him square in the eyes. "Are you scared?"

He wets his lips while he nods.

"It's okay to be scared. I get that, but please know, I'll be making the smartest decisions to keep safe, okay?"

"Promise?"

The insecurity in his eyes.

The trepidation.

It nearly shatters me.

"I promise," I say.

Nodding, he cups my cheek one last time for a kiss before helping me off the counter.

"Thank you," he says softly as he picks up my bag for me and helps me to the door with my suitcase. "For understanding."

"You never have to thank me for something like that," I say.

I take my bag and suitcase from him, then place my hand on his chest. "I'll miss you."

He sighs heavily. "Miss you too, baby. I'll see you in California."

I kiss him gently. "See you in California."

Chapter Twenty-Three

HALSEY

I stare down at my phone and take a deep breath.

You can do this.

Holden would want you to do this.

But fuck am I nervous.

I drop my phone on my hotel bed, and for the second time in thirty seconds, I pace my hotel room.

We arrived in Vegas about an hour ago. Blakely is in training, but we don't have to report in for training until tomorrow. If I'm ever going to do this, now is the time.

But what the hell do I say?

Hey, it's been a long time, but it's good to hear your voice?

Oh hey, yeah, it's your son, the one who didn't die?

You know, the last time I heard from you was at Holden's funeral, pretty sad day, wasn't it?

"Jesus," I mutter as I rub my eyes. "Just fucking call him."

I sit down on my bed, grab my phone again, and pull up my dad's name in the contacts.

On a deep breath, I call him, and then put the phone on speaker.

Nausea and nerves roll through me as I stand, waiting for the phone to ring.

But it never does.

Instead, I hear, "We're sorry, but the number you're trying to reach is no longer in service."

My brow creases as I hang up.

Does he not have that phone number anymore?

Just because I need to double-check, I try calling it again, and the same response plays.

I scratch the back of my head and hang up.

Maybe . . . maybe my mom would know.

My teeth roll over the corner of my lip, and I contemplate whether this is worth it.

I want to mend things with my family. I know Holden would hate that it's gone on this long. He'd be so mad at us. And now with Blakely in my life, I want . . . I want this off my chest. I love her, I want to marry her, and I want to start a family. Deep down, I know I need to make things right with my family first. They need to know that I'm okay, and I need to know they're okay. And maybe, if we can, perhaps we can be in each other's lives once more.

And because of that, I find myself searching through my phone for my mom's home number.

When I find it, I don't even think twice and press the call button.

Once again, I feel sick with anxiety. I try to tamp it down with deep breaths.

On the third ring, the phone picks up.

"Hello?"

Jesus, I haven't heard that voice in years.

I swallow down my nerves and say, "Hey, uh . . . Mom, it's Halsey."

I'm met with silence.

After a few seconds, I add, "Are you there?"

"Wh-why are you calling me?"

I squeeze my eyes shut as I answer, "Well, I tried calling Dad, but—"

"He's dead."

"What?" I croak out, my throat growing tight. My heart sinks to the floor, and I immediately sit down on the bed.

"He died a few months ago. Heart attack."

"Why . . . why didn't anyone tell me?"

"Why do you think, Halsey?" she says in such a strong, menacing tone that there's no mistaking the anger she still carries.

Why do I think? I have no idea.

I'd like to think that it would be important to relay news of my father's death to me, but this family has fallen apart so tragically that I don't think we know how to treat each other like decent human beings anymore.

"Mom, I know—"

"You know nothing, Halsey. You know absolutely nothing. And why are you even calling? Trying to open a wound that has barely healed?"

I press my hand to my eye as my heart races, laboring my breath as I try to wrap my head around both the disdain blistering from my mom's mouth and my dad's death.

A heart attack?

Was he alone?

Did the loss of Holden kill him?

"I don't understand," I mumble into the phone.

"What don't you understand?" she asks.

For one, why do you hate me?

Why don't you love me anymore?

Why has this family exploded into nothing?

Why can't we find each other again?

Why does my mom hold such hostility toward me?

Shouldn't she have unconditional love for me? I don't understand why she doesn't.

Lip trembling, I say, "Why . . . why are you so angry with me?"

"Why am I angry with you?" she asks on a sardonic laugh, the type of laugh I've never heard my mom use. She was a sweet, loving woman. "Are you really that dense, Halsey?"

Her words cut through me, one at a time, and I steel myself, trying to stay strong, but I can feel this dark, ominous cloud looming over me. "Maybe I am," I say, my voice barely above a whisper. "We lost Holden, and we haven't—"

"You lost Holden," my mom says.

I pause and ask, "What?"

"You're the one who lost Holden. You're the one who wasn't paying attention. You're the one who let this happen. You're the reason he drove home drunk. You, Halsey. You are the reason."

I feel all the blood drain from my body as her words swirl around in my head.

She can't possibly think that. I wasn't even there that night. He was the one who got drunk. He was the one who decided to drive home. He was the one who drove into a tree.

That was on him. Not me.

"He made the choice to drive," I say.

"Do not start on that with me. I asked you to watch out for him. I told you he was going to be wild. And it was your responsibility to guide him down the right road when you both left the house. You promised me and you broke that promise." Hurt and anger pervade her every word. "You are the reason he died."

"That's not fair."

"Do you know what's not fair?" Mom asks. "That the wrong twin died."

The air is completely knocked out of my lungs as I feel the room, the world melt into nothing around me.

Th-there's no way she meant that.

She couldn't possibly be that cruel.

"Mom . . ." I croak out.

"Please don't use this phone number again. I consider you

dead to me as well." And then she hangs up, leaving me in a state of shock.

I drop my phone to the bed and curl into a ball as panic seizes me. And then I see it all again. The same horror.

The smashed, mangled car.

The bent, broken tree.

The gnarled limb that had penetrated the windshield.

The blood.

And then . . . the smells.

The dank soil.

The acrid yet sweet smell of gasoline.

The officer's gum to hide the cigarette smell.

The blood and metal maliciously fused together.

She hates me. Not only does she place all the blame on my shoulders, but she despises me. Her son.

My stomach roils. Nausea pulses through me.

He's dead. The wrong twin died.

"You're the one who lost Holden. You're the one who wasn't paying attention. You're the one who let this happen. You're the reason he drove home drunk. You, Halsey. You are the reason."

I leap toward the bathroom and barely make it to the tile before I'm throwing up all over the bathroom floor, wave after wave of nausea hitting me, creating a sheen of sweat all over my body.

Four words.

Four powerful, excruciating words.

The wrong twin died.

I feel every aspect of the life I've tried to build after losing Holden slip from my grasp, that dark cloud swallowing them up and leaving me in a painful state of agony where I don't belong on this earth.

Maybe she's right. Maybe the wrong twin did die. *Isn't that what I've thought all along? I am the cause? He should be alive?*

Not me.

If Holden was alive, he would have been stronger.

If Holden was alive, he would have mourned but carried on my spirit.

If Holden was alive, he wouldn't have hidden in a world of denial.

If Holden was alive, he would have kept the family together. And he wouldn't have let Dad die.

He would have been there for him.

He would have made sure everyone in our life was good. He would have called. He would have visited.

He wouldn't have holed up in a summer cabin, pretending nothing was wrong and escaping into books.

And there's the difference.

He would have lived.

He wouldn't have let any of this happen.

Unlike me . . .

So yeah, she's probably right. The wrong twin did die.

―――

"DUDE, what the fuck are you doing?" Eli says as he comes up to where I'm sitting at the bar, a glass of whiskey in my hand, sweat beading down my forehead, as I try to get so obliterated that I black out and forget everything.

"What does it look like?" I ask, hearing my words slur ever so slightly. Good. I'm right where I want to be.

"Fuck, Halsey." He peels the cup out of my hand and places it on the other side of the bar. He then addresses the bartender and says, "Close his tab. Now. Do not open another."

"Don't listen to him," I say, but unfortunately, the bartender does. "What the fuck, man?"

"You have a goddamn game tomorrow. You shouldn't be drinking."

"Fuck off," I say, but then I'm dragged off my stool by the shoulder. "What the fuck?"

Eli doesn't say anything. Instead, he pockets my card, signs the receipt for me, then pushes me toward the hotel elevators.

Irritated, I spin around and push him back.

Eli's eyes sear into me. "Not fucking here," he says as he punches the up button on the elevator.

Unlucky for me, the elevator door opens immediately, and he moves me inside. When the door closes, he asks, "What the fuck are you doing? Blakely said she's been trying to call you all night, and you haven't answered. She texted Penny, and Penny texted me. When I saw you weren't in your room, I came downstairs to find you in the bar. So explain to me what the hell is going on."

I push my hand through my hair and lean against the wall. "Nothing," I say.

"Bullshit. You don't drink before games. So what happened?"

"I said nothing." The elevator door opens, and I stumble out, confused as to where to go.

Sighing, Eli pushes me toward the right.

"Stop fucking pushing me," I yell.

"Keep your goddamn voice down unless you want people hearing that the center for the Vancouver Agitators is drunk off his ass."

"Who fucking cares," I mutter as I slam into a door that's not mine.

"Jesus fuck," Eli says as he grabs me by the shoulder and moves me forward, staying right behind me.

A door opens behind us, and we hear, "What's going on?" I glance over my shoulder to see Silas pop his head out.

"I need help," Eli says.

"One second," Silas replies.

"Just leave me the fuck alone," I say as I try to move away from Eli, but he doesn't let me.

He keeps his hand on my shoulder and brings me to my room just as Silas catches up.

"What's happening?" he asks.

"Holmes is drunk. Blakely hasn't heard from him all night. Something's up."

"Nothing is up." I push him away but he doesn't budge.

Instead, he takes my key card from my pocket and opens my

door right before pushing me in with a giant shove. I stumble in, hit the wall, and fall to the ground.

"How is that productive?" Silas asks as he leans down and helps me up.

"I didn't mean to send him to the floor. He clearly doesn't have good balance."

"All the more reason not to shove him. The last thing we need is for him to roll his ankle again."

"Right . . . sorry," Eli says before dragging his hand over his face. "I'm exhausted and not thinking right."

"Then let me handle this."

Eli shakes his head. "No, I promised Blakely I'd take care of it."

"Don't promise Blakely anything," I say as Silas brings me over to the bed and sits me down.

Two of my best friends stand in front of me, probably trying to figure out what to do with me. I can tell them . . . let me go back to the bar. Their presence just reminds me of all the reasons I don't want to be in this room, near my phone.

"What happened?" Eli asks.

"Nothing," I reply.

"And like I said earlier, bullshit." He reaches for my phone on the nightstand and flashes the screen at my face to unlock it.

"What are you doing?" I ask as I reach for it, but Silas steps in front of me and settles me back down on my ass.

"You have ten missed calls from Blakely, a bunch of texts." He flips through the phone, then his eyes lift to mine. "Why the fuck were you calling your parents?"

Silas's head whips toward me. "You called your parents?"

God, they're so invasive.

I lie back on the bed and cover my eyes. "None of your fucking business."

"Halsey—"

"I said it's none of your fucking business." I yell loud enough that it probably woke up the whole floor.

Silas turns to Eli and says, "Not the right time, man."

Eli nods and sets my phone down. "Okay." He sets his hands on his hips. "Well, might as well get comfortable." He moves around to the other side of the bed and pulls back the sheets before knocking his slides off and getting into bed.

"What are you doing?" I ask.

"You're not sleeping alone, so get comfortable . . . buddy."

"Jesus fuck," I say as I stand, but Silas gets in front of me.

"Where are you going?"

"To take a piss," I shout. "Can I do that?"

"I prefer he doesn't pee the bed," Eli says.

"I prefer that he does," Silas says with a smirk before I blow past him.

BLAKELY

"ELI'S WITH HIM?" I ask Penny. I'm trying not to lose my freaking mind over the fact I've been trying to contact Halsey all freaking night with no response.

"He is. He just texted me and told me to tell you," Penny replies over the phone.

"Did he say what he was doing?"

Penny is silent for a second before she says, "He was down at the bar, drunk."

"Drunk?" I ask. "Halsey doesn't drink before games. Did he say what was wrong?"

"Well, they aren't sure. Halsey won't say anything, but Eli did look in his phone and saw that Halsey called his parents."

"Oh no," I say softly. "He called them today?"

"That's what it seemed like. When they asked him about it, he said nothing. He's passed out now in bed and will be hurting tomorrow for sure."

"Fuck," I whisper. "This isn't good, Penny."

"I remember you saying he wanted to contact his family. Do you think it went wrong?"

"It had to," I say as I stand from my hotel bed and grip my forehead, wishing I could be in Vegas with Halsey right now to tell him whatever they said, it's going to be okay. That he's loved and cherished. "I know he's wanted to contact them for a bit, but I didn't think . . . I don't know. I didn't think it would go so wrong that he'd end up at a bar the night before a game. Halsey doesn't do that. He's very cautious about what he does before games. He wouldn't even drink when he was injured."

"Well, from what Eli said, there doesn't seem to be anything you can do until tomorrow, so I think you should probably just get some sleep—at least try, I know that's easier said than done—and hopefully he calls you in the morning."

"And what if he doesn't?" I ask in a panic. "What if he uses this as an excuse to push me away?"

"Don't let him," she says. "No matter what he says to you, you have to know this isn't the real Halsey talking. It's the scared, hurt Halsey."

"Do you think he'll push me away?" I bite on the tip of my finger, my stomach roiling with anxiety.

"Honestly . . . yes. Knowing how these men work, he'll do everything to ensure he can feel as shitty as possible. And that means eliminating the one thing that brings him joy. And that's you."

Tears spring to my eyes. "I don't want to be pushed away. I want to help him, hold him, and nurture him through this."

"Which means no matter what he says or does, you need to hold strong. You said it yourself, you love him deeper than anything or anyone you've loved before. Don't let that feeling be taken away from a hurt man who is drowning. You are the lifeline, so be the lifeline."

I nod even though she can't see me. "You're right."

"Fight for him, Blakely."

"I will."

"And I'm here for you if you need anything."

"Thank you, Penny."

―――――

HALSEY

BLAKELY: *Can you at least let me know that you're okay? Please, Halsey?*

I stare down at her text message and all the other text messages she's sent as I nurse a bottle of water in the locker room.

Fuck, do I feel like shit.

I woke up this morning with Eli next to me, his arm splayed out across the bed and a light snore coming from his mouth. I proceeded to throw up in the bathroom, which of course woke him up. He tossed me some water and ordered breakfast for us both.

I watched him inhale a large plate of eggs, bacon, and fruit, and I proceeded to throw up two more times after that.

He urged me to at least eat some bacon to settle my stomach, but that did nothing for me. So he ordered a hangover cure from the kitchen. I have no idea what the hell was in that, but it eased my stomach and brought me back from hell. Now I just feel like a goddamn zombie walking around the earth with a game ahead of me.

Yet it doesn't feel as bad as what my mom said to me and the realization of all of that.

"Text her back," Eli says when he sits beside me in the locker room.

"Mind your own fucking business."

"Funny you say that, I don't recall you minding your own business when it came to me and Penny."

"This has nothing to do with my relationship with Blakely," I say as I set my phone down and lift my drink to my lips. I've been doing my damnedest to try to hydrate before the game. It's been slow. If I make it through the three hours of gameplay tonight, it will be a goddamn miracle.

"Then why not text her back?" He nudges me with his shoulder. "Go ahead. I'll wait."

"Can you leave me the fuck alone?"

"No."

And he leaves it at that, so I pick up my phone and text Blakely back.

Halsey: *I'm fine.*

"That's all you're going to say to her?" Eli asks. "That you're fine? She called and texted you several times last night, and that's what you're going to say? You're fine. Are you trying to be a dick?"

"I'm trying to fucking hydrate and get my mind on the game. I don't need you chattering in my ear."

He tugs on my shoulder so I'm forced to look at him. "What the hell did your parents say to you last night?"

"How . . . how do you know—"

"I saw that you called them. It was in your call history. So what the fuck did they say to you that has put you in this frame of mind? Whatever it is, it isn't fucking true. And do not for a second believe it. Don't let them get in your goddamn head. Don't let them rule over everything you've been able to move toward with Blakely. You have a good thing, man. Don't waste it on their empty words."

I look away from him as my phone dings with a text. I glance at the preview and read her text.

Blakely: *Okay. Well, I miss you. Please call me if you can.*

I set my phone down again and lean my head back so I can close my eyes. "My mom's words were not empty. They were true."

"What did she say?"

Keeping my eyes closed, I say, "My dad is dead."

"Jesus." Eli turns toward me. "Fuck, man. I'm sorry."

My throat grows tight, and I shake my head. "It is what it is."

"No, Halsey. That's awful, and you're allowed to feel that pain."

Little does he know.

"Okay, so can you just leave me the fuck alone now?"

"No," he says, and I feel him scoot closer. "I'm not leaving you alone."

I place my hands over my face and groan. "I don't want to fucking talk about this. Okay? I just want to . . . fuck." I stand from the bench and place my hands on my hips. "I just want to be . . . be done."

"Done with what?" Eli asks.

"Everything," I shout before pulling on my hair. "I want to be done with this guilt, I want this heaviness resting on my chest, the responsibility of it all, taken away. I want it to be done. I want it to end. She was right. She was so fucking right."

"Who was right?" Eli asks, standing now. "Your mom?"

"Don't worry about it." I step forward, but Eli stops me. And I don't know what comes over me, but between my frustration, hurt, and irritation, I whip around and plow my fist right into Eli's face, sending him back against the locker.

"What the fuck?" Pacey says as he comes into the locker room.

Eli doesn't move, though. He just looks up at me, his cheekbone red from my fist. "Do it again," he says. When I don't move, still stunned from what I did, he lifts to his feet and gets right in my face. "Do it again, Holmes. Punch me. If that's what's going to help you, then fucking punch me again." He pokes my chest and says, "But it won't stop me from continuing to love you, care for you, and be there every step of the way." He wets his lips. "I was there that night. I was at the bar with him. I watched him sling back shot after shot, and I didn't do anything about it. I've held on to that feeling, the one where I think to myself . . . if only. But do you know where holding on to that has gotten me?" He pushes my chest, sending me a step back and causing Pacey to come up to us. "It got me fucking nowhere. Holding on to what your mom said to you will get you nowhere.

Punching me will get you nowhere. Drinking like your fucking brother who had a goddamn problem that no one could fix BUT HIM won't get you anywhere. So punch me." He holds his arms out. "Fucking punch me, Holmes, and get it all out."

"He was my responsibility," I yell. "That's what my mom said. *And it was true.* I should have looked after him. He was my—"

"No, Holmes. She's wrong. So fucking wrong. He was a man. He was responsible for his own actions. He—"

"But I knew he was wild. I should have taken better care of him. I—"

"The only thing you should be doing is grieving the loss of your brother. That's it. He made choices. And not just that night. You know this. It's not your fault."

"It should have been me, though. My mom was right. The wrong twin died."

"Fucking hell. She said that?" Pacey rasps.

"Of course she did. It's true."

"It's not. She's bitter and angry, but that cannot live on your shoulders. It can't. He made choices. And we grieve."

"But—"

"No, man. No buts. You gotta let this go. You gotta get this anger out. Punch me. I'll take it. And when you're done, I'm going to be here with these open arms, ready to hold you and help you. So just . . . fucking . . . punch me."

I crash into him, but without my fists as weapons or anger being stored in my brow. Instead, my silent tears guide the way, followed by the pain that's been funneled deeply into my heart. I wrap my arms around him and quietly shake against his chest as he holds me close to him.

And that's how we stand for I don't know how long. Eli holding me, Pacey gently placing his hand on my back, and me sobbing into my teammate.

BLAKELY

BLAKELY: *I can't tell you how grateful I am, Huxley. I will forever owe you.*

Huxley: *You owe me nothing. I'll see you tomorrow.*

I stare out the window as my taxi driver drives me from the private airport in Vegas to Halsey's hotel room. I checked the score of the game, and the boys lost terribly. Zero to three. Pacey didn't play. Eli was out for a lot of the game, and Halsey . . . well, he didn't play at all. It was a second-string game that they could afford to lose, but it only leads me to believe that nothing is fine like Halsey said.

The only thing he's said to me all day.

Huxley saw how distracted I was and pulled me to the side to ask me what was going on. I apologized profusely and told him that I'd do better, but he didn't let me leave his office. He wanted to know what was distracting me, so I told him I was worried about Halsey. That's when he offered his private plane so I could get to him. He didn't care how long I had it for as long as I was back in the office in the morning for training.

I've never been more grateful.

I brought a small overnight bag with me, just in case, and could change on the plane into a pair of shorts and a regular shirt so that I'm at least comfortable and not walking around in a business suit and heels.

"This is it," the driver says. I hand him over forty dollars, tell him to keep the change, and walk into the upscale hotel and straight to the lobby. The immediate smell of smoke from the casino filters into the air, but the sound of the slot machines goes undetected by the blaring music in the lobby.

Penny worked with the team to get me the information I needed as to where Halsey's room is, so I head straight to the elevators and up to his floor. Depending on where the boys play next, they fly to their next city after the game or stay one more night for some good sleep. Since they're off to Arizona next and then California, I couldn't wait. I had to see him now.

When I get off the elevator, I head to the right and down the hall where I find his room. I knock on the door, and while I wait for him to answer, I adjust the strap of my bag on my shoulder and try not to fidget too much from the anxiety rolling through me.

It takes a second, but when the door opens, I steel my breath, only to see Eli on the other side sporting a black eye.

"Blakely," he says quietly as he steps out into the hall with me but keeps his foot propping the door open slightly. "What are you doing here?"

"I hadn't heard from Halsey all day besides one text, and I was worried. Huxley Cane lent me his private plane. How is he?"

Eli shakes his head. "Not good."

My stomach twists. "What's going on?"

"It's not for me to say." He shakes his head. "But it's not good."

"Well, can I see him?"

"Yes," he says. "But I need to warn you, he's not in a good headspace, okay? I wouldn't expect much from him. It's been rough for me and the boys, so I can only imagine what he'll do when he sees you. Just . . . be prepared."

"I am," I say even though I feel like I'm going to throw up.

Fight for him.

Just keep fighting for him.

That's what Penny told me to do and that's what's going to happen. I'm going to fight for him no matter what.

"Okay." Eli props the door open and leads me inside, where the nightstand light is on. Halsey is curled up on the bed wearing nothing but a pair of shorts. Pacey is on the other side of the bed with a worried look on his face.

When he sees me approach, I watch him wince, but then he stands from the bed and offers me a silent wave.

"I'll give you some time alone," Eli says and then nods at Pacey to join him.

They slip out of the room, and when the door shuts behind them, I set my bag on the floor. Halsey doesn't move.

Not even a flinch.

So I walk over to the side of the bed he's facing, and I take a seat on the edge to find him with his eyes closed.

Gently, I place my hand on his side and say, "Hey, you."

His eyes part open, and he pauses for a moment, not making a move, not reacting to seeing me. He just stares, which scares me more than anything because I've seen how he reacts when I enter a room. I know the way he looks at me when we're in bed together, and the man staring back at me is just a shell.

After a few moments of silence, I can't take it anymore, so I say, "Are you doing okay?"

His eyes are tired. Bloodshot.

His face looks gaunt.

And he almost seems very feeble at this moment.

Finally he says, "No." It comes out strangled. His eyes well up with tears, and my heart shatters into a million pieces.

"Halsey—"

I don't have time to finish because he reaches out and pulls me into his chest, wrapping his arm around my waist, securing me into his fetal position.

At this moment, I can feel it all the way down to my bones. I'm his lifeline right now. He's holding on to me, silently begging and pleading to help him stay afloat, and I will do everything within me to do that.

I twist to my back, and he snuggles into me, his head to my chest. I put my arm around him and kiss the top of his head as I feel his tears cascade down to my shirt as his body quietly wracks against mine.

It breaks me.

He breaks me.

I find myself fighting off my own tears as I hold him close.

Oh, you poor, poor man. I hate that you're hurting. I love you. I will always love you. And I'm here for you. Always.

HALSEY IS SLEEPING, and I was able to slip out of his arms for a brief second to go to the bathroom, brush my teeth, and grab my phone from my bag, where a text waits for me from Huxley from a few minutes ago.

Huxley: *I've been informed by my pilot that you haven't contacted them yet.*

I glance up at Halsey, still curled into a ball, and I know exactly what I need to do.

Blakely: *Sorry. This is more serious than I expected it to be. I know this is probably not what you want to hear, and I understand the repercussions, but I won't be able to make it in tomorrow. Or the next day. Not sure how long it might take me to get back. I understand if you need to look elsewhere for someone more reliable, but this is too important for me not to be here.*

I heave a heavy sigh.

But, I know I've made the right decision.

Jobs will come and go, but a man like Halsey? He's once in a lifetime, and if that means I need to go back to ground zero, give up the dream job, and be here for him, then I will do it.

I'll do anything for this man.

It's a far cry from the thoughts going through my head when Perry asked me to move with him. I didn't even give Australia a thought. I didn't want to move. I didn't want to give up what I had.

But with Halsey, I'd give up the world to be by his side. And that's what he needs. He needs me by his side. And I know, with absolute certainty, that he'd do the same for me.

That's what love is.

My phone buzzes with a text, and I know I'll see the words HR in his text. *I'm about to lose this job.*

But . . . worth it.

Huxley: *Take all the time you need. When it comes to reliability, your choice to be with your man just proved to me how reliable you really are. We'll talk when you're ready to start back up. Wishing you luck.*

I stare at his text, dumbfounded.

And that's probably why he's one of the most brilliant men to work with.

Blakely: *I'm not even going to ask you if you're sure because you told me you mean everything that comes out of your mouth. I appreciate it, Huxley, and I promise, when I start with the company, I'll give you everything I've got plus more.*

Huxley: *I don't doubt it.*

Halsey shifts in bed and reaches across the empty mattress. When he doesn't find me, his head pops up and he looks around the room.

"Right here," I say to ease his panic. I set my phone down and climb back into bed with him. He spoons me around the waist and buries his head in my hair.

And once again, he holds me tightly, never letting go the entire night.

HALSEY

"GOOD MORNING," Blakely's sweet voice says as her hand strokes over my forehead.

I open my eyes and find her standing over me, hair wet and fresh from the shower with a towel wrapped around her body.

"I packed you all up so you're ready to go. Eli said you leave in about forty-five minutes." Her fingers continue to stroke my forehead, and it's just enough of a touch to put me back in my safe space with her.

"I'm . . . I'm sorry," I say.

Because how could I not be sorry?

I was such an idiot thinking that not talking to Blakely would help me when, in reality, I needed her more than anything. I needed her warm body, her touch . . . her love. Her presence.

I couldn't get myself together enough to play last night, which only made me feel more like shit because I was letting my team down, and we lost. Thankfully, it was a game where our coach rested players, so it didn't seem like I was missing for any serious reason.

Eli and Pacey helped me back to my room, didn't ask questions, didn't bother me to talk about anything. They sat with me until Blakely showed up, and I'm not sure they even knew she was coming. They would have stayed there all night probably.

Blakely takes a seat next to me on the bed and runs her hand over my cheek. "Don't apologize. There's no need to."

"Yes, there is. I never should have ignored you."

She leans over, touching her forehead to mine. I catch her towel fall open, and her breasts rest against my bare chest. "Don't, Halsey," she whispers as she straddles my lap. "Don't feel like you need to apologize. I appreciate you realizing what happened, but I also understand how pain can determine your decisions."

My hands smooth up her back as she presses a very soft kiss to my lips.

The fear, the anxiety, the pain all washes away because her lips are like a drug, making me forget and helping me escape.

I roll her to her back, the towel falling from her completely and leaving her naked in my arms, then caress her cheek with my thumb.

Those eyes captivate me. They offer me peace and calm.

Those lips make me feel alive.

And her body is the warm, comforting blanket I've needed for so many fucking years.

"You're everything I need," I say to her. "And I'm such a fucking fool for ignoring you. I'm lost, Blakely. Hurt. Teetering on the edge of whether I'm worth this life or not."

"You are," she says so quickly that I can feel the words break through to me. They aren't empty. They aren't a gut reaction. They're full of meaning. "You are so worth this life, Halsey. You bring so much joy to people. You are such a beacon, a kind, thoughtful, loving soul. Your boys love you more than anything." She swallows and says, "I love you more than anything." Her eyes fill with tears as I lift, stunned, but she loops her arm around my neck and pulls me closer. "I love you, Halsey. And I'd be devastated if you didn't know that, if you believed you don't deserve to spend time on this earth, because you do. I love you, and I need you. I don't need your family. I don't need you to solve any issues settled on your shoulders. Because none of that matters. What matters is you and me."

"Blakely . . ." I choke out.

"And I'm sorry if you're not ready to say I love you, but I—"

I don't let her finish as I crash my mouth to hers, parting her lips with mine and driving my tongue against hers. She matches my energy, my strokes, my desire to be close. I cup her cheeks and move my thumb to under her chin where I tip it up, giving me a better angle. Her hands travel to my shorts, where she pushes them down and uses her legs to maneuver them the rest of the way, leaving us both naked.

She spreads her legs and reaches between us, where she grips my cock and starts pumping my length. It takes seconds before I'm so hard I can feel my entire body tingle. That's when she positions me at her entrance. But I don't enter her.

Instead, I lift and stare into her questioning eyes.

"What's wrong?" she asks.

I shake my head. "Nothing. I . . . I wanted to say." I wet my lips. "Fuck . . . I love you, too, Blakely." Her eyes soften. "I've loved you from the very fucking moment I laid eyes on you. I knew you were supposed to be mine, I just didn't know how I'd make it happen."

"I'm yours," she says. "All yours."

"And I'm never letting you go," I say as I enter her, pushing all the way to the hilt.

I bring my mouth to hers, our lips melt together, our tongues colliding, and our hands strive for a touch, a feel. And I sink into her, lightly pulsing my hips and relishing in the feel of her wrapped around me, our undeniable energy, attraction, connection molding into one.

Her hands grasp my cheeks, holding me in place as her tongue dives against mine, swirling, taking.

This woman. This stunning, selfless woman loves me.

"I love you, and I need you. What matters is you and me."

And it's in her arms that I begin to see a chance to heal. Her love. Her belief in me.

She loves me.

My hips start to pump faster as my desire grows, my need pounding on my back, telling me to take more. Her fingers dig into my shoulder as she arches into my chest, her hard nipples rubbing against my pecs.

"Fuck, baby," I whisper. "You are everything I'll ever need. This body, *your* heart. It's all I fucking need." I glance down and watch my greedy cock sink into her deep warmth. The visual brings me to the edge. "I'm right there."

"Me . . . too," she moans right before taking my mouth again, and as her tongue dives deeper, swiping and tangling against mine, her body shivers and quakes beneath me. "Oh . . . God," she cries into my mouth just as she constricts around my cock.

Her cries echo through the hotel room, and I'm wrapped up inside her, her contracting pussy sending me right over the fucking edge.

I groan into her shoulder as my hips still, and I come.

"Jesus . . . Christ," I say as I let my hips lightly pump for a few more seconds. Once we're both satisfied, I look her in the eyes. Cupping her cheek softly, I say, "I love you, Blakely. So fucking much and this . . . this is what I need. I need you. I want you. I never want this to end."

"Me neither," she says with a smile. "But you have a plane to catch."

"Fuck, I know." I give her one more kiss, then I pull out before hopping off the bed and lifting her into my arms.

I carry her into the bathroom, and we wash up in the shower

together. I try to keep my hands to myself as much as possible, because the last thing I need is to get caught up in my desire for this woman all over again.

Once we dry off, we both get dressed—her into comfortable clothes and me into a suit.

I'm buttoning up my shirt when she says, "I don't want to pressure you to tell me what happened, but just know, Halsey, I'm always here for you whenever you're ready, if you're ever ready."

"I know you are." I walk up to her, press my finger under her chin, and lift her mouth to mine. I softly kiss her as her hands find my shirt. She helps me button it up as I say, "I called my mom." She moves slower. "She told me my dad died." Her eyes snap up to mine.

"Oh my God, Halsey, I'm so sorry."

I take a piece of her hair and twirl it around my finger. "Still don't think I believe it. Processing all of that. But then . . ." I take a deep breath, knowing that when she hears what I'm about to say, she'll help take the pain away. "She, uh, she told me that the wrong twin died."

A gasp falls past her lips before she stands and brings her hands to my face. "Don't for one second," she says, staring me in my eyes, "believe anything about that statement. Because it's not true, it's a pathetic thing to say by a lost woman searching to hurt anyone and everyone because she's hurting." My throat grows tight as tears form in my eyes. "Do you hear me, Halsey? There is no validity behind that statement. You are worthy of this life, of this air I share with you, of this love we feel. You are worthy of it all."

My tears stream down my cheeks, and she wipes them away with her thumbs.

"I'm so sorry you had to hear that," she continues. "I'm so sorry that you had to feel her pain, that she transferred that over to you. It wasn't right, and it was undeserved. But you have to know that Holden would never think that. He'd be proud of you for the man you are and the hurdles you've faced. The changes you've made. The love you've accepted. This is your life to live and don't let anyone else tell you differently. Promise me." She grips me tightly. "Promise me, Halsey."

More tears fall past my eyes as I lightly nod. "I promise you."

"Thank you." She then lifts on her toes and presses a deep, loving kiss to my lips while looping her arms around me, holding me close.

She rubs her hand over my chest. "I know it will take time to sift through everything you're feeling and this won't just magically disappear. That's not how hurt works. But I will be here for you every step of the way. I'll stand by your side, reminding you just how special you are to this world."

Just then, there's a knock on the door.

It has to be one of the guys.

"I'll get it," she says before giving me one more kiss and answering the door.

I finish buttoning my shirt just as Eli, Posey, Silas, and Pacey walk into the room, all shuffling inside wearing their suits.

All it takes is a moment of eye contact before they each walk up to me and pull me into a hug.

Posey is first. He pats me on the back and says, "I love you, man."

Silas is next. He clasps my hand with his and gives me a shoulder hug before saying, "I love you."

Pacey follows Silas and offers me a large hug while quietly saying, "I love you."

Eli is last. And as I look him in his watery eyes, I realize just how much this path we've been down has wrecked us both. When he pulls me into a hug, I nearly feel myself crumble as he squeezes me tight. "You mean so much to us, to this team, to this world. You're supposed to be here. You're here for a reason, and never forget that." When he pulls away, he grips my face and forces me to look him in the eyes. "Holden was an alcoholic. I knew that; you knew that. We tried to fucking help him, but he wouldn't help himself. No one is to blame but him. Got that? No one." More tears stream down my cheeks as I silently nod. "You have a family, right here in this room. You have brothers, you have sisters, and you have your girl. We are the ones who matter. Our opinions. And collectively, we need you walking by our sides because we love you, Halsey. Okay? We fucking love you."

I nod, and Eli pulls me into a hug one more time, squeezing me tight.

The hold he has on me reminds me just how right he is.

I have everything I need right here in this room.

I have people who care.

People who love me.

Who want me to do well in this life.

I can't dwell on the past and the spiteful words tossed my way from damaged people.

My brothers, they're the ones that are important, they are my rocks, my foundation, and this is what I build on.

"Thank you," I say, my voice so tight, I barely hear it. "I love you all."

Posey sniffs off to the side, grabbing all of our attention. When he looks around the room, he says, "I think . . . I think there's something in my eye."

Silas pushes his shoulder. "Just fucking cry if you're going to cry. Be a goddamn man about it."

"Yeah, look at Halsey. He's not trying to hide his emotions," Pacey says. "Or Eli."

"I'm not hiding it," Posey says as he turns away and wipes at his eyes.

"You're an idiot." Silas loops his arm over Posey's shoulders and guides him to the door. "See you downstairs, man."

Pacey offers me a salute.

And Eli gives me one last hug before taking off, leaving me alone with Blakely.

With a large smile on her face, she walks up to me and says, "You are so lucky you have those nitwits in your life."

I chuckle. "Yeah, I am. But most importantly, I'm lucky to have you." I loop my arms around her. "I'm assuming you're going back to California, and I'll see you there?"

She shakes her head. "Nope. I told Huxley I needed time and if he fired me, I was okay with that, but I needed to be with you."

"You said that?" I ask, surprised.

"Yes, Halsey." Her hand smooths up my chest. "I can live without the new job, but I can't fathom walking this life without you by my side." I stroke her hair, staring at those beautiful eyes that captured me from day one.

"You chose me."

"And I'll choose you every single time."

My heart swells, and I angle her head up, capturing her mouth with mine.

During the darkest time of my life, when I was walking through every day with no purpose and simply going through the motions, a sliver of light awoke the dead inside me. That light was Blakely. And the more I got to know her, the more I realized she was sent to me and meant to be in my life.

And I like to believe Holden had a big part in making that happen.

Epilogue

HALSEY

"Do you want me to come inside with you or wait in the car?" Blakely asks as she holds my hand.

"I want you there," I say as I stare up at the large coastal house in front of us.

Visiting Hayden has been on my mind ever since Blakely and I started to get close. I wanted to share this amazing woman with my family, but after the incident with my mom, I had to step back and reassess if contacting my family would be healthy for me or if it would just put another hole in my heart.

So I put the idea on pause.

I focused on what mattered at the moment.

That was Blakely and the playoffs.

And now . . . Blakely and I are engaged, and we have another championship win under our belt.

I'm not going to say it was easy because it wasn't. There were games when I thought we weren't going to make it to the next round, but time and time again, we were able to pull it together, string plays in a row, and attack the defense, confusing them with our quick, sly passes and scoring.

And the night we won the Cup, I looked over at Blakely, who was crying hysterically, tears of joy falling down her face, and I told myself she was going to be my wife.

The next day, I bought a ring, and that night, while we were out on the patio, staring up at the stars from the privacy of our apartment, I asked her to be my wife.

It was an immediate yes from her followed by a night I'll never forget.

I thought winning the championship would be the pinnacle of my life, but I was so fucking wrong. Hearing Blakely say she wanted me to be her husband, that was it.

So now that I'm engaged and a small wedding is in the works for this summer—because I don't want to wait like my "nitwit" friends—I know I need to do one more thing. And that's speak to my brother.

I've mentally prepared for every scenario.

Blakely has told me over and over again that she's here for me no matter what.

And we even planned to meet the boys at the cabin in Banff after so that I'm surrounded by those I love.

"Tell me when you're ready," she says.

I stare at the black door, the potted plants on the front porch adding a pop of color. "I'm ready."

I open my door and meet her on her side, then I take her hand in mine.

She squeezes my hand, and we walk up to the house together.

"I love you," she whispers.

I glance down at her. "I love you, too."

And then I ring the doorbell, nerves bouncing off in my stomach. We wait a few minutes but when the door is unlocked and opened, I steel myself for his reaction.

On the other side, a tall, familiar figure appears at the door. With a spot of gray at his temples and laugh lines in the corners of his eyes, stands my brother, recently retired and looking like the brother I grew up with, just older.

It takes him a few seconds, but when I see the recognition fall over his face, my stomach roils with anxiety.

"Halsey?" he says, his voice almost a whisper.

"Hey . . . Hayden," I say.

And then, before I can even blink, he steps forward out onto the porch, wraps his arms around me, and pulls me into the biggest hug I've ever felt.

"Fucking hell, I missed you so much."

And just like that . . . it feels like I'm not only surrounded by my older brother but by Holden as well. Fuck, this feels right.

Losing Holden was the toughest thing I've ever endured. But if I've learned one thing through such devastating loss, it's that the sun still rises the next day. And the day after that. Life continues its motion. Waiting for your return.

It's okay to stay in that darkness for a while. It's okay to grieve your loss. Live the pain. Mourn.

But then, when you can, it's time to climb out. When you can, it's time to look at every element of your life and see that there is still joy in it. *Even in the shape of four crazy-ass hockey players.*

It's time to lean on those who've walked alongside you. And if you're really lucky, you might find a love that reaches deep inside, finds the pain-filled hole, and holds it. Shares it with you. Carries it. I have no idea what I ever did to deserve Blakely White's love, but I will treasure it for the rest of my days.

Made in the USA
Monee, IL
02 May 2024

57891402R00216